THE MANCHURIAN CANDIDATE

Berezovo was thinking of Yen Lo's proud claim of prolonging post-hypnotic amnesia into eternity. Berezovo had been life-trained in security work, particularly that having to do with Soviet security problems in North America, where this killer would operate. If a normally conditioned Anglo-Saxon could be taught to kill and kill, then to have no memory of having killed, or even of having had the thought of killing, he could feel no guilt. If he could feel no guilt he could not fall into the trap of betraying fear of being caught. If he could not feel guilt, or the fear of being caught, he would remain an outwardly normal, productive, sober, and respectful member of his community so that as Berezovo saw it, this killer was very close to being police-proof and the method by which he was created must be very, very carefully controlled in its application to other men within the Soviet Union. Specifically, within Moscow. More specifically within the Kremlin.

Richard Condon

THE MANCHURIAN CANDIDATE

ARROW BOOKS

Arrow Books Limited
62–65 Chandos Place, London WC2N 4NW

An imprint of Century Hutchinson Limited

London Melbourne Sydney Auckland
Johannesburg and agencies
throughout the world

First published by Michael Joseph 1960
Arrow edition 1982
Reprinted 1985

Printed and bound in Great Britain by
Anchor Brendon Ltd, Tiptree, Essex

ISBN 0 09 928400 6

To

MAX YOUNGSTEIN
*and not only for reasons
of affection and admiration,
this book is warmly dedicated*

The order of Assassins was
founded in Persia at the end of
the 11th Century. They were committed to anyone willing to pay
for the service. Assassins were
sceptical of the existence of
God and believed that the world
of the mind came into existence
first, then, finally, the rest of creation.

*Standard Dictionary of
Folklore, Mythology and Legend*

I am you and you are me and
what have we done to each other?

The Keener's Manual

I

It was sunny in San Francisco; a fabulous condition. Raymond Shaw was not unaware of the beauty outside the hotel window, across from a mansion on the top of a hill, but he clutched the telephone like an *osculatorium* and did not allow himself to think about what lay beyond that instant: in a saloon some place, in a different bed, or anywhere.

His lumpy sergeant's uniform was heaped on a chair. He stretched out on the rented bed, wearing a new one-hundred-and-twenty-dollar dark blue dressing-gown, and waited for the telephone operator to complete the chain of calls to locate Ed Mavole's father, somewhere in St Louis.

He knew he was doing the wrong thing. Two years of Korean duty were three days behind him and, at the very least, he should be spending his money on a taxicab to go up and down those hills in the sunshine, but he decided his mind must be bent or that he was drunk with compassion, or something else improbable like that. Of all of the fathers of all of the fallen whom he had to call, owing to his endemic mopery, this one had to work nights, because, by now, it must be dark in St Louis.

He listened to the operator get through to the switchboard at the *Post-Dispatch*. He heard the switchboard tell her that Mavole's father worked in the composing room. A man talked to a woman; there was silence. Raymond stared at his own large toe.

'Hello?' A very high voice.

'Mr Arthur Mavole, please. Long distance calling.' The steady rumble of working presses filled the background.

'This is him.'

'Mr Arthur Mavole?'

'Yeah, yeah.'

7

'Go ahead, please.'

'Uh—hello? Mr Mavole? This is Sergeant Shaw. I'm calling from San Francisco. I—uh—I was in Eddie's outfit, Mr Mavole.'

'My Ed's outfit?'

'Yes, sir.'

'Ray Shaw?'

'Yes, sir.'

'The Ray Shaw? Who won the Medal of——'

'Yes, sir.' Raymond cut him off in a louder voice. He felt like dropping the phone, the call, and the whole soggy, masochistic, suicidal thing in the wastebasket. Better yet, he should whack himself over the head with the goddam phone. 'You see, uh, Mr Mavole, I have to, uh, go to Washington, and I——'

'We know. We read all about it and let me say with all my heart I got left that I am as proud of you, even though I never met you, as if it were Eddie, my own kid. My son.'

'Mr Mavole,' Raymond said rapidly, 'I thought that if it was O.K. with you maybe I could stop over in St Louis on my way to Washington, you know? I thought, I mean it occurred to me that you and Mrs Mavole might get some kind of peace out of it, some kind of relief, if we talked a little bit. About Eddie. You know? I mean I thought that was the least I could do.'

There was a silence. Then Mr Mavole began to make a lot of slobbering sounds so Raymond said roughly that he would wire when he knew what flight he would be on and he hung up the phone and felt like an idiot. Like an angry man with a cane who pokes a hole through the floor of heaven and is scalded by the joy that pours down upon him, Raymond had a capacity for using satisfactions against himself.

When he got off the plane at St Louis airport he felt like running. He decided Mavole's father must be that midget with the eyeglasses like milk-bottle bottoms who was enjoying sweating so much. The man would be all over him like a charging elk in a minute. 'Hold it! Hold it!' the pimply press photographer said loudly.

'Put it down,' Raymond snarled in a voice which was even

more unpleasant than his normal voice. All at once the photographer was less sure of himself. 'Whassa matter?' he asked in bewilderment—because he lived at a time when only sex criminals and dope peddlers tried to refuse to have their pictures taken by the press.

'I flew all the way in here to see Ed Mavole's father,' Raymond said, despising himself for throwing up such corn. 'You want a picture, go find him, because you ain't gonna take one of me without he's in it.'

Listen to that genuine, bluff sergeant version of *pollice verso*, Raymond cried out to himself. I am playing the authentic war buddy so deeply that I will have to mail in a royalty check for the stock rights. Look at that clown of a photographer trying to cope with phenomena. Any minute now he will realise that he is standing right beside Mavole's father.

'Oh, Sergeant!' the girl said, so then he knew who *she* was. She wasn't red-eyed and runny-nosed with grief for the dead hero, so she had to be the cub reporter who had been assigned to write the big local angle on the White House and the Hero, and he had probably written the lead for her with that sappy grandstand play.

'I'm Ed's father,' the sweat manufacturer said. It was December, fuh gossake, what's with all the dew? 'I'm Frank Mavole. I'm sorry about this. I just happened to mention at the paper that you had called all the way from San Francisco and that you had offered to stop over and see Eddie's mother on the way to the White House, and the word somehow got upstairs to the city desk and well—that's the newspaper business, I guess.'

Raymond took three steps forward, grasped Mr Mavole's hand, gripped his right forearm with his own left hand, transmitted the steely glance and the iron stare and the frozen fix. He felt like Captain Idiot in one of those space comic books, and the photographer got the picture and lost all interest in them.

'May I ask how old you are, Sergeant Shaw?' the young chick said, notebook ready, pencil poised as though she and Mavole were about to give him a fitting, and he figured reflexively that

9

this could be the first assignment she had ever got after years of journalism school and months of social notes from all over. He remembered his first assignment and how he had feared the waffle-faced movie actor who had opened the door of the hotel suite wearing only pyjama bottoms, with corny tattoos like So Long, Mabel on each shoulder. Inside the suite Raymond had managed to convey that he would just as soon have hit the man as talk to him and he had said, 'Gimme the handout and we can save some time.' The travelling press agent with the actor, a plump, bloodshot type whose glasses kept sliding down his nose, had said, 'What handout?' He had snarled that maybe they would prefer it if he started out by asking what was the great man's hobby and what astrology sign he had been born under. It was hard to believe but that man's face had been as pocked and welted as a waffle, yet he was one of the biggest names in the business, which gives an idea what those swine will do to kid the jerky public. The actor had said, 'Are you scared, kid?' Then, after that, everything seemed to go O.K. They got along like a bucket of chums. The point was, everybody had to start some place.

Although he felt like a slob himself for doing it, he asked Mr Mavole and the girl if they would have time to have a cup of coffee at the airport restaurant because he was a newspaperman himself and he knew that the little lady had a story to get. The little lady? That was overdoing it. He'd have to find a mirror and see if he had a wing collar on.

'You were?' the girl said. 'Oh, Sergeant!' Mr Mavole said a cup of coffee would be fine with him, so they went inside.

They sat down at a table in the coffee shop. The windows were steamy. Business was very quiet and unfortunately the waitress seemed to have nothing but time. They all ordered coffee and Raymond thought he'd like to have a piece of pie but he could not bring himself to decide what kind of pie. Did everybody have to look at him as though he were sick because he couldn't set his taste buds in advance to be able to figure which flavour he would favour before he tasted it? Did the waitress just have to start out to recite 'We have peach pie, and pumpk—' and they'd just yell out peach, peach, peach? What was the sense of eating in a place where they gabbled the menu at you, anyway? If a man were intelligent and he sorted through the memories of past tastes he not only could get exactly what he wanted sensually and with a flavour sensation, but he would probably be choosing something so chemically exact that it would benefit his entire body. But how could anyone achieve such a considerate deliberate result as that unless one were permitted to pore over a written menu?

'The prune pie is very good, sir,' the waitress said. He told her he'd take the prune pie and he hated her in a hot, resentful flash because he did not want prune pie. He hated prune pie and he had been manœuvered into ordering prune pie by a rube waitress who would probably slobber all over his shoes for a quarter tip.

'I wanted to tell you how we felt about Ed, Mr Mavole,' Raymond said. 'I want to tell you that of all the guys I ever met, there was never a happier, sweeter, or more solid guy than your son Ed.'

The little man's eyes filled. He suddenly choked on a sob so loud that people at the counter, which was quite a distance away, turned round. Raymond spoke to the girl quickly to cover up. 'I'm twenty-four years old. My astrological sign is Pisces. A very fine lady reporter on a Detroit paper once told me always to ask for their astrology sign because people love to read about astrology if they don't have to ask for it directly.'

'I'm Taurus,' the girl said.

'We'd be very good,' Raymond said. She let him see just a little bit behind her expression. 'I know,' she said.

Mr Mavole spoke in a soft voice. 'Sergeant—you see—well, when Eddie got killed his mother had a heart attack and I wonder if you could spare maybe a half an hour out and back. We don't live all the way into the city, and——'

O Jesus! Raymond saw himself donning the bedside manner. A bloody cardiac. The slightest touchy thing he said to her could knock the old cat over sideways with an off-key moan. But what could he do? He had elected himself Head Chump when he had stepped down from Valhalla and telephoned this sweaty little advantage-taker.

'Mr Mavole,' he said, slowly and softly, 'I don't have to be in Washington until the day after tomorrow, but I figured I would allow a day and a half in case of bad weather, you know? On account of the White House? I can even get to Washington by train from here overnight, the Spirit of St Louis, the same name as that plane with that fella, so please don't think I would even think of leaving town without talking to Mrs Mavole—Eddie's mother.' He looked up and he saw how the girl was looking at him. She was a very pretty girl; a sweet-looking, nice, blonde girl. 'What's your name?' he asked.

'Mardell,' she said.

'Do you think I'll be able to get a hotel here tonight?'

'I'm absolutely sure of it.'

'I'll take care of that, Sergeant,' Mr Mavole said hurriedly. 'In fact, the paper will take care of everything. You would certainly be welcome to stay at our place, but we just had the painters. Smells so sharp your eyes water.'

Raymond called for the check. They drove to the Mavoles'. Mardell said she'd wait in the car and just to forget about her. Raymond told her to get on in to the paper and file her story, then drive back out to pick him up. She stared at him as if he had invented balk-line billiards. He patted her cheek, then went into the house. She put her hand on her stomach and took three or four deep breaths. Then she started the car and went into town.

The session with Mrs Mavole was awful and Raymond vowed that he would never take an intelligence test because they might lock him up as a result of what would be shown. Any cretin could have looked ahead and seen what a mess this was going to be. They all cried. People can certainly carry on, he thought, holding her fat hand because she had asked him to, and feeling sure she was going to drop dead any minute. These were the people who let a war start, then they act surprised when their own son is killed. Mavole was a good enough kid. He certainly was a funny kid and with a sensational disposition but, what the hell, twenty thousand were dead out there so far on the American panel, plus the U.N. guys, and maybe sixty, eighty thousand more all shot up, and this fat broad seemed to think that Mavole was the only one who got it.

Could my mother take it this big if I got it? Would anyone living or anyone running a legitimate seance which picked up guaranteed answers from Out Yonder ever be able to find out whether she could feel anything at all about anything or anybody? Let her liddul Raymond pull up dead and he knew the answer from his liddul mommy. If the folks would pay one or more votes for a sandwich she would be happy to send for her liddul boy's body and barbecue him.

'I can tell you that it was a very clear action for a night action, Mrs Mavole,' Raymond said. Mr Mavole sat on the other side of the bed and stared at the floor, his eyes feverish captives in black circles, his lower lip caught between his teeth, his hands clasped in prayer as he hoped he would not begin to cry again and start her crying. 'You see, Captain Marco had sent up some low flares because we had to know where the enemy was. They knew where we were. Eddie, well—' He paused, only infinitesimally, to try not to weep at the thought of how bitter, bitter, bitter it was to have to lie at a time like this, but she had sold the boy to the recruiters for this moment, so he would have to throw the truth away and pay her off. They never told The Folks Back Home about the filthy deaths—the grotesque, debasing deaths which were almost all the deaths in war. Dirty deaths were the commonplace clowns smoking idle cigarettes backstage at a circus filled with clowns. Ah, no. No, no, no, no, no, no, no. Only a clutch of martial airs played on an electric guitar and sung through the gaudy juke box called Our Nation's History. He didn't know exactly how Mavole caught it, but he could figure it close. He'd probably gotten about sixteen inches of bayonet in the rectum as he turned to get away and his screaming had scared the other man so much that he had fought to get his weapon out and run away, twisting Mavole on it until the point came out under Mavole's ribs where the diaphragm was and the man had had to put his foot on the back of Mavole's neck, breaking his nose and cheekbone, to get the sticker out, while he whimpered in Chinese and wanted to lie down somewhere, where it was quiet. All the other people knew about how undignified it was to lose a head or some legs or a body in a mass attack, except his people: the innocents hiding in the jam jar. Women like this one might have had that li'l cardiac murmur stilled if her city had been bombed and she had seen her Eddie with no lower face and she had to protect and cherish the rest, the ones who were left. '—well, there was this very young lad in our outfit, Mrs Mavole. He was maybe seventeen years old, but I doubt it. I think sixteen. Eddie had decided a long time ago to help the kid and look out for him because that was the kind of man your son was.' Mr Mavole was sobbing very softly on the other side of the bed. 'Well, the boy, little Bobby Lembeck, got separated from the rest of us. Not by far; Ed went out to cover him. The boy was hit just before Eddie could make it to him and, well, he just couldn't leave him there. You know? That's the kind of a man, I mean; that was Ed. You know? He couldn't. He tried to bring the youngster back and by that time the enemy had a fix on them and they dropped a mortar shell on them from away up high and it was all over and all done, Mrs Mavole, before those two boys felt a single thing. That's how quick it was, Mrs Mavole. Yes, ma'am. That quick.'

'I'm glad,' Mrs Mavole said. Then suddenly and loudly she said, 'O my God, how can I say I'm glad? I'm not. I'm not. We're all a long time dead. He was such a happy little boy and he'll be a long time dead.' She was propped up among the pillows of the bed and her body moved back and forth with her keening.

What the hell did he expect? He came here of his own free will. What did he expect? Two choruses of something mellow, progressive, and fine? O man, O man, O man! A fat old broad in a nine-by-nine box with a sweat-maker who can't get with it. How can I continue to live, he shouted at high scream under the

14

nave of his encompassing skull, if people are going to continue to carry bundles of pain on top of their heads like Haitian laundresses, then fling the bundles at random into the face of any bright stroller who happened to be passing by? All right. He had helped this fat broad to find herself some ghoulish kicks. What else did they want from him?

'The wrong man died, Mrs Mavole,' Raymond sobbed. 'How I wish it could have been me. Not Eddie. Me. Me.' He hid his face in her large, motherly breasts as she lay back on the pillows of the bed.

Through arrangements beyond his control, Raymond had developed into a man who sagged fearfully within a suit of stifling armour, imprisoned for the length of his life from casque to solleret. It was heavy, immovable armour, this thick defence, which had been constructed mainly at his mother's forge, hammered under his stepfather's noise, tempered by the bitter tears of his father's betrayal. Raymond also distrusted all other living people because they had not warned his father of his mother.

Raymond had been shown too early that if he smiled his stepfather was encouraged to bray laughter; if he spoke, his mother felt compelled to reply in the only way she knew how to reply, which was to urge him to seek popularity and power with all life-force. So he had deliberately developed the ability to be shunned instantly no matter where he went and notwithstanding extraneous conditions. He had achieved this state consciously after year upon year of unconscious rehearsal of the manifest paraphernalia of arrogance and contempt, then exceeded it. The shell of armour that encased Raymond, by the horrid tracery of its design, presented him as one of the least likable men of his century. He knew that to be a fact, and yet he did not know it because he thought the armour was all one with himself, as is a turtle's shell.

He had been told who he was only by his whimpering unconscious mind: a motherless (by choice), fatherless (by treachery), friendless (by circumstance), and joyless (by consequence) man who would continue to refuse emphatically to live and who, autocratically and unequivocally, did not intend to die. He was a marooned balloonist, supported by nothing visible, looking down on everybody and everything, but yearning to be seen so that, at least, he could be given some credit for an otherwise profitless ascension.

That was what Raymond's ambivalence was like. He was held in a paradox of callousness and feeling: the armour, which he told the world he was, and the feeling, which was what he did not know he was, and blind to both in a darkness of despair which could neither be seen nor see itself.

He had been able to weep with Mr and Mrs Mavole because the door had been closed and because he knew he would be careful never to be seen by those two slobs again.

At seven-twenty on the morning after he had reached St Louis, there was a discreet but firm knocking at Raymond's hotel room door. These peremptory sounds just happened to come at a moment when Raymond was exchanging intense joy with the young newspaperwoman he had met the day before. When the knocking had first hit the door, Raymond had heard it clearly enough but he was just busy enough to be determined to ignore it, but the young woman had gone rigid, not in any attitude of idiosyncratic orgasm, but as any healthy, respectable young woman would have done under similar circumstances in a hotel room in any city smaller than Tokyo.

Lights of rage and resentment exploded in Raymond's head. He stared down at the sweet, frightened face under him as though he hated her for not being as defiant as a drunken whore in a night court, then he threw himself off her, nearly falling out of bed. He regained his balance, slowly pulled on the dark blue dressing gown, and walking very close to the door of the room, said into the crack, 'Who is it?'

'Sergeant Shaw?'

'Yes.'

'Federal Bureau of Investigation.' It was a calm, sane, tenor voice.

'What?' Raymond said. 'Come on!' His voice was low and angry.

'Open up.'

Raymond looked over his shoulder, registering amazement, either to see whether Mardell had heard what he had heard or to find out if she looked like a fugitive. She was chalk-white and solemn.

'What do you want?' Raymond asked.

'We want Sergeant Raymond Shaw.' Raymond stared at the door. His face began to fill with a claret flush that clashed unpleasantly with the Nile-green wallpaper directly beside him. 'Open up!' the voice said.

'I will like hell open up,' Raymond said. 'How dare you pound on this door at this time of the morning and issue your country constable's orders? There are telephones in the lobby if you needed to make some kind of urgent inquiry. I said, how dare you?' The hauteur in Raymond's voice held no bluster and its threat of implicit punishment startled the girl on the bed even more than the FBI's arrival. 'What the hell do you want from Sergeant Raymond Shaw?' he snarled.

'Well—uh—we have been asked——'

'Asked? *Asked*?'

'—we have been asked to see that you meet the Army plane which is being sent to pick you up at the Lambert Airport in an hour and fifteen minutes. At eight forty-five.'

'You couldn't have called me from your home, or some law-school telephone booth?'

There was a strained silence, then: 'We will not continue to discuss this with you from behind a door.' Raymond walked quickly to the telephone. He was stiff with anger, as though it had rusted his joints. He picked up the receiver and rattled the bar. He told the operator to please get him the Mayflower Hotel in Washington, D.C.

'Sergeant,' the voice said distinctly through the door, 'we have orders to put you on that plane. Our orders are just as mandatory as any you ever got in the Army.'

'Listen to what I'm going to say on this phone, then we'll talk about orders,' Raymond said nastily. 'I don't take any orders from the FBI or the Bureau of Printing and Engraving or the Division of Conservation and Wild Life, and if you have any written orders for me from the United States Army, slide them under the door. Then you can wait for me in the lobby, if you still think you have to, and the Air Force can wait for me at the airport until I make my mind up.'

'Now, just one minute here, son——' The voice had turned ominous.

'Did they tell you I am being flown to Washington to get a Medal of Honour at the White House?' Maybe that silly hunk of iron he had never asked for would be useful for something just once. This kind of a square bought that stuff. A Medal of Honour was like a lot of money; it was very hard to get, so it took on a lot of magic powers.

'Are you that Sergeant Shaw?'

'That's me.' He spoke to the phone. 'Right. I'll hold on.'

'I'll wait in the lobby,' the FBI man said. 'I'll be standing near the desk when you come down. Sorry.'

Holding the telephone and waiting for the call, Raymond sat down on the edge of the bed, then leaned over and kissed the girl very softly at a soft place right under her rigid right nipple, but he didn't smile at her because he was preoccupied with the call. 'Hello, Mayflower? This is St Louis, Missouri, calling Senator John Iselin. Sergeant Raymond Shaw.' There was a short wait. 'Hello, Mother. Put your husband on. It's Raymond. *I said put your husband on!*' He waited.

'Johnny? Raymond. There's an FBI man outside my hotel room door in St Louis to say that they are holding an Army plane for me. Did you tell the Army to request FBI co-operation, and did you have that plane sent here?' He listened. 'You did. Well, I knew damn well you did. But why? What the hell did you decide to do a thing like that for?' He listened. 'How could I be late? It's Wednesday morning and I don't have to be at the White House until Friday afternoon.' He listened. He went totally pale. 'A parade? *A par—ade?*' He stared at the details offered by his imagination. 'Why—you cheap, flag-rubbing bastard!'

Mardell had slipped out of bed and was starting to get dressed, but she didn't seem to be able to find anything and she looked frightened. He signalled her with his free hand, caught her attention, and smiled at her so warmingly and so reassuringly that she sat down on the edge of the bed. Then she leaned back slowly and stretched out. He reached over and took her hand, kissed it softly, then placed it on top of her flat smooth stomach, while the telephone squawked in his ear. She reached up and just barely allowed her hand to caress the length of his right cheek, unshaven. Suddenly his face went hard again and he barked into the telephone. 'No, don't put my mother on again! I know I haven't spoken to her in two years! I'll talk to her when I'm good and ready to talk to her. Aaah, for Christ's sake!' He gritted his teeth and stared at the ceiling.

'Hello, Mother.' His voice was flat.

'Raymond, what the hell is this?' his mother asked solicitously. 'What's the matter with you? If we were in the mining business and you struck gold you'd call us, wouldn't you?'

'No.'

'Well, it just so happens that you're a Medal of Honour winner—incidentally, congratulations—I meant to write but we've been jammed up. Johnny is a public figure, Raymond. He represents the people of your state just the same as the President represents the people of the United States, and I notice you aren't making any fuss about going to the White House. Is there something so slimy and so terrible about having your picture taken with your father——'

'He is *not my father!*'

'—who represents the pride the people of this nation feel for what you have sacrificed for them on the field of battle?'

'Aaah, fuh crissakes, Mother, will you please——'

'You didn't mind having your picture taken with that stranger in St Louis yesterday. Incidentally, what happened? Did the Army PRO send you in there to slobber over the Gold Star Mother?'

'It was my own idea.'

'Don't tell me that, Raymond darling. I just happen to know you.'

'It was my own idea.'

'Well, wonderful. It was a wonderful idea. All the papers carried it here yesterday and, of course, everywhere this morning. Marty Webber called in time so we were able to work in a little expression from Johnny about how he'd do anything to help that dead boy's folks and so forth, so we tied everything up from this end. It was great, so you certainly can't stand there and tell me that you won't have your picture taken with the man who is not only your own family but who happens to have been the governor and is now the senator from your own state.'

'Since when do you have to get the Army to ask the FBI to set up a picture for Johnny? And that's not what we're arguing about, anyway. He just told me about a filthy idea for a parade to commemorate a medal on which you and I might not place any particular value but which the rest of this country thinks is a nice little thing—for a few lousy votes for him, and I am not going to hold still for any cheap, goddam parade!'

'A parade? That's ridiculous!'

'Ask your flag-simple husband.'

Raymond's mother seemed to be talking across the mouthpiece in an aside to Johnny, but Johnny had left the apartment some four minutes before to get a haircut. 'Johnny,' she said to nobody at all, 'where did you get the idea that they could embarrass Raymond with a parade? No wonder he's so sore.' Into the telephone she said, 'It's not a parade! A few cars were going out to the airport to meet you. No marching men. No colour guard. No big bands. You know you are a very peculiar boy, Raymond. I haven't seen you for almost two years--your mother—but you go right on mewing about some parade and

Johnny and the FBI and some Army plane, but when it comes
to——'

'What else is going to happen in Washington?'

'I had planned a little luncheon.'

'With whom?'

'With some very important key press and television people.'

'And Johnny?'

'Of course.'

'No.'

'What?'

'I won't do it.'

There was a long pause. Waiting, staring down at the girl, he
became aware that she had violet eyes. His mind began to spin
off the fine silk thread of his resentment in furious *moulinage*. For
almost two years he had been free of his obsessed mother, this
brassy bugler, this puss-in-boots to her boorish Marquis de
Carrabas, the woman who could think but who could not feel.
He had had three letters from her in two years. (1) She had
arranged for a life-sized cut-out of Johnny to be forwarded to
Seoul. General MacArthur was in the area. Could Johnny
arrange for a picture of the two of them with arms around the
photographic cut-out of Johnny, as she could guarantee that this
would get the widest kind of coverage? (2) Would he arrange for
a canvass of fighting men from their state to sign a scroll of
Christmas greetings, on behalf of all Johnny's fighting buddies
everywhere, to Johnny and the people of his great state? And (3)
she was deeply disappointed and not a little bit shocked to find
out that he would not lift one little finger to carry out a few
simple requests for his mother who worked day and night for
both of her men so that there might be a better and more secure
place for each of them.

He had been two years away from her but he could feel his
defiance of her buckling under the weight of her silence. He had
never been able to cope with her silence. At last her voice came
through the telephone again. It was charged. It was rough and
sinister. It was murderous and frightening and threatening. 'If

you don't do this, Raymond,' she said, 'I will promise you on my father's grave right now that you will be very, very sorry.'

'All right, Mother,' he said. 'I'll do it.' He shuddered. He hung up the telephone from a foot and a half above the receiver. It fell off, but he must have felt he had made his point because he picked it up from the bed where it had bounced and put it gently into its cradle.

'That was my mother,' he explained to Mardell. 'I wish I knew what else I could say to describe her in front of a nice girl like you.'

He walked to the locked door. He leaned against the crack in despair and said, 'I'll be in the lobby in about an hour.' There was no answer. He turned towards the bed, untying the belt of his new blue robe, as a massive column of smoke began to spiral upward inside his head, filling the eyes of his memory and opaquing his expression from behind his eyes. Mardell was spilled out softly across the bed. The sheets were blue. She was blonde-and-ivory, tipped with pink; lined with pink. It came to him that he had never seen another girl, named Jocie, this way. The thought of Jocie lying before him like this lovely moaning girl excited him as though a chemical abrasive had been poured into his urethra and she was assaulted by him in the most attritive manner, to her greater glory and with her effulgent consent, and though she lived to be an old, old woman she never forgot that morning and could summon it back to her in its richest violence whenever she was frightened and alone, never knowing that she was not only the first woman Raymond had ever possessed, but the first he had ever kissed in passion, or that he had been given his start towards relaxing his inhibitions against the uses of sex not quite one year before, in Manchuria.

II

A Chinese Army construction battalion arrived at Tunghwa, forty-three miles inside the Korean frontier, on July 4, 1951, to set underway the housing for events, planned in 1936, that were to reach their conclusion in the United States of America in 1960. The major in charge of the detail, a Ssu Ma Sung, is now a civilian lawyer in Kunming.

Manchuria is in the subarctic zone, but the summers are hot and humid. Tunghwa handles industry, such as saw milling and food processing with hydro-electric power. It is a city of approximately ninety thousand, about the size of Terre Haute, Indiana, but lacking a public health appropriation.

The Chinese construction battalion set up the job near a military airfield nearly three miles out of town. Everything they put up was prefabricated, the sections keyed by different colours; this, when the pieces were scattered around the terrain, made the men seem like toy figures walking among the pieces of a giant jigsaw puzzle. When these were assembled into a building, they were sprayed with barn-red lead paint to banish the quilted effect. By July 6, at seventeen-nineteen, the battalion had completed a two-storey, twenty-two-room structure with a small auditorium. The building was called the Research Pavilion and had some one-way transparent glass walls. It also had a few comfortably furnished guest rooms without glass walls on the first floor; these had been reserved for the brass from Moscow and Peiping.

Each floor held different-coloured, vari-patterned asphalt tile as a guide for furniture and equipment placement. Each wall, as it was erected, had decorations riveted into it. The windows, cut through each outer wall, had curtains and drapes fastened to them. The thousand pieces of that house gave the impression that it was a travelling billet for political representatives of the allied People's Governments: a structure forever being built, struck, then sent on ahead to be built again for the next series of meetings and discussions. All of the furniture was made of blonde wood in mutated, modern Scandinavian design. All of the interior colouring, except the bright yellow rattan carpeting on the second floor, was the same green and apricot utilised by new brides during their first three years of marriage.

The second floor of the building held one large corner suite of rooms and ten other compact cubicles that had three solid walls each and one building-long common wall of one-way transparent glass facing a catwalk that was patrolled day and night by two Soviet Army riflemen. Each cubicle contained a cot, a chair, a closet, and a mirror for reassurance that the soul had not fled. The large apartment had similar fittings, plus a bathroom, a large living room, and an additional bedroom. All of the walls here were opaque. The invigorating scent of pine-tree incense pervaded the upper floors, subtly and pleasantly.

The marvellous part of what they were doing several hundred miles to the south of Tunghwa was that every time Mavole moved, the girl moved, and every time Mavole bleated, the girl bleated. It was really a money's worth and after Mavole came downstairs he told the guys that the classy part about the joint was that when he took the broad upstairs in the first place, there had been no jeers or catcalls. Mavole's co-mover and bleater was a young Korean girl who had adapted to prostitution a variation of the Rochdale principle on which had been based the first co-operative store in 1844, in that she extended absolutely no credit but distributed part of the profits in the form of free beer. Her name was Gertrude.

Freeman had left to check gear, but Mavole and Bobby Lembeck sat around and drank a few more beers while they waited for the corporal to get finished upstairs. They tried to explain to the two little broads that it was not necessary to smile so hard but they couldn't speak Korean, except for a few words, and the girls couldn't speak American, so Bobby Lembeck put his two forefingers at the corners of his mouth and pulled an inane prop smile down. The girls caught on but it looked so

24

funny the way he did it that Bobby and Mavole started laughing like crazy, which started the girls laughing again so that when they stopped laughing they were still smiling.

To the extent that wartime zymurgists imperil the norm, the Korean beer was about as good as local Mississippi beer or Nebraska beer, which is pretty lousy, but it was hot. That was one thing you could say about it, Mavole pointed out.

'Eddie, why do we have to spend all of our time off in a whorehouse?' Bobby asked.

'Yeah. Rough, ain't it?'

'I don't mean it's hard to take, but my hobby is birds. There are a lot of new birds around this part of the world.'

'We spend our time off here because it's the only place on the entire Korean peninsula that Sergeant Raymond Shaw doesn't walk into.'

'You think he's a fairy, or very religious?'

'What?'

'Or both?'

'Sergeant Shaw? Our Raymond?'

'Yeah.'

'What are you? Out of your mind? It's just that Raymond doesn't give to anybody. And it's a common vulgar thing—sex—to Raymond.'

'He happens to be right,' Bobby Lembeck said. 'It sure is. I'm only a beginner but that's one of the things I like about it.'

Mavole looked at him, nodding his head in a kind of awe. 'It's a very funny thing,' he said slowly, 'but every now and then I think about you coming all the way to Korea from New Jersey to get your first piece of poontang and it makes me feel like I'm sort of a monument—part of your life. You know? And Marie Louise too. Of course.' He nodded equably to indicate the small Japanese girl who was sitting beside Bobby Lembeck, holding his right wrist like a falcon.

'She certainly is,' Bobby agreed. 'What a monument.'

'It's kind of a very touching thing to me that you have never had a fat broad or a tall broad, say.'

25

'It's different?'

'Well—yes and no. It's hard to explain. These little broads, while very nice and with lovely dispositions and with beer included, which is very unusual, they *are* very little—spinners, we used to call them—and although I hate to say this even though I know they can't understand me, they are very, very skinny.'

'Just the same,' Bobby said.

'Yeah. You're right.'

Melvin, the corporal, came rushing down the stairs. He was combing his hair rapidly, head tilted to one side, like a commuter who had overslept. 'Great!' he said briskly. 'Great, great, great!' he repeated, running the words together. 'The greatest.'

'You're telling me?' asked Bobby Lembeck.

'Look at him,' Mavole said proudly. 'Already he's an expert on getting laid.'

'All right, you guys,' Melvin said in a corporal's voice. 'We move up north in a half an hour. Let's go.'

Bobby Lembeck kissed Marie Louise's hand. '*Mansei!*' he said, using the only Korean word he knew; it voiced a gallant hope, for it meant 'May our country live ten thousand years.'

Sergeant Shaw was capable of weeping objective, simulated tears at several points in the story of his life, which Captain Marco always encouraged him to tell to pass the time during quiet hours on patrol. The sergeant's rage-daubed face would shine like a ripped-out heart flung on to stones in moonlight, and the captain liked to hear the story because, in a way, it was like hearing Orestes gripe about Clytemnestra. Captain Marco treasured poetic, literary, informational, and cross-referenced allusions, military and non-military. He was a reader. His point of motive was that on many Army posts one's off-time could only be spent drinking, bridge-playing, or reading. Marco enjoyed beer, abjured spirits. He had no head for cards; he always seemed to win from his superior officers. His fellow officers were used up on conversations of a non-professional nature, so he transhipped boxes of books about anything at all, back and forth between San Francisco and wherever he was stationed at the time, because he was deeply interested in the problems of Bilbao bankers, the history of piracy, the paintings of Orozco, the modern French theatre, the jurisprudential factors in Mafia administration, the diseases of cattle, the works of Yeats, the ramblings of the Bible, the novels of Joyce Cary, the lordliness of doctors, the psychology of bullfighters, the ethnic choices of Arabs, the origin of trade winds, and very nearly anything else contained in any of the books which he paid to have selected at random by a stranger in a bookstore on Market Street and shipped to him wherever he happened to be.

The sergeant's account of his past was ancient in its form and confusingly dramatic, as perhaps would have been a game of three-level chess between Richard Burbage and Sacha Guitry. It all seemed to revolve around his mother, a woman as ambitious as Daedalus. The sergeant was twenty-two years old. He was as ambivalent as a candle burning at both ends. Awake, his resentment was almost always at full boil. Asleep, Captain Marco could understand, it simmered and bubbled in the blackened iron pot of his memory.

Raymond had made tech sergeant because he was a bleakly good soldier and because he was the greatest natural marksman in the division. Any weapon he could lift, he could kill with. He pointed it languidly, pulled the trigger, and something always fell. Some of the men appreciated this quality very much and liked to be with or near Raymond when any action occurred, but otherwise he was scrupulously shunned by all of them.

Raymond was a left-handed man of considerable height—to which he soared from wide hips, narrower shoulders—with a triangular face which suspended a pointed chin that was narrow and not very firm. The vertical halves of his face pouted together sullenly, projecting the effluvia of self-pity. His skin was immoderately white, which made the prominent veins of his arms and legs seem like blue neon tubing. His cropped hair was light blonde and it grew down low and in a round shape over his forehead in a style affected by many American businessmen of a juvenile or eunuchoid turn.

Despite that specific inventory of his countenance, Raymond was a very handsome man, very nearly a pretty man, who had heavy bones, great physical strength, and large glaucous eyes with very large whites, like those of a carousel horse pursued by the Erinyes, those female avengers of antiquity.

When the flautist Boehm engineered the new design and the new note value system for the clarinet, his system took a half note away from the thumb and a half note away from the third finger on each hand, as it would have been played on the standard Albert clarinet. By so doing he created an aural schism and brought a most refined essence of prejudice to a world of music. He created two clarinetists with two subtly different qualities of sound, where there had been one before, and provided, amid this decadence, many bitter misunderstandings. It was as if Raymond had been built by Herr Boehm to have had his full notes dropped to half notes, then to quarter notes, then to eighth notes, for his was an almost silent music, if music Raymond contained at all.

In spite of himself the captain liked Shaw, and the captain was a matured and thoughtful man. He liked Raymond, he had decided after much consideration of the phenomenon, because, in one way or another, Shaw was continuously demonstrating that he liked the captain and the captain was too wise a man to believe he could resist a plea like that.

Nobody else in Company C liked Raymond, and perhaps no one else in the U.S. Army did. His comrades skirted him charily or they pretended he was not there, as the fathers of daughters might regard an extremely high incidence of rape in their neighbourhood.

It was not that Raymond was hard to like. He was impossible to like. The captain, a thoughtful man, understood that Shaw's attention to him was merely the result of the pressure of a lifetime of having his nose rubbed in various symbols of authority, and as the sergeant's life story droned on and on the captain came to realise that Raymond was pouring out a cherished monologue upon the beloved memory of his long-dead, betrayed father, who had been cast off by that bitch before Raymond could begin to love him. Amateur psychiatric prognosis can be fascinating when there is absolutely nothing else to do. Also fascinating was the captain's unending search for one small, even isolated address of Raymond's that was warm or, in any human way, attractive.

Raymond's crushing contemptuousness aside, examining such a minute thing as the use of his hands while talking could be distressing, and the captain could see how little fragments of Raymond's personality had formed one great, cold lump. Raymond could not stop using one horrid gesture: a go-way-you-bother-me, flicking sort of gesture that he managed by having his long, fish-belly white fingers do small, backhand, brushing gestures to point up anything he said. Anything. He made the brush if he said good morning. If. He flicked air away from himself when he talked about the weather, politics (his field), food, or gear: anything. This *digitorum gesticulatione* was about the most irritating single bit of movement that the captain could ever remember seeing, and the captain was a thoughtful man. He had burst out against it early one morning while the sky was flinging light all around them, and Raymond had responded with a look of confusion, unaware of his fault, and disturbed. He had said to the captain that he, flick-flick, did not understand what the captain meant, brush-brush, and at last the captain had chosen to overlook it, as it was a relatively minor thing to a man who planned to be a war-time or a peace-time general of four stars some day and who had permitted himself to decide that he would be crazy to refuse to understand a hero-worshipping sergeant whose relative might some day be chairman, or have direct influence on the chairman, of the Armed Services Committee of the Congress.

It took that kind of objectivity to begin to tolerate Raymond, who was over full of haughtiness. Raymond stood as though someone might have just opened a beach umbrella in his bowels.

His very glance drawled when he deigned to look, seldom deigning to speak. There were wags in the company who said he put his lips up in curl papers each night, and all of these things are sure ingredients for arousing and sustaining the hostility of others. In theory, Shaw possessed a manner that should become a sergeant, and perhaps would become a drill sergeant or a Marine Corps public-relations sergeant, but not a combat noncom because under heightened realism any attitude of power must always be accompanied by something that makes the privilege of power pardonable, and Shaw possessed no such rescuing qualifiers. His resentment of people, places, and things was a stifling, sensual thing.

The captain's name was Ben Marco. He was a professional officer. He had been sixth in his class at the Academy. His family had claimed the Army as a trade ever since a gunnery lieutenant who had grown up with Hernando de Soto at Barcarrota, Spain, had left Pizarro for a look at the upper Mississippi River. Marco followed his father's vocation because it was the last preserve of intimate feudalism: terraced ranks of fief and lord, where a major can always remain a peasant to a general and a lieutenant a peon to a major.

Marco was an intelligent intelligence officer. He looked like an Aztec crossed with an Eskimo, which was a fairly common western American type because the Aztec troops had drifted down from Siberia quite a long time before the Spaniards of Pizarro and Cortez had drifted north out of the Andes and Vera Cruz. He had metallic (copper-coloured) skin and strong (very white) teeth but, aside from pigmentation, the straight (black) hair, the aboriginal look, and the eyes coloured like Pôtage St Germaine, the pôtage's pôtage (green); he had had the contrasting fortune of being born in New Hampshire, where his father had been stationed at the time, just prior to duty in the Canal Zone. He stood five feet eleven and three-quarter inches and looked small when standing beside Raymond. He had a powerful frame and the meat on it was proportioned like the stone meat on an Epstein statue. He had the superior digestive system which affords almost every man blessed with it the repose to become thoughtful.

They were an odd combination: the civilian who tried to talk like a soldier and the soldier who had been ordered by the Joint Chiefs in this new and polite Army to damn well learn how to talk like a civilian; the frosty Brahmin with the earthy, ambitious man; the pseudomystagogue with the counter-puncher; the inhibitory with the excitatory, the latter being a designation used by the physiologist Ivan Petrovich Pavlov.

Marco led the Intelligence and Reconnaissance patrol of nine men and his sergeant, Ray Shaw, on their fourteenth reconnaissance that night. Chunjin, Marco's orderly, appeared suddenly at his elbow, out of the almost total darkness and persistent silence. Chunjin was the captain's interpreter, the general guide over terrain, who, no matter where they were sent in Korea always insisted gravely that he had been born within two miles of the spot. Chunjin was a very good man with a frying pan, a shoe brush, a broom, a shaving kit, and at crating and transhipping books to San Francisco. He was small and wiry. He was a very, very tough-looking fellow against any comparison. He had the look of a man who maybe had been pushed around a lot and then had taken his life into his hands by deciding not to take any more of that kind of stuff. He always looked them right in the eyes, from private to colonel, and he did not smile at any time.

'What?' Marco said.

'Bad here.'

'Why?'

'Tricky.'

'How?'

'Swamp all around thirty yards up. May be quicksand.'

'Nobody told me about any quicksand.'

'How they know?'

'All right! All right! What do you want?'

'All walk in single line next two hundred yards.'

'No.'

'Patrol sink.'

'It is tactically unsound to go forward in a single file.'

'Then patrol sink in thirty yards.'

'Only for two hundred yards ahead?'

'Yes, sir.'

'We can't go around it?'

'No, sir.'

'All right. Pass the word.'

Raymond was at the head of the line, right behind Chunjin, in guide position. Marco finished the twelve-man line. I & R patrols go out at night, unarmed except for knives. They are unarmed because rifle fire draws other fire and I & R patrols do what they do by staying out of trouble. There was very little light from a pallid crescent of moon. There was about twenty feet distance between each man. The line was about seventy yards long. When it had moved forward about sixty yards, two human forms rose up in front of and behind each man on the line. The forward form hit its man at the pit of the stomach with a rifle butt, while the back man brought the stock down hard at the back of each man's head when the bodies doubled forward. Excepting Chunjin, they all seemed to go down at the same time. It was an extremely silent action, a model action of its kind. Without pause each two-man team of attackers built a litter out of the two rifles and rolled their charges aboard. Two noncoms checked each team out, talking quietly and occasionally slapping a man on the shoulder with approval and self-pleasure.

Chunjin led the litter teams on a route that was at right angles to the direction taken by the patrol, across the dark, firm terrain. Twenty-two men carried eleven bodies in the improvised stretchers at a rapid dogtrot while the noncoms sang the cadence in soft Russian. The patrol had been taken by Three company of the 35th Regiment of the 66th Airborne Division of the Soviet Army, a crack outfit that handled most of the flashy assignments in the sector, and dined out between these jobs with available North Korean broads and the young ladies of the North-east Administrative Area, on the stories emanating therefrom.

The patrol was taken to two trucks waiting a quarter mile away. The trucks rode them twelve miles over bad terrain to a temporary airfield. A helicopter took them north at about twelve hundred feet. They had cleared the Yalu before the first man began to climb back into sluggish consciousness to see a uniformed country boy from Ukhta holding a machine rifle at ready and grinning down at him.

Dr Yen Lo and his staff of thirty technicians (all of whom were Chinese except two overawed Uzbek neuropsychiatrists who had jointly won an Amahlkin award; as a reward, their section had arranged for them to spend a thirty-day tour with this man whom they had always thought of as a shelf of books or the voice behind the many professors in their short lives—the living monument to, and the continental expander of, the work of Pavlov) installed their peculiar establishment during the night of July 6 and worked at the fixtures necessary until mid-morning of July 7. Their pharmacy was an elaborate affair, for one thing. For another, they had brought in four compact electronic computers. Included in the effects was an electrical switchboard that seemed large enough to have handled the lighting for the State Opera in Vienna, where, quite possibly, it originated.

Old Yen was in fine spirits. He chatted freely about Pavlov and Salter, Krasnogorski and Meignant, Petrova and Bechtervov, Forlov and Rowland, as though he had not made his departure from the main stream of their doctrine some nine years before when he had come upon his own radical technology for descent into the unconscious mind with the speed of a mine-shaft elevator. He made jokes with his staff. He taunted the two Uzbeks just as though he were not a god, about Herr Freud, whom he called 'that Austrian gypsy fortuneteller' or 'the Teuton fantast' or 'that licensed gossip,' and he permitted his chief of staff to visit General Kostroma's chief to arrange for the mess and the billeting of his people.

During the pleasantly cool evening before the morning when the American I & R patrol was brought in for him, Yen Lo and his staff of thirty men and women sat in a large circle on a broad, grassy space, and as the moon went higher and the hour got later, and all of the voices seemed to fall into lower pitch preparing for sleepiness, Yen Lo told them a fairy story, which was set thirty-nine centuries before they had been born, about a young fisherman and a beautiful princess who had journeyed through the province of Chengtu.

The American patrol was brought to the Research Pavilion at six-nine the following morning, July 8. Yen Lo had them bathed, then inoculated each of them personally. They were dressed again while they slept and set down, excepting for Raymond Shaw, one man to a cot to a cubicle, where Yen Lo got three implantation teams started on them, staying with each team through the originating processes until he had assured himself that all had been routined with smoothness. When he had assured himself to the point of downright fussiness, he brought his assistant and two nurses with him into the corner apartment where Raymond slept and began the complex work on the reconstruction of the sergeant's personality.

The principles of excitation, as outlined by Pavlov in 1894, are immutable and apply to every psychological problem no matter how remote it may appear at first. Conditioned reflexes do not involve volitional thinking. Words produce associative reflexes. 'Splendid,' 'marvellous,' and magnificent' give us an unconscious lift because we have been conditioned to that feeling in them. The words 'hot,' 'boiling,' and 'steam' have a warm quality because of their associativity. Inflection and gesture have been conditioned as intensifiers of word conditionings, as Andrew Slater, the Pavlovian disciple, writes.

Salter shows that when one sees the essence of the unconscious mind to be conditioning, one is in a strategic position to develop a sound understanding of the deepest wellsprings of human behaviour. Conditioning is based upon associative reflexes that use words or symbols as triggers of installed automatic reactions. Conditioning, called brain-washing by the news agencies, is the production of reactions in the human organism through the use of associative reflexes.

Yen Lo approached human behaviour in terms of fundamental components instead of metaphysical labels. His meaningful goal was to implant in the subject's mind the predominant motive, which was that of submitting to the operator's commands; to construct behaviour which would at all times strive to put the operator's exact intentions into execution as if the subject were playing a game or acting a part; and to cause a redirection of his movements by remote control through second parties, or third or fiftieth parties, twelve thousand miles removed from the original commands if necessary. The first thing a human being is loyal to, Yen Lo observed, is his own conditioned nervous system.

On the morning of July 9, the members of the American patrol, excepting Shaw, Marco, and Chunjin, the Korean interpreter, were allowed to walk in and out of each other's rooms and to lounge around in a comfortable common room where there were magazines only two or three years old, printed in Chinese and Russian, and an Australian seed catalogue dated Spring 1944, with attractive colour pictures. Yen Lo had conditioned the men to enjoy all the Coca-Cola they could drink, which was, in actuality, Chinese Army issue tea served in tin cups. There were playing cards, card tables, and some dice. Each man had been given twenty strips of brown paper and told that these were one-, five-, ten- and twenty-dollar bills of U.S. currency, depending on how they had been marked in pencil on the corners.

The yellow rattan carpet, the simulated sunlight from the fluorescent tubing, and the happy, blonde furniture in the windowless room were quite cheery and bright and the men had been instructed to enjoy their surroundings. About thirty pin-up pictures of Chinese and Indian movie stars were clustered thickly on one wall around a calendar that advertised Tiger Beer of Singapore (fourteen per cent by volume) and offered a deminude Caucasian cutie dressed for Coney Island in the mode of the summer of 1931. There were cigarettes and cigars for everyone, and Yen Lo had allowed his boys to have a little fun in the selection of outlandish tobacco substitutes because he knew that word of it would pass through the armies, based upon the sure knowledge of what made armies laugh, rubbing more sheen into the legend of the Yen Lo unit. They would be talking about how much those Americans had savoured those cigars and cigarettes from Lvov to Cape Bezhneva inside of one week, as yak dung tastes good like a cigarette should.

The nine men had been conditioned to believe that they were levelling off on a Sunday night after a terrific three-day pass from a post forty minutes outside of New Orleans. They were all convinced that each had won a lot of money and that in spending most of it they had reached exhaustion with warm edges and an expensive calm feeling.

Ed Mavole had received the spirit of Yen Lo's suggestion so strongly that he confided to Silvers that he was slightly worried and wondered if maybe he wouldn't be doing the right thing if he stepped out for a minute to a prophylactic station.

They were worn down from all that whisky and those broads, but they were relaxed and euphoric. Three times a day Yen's staff men gave each man his deep mental massage, stacking up the layers of light and shadow neatly within each unconscious mind, as ordered. The men spent two days in and out of the common room, sleeping and eating when they felt like it, believing it was always the same time on the same Sunday night, remembering that clutch of sensational broads as if they had just rolled off them.

The distinguished commission of distinguished men, including one who was a member of the Central Committee, and another who was a security officer wearing the uniform of a lieutenant general of the Soviet Army inasmuch as he was travelling through a military zone and because he happened to like to wear uniforms, arrived with their staffs at the Tunghwa military airport, accompanied by two round Chinese dignitaries, at five minutes

36

to noon on the morning of July 12, 1951. There were fourteen in the group. Gomel, the Politburo man, in mufti, had a staff of five men who were in uniform. Berezovo, the security officer, in uniform, had a staff of four men and a young woman, in mufti. The two Russian groups seemed remote from each other and from the two young Chinese who may only have seemed young because of an eighty-three per cent vegetable diet.

They all ate at General Kostroma's mess. He was the army corps commander who had been transferred too suddenly from work that had suited him so well at the Army War College to be pressed into supervising Chinese who seemed to have no understanding of military mission and who were fearfully spendthrift with troops.

There appeared to be four entirely separate groups dining at the same large table.

First, Kostroma and his staff: bravely silent men who realised now that they had made a chafing mistake when they had wangled places with this general; they were continuously wondering where they had gone wrong in their judgement, trying to analyse retrospectively whether anyone along the line had encouraged them to think that a berth with Kostroma would be a shrewd move. General Kostroma himself remained mute because a Central Committee member was present, and as Kostroma had evidently made mistakes in the past which he had not known he had been making, he did not want to make another.

The second group, Gomel's, was made up of men whose average length of service among the trench-mortar subtleties of party practice and ascent through the ranks had been a total of eighteen years and four months each. They were professional politicians, wholly independent of the whims of popular vote. They saw their community duty as that of appearing wise and stern, hence they observed silence.

The Berezovo group was silent because they were security people. Berezovo is dead now. For that matter, so is General Kostroma.

Those three groups, however silent, were well aware of the

fourth, chaired by Yen Lo (D.M.S., D.Ph., D.Sc., B.S.P., R.H.S.) who kept his own executive staff and the two young (one should call them young-looking rather than young) Chinese dignitaries in high-pitched, continual laughter until the meal had spent itself. All jokes were in Chinese. Even without pointed gestures, Yen managed to convey the feeling that all of the gusty sallies were at their gallant Russian ally's expense. Gomel glared and sweated a form of chicken fat. Berezovo picked at his food expressionlessly, and pared an apple with a bayonet.

Gomel, who established himself as being hircine before anything else, was as stocky as an opera hat, with a bullet head and stainless-steel false teeth. It would be difficult to be more proletarian-seeming than Gomel. The teeth had made him carnivorously unphotogenic and therefore unknown to the newspaper readers of the West. He dressed in the chic moujik style affected by his leader; loose silk everythings rushing downward into the tops of soft black boots. His smell tended to worry his personal staff lest their expressions make it seem as though they were personally disloyal to him. He was a specialist in heavy industrial management.

Berezovo, who was younger than Gomel, represented the new Soviet executive and resembled a fire hydrant in a rundown neighbourhood: short, squat, stained, and seamed, his head seeming to come to a point and his fibrous hair parted in several impossible places, like a coconut's. Berezovo was all brass; a very important person. Gomel was important, no doubt about that. He had *dachi* in both Moscow and the Crimea, but there were only two men higher than Berezovo in the entire, exhaustingly delicate business of Soviet security.

Each man had successfully concealed from the other that he was present at the seminar as the personal and confidential representative of Josef Stalin, proprietor.

Yen Lo's lectures began at 4 p.m. on July 11. General Kostroma was not invited to attend. The group strolled in pairs, not unlike dons moving across a campus, towards the lovely copse

38

which framed that little red schoolhouse wherein Yen Lo had inserted so many new values and perspectives into the minds of the eleven Americans. It was a glorious summer afternoon: not too hot, not too cool. The excessive humidity of the morning had disappeared. The food had been excellent.

The single extraordinary sight in the informal but stately procession led by Yen Lo and Pa Cha, the senior Chinese statesman present, was that of Chunjin, the Korean interpreter hitherto attached to the U.S. Army as orderly and guide for Captain Marco, walking at Berezovo's side, chewing on and smoking a large cigar which was held in his small teeth at a jaunty angle. Had any member of the American patrol still retained any semblance of normal perspective he would have been startled at seeing Chunjin there, for when natives were captured by a military party of either side their throats were always cut.

Yen Lo had telephoned ahead from the mess so that when the commission entered the auditorium of the Research Pavilion the American patrol had been seated in a long line across the raised stage, behind a centred lectern. They watched the Sino-Soviet group enter with expressions of amused tolerance and boredom. Yen Lo moved directly to the platform, rummaging in his attaché case while the others found seats, by echelon, in upright wooden chairs.

Large, repeated, seven-colour lithographs of Stalin and Mao were interspersed on three walls between muscularly typographed yellow-on-black posters that read: *LET US STOP IMITATING!!!* as a headline, and as text: *Piracy and imitations of designs hamper the development and expansion of export trade. It is regrettable that there are quite a few cases of piracy in the People's Republic. Piracy injures the Chinese people's international prestige, causes the boycott of Chinese goods, and makes Chinese designers lose interest in making creative efforts.* The smell of new paint and shellac and the delicious clean odour of wood shavings floated everywhere in the air of the room, offering the deep, deep luxury of absolute simplicity.

On stage, Ben Marco sat on the end of the line at stage right, in the Mr Bones position. Sergeant Shaw sat on the other end of the line, stage left. Between them, left to right, were Hiken, Gosfield, Little, Silvers, Mavole, Melvin, Freeman, Lembeck. Mavole was at stage centre. All of the men were alert and serene.

The audience was divided, physically and by prejudice. Gomel did not approve of Yen Lo or his work. Berezovo happened to see in Yen Lo's methods possibilities that would hasten revolutionary causes by fifty years. Five staff members sat behind each of these men who sat on opposite sides of the room, re-creating an impression of two Alphonse Capones (1899–1947) attending the Chicago opera of 1927. The two Chinese representatives sat off to the left, closer to the platform than the others, as bland as two jars of yoghurt. Yen Lo winked at them now and again as he made his address with asides in various Chinese dialects to annoy Gomel.

The stage was raised about thirty inches from the floor and was draped with bunting of the U.S.S.R. and the People's Republic of China. Yen Lo stood behind the centred lectern. He was wearing an ankle-length dress of French blue that buttoned at the side of his throat and fell in straight, comfortable lines. The skin of his face was lapstreaked, or clinker-built, into overlapping horizontal folds like the sides of some small boats, and it was the colour of raw sulphur. His eyes were hooded and dark, which made him seem even older than did the wrinkles. His entire expression was theatrically sardonic as though he had been advised by prepaid cable that the late Dr Fu Manchu had been his uncle.

Yen Lo instructed the Russians with bright contempt, with the slightly nauseated fixity of a vegetarian who must remain in a closed room with carnivores. He used a pointer to indicate the various U.S. Army personnel behind him. He introduced each man courteously and by name. He explained their somewhat lackadaisical manners by saying that each American was under the impression that he had been forced by a storm to wait in a small hotel in New Jersey where space restrictions made it necessary for him to watch and listen to a meeting of a ladies' garden club.

Yen motioned to Raymond Shaw. 'Pull your chair over here, Raymond, if you please,' he said in English. Raymond sat beside Yen Lo, who placed his hand lightly on the young man's shoulder as he spoke to the group. Raymond's bearing was superciliously haughty. His pose, had it been executed in oils, might have been called 'The Young Duke among the Fishmongers.' His legs were crossed and his head was cocked with his chin outstretched.

The male stenographer on Gomel's team and the female stenographer on Berezovo's squad flipped their notebooks open on their laps at the same instant, preparing to record Yen's remarks. The shorter Chinese emissary, a chap named Wen Ch'ang, got his hand under his dress and scratched his crotch.

'This, comrades, is the famous Raymond Shaw, the young man you have flown nearly eight thousand miles to see,' Yen Lo said in Russian. 'Your chief, Lavrenti Pavlovich Beria, saw this young man in his mind's eye, only as a disembodied ideal, as long as two years before he was appointed to head the Ministry of Internal Affairs and Security in 1938, and that was thirteen eventful years ago. I feel I must add at this point my humble personal gratitude for his warm encouragement and fulfilling inspiration. It is to Lavrenti Pavlovich that this little demonstration will do homage today.'

Berezovo nodded his head graciously in silent acknowledgment of the tribute, then the five staff people behind him just as graciously nodded their heads.

Yen Lo told the group that Raymond Shaw was a unique combination of the exceptional: both internally and externally. With oratorical roundness he presented Raymond's external values first. He told them about Raymond's stepfather, the governor; of Raymond's mother, a woman of wealth and celebrity; of Raymond's uncle, a distinguished member of the U.S. diplomatic service. Raymond himself was a journalist and when this little war was over might even rise to become a distinguished journalist. All of these attributes, he said, made Raymond welcome everywhere within the political hierarchy of the United States, within both parties.

The line of American soldiers listened to the lecture politely, as though they had to make the best of listening to club women discuss fun with hydrangeas. Bobby Lembeck's attention had strayed. Ed Mavole, who was still firmly convinced that he had just finished the most active three-day pass of his Army career, had to stuff a fist into his mouth to conceal a yawn. Captain Marco looked from Shaw to Yen Lo to Gomel to Berezovo's recording assistant, a fine-looking piece with a passionate nose who was wearing no lipstick and no brassiere. Marco mentally fitted her with a B cup, enjoyed the diversion, then turned back to try to pay attention to Yen Lo, who was saying that as formidable as were Raymond's external attributes, he possessed internal weaknesses that Yen would show as being incredible strengths for an assassin.

'I am sure that all of you have heard that old wives' tale,' Yen stated, 'which is concerned with the belief that no hypnotised subject may be forced to do that which is repellent to his moral nature, whatever that is, or to his own best interests. That is nonsense, of course. You note-takers might set down a reminder to consult Brenmen's paper, "Experiments in the Hypnotic Production of Anti-social and Self-injurious Behaviour," or Wells' 1941 paper which was titled, I believe, "Experiments in the Hypnotic Production of Crime," or Andrew Salter's remarkable book, *Conditioned Reflex Therapy*, to name only three. Or, if it offends you to think that only the West is studying how to manufacture more crime and better criminals against modern shortages, I suggest Krasnogorski's *Primary Violence Motivation* or Serov's *The Unilateral Suggestion to Self-Destruction*. For any of you who are interested in massive negative conditioning there is Frederic Wertham's *The Seduction of the Innocent*, which demonstrates how thousands have been brought to anti-social actions through children's cartoon books. However, enough of that. You won't read them anyway. The point I am making is that those who speak of the need for hypnotic suggestion to fit a subject's moral code should revise their concepts. The conception of people acting against their own best interests should not startle us. We see it occasionally in sleepwalking and in politics, every day.'

Raymond sighed. The youngest man on Gomel's staff, seated farthest back in the rows of irregularly placed chairs, picked his nose surreptitiously through the ensuing silence. Berezovo's recording assistant, her breasts pointing straight out through the cotton blouse without benefit of B cup, stared at Marco just below the belt buckle. The Chinese had become aware of how much Comrade Gomel smelled like a goat. Bobby Lembeck was thinking about Marie Louise.

Most of the Russians understood clearly that what Yen Lo had done was to concentrate the purpose of all propaganda upon the mind of one man. They knew that reflexes could be conditioned to the finest point so that if the right person levelled his finger from the right place at the right time and cried 'Deviationist!' or 'Trotskyite' that any man's character could be assassinated or a man could be liquidated. Conditioning was intensified repetition.

Ed Mavole had to go to the john. He looked furtively to the right and left, then he caught Marco's eye and made a desperate series of lifts with his eyebrows combined with some compulsive face tics. Marco coughed. Yen Lo looked over at him serenely, then nodded. Marco went to Yen's side and whispered a message. Yen shouted a command in Chinese and a man appeared in the open doorway at the back of the auditorium. Yen suggested that Mavole follow that man and he told Mavole not to be embarrassed, because the ladies did not understand Chinese. Mavole thanked him, then he turned to the line of sitting soldiers and said, 'Anybody else?' Bobby Lembeck joined him and they left the room. Marco returned to his chair. Gomel demanded to know what the hell was going on anyway. Yen Lo explained, deadpan, in Russian, and Gomel made an impatient, exasperated face.

Yen Lo carried his thesis forward. Neurotics and psychotics, he

43

told the group, are too easily canted into unpredictable patterns and the constitutional psychopaths, those total waste products of all breeding, were too frivolously based. Of course, he explained, the psychotic group known as paranoiacs had always provided us with the great leaders of the world and always would. That was a clinical, historical fact. With their dedicated sense of personal mission (a condition that has been allowed to become tainted semantically, he pointed out, with the psychiatric label of megalomania), with their innate ability to falsify hampering conditions of the past to prevent unwanted distortion of the future, with that relentless, protective cunning that places the whole world, in revolving turn, into position as their enemies, paranoiacs simply had to be placed in the elite stock of any leader pool.

Mavole and Lembeck came back, picking their way carefully through the chairs and moving very properly, Mavole leading. They climbed back upon the platform almost daintily while the speaker and the audience waited politely. Mavole inadvertently broke wind as he sat down. He excused himself with a startled exclamation and flushed with embarrassment before all those garden ladies. His consternation sent Gomel into barking laughter. Yen Lo waited icily until the commissar had finished his pleasure, whacking his packed thighs and wheezing, then pointing his stunted finger up at Mavole on the platform while he guffawed helplessly. When the laughter finally subsided, Yen threw an aside at his countrymen in Chinese. They tittered like *thlibii*, which shut Gomel up. Yen Lo continued blandly.

'Although the paranoiacs make the great leaders, it is the resenters who make their best instruments because the resenters, those men with cancer of the psyche, make the great assassins.' His audience was listening intently again.

'It is difficult to define true resentment for you. The Spanish medical philosopher Dr Gregorio Marañón described it as a passion of the mind. Some blow of life which produces a sharp moan of protest, when it is not transformed by the normal mental mechanism into ordinary resignation, ends by becoming

44

the director of our slightest reactions. Raymond's mother helped
to bring about his condition to the largest and most significant
extent for, in Andrew Salter's words, "the human fish swim about
at the bottom of the great ocean of atmosphere and they develop
psychic injuries as they collide with one another. Most mortal of
all are the wounds got from the parent fish." '

'It has been said,' the Chinese doctor continued, 'that only
the man who is capable of loving everything is capable of
understanding everything. The resentful man is a human with
the capacity for affection so poorly developed that his understanding for the motives of others very nearly does not exist.'
Yen Lo patted Raymond's shoulder sympathetically and smiled
down at him regretfully. 'Raymond is a man of melancholic and
reserved psychology. He is afflicted with total resentment. It is
slowly fomenting within him before your eyes. Raymond's heart
is arid. At the core of his defects is his concealed tendency to
timidity, sexual and social, both of which are closely linked,
which he hides behind that formidably severe and haughty cast
of countenance. This weakness of will is compounded by his
constant need to lean upon someone else's will, and now, at last,
that has been taken care of for the rest of Raymond's life.'

'Has the man ever killed anyone?' Berezovo asked loudly.

'Have you ever murdered anyone, Raymond?' Yen Lo asked
the young man solicitously.

'No, sir.'

'Have you ever killed anyone?'

'No, sir.'

'Not even in combat?'

'In combat, yes, sir. I think so, sir.'

'Thank you, Raymond. Dr Marañon tells us that resentment
is entirely impersonal, as opposed to hatred, which has a strictly
individual cast and presupposes a duel between the hater and
the hated. The reaction of the resenter is directed against
destiny.' The pace of Yen Lo's voice slowed and it had softened
when he spoke again. 'Pity Raymond, if you can. Beneath his
sad and stony mask, wary and hypocritical, you must remember

45

that his every act, every thought, and all of his ends, are permeated with an indefinable bitterness. An infinite anguish must mark his life. He flees the world to find himself in solitude and solitude terrifies him because it is too close to his despair. His soul has been rubbed to shreds between the ambivalence of wanting and not wanting; of being able and unable; of loving and hating; and, as Dr Marañon has demonstrated, his feeling lives like two brothers, at one and the same time Siamese twins and deadly enemies.'

The commission stared at this dream by Lavrenti Beria: the perfectly prefabricated assassin, this bored, too handsome, blonde young man with the pointed chin and the pointed ears, whose mustard-coloured eyes looked through them as a cat's would, and who would not be able to stop destroying once the instructions had been fed into him. All but four of them had had experience in one soviet or another with the old-fashioned, wild-eyed, cause-torn name-killers of the domestic politics of the past twenty-five years, and every one of those had been a shaky, thousand-to-one shot as far as being able to guarantee success, but here was Caesar's son to be sent into Caesar's chamber to kill Caesar. Steady, responsible, shock-proof assassins were needed at home because assassination was a stratagem requiring secrecy and control, and if an assassination were not to be committed secretly then it had to be arranged discreetly and smoothly so that the ruling cliques realised that it was an occasion not to be advertised. If the assassin were to be used in the West, as this one would be, where sensationalism is not only desirable but politically essential, the blow needed to be struck at exactly the right time and place, at a national emotional apogee, as it were, so that the selected messiah who would succeed the slain ruler could then defend all of his people from the threatening and monstrous element at whose doorstep the assassination of an authentic national hero could swiftly and effectively be laid.

Berezovo was thinking of Yen Lo's proud claim of prolonging post-hypnotic amnesia into eternity. Berezovo had been life-

46

trained in security work, particularly that having to do with Soviet security problems in North America, where this killer would operate. If a normally conditioned Anglo-Saxon could be taught to kill and kill, then to have no memory of having killed, or even of having had the thought of killing, he could feel no guilt. If he could feel no guilt he could not fall into the trap of betraying fear of being caught. If he could not feel guilt, or the fear of being caught, he would remain an outwardly normal, productive, sober, and respectful member of his community so that, as Berezovo saw it, this killer was very close to being police-proof and the method by which he was created must be very, very carefully controlled in its application to other men within the Soviet Union. Specifically, within Moscow. More specifically within the Kremlin.

Gomel was multiplying Raymond. If Yen Lo could manufacture one of these he could manufacture an elite corps of what could be the most extraordinary personal troops a leader could have. By having immutable loyalty built into a cadre of perhaps one hundred men a leader could not only take power but he would become unseatable because after the flawless, selfless guardians had removed the others they could be conditioned to take portfolios under the new leader from which they would never, never plot against the new leader and would reflexively choose to die themselves rather than see any harm come to him. Gomel felt himself grow taller but, all at once, he thought of the power of Yen Lo and it spoiled his vision. Yen Lo would have to manufacture these assistants. Who would ever know what else he had built into their minds, such as acting to kill within an area where they were supposed to be utterly immobile? He had disliked Yen Lo before this but now he began to feel a bitter hatred towards him. But what could be done to such a man? How could fear be put into him to control him? Who knew but that he had conditioned other unknown men to strike at all authority if they were to hear of Yen Lo's arrest or death by violence, or for that matter, death under any circumstances whatsoever?

Marco knew he was sick but he did not know, nor did he seem

47

to be able to make himself learn how to know why he thought he was sick. He could see Raymond sitting in calmness. He knew they were waiting out a storm in the Spring Valley Hotel, twenty-three miles from Fort Monmouth in New Jersey, and that they had been lucky indeed to have been offered the hospitality of the lobby, which, as everyone knew, in the off season was reserved almost exclusively on Wednesday afternoons for the Spring Valley Garden Club. He was conscious of boredom because he had little interest in flowers except as a dodge to jolly a girl into bed, and although these ladies had been very kind and very pleasant they were advanced in terms of years beyond his interest in women. That was it. There it was. Yet he sat among them distorted by the illusion that he was facing a lieutenant general of the Soviet Army, three Chinese, five staff officers, and six civilians who were undoubtedly Russian because the bottoms of their trousers were two feet wide and the beige jackets seemed to have been cut by a drunken chimpanzee, plus one randy broad who never took her eyes off his pants. He knew it was some kind of psychiatric hallucination. He knew he was sick, but he could not, on the other hand, figure out why he thought he was sick. Spring Valley was a beautiful, lazy place. A lovely, lovely, lazy, lazy place. Spring Valley.

Yen Lo was explaining his methods of procedure. The first descent into the deep unconscious, he explained, was drug-induced. Then, after the insistence of various ideas and instructions which were far too tenuous to take up time with, the subject was pulled out for the first time and four tests were made to determine the firmness of the deep control plant. The total immersion time into the unconscious mind of the subject during the first contact had been eleven hours. The second descent was light-induced. The subject, after further extensive suggestion which took up seven and three-quarter hours and required far less technique than the first immersion, was then pulled out again. A simple interrogation test based upon the subject's psychiatric dossier, which the security force had so skilfully assembled over the years, and a series of physical reflexive tests, were followed by conditioning for control of the subject by hand and symbol signal, and by voice command. The critical application of deep suggestion was observed during the first eleven hours of immersion when the primary link to all future control was set in. To this unbreakable link would be hooked future links that would represent individual assignments which would motivate the subject and which would then be smashed by the subject's own memory, or mnemonic apparatus, on a pre-signalled system emanating from the first permanent link. At the instant he killed, Raymond would forget forever that he had killed.

Yen Lo looked smug for an instant, but he wiped the expression off before anyone but Berezovo had an opportunity to register it. So far, so good, he said. The subject could not ever remember what he had done under suggestion, or what he had been told to do, or who had instructed him to do it. This eliminated altogether the danger of internal psychological friction resulting from feelings of guilt or from the fear of capture by authorities, and the external danger existent in any police interrogation, no matter how severe.

'With all of that precision in psychological design,' Yen said, 'the most admirable, the most far-reaching characteristic of this extraordinary technology of mine is the manner in which it provides for the refuelling of the conditioning, and this factor will operate wherever the subject may be—two feet or five thousand miles away from Yen Lo—and utterly independently of my voice or any assumed reality of my personal control. Incidentally, while we're on that subject, we presented one of these refuelling devices to the chairman of your sub-rural electrification programme who faced a somewhat lonely and uncomfortably cold winter on the Gydan Peninsula. Our subject was a thoroughly conditioned young ballet dancer whom the commissar had long admired, but she was most painfully, from his view, married to a young man whom she loved not only outrageously but to the exclusion of all others. Comrade Stalin took pity on him and called me. By using our manual of operating instructions he found himself with the beautiful, very young, very supple dancer

49

who never wore clothes because they made her freezing cold and who undertook conditioned sexual conceptions which were so advanced that the commissar's winter passed almost before he knew it had started.'

They roared with laughter. Gomel slapped welts on his thighs with his horny hand. The recording assistant beside Berezovo couldn't stop giggling: a treble one-note giggle which was so comical that soon everyone was laughing at her giggle as well as Yen Lo's story. Berezovo finally rapped on the wooden back of the chair in front of him with the naked bayonet he was carrying. Everyone but Gomel stopped laughing in mid-note, but Gomel had just about laughed himself out and was wiping his eyes and shaking his head, thinking of what could be done with a beautiful, nubile young woman who had also been conditioned to kill efficiently.

'Now,' Yen Lo said, 'to operate Raymond it amused me to choose as his remote control any ordinary deck of playing cards. They offer clear, colourful symbols that, in ancient, monarchical terms, contain the suggestion of supreme authority. They are easily obtainable by Raymond anywhere in his country and, after a time, he will probably take to carrying a deck of the cards with him. Very good. I will demonstrate.' He turned to the sergeant. 'Raymond, why don't you pass the time by playing a little solitaire?' Raymond sat erect and looked alertly at Yen Lo. 'Pull that table over, Raymond,' the old Chinese said. Raymond walked to stage right and carried back with him a small table on whose top had been placed a pack of cards. He sat down.

'The first refuelling key was the sentence suggesting solitaire in those exact words, which unlocks his basic conditioning. Then the queen of diamonds, in so many ways reminiscent of Raymond's dearly loved and hated mother, is the second key that will clear his mechanism for any assignments.' As Yen spoke, Raymond had been shuffling the cards and was laying out the seven-card spread that is variously called solitaire, Klondike, or patience.

'He will play the game until the queen of diamonds enters the play, which will be soon because we arranged it that way to save your time. Ah, here it is.' Raymond's play had turned up the queen. He scooped all the other cards together neatly. He squared them, placed them face down on the table, and put the queen of diamonds face up on top of the pack, then sat back to watch the card with off-hand interest, his manner entirely normal.

'May I have that bayonet, please?' Yen Lo asked General Berezovo.

'Not with the knife,' Gomel barked. 'With the hands.'

'His hands?' Yen responded distastefully.

'Here,' Berezovo said. 'Have him use this.' He handed a white silk scarf to an assistant who carried it to Yen Lo. Yen knotted the scarf tightly in three close places, speaking to Raymond as he did so.

'Raymond, whom do you dislike the least in your group who are here today?'

'The least?'

'That's right.'

'Well—I guess Captain Marco, sir.'

'Notice how he is drawn always to authority?' Yen asked the group. Then he said to Raymond. 'That won't do. We will need the captain to get you your medal. Whom else?' Both Gomel's and Berezovo's translators were right at their master's ears, keeping up with the conversation in English on the stage.

'Well—' It was a difficult question. Raymond disliked the rest of them in the same detached and distant way. 'Well, I guess Ed Mavole, sir.'

'Why?'

'He is a funny fellow, sir. I mean very humorous. And he never seems to complain. Not while I'm around, anyway.'

'Very good, Raymond. Now. Take this scarf and strangle Ed Mavole to death.'

'Yes, sir.'

Raymond got up from the table and took the scarf from Yen. He walked to the end of the line of seated men at stage left, then moved along behind the row to a position directly behind Mavole, fifth man from the end. Mavole was chewing gum rapidly and trying to watch both Yen and Raymond at the same time. Raymond looped the scarf around Mavole's throat.

'Hey, Sarge. Cut it out. What is this?' Mavole said irritably, only because it was Raymond.

'Quiet, please, Ed,' Yen said with affectionate sternness. 'You just sit there quietly and co-operate.'

'Yes, sir,' Mavole said.

Yen nodded to Raymond, who pulled at either end of the white scarf with all of the considerable strength of his long arms and deep torso and strangled Ed Mavole to death among his friends and his enemies in the twenty-first year of his life, producing a terrible sight and terrible sounds. Berezovo dictated steadily to his recording assistant who made notes and watched Mavole at the same time, showing horror only far back behind the expression in her eyes. As she set down the last Berezovo observation she excused herself, turned aside, and vomited. Leaning over almost double, she walked rapidly from the room, pressing a handkerchief to her face and retching.

Gomel watched the strangling with his lips pursed studiously and primly. He belched. 'Pardon me,' he said to no one at all.

Raymond let the body drop, then walked along the line of men to the end of the row, rounded it, and returned to his chair. There was a rustle of light applause which Yen Lo ignored, so it stopped almost instantly, as when inadvertent applause breaks out during an orchestral rest in the performance of a symphony.

'Very good, Raymond,' Yen said.

'Yes, sir.'

'Raymond, who is that little fellow sitting next to the captain?'

The sergeant looked to his right. 'That's Bobby Lembeck, sir. Our mascot, I guess you could call him.'

'He doesn't look old enough to be in your Army.'

'Frankly, sir, he isn't old enough but there he is.'

Yen opened the only drawer in the table in front of Raymond and took out an automatic pistol. 'Shoot Bobby, Raymond,' he ordered. 'Through the forehead.' He handed the pistol to

Raymond who then walked along the front of the stage to his right.

'Hi, Ben,' he said to the captain.

'Hiya, kid.'

Apologising for presenting his back to the audience, Raymond then shot Bobby Lembeck through the forehead at point-blank range. He returned to his place at the table, offering the pistol butt to Yen Lo who motioned that it should be put in the drawer. 'That was very good, Raymond,' he said warmly and with evident appreciation. 'Sit down.' Then Yen turned to face his audience and made a deep, mock-ceremonial bow, smiling with much self-satisfaction.

'Oh, marvellous!' the shorter Chinese, Wen Ch'ang, cried out in elation.

'You are to be congratulated on a most marvellous demonstration, Yen Lo,' said the other Chinese, Pa Cha, loudly and proudly, right on top of his colleague's exclamation. The Russians broke out into sustained applause and were tasteful enough not to yell 'Encore!' or 'Bis!' in the bourgeois French manner. The young lieutenant who had been picking his nose shouted 'Bravo!' then immediately felt very silly. Gomel, who was applauding as heavily and as rapidly as the others, yelled hoarsely, 'Excellent! Really, Yen, really, really, excellent!' Yen Lo put one long forefinger to his lips in an elaborate gesture. The line of soldiers watched the demonstration from the stage with tolerance, even amusement. Yen turned to them. The force of the bullet velocity at such close range had knocked little Bobby Lembeck over backward in his chair. His corpse without a forehead, never having known a fat lady or a tall one, sprawled backward with its feet still hooked into the front legs of the overturned chair, as though it were a saddle which had slipped off a running colt.

Mavole's body had fallen forward. The colour of the face was magenta into purple and the eyes seemed to pop out towards Yen in a diligent effort to pay him the utmost attention.

The other men of the patrol sat relaxed, with the pleasant look

53

of fathers with hangovers who are enjoying watching a little girls' skating party in the moist, cool air of an indoor rink on a Saturday morning.

'Captain Marco?' Yen said briskly.

'Yes, sir.'

'To your feet, Captain, please.'

'Yes, sir.'

'Captain, when you return with your patrol to your command headquarters what will be among the first duties you will undertake?'

'I will submit my report on the patrol, sir.'

'What will you report?'

'I will recommend urgently that Sergeant Shaw be posted for the Medal of Honor, sir. He saved our lives and he took out a full company of enemy infantry.'

'A full company!' Gomel said indignantly when this sentence was translated to him. 'What the hell is this?'

'We can spare an imaginary company of infantry for this particular plan, Mikhail,' Berezovo said irritably.

'All right! If we are out to humiliate our brave Chinese ally in the newspapers of the world we might as well go ahead and make it a full battalion,' Gomel retorted, watching the Chinese representatives carefully as he spoke.

'We don't object, Comrade,' the older Chinese said. 'I can assure you of that.'

'Not at all,' said the younger Chinese official.

'However, thank you for thinking of the matter in that light, just the same,' said the first Chinese.

'Not at all,' Gomel told him.

'Thank you, Captain Marco,' Yen Lo told the officer. 'Thank you, everyone,' he told the audience. 'That will be all for this session. If you will assemble your questions, we will review here in one hour, and in the meantime I believe General Kostroma has opened a most pleasant little bar for all of us.' Yen motioned Raymond to his feet. Then, putting an arm around his shoulders, he walked him out of the auditorium saying, 'We will have some

54

hot tea and a chat, you and I, and to show my appreciation for the way you have worked today, I am going to dip into your unconscious and remove your sexual timidity once and for all.' He smiled broadly at the young man. 'More than that no man can do for you, Raymond,' he said, and they passed from the room, out of the view of the patient, seated patrol.

There was a final review for the patrol that evening, conducted by Yen Lo's staff as a last brush-up to recall the details of the imaginary engagement against the enemy that, in fantasy, Raymond had destroyed. In all, Yen Lo's research staff provided four separate versions of the over-all feat of arms, as those versions might have been witnessed from four separate vantage points in the action and then later exchanged between members of the patrol. Each patrol member had been drilled in individual small details of what Raymond had done to save their lives. They had been taught to mourn Mavole and Bobby Lembeck who had been cut off before Raymond could save them. They had absorbed their lessons well and now admired, loved, and respected Raymond more than any other man they had ever known. Their brains had not merely been washed, they had been dry-cleaned.

The captain was taught more facets of the lie than the others because he would have observed the action with a schooled eye and also would have assembled everyone else's report. Raymond did not attend the final group drill. Yen had locked in his feat of valour personally, utilising a pioneer development of induced autoscopic hallucination which allowed Raymond to believe he had seen his own body image projected in visual space, and he had given the action a sort of fairy-tale fuzziness within Raymond's mind so that it would never seem as real to him as it always would remain to most of the other members of the patrol. By seeming somewhat unreal it permitted Raymond to project a sense of what would seem like admirable modesty to those who would question Raymond about it.

The patrol, less Ed Mavole and Bobby Lembeck, was loaded aboard a helicopter that night and flown into central Korea, near the west coast, not too far from where they had been captured. The Soviet pilot set the plane down on a sixteen-foot-square area that had been marked by flares. After that, no more than seventy minutes after they had been pointed on their way, the patrol came up to a U.S. Marine Corps outfit near Haeju, and they were passed back through the lines until they reached their own outfit the next afternoon. They had been missing in action for just less than four days, from the night of July 8 to the mid-afternoon of July 12. The year was 1951.

In the deepening twilight hours after the Americans had been sent back to their countrymen and his own work in the sector had been completed, Yen Lo sat with the thirty boys and girls of his staff in the evening circle on the lovely lawn behind the pavilion. He would tell them the beautiful old stories later when the darkness had come. While they had light he made his dry jokes about the Russians and amused them or startled them or flabbergasted them with the extent of his skill at *origami*, the ancient Japanese art of paper-folding. Working with squares of coloured papers, Yen Lo astonished them with a crane that flapped its wings when he pulled its tail, or a puffed-up frog that jumped at a stroke along its back, or a bird that picked up paper pellets, or a praying Moor, a talking fish, or a nun in black and grey. He would hold up a sheet of paper, move his hands swiftly as he paid out the gentle and delicious jokes, and lo!—wonderment dropped from his fingers, the paper had come to life, and magic was everywhere in the gentling evening air.

III

The nation guards its highest tribute for valour jealously. In the Korean War only seventy-seven Medals of Honour were awarded, with 5,720,000 personnel engaged. Of the 16,112,566 U.S. armed forces mobilised in World War II, only two hundred and ninety-two Medals of Honour were awarded. The Army reveres its Medal of Honour men, living and dead, above all others. A theatre commander who later became President and a President who had formerly been an artillery captain both said that they would rather have the right to wear the Medal of Honour than be President of the United States.

After Abraham Lincoln signed the Medal of Honour bill on July 12, 1862, the decoration was bestowed in multitude; on one occasion to every member of a regiment. The first Medal of Honour was awarded by Secretary of War Stanton on March 15, 1863, to a soldier named Parrott who had been doing a bit of work in mufti behind enemy lines. Counting medals that were later revoked, about twenty-three hundred of them were awarded in the Civil War era, up to 1892. Hundreds were poured out upon veterans of the Indian campaigns, specifying neither locales nor details of bravery beyond 'bravery in scouts and actions against the Indians.'

In 1897, for the first time, eyewitness accounts were made mandatory and applications could not be made by the candidate for the honour but had to be made by his commanding officer or some other individual who had personally witnessed his gallantry in action. The recommendation had to be made within one year of the feat of arms. Since 1897, when modern basic requirements were set down, only five hundred and seventy-seven Medals of Honour have been awarded to a total of 25,000,000 Americans in arms, which is why the presence of a medal winner can bring full generals to their feet, saluting, and has been known to move them to tears.

In 1904 the medal was protected from imitators and jewelry manufacturers when it was patented in its present form by its designer, Brigadier General George L. Gillespie. On December 19, 1904, he transferred the patent to 'W. H. Taft and his successor or successors as Secretary of War of the United States of America.' In 1916, the Congress awarded to Medal of Honour winners a special status, providing the medal had been won by an action involving actual conflict with the enemy, distinguished

57

by conspicuous gallantry or intrepidity at the risk of life above and beyond the call of duty. The special status provided that the Medal of Honour winner may travel free of charge in military aircraft; his son may get Presidential assistance in an appointment to West Point or Annapolis; if he is an enlisted man two dollars extra per month is added to his pay, and when he reaches the age of sixty-five he becomes eligible to receive a pension of $120 per year from which, if he smokes one packet of cigarettes a day, he would have $11.85 left over for rent, food, hospitalisation, entertainment, education, recreation, philanthropies, and clothing.

An Army board was convened in 1916 to review all instances of the award of the Medal of Honour since 1863 to determine whether or not any Medal of Honour had been awarded or issued 'for any cause other than distinguished conduct involving actual conflict with the enemy,' Nine hundred and eleven names were stricken from the list, and lesser decorations were forthwith created so that, as Congress had demanded, 'the Medal of Honour would be more jealously guarded.'

There was every reason for the awe in which Medal of Honour men were held. Some of their exploits included such actions as: had taken eight prisoners, killing four of the enemy in the process, while one leg and one arm were shattered and he could only crawl because the other leg had been blown off (Edwards); had captured a hundred and ten men, four machine guns, and four howitzers (Mallon and Gumpertz); wounded five times, dragged himself across the direct fire of three enemy machine guns to pull two of his wounded men to safety amid sixty-nine dead and two hundred and three casualties (Holderman); singly destroyed a fourteen-man enemy ambush of his battalion and, in subsequent actions, with his legs mangled by enemy grenade and shot through the chest, died taking a charge of eight enemy riflemen, killing them (Baker); held his battalion's flank against advancing enemy platoons, used up two hundred rounds of ammunition, crawled twenty yards under direct fire to get more, only to be assailed by another platoon of the enemy, ultimately firing six hundred rounds, killing sixty and holding off all others to be one of twenty-three out of two hundred and forty, of his comrades to survive the action (Knappenburger); a defective phosphorus bomb exploding inside his plane, blinding and severely burning him, the radio operator scooped up the blazing bomb in his arms and, with incalculable difficulty, hurled it through the window (Erwin).

Raymond waited in the Rose Garden of the White House while an assistant press secretary tried to talk to him. It was a bonny sunny day. Raymond was stirred by the building near him; moved by the colour of the green, green grass. Raymond was torn and shamed and he felt soiled everywhere his spirit could feel. Raymond felt exalted, too. He felt proud of the building near him and proud of the man he was about to meet.

Raymond's mother was across the garden with the press people, pulling her husband along behind her, explaining with brilliant smiles and leers when necessary that he was the new senator and Raymond's father. Raymond, fortunately, could not hear her but he could watch her hand out cigars. They both handed out cigars whether the press people wanted cigars or not. Raymond's mother was dressed up to about eight hundred dollars' worth of the best taste on the market. The only jarring note was the enormous black purse she carried. It looked like a purse. It was a portable cigar humidor. She would have given the press people money, Raymond knew, but she had sensed somehow that it would be misunderstood.

All the cameras were strewn about in the grass while everybody waited for the President to arrive. Raymond wondered what would they do if he could find a sidearm some place and shoot her through the face—through that big, toothy, flapping mouth? Look how she held Johnny down. Look how she could make him seem docile and harmless. Look how she had kept him sober and had made him seem quiet and respectable as he shook hands so tentatively and murmured. *Johnny Iselin was murmuring!* He was crinkling his thick lips and making them prissy as he smirked under that great fist of a nose and two of the photographers (they must be his mother's tame photographers) were listening to him as though he were harmless.

The airport. O Jesus, Jesus, Jesus. She had got the AP photographer by the fleshy part of his upper right arm and she had got Johnny by the fleshy part of his upper left arm and she had charged them forward across that concrete apron at the National Airport yelling at the ramp men, 'Get Shaw off first! Get that sergeant down here!' and the action and the noises she made had pulled all thirty news photographers and reporters along behind her at a full run while the television newsreel truck had rolled along sedately abreast of her, filming everything for the world to see that night, and thank God they were not shooting with sound.

The lieutenant had pushed him out of the plane and his mother had pushed Johnny at him and Johnny had pulled him down the ramp so he wouldn't look too much taller in the shot. Then to make sure, Raymond's mother had yelled, 'Get on that ramp, Johnny, and hang on to him.' Johnny gripped his right hand and held his right elbow, and towered over him. Raymond's mother didn't say hello. She hadn't seen him for over two years but she didn't say hello and neither did Johnny. Thank God they were a family who didn't waste a lot of time on talking, Raymond thought.

Johnny kept grinning at him insanely and the pupils of his eyes were open at about $f.09$ with the sedation she had loaded into him. The pressmen were trying to keep their places in a tight semicircle and, as always at one of those public riots where every man had been told to get the best shot, the harshest, most dominating shouter finally solved it for all the others: one big Italian-looking photographer yelled at nobody at all, 'Get the mother in there, fuh crissake! Senator! Get your wife in there, fuh crissake!' Then Raymond's mother caught on that she had goofed but good and she hurled herself in on Raymond's offside and hung off his neck, kissing him again and again until his cheek glistened with spit, cheating to the cameras about thirty degrees, and snarling at Johnny between the kisses, 'Pump his hand, you jerk. Grin at the cameras and pump his hand. A TV newsreel is working out there. Can't you remember anything?' And Johnny got with it.

It had taken about seven minutes of posing, reposing, standing, walking towards the cameras, then the photographers broke ranks and Raymond's mother grabbed Johnny's wrist and took off after them.

The assistant press secretary from the White House steered Raymond to a car, and the next time Raymond saw his mother she was handing out cigars in the Rose Garden and paying out spurts of false laughter.

Everybody got quiet all of a sudden. Even his mother. They all looked alert as the President came out. He looked magnificent. He was ruddy and tall and he looked so entirely sane that Raymond wanted to put his head on the President's chest and cry because he hadn't seen very many sane people since he had left Ben Marco.

He stood at attention, eyes forward.

The President said, 'At ease, soldier.' The President leaned forward to pick up Raymond's right hand from where it dangled at his side and as he shook it warmly he said, 'You're a brave man, Sergeant. I envy you in the best sense of that word because there is no higher honour your country has to give than this medal you will receive today.' Raymond watched his mother edge over. With horror, he saw the jackal look in her eyes and in Johnny's. The President's press secretary introduced Senator Iselin and Mrs Iselin, the sergeant's mother. The President congratulated them. Raymond heard his mother ask for the honour of a photograph with the President, then moved her two tame photographers in with a quick low move of her left hand. The others followed, setting up.

The shot was lined up. Raymond's mother was on the President's left. Raymond was on the President's right. Johnny was on Raymond's right. Just before the bank of press cameras took the picture, Mrs Iselin took out a gay little black-on-yellow banner on a brave little gilded stick and held it over Raymond's head.

At least it seemed that she must have meant it to be held only over Raymond's head, but when the pictures came out in the newspapers the next day, then in thousands of newspapers all over the world beginning three and a half years hence, and with shameful frequency in many newspapers after that, it was seen that the gay little banner had been held directly over the President's head and that the lettering on it read: JOHNNY ISELIN'S BOY.

IV

In 1940, Raymond's mother had divorced his father, a somewhat older man, while she was six months pregnant with a second child, to marry Raymond's father's law partner, John Yerkes Iselin, who had a raucous laugh and a fleshy nose. There was more than the usual talk in their community that loud, lewd Johnny Iselin was the father of the unborn child.

Raymond had been twelve years old at the time of his mother's remarriage. He hadn't particularly liked his father but he disliked his mother so much more that he felt the loss keenly. In later years the second son, Raymond's brother, could have been said to have favoured noisy Johnny more than did the dour and silent Raymond, as he had many of the identical interests in making sounds for the sake of making sounds, and also the early suggestion of a nose that promised to be equally fleshy—but Raymond's brother died in 1948, greatly helping John Iselin's bid for the governorship by interjecting that element of human sympathy into the campaign.

The unquestionable fact was that Eleanor Shaw's marriage to John Iselin was a scandal and the questions that aroused curiosity must have been an insufferable torment in the mind of young Raymond as his awakening consciousness absorbed the details which kept filtering fresh drops of bitterness into his memory.

Raymond's father had paused with his grief for six years before killing himself. At this disposition, Raymond, if no one else, was inconsolable. In the driving rain, in the presence of so few witnesses, most of whom having been rented through the funeral director, he made a graveside oration. As he spoke he looked only at his mother. He told, in a high-pitched, tight voice, of what an incomparably noble man his father had been and other boyish balderdash like that. To Raymond, from that day in 1940 when he had seen his father's tears, his mother would always be a morally adulterous woman who had deserted her home and had brought sadness upon her husband's venerable head.

Iselin, the stepfather, was doubly hateful because he had offended, humiliated, and betrayed a noble man by robbing him of his wife, and because he seemed to make noises with every movement and every part of his body, forsaking silence awake and asleep; belching, bawling, braying, blaspheming; snoring or shouting; talking, always, always, never stopping talking.

Raymond's father and Johnny Iselin had been law partners until 1935 when Johnny had switched his party affiliations to run for judge of the three-county Thirteenth Judicial District. The announcement of his candidacy had come as a staggering blow to his partner and benefactor who had had his heart set for some time on running for the circuit judgeship in that district, so words were exchanged and the partnership was dissolved.

Johnny had noise and muscle on his side in anything he ever decided to do. He won the election. He served for four years before the State Supreme Court rebuked him for improper conduct on the bench. Judge Iselin had found it necessary to order the destruction of a portion of the record and had, in general, created 'a highly improper and regrettable state of affairs,' but, simultaneously, he had earned himself a nice thirty-five hundred dollar off-bench fee.

Johnny always kept his gift for merchandising justice. Just

about ten months after the exhibitionistic politicking by the State Supreme Court against him, he began to grant quickie divorces to couples not resident in his judicial district. Later, records indicated that in several of these cases, one of the principals, or their attorneys, or both, were active in supporting Johnny's political pretensions, sometimes with cash. His practice of favouring the generous gave at least one editorial writer his morning angle when the *Journal*, the state's largest daily, wrote: 'Is state justice to be used to accommodate the political supporters of the presiding judge? Are our courts to become the place in which to settle political debts?' By this time Raymond's mother had seen her duty and had taken to lolling around on a bed with Johnny in a rented-by-the-hour-or-afternoon summer home near a gas station off a secondary highway. When she finished reading that editorial aloud to Johnny she snorted and described the editorial writer, whom she had never met, as a jerk.

'You are so right, baby,' Johnny had answered.

The most famous case Judge Iselin ever disposed of on the circuit bench was reflected in the consequences of his granting a divorce in the case of Raymond's mother versus Raymond's father. The newspapers paid out the juicy facts that Mr Shaw had been Judge Iselin's law partner. Second, they announced that Mrs Shaw was six months pregnant and ran a front-page picture that made her look as though she had strapped a twenty-one-inch television set to her middle. Thirdly, the readers were told that Mrs Shaw and Judge Iselin would become man and wife as soon as the divorce became final. Raymond's mother had been twenty-nine years old at the time. Judge Iselin was thirty-two. Raymond's father was forty-eight.

Mr Shaw had married Raymond's mother when she was sixteen years old, after two ecstatic frictions on an automobile seat. Raymond had been born when she had just reached seventeen. During the thirteen years of her marriage to Raymond's father she had been a member or officer or founder or affiliate of organisations including: the St Agnes Music Club, the Parent-Teachers' Association, the Association of Inner Wheel Clubs, the

Honest Ballot Association, the International Committee for Silent Games, the Auxiliary Society of the Professional Men's League, the Third Way Movement, the Society for the Prevention of Cruelty to Animals, the Permanent International Committee of Underground Town Planning, the Good Citizen's Shield, the Joint Distribution Committee for Anti-Fascist Spain, the Scrap Metal User's Joint Bureau, the International Symposium on Passivity, the American Friends of the Soviet Union, the Ladies' Auxiliary of the American Legion, the Independent Order, the English-Speaking Union, the International Congress for Surface Activity, the Daughters of the American Revolution, the International Union for the Protection of Public Morality, the Society for the Abolition of Blasphemy Laws, the Community Chest, the Audubon League, the League of Professional Women, the American-Scandinavian Association, the Dame Maria Van Slyke Association for the Abolition of Canonisation, the Eastern Star, the Abraham Lincoln Brigade Memorial Fund, and others. Raymond's mother had, quite early in life, achieved an almost abnormal concentration upon an interest in local, state, and national politics. She used all organisations to claw out recognition for herself within her chosen community. Her ambition was an extremely distressing condition. She sought power the way a superstitious man might look for a four-leaf clover. She didn't care where she found it. It would make no difference if it were growing out of a manure pile.

The newspapers knew the three sets of facts about Raymond's mother's divorce because Raymond's mother, always keeping an eye upon a public future, had made sure they were told about it in a series of letters which she had typed without signature and mailed herself the day before the divorce action had reached Judge Iselin's court. She had explained to Johnny why she was going to do it before she did it. She made it clear that the entire thing would serve to humanise him like nothing else could, later on. 'Every one of the jerks lives in the middle of one continuous jam,' she had explained sympathetically, the jerks being the great American people in this instance. 'Isn't it better if they think you got me this way than if they get the idea the baby is his and I walked out on him for you? You see what I mean, Johnny? We'd be taking his own child away from him, which is a very precious possession—as the jerks pretend about kids while they knock them out like hot cross buns, then abandon them or ignore them. And we'll get married right away. At the split second that it becomes legal under the great American flag, see, lover? We'll be as respectable as anybody else right at that instant, except just like everybody else, underneath. You know what I mean, lover? They're all tramps in their hearts and we'll want them to identify with us when the time comes to line up at the polls. Right, sweetheart?'

Raymond's mother had not been unfaithful to his father until he had forced her into it. She had used exactly the same political blandishments on him first that she had had to use on Johnny later, and long before she had exposed either them or her body to John Iselin, which is to say that Raymond's father could have become just as big a man in the United States and the world as she eventually made Johnny, a fact that Raymond never realised in his harsh evaluation of his mother. After she had finished detailing her political plan to Raymond's father, instead of striking her, the man had actually tried to instil into her a devotion to the ancient ideals of justice, liberty, fair play, and the Republic until she had at last needed to cuckold him to be rid of him. Later on she had explained the whole thing to Johnny as though the entire sordid mess had come about as the result of her shrewd design.

The most sordid part of the sordid, rationalised mess was what it did to Raymond, but even if she had acknowledged that to herself as a mother, she knew it was worth it because for more than five years Johnny Iselin was a very big man in the United States of America and Raymond's mother ruled Johnny Iselin. So, it can be seen that Raymond's mother had been assiduously fair with her first husband. She told him how she had worked and worked behind the scenes in politics to have him run for the Senate and she laid out her sure-fire platform for him. When he heard what she proposed to have him do, her husband gave her a tongue lashing that finally made her plead for relief, so long and so hostile was its address. After that she was silent. Not for the rest of the day nor the rest of the week; she did not speak to him again until the day she left him, six months later, after deliberately seeking insemination from Judge Iselin, then leaving Raymond's father forever, holding one son by the hand and the other by the umbilicus.

Judge Iselin had been the marital candidate in reserve for some years. They had all been close friends during the time the judge and Raymond's father had been partners. As she had anticipated he would, Johnny Iselin had agreed with everything she said, which, when boiled down, expressed the conviction that the Republic was a humbug, the electorate rabble, and anyone strong who knew how to manœuvre could have all the power and glory that the richest and most naïve democracy in the world could bestow. Boiled down, Judge Iselin's response expressed his lifelong faith in her and in her proposition: 'Just you tell me what to do, hon, and I'll get it done.' Falling in love had been as simple as that because she had set out, from that moment on, to bring his appreciation of her and dependence on her to a helpless maximum, and when she had finished her work he was never again to be able to recall his full sanity.

Raymond's father, having been told by his beautiful, young wife that she was with child and that he was not the father and that she would die before she would have another child by him, a coward, took it all like the booby that he was, a willingness aided and abetted by the fact that there can be no doubt that he was a registered masochist. He marched like a little soldier to the man who had doublecrossed him once before, mumbling something ludicrous, such as: if you love this woman and will marry her honourably, take her; only let the decencies be observed.

The lout Iselin made a loud, garbled fuss (the whole thing took place on the porch of the country club in August), swearing and sweating that he would marry Raymond's mother just as soon as he could confer a divorce upon her, presumably even if he had to open his court on a Sunday, then marry her immediately, and never, never, never, ever, ever cast her off. He bound himself, in the presence of nine per cent of the membership, by the most frightful, if meaningless, oaths.

Secretly, Raymond's father, loving Raymond's mother as deeply as he did, regarded this infatuation of hers as a form of divine punishment on himself, having a capacity exceeded only by other humans for taking himself so seriously as to know he had been under continuous divine scrutiny, because over the period of sixteen years past as the sole executor of two large estates he had been looting, systematically, the substance of two maiden ladies and an institution-committed schizophrenic. He was so affected by these secret sins that, while he never stopped looting the two estates and it was never revealed that he had done so, it was quite clear that it would have been a matter of only slight effort to have persuaded him to give the bride away at the Iselin wedding as part of due punishment.

The result of this attitude was, naturally, that Raymond's mother felt angry and ashamed; humiliated, as it were, in the eyes of their common community, that he seemed to take the matter so calmly, giving her up so tamely as though she were a thing of little worth. She had a not inconsiderable fortune, by inheritance, as did Raymond, all from her father's estate, then her mother's estate, and she spent a fraction of it on private detectives from Chicago, trying to uncover other women in his life. She told Johnny that she would take the old bastard's skin off if he had been setting her up all this time just to get rid of her but, of course, nothing came of the investigations, and she had to wait six years for the afternoon when he killed himself out of yearning and loneliness, by administering a large dose of bar-biturate Thiopentone by intercardiac injection, causing permanent cessation of respiration within two seconds, which was little enough punctuation to fifty-four years of living. Raymond's mother admired him, technically, for the method used, and also emotionally for the act itself because, in a way, it made her look good to those who still remembered what effect he had achieved with his public dignity and cool indifference at the time she had left him. On many counts beyond his thoughtful suicide, however, she had been very, very fond of him.

Throughout their eventful life together Raymond's mother was to maintain a remarkable hold over Johnny Iselin, whom she had immediately taken to calling Big John because it sounded so bluff and hearty, so open and honest. Perhaps the truth of her hold on him will not easily be credited. The truth is that the marriage was never consummated. Johnny, that old-time mattress screamer and gasper, although throughout his life quite capable of getting and giving full satisfaction with other women, found himself as impotent as a male butterfly atop a female pterodactyl when he tried to have commerce with Raymond's mother. The only reasonable explanation was that, at bottom, Johnny was the caricature of a pious man. He was a superstitious Catholic who had ignored his faith for years, who supported none of the beauty of the religion he had been born into, but rooted and snouted out all the aboriginal hearsay it could imply concerning sin and its consequences. Johnny knew in his super-stitious heart of hearts that his marriage to Raymond's mother was an impious thing and his knowledge, it seems, affected him nervously, putting an inner restraint upon his flesh. Raymond's mother, who wanted her Big John as a striking force of her ambition rather than as a lover, was extremely pleased at this response, or lack of it, and counted her blessings when she considered his sudden but continuing impotence where the celebration of her body was concerned. She calculated without hesitation that she could use it as an irresistible weapon against him.

She played all of the key scenes with consummate art; reproaching him for having lured her away from the base of her virtue, an incredible inversion of moral usage; for having torn her away from Raymond's father whom she had loved distract-edly, she protested so very bitterly, by moaning, rocking, bleating, and rolling all over the bed and across the floor, if need be, as she simulated the tearing, roiling, rutting, ripping passion which she felt for him, her very own Big John.

69

Iselin's knowledge of these things (and he was not the first man to be so confused by this sort of excellence) was so juveniley subjective that he made the automatic responses, as though directions for using him had come with him, clipped to the marriage certificate. She had been tricked! she would cry out, turning away and holding one hand over her heart. That distant-day passionate lover who had bounded about her body with such ardour and so inexhaustibly in that rented summer bed had turned out to be no man at all! Any bellhop, any delivery man was more of a man than he! All he could do was to bring a madness of fondling and fumbling with the flaccid kisses of a boarding-school room-mate. In vain did Big John protest that with other women he was like a squad of marines after eleven weeks at sea. Either she would refuse to believe it or she would accuse him of wasting on other women what he was, at that instant, denying her. She made it clear however, that she would protect him forever from any scandal because she loved him so deeply, if never orgastically. Constant shame, unreasonable gratitude, and unslakeable passion welded him to her more closely than if they had been sharing the same digestive system— far closer than if their mutual longings had been nightly satisfied or she had borne him a dozen fine children. Later on, after they had reached the pinnacles in Washington, when she would see to it that nubile young women were let into his chamber late at night in utter darkness to leave before dawn, felt but never seen by him, as though they had been a carnal dream, she contrived all this with such precision and remained so immutably constant to him herself that he considered this perfect proof of her love for him.

She took the most enveloping care of his health, his comfort, and his career. She was memorably faithful to him, not being naturally lustful herself except for power. In consequence he was so grateful that he let her rule all of his public and private acts. She could think much better than he could, anyway. Her basic, effective policy was to recognise that her own strength lay in her sexual austerity and in her cultivated understanding of the astonishingly simple reproductive plumbing of the human male.

Throughout their lives together, no matter how melodramatic the intrigue, not only could no one ever level at her the accusation of sexual immorality, but because Big John's occasional good health sometimes overflowed too impulsively, her enemies and his enemies had to give her credit on the angel's side for her loyalty and forbearance. Frigidity preserved her from temptation. Her ambition kept her insatiably excited. Johnny's panting and clutching at the passing parade of paid virgins she happily accepted, even though this avid forgiveness betrayed her own eternal inability to reach out in darkness towards fulfilment.

One year after they had arranged for all of this bliss, the nation entered World War II, elating Raymond's mother because she saw the occasion as an acceleration of opportunity which would pull her John up the ladder of politics. She lost no time getting him set, in cartouche, against that martial background.

Raymond's mother's brother, the clot, had become a non-political federal commissioner of such exalted station that it often brought her to the point of retching nausea when she encountered its passing mention in a news story. She had despised this son-of-a-bitch of a sibling ever since the far-off summer afternoon when her beloved, wonderful, magnetic, pleasing, exciting, generous, kind, loving, and gifted father had died sitting upright in the wooden glider-swing with a history of Scandinavia in his lap and this fool they said was her brother had announced that he was head of the family. This foolish, insensitive, ignorant, beastly nothing of a boy who had felt that he could in any way, in any shocking, fractional way, take the place of a magnificent man of men. Then he had beaten her with a hockey stick because he had objected to her nailing the paw of a beige cocker spaniel to the floor because the dog was stubborn and refused to understand the most elemental instructions to remain still when she had called out the command to do so. Could she have called out and made her wondrous father stay with her when he was dying?

She had loved her father with a bond so secret, so deep, and

71

so thrilling that it surpassed into eternity the drab feelings of the other people, all other people, particularly the feelings of her brother and her clot of a mother. She had had woman's breasts from the time she had been ten years old, and she had felt a woman's yearnings as she had lain in the high, dark attic of her father's great house, only on rainy nights, only when the other slept. She would lie in the darkness and hear the rain, then hear her father's soft, soft step rising on the stairs after he had slipped the bolt into the lock of the attic door, and she would slip out of her long woollen night dress and wait for the warmth of him and the wonder of him.

Then he had died. Then he had died.

Every compulsively brutal blow from that hockey stick in the hands of that young man who wanted so badly to be understood by his sister but who could not begin to reach her understanding or her feeling had beaten a deep distaste and contempt for all men since her father into her projective mind, and, right then, when she was fourteen years old, she entered her driving, never-to-be-acknowledged life competition with her only brother to show him which of them was the heir of that father and which of them had the right to say that he should stand in that father's shoes and place and memory. She vowed and resolved, dedicated and consecrated, that she would beat him into humiliation at whatsoever he chose to undertake, and it was to the eternal shame of their country that he chose politics and government and that she needed therefore to plunge in after him.

Her clot of a brother had absorbed the native clottishness of her mother, a clot's clot. How could her father have loved this woman? How could such a shining and thrilling and valiant knight have lain down with this great cow? Everyone who knew them said that Raymond's mother was the image of her mother.

After her beating with the hockey stick she had given her family no rest until she had been sent away to a girl's boarding-school of her own choice in the Middle West. It was chosen as her natural base of operations in politics because it was in the heart of the Scandinavian immigrant country; at the chosen time the outstanding Norse nature of her father's name and his heroic origins could be turned into blocks of votes.

At sixteen, because she had taught herself to believe that she knew exactly what she wanted, no matter what she got, she escaped from the school every weekend, dressed herself to look older, and arranged to place herself in locations where she could use herself as bait. She seduced four men between the ages of thirty and forty-six, got no pleasure from it nor expected any, had definitely lost two of the contests after a gluttonous testing period, could have turned either of the remaining two in any direction she chose, decided on Raymond's father because the man had a good, open face for politics and hair that was already grey although he was only thirty-six years old. She married him and bore him Raymond as soon as the gestation cycle allowed.

Generalities, specifics, domestic manifestations, or her youth never made Raymond's mother's thinking fuzzy or got in the way of her plan. She knew, like a mousetrap knows the back of a mouse's neck, that she was far too immature to be accepted publicly as the bride of a man seeking public office. She knew that it was possible that her husband might even get slightly tarred because of her age, so she had set her own late twenties as the time when she would have Raymond's father make his move. Her reasoning was sound: by that time, when it was reported during a campaign that Raymond's father had taken a child bride of sixteen some twelve faithful, productive years before, it would have become a romantic asset and Raymond's father would be seen by women voters as a suggestively virile candidate. meanwhile, she had accomplished her primary objective of escaping the authority of her mother, her brother, and the school. She had her share of her father's substantial estate. She had started a family unit that, with few modern exceptions, was essential to success in American politics.

Raymond's mother was an exceptionally handsome woman who was dressed in France. This was quite shrewd, because money displaces one's own taste when one chooses to be dressed in France. She was coiffed in New York and her very laundry seemed to have been washed in Joy de Patou. Her hair was straw blonde, in the Viking tradition, and it was kept that way, no matter the inconvenience. Her sense of significant birth, her grinding virtue, and her carriage completed her pre-eminence in any group of women, and she assiduously recultivated all three attributes as a fleshy-plant fancier might exalt and extend orchid graftings. What was especially striking in the earlier photographs of Raymond's mother was the suggestion of a smile on her full lips as they counterfeited sensuality, and in her large ecstatic eyes, which were like those of a sexually ambitious girl. In later likenesses, such as the *Time* cover in 1959 (and she being of the same political party as *Time's* persuasion, its editors therefore made an effort to supervise a most honest likeness) where she was clad as a matron, the supple grace was gone but the perfect features and the whole figure were stamped with the adaptable and flexible energy that marked her maturity.

One of Big John Iselin's favourite perorations in campaign oratory after the war, or rather, after Johnny's interrupted service in the war, was the recollection of what he had seen and done in battle and what he would never be able to forget 'up there at the top of the world, alone with God in a great cathedral of ice and snow in the stark loneliness of arctic night where the enemy struck out of nowhere and my boys fell and I cried out piteously, "O Lord, they are young, why must they die?" as I raced forward over ice which was thirty miles deep, pumping my machine rifle, to even the score with those Nazi devils who, in the end, came to have a superstitious fear of me.'

The point Johnny seemed to want to make in this section of this speech, his favourite speech, was never quite clear, but the story carried a powerful emotional impact to those whose lives had been touched by the tragedy of war. 'At night while my spent, exhausted buddies slept,' he would croon into the platform microphone, 'I would prop my eyes open with matchsticks and write home—to you—to the wives and the sweethearts and the blessed mothers of our gallant dead—night after night as the casualties mounted—to try to do just a little more than my part to ease the heartbreak which Mr Roosevelt's war had caused.'

The official records of the Signal Corps of the U.S. Army show that Johnny's outfit (SCB-52310) had lost all together, during the entire tour outside the continental United States, one chaplain and one enlisted man, the former from a nervous breakdown and the latter from delirium tremens (a vitamin deficiency). The outfit, whose complement was a half-company of men, had been posted in northern Greenland as defences for the comprehensive meteorological installations that predicted the weather for the military brass lower down on the globe, operating in mobile force far up on the ice cap, mostly between Prudhoe Land and the Lincoln Sea.

The enemy's weather forecasting installations were mostly based somewhere above King Frederick VIII Land, on the other side of the sub-continent, below Independence Sea. Greenland is the largest island in the world. Both sides, although continually aware of each other, remained strictly aloof and upon those occasions where they found that they were working in sight of each other they would both move out of sight without acknowledgment, as people will act following a painful social misunderstanding. There was no question of shooting. Their work was far too important. It was essential that both sides maintain an unbroken flow of vital weather data, which was an extremely special contribution when compared to the basically uncomplicated work of fighting troops.

It just did not seem likely that even Johnny would send the families of those two casualties a different letter every night, harping on a nervous breakdown and the D.T.'s, and besides the mail pickup happened only once a month when the mail plane was lucky enough to be able to swoop low enough and at the right ground angle to be able to bring up the gibbeted mail sack on a lowered hook. If they missed after three passes they let it go until the next month, but they did bring the mail in, which was far more important, and did maintain a reasonably high average on getting it out, considering the conditions.

No citizen of the United States, including General Mac-Arthur and those who enlisted from the film community of Los Angeles, California, entered World War II with more fanfare from the local press and radio than John Yerkes Iselin. When the jolly judge arrived at the State Capitol on June 6, 1942, and announced to the massive communications complex that Raymond's mother had assembled over a two-day period from all papers throughout the state, from Chicago, and three from Washington, at an incalculable cost in whisky and food, that he had seen his duty to join up as 'a private, an officer, or anything else in the United States Marine Corps,' the newspapers and radio foamed with the news and the UP put the story on the main wire as a suggested boxed news feature because of Raymond's mother's angle, which had Johnny saying: 'They need a judge in the Marines to judge whether they are the finest fighting men in the world, or in the universe.' The Marines naturally had gotten Raymond's mother's business because, she told Johnny, they had the biggest and fastest mimeographing machines and earmarked one combat correspondent for every two fighting men.

She started to run her husband for governor as of that day, and the first five or six publicity releases emphasised strongly how this man, whose position as a public servant demanded that he *not* march off to war but remain home as part of the civilian task force to safeguard Our Liberties, had chosen instead, had volunteered even, to make the same sacrifices which were the privileged lot of his fellow Americans and had therefore enlisted as a buck-private marine. She had only two objectives. One was to make sure Johnny got overseas somewhere near, but not too near, the combat zones. The second was that he be assigned to a safe, healthy, pleasant job.

It was at that point that something got screwed up. It was extremely embarrassing, but fortunately she was able to patch

76

it up so that it looked as if Johnny was even more of a patriotic masochist, but it brought her anger she was careful never to lose, and because of what happened to outrage her, it spelled out her brother's eventual ruin.

This is what happened. Through her brother, whom she had never hesitated to use, Raymond's mother had decided to negotiate for a Marine Corps commission for Johnny. She would have preferred it if Johnny had enlisted as a private so that she could arrange for a field commission for him, following some well-publicised action, but Johnny got stubborn at the last minute and said he had agreed to go through all this rigmarole to please her but he wasn't going to sit out any war as a goddam private when whisky was known to cost only ten cents a shot at all officers' clubs.

Her brother was sitting on one of the most influential wartime government commissions that spring of 1942, and the son-of-a-bitch looked her right in the eye in his own office in the Pentagon in Washington and told her that Johnny could take his chances just like anybody else and that *he didn't believe in wire-pulling in wartime!* That was that. Furthermore, she found out immediately that he wasn't kidding. She had had to move fast and think up some other angle very quickly but she hung around her brother's office long enough to explain to him that her turn would come some day and that when it came she was going to break him in two.

She rode back to the Carlton, shocked. She blamed herself. She had underestimated that mealy-mouthed bastard. She should have seen that he had been waiting for years to turn her out like a peasant. She concentrated upon preserving her anger.

Johnny was pretty drunk when she got back to the hotel, but not too bad. She was sweet and amiable, as usual. 'What am I, hon?' he asked thickly, 'A cappen?' She threw her hat away from her and walked to the small Directoire desk. 'A cappency is good enough for me,' he said. She pulled a telephone book out of the desk drawer and began to flip through the pages. 'Am I a cappen or ain't I a cappen?' he asked.

'You ain't a cappen.' She picked up the phone and gave the operator the number of the Senate Office Building.

'What am I, a major?'

'You're gonna be a lousy draftee if something doesn't give,' she said. 'He turned us down.'

'He never liked me, honey.'

'What the hell has that got to do with anything. He's my brother. He won't lift a finger to help with the Marines and if we don't get an understanding set in about forty-eight hours you're going to be a draftee just like any other jerk.'

'Don't worry, hon. You'll straighten it out.'

'Shaddup! You hear? Shadd*up*!' She was pale with sickening bad temper. She spoke into the phone and asked for Senator Banstoffsen's office, and when she got the office she asked to speak to the senator. 'Tell him it's Ellie Iselin. He'll know.'

Johnny poured another drink, threw some ice into the glass, put some ginger ale on top of it, then shambled off towards the john, undoing his suspenders as he walked.

Raymond's mother's voice had suddenly gotten hot and sweet, although her eyes were bleak. 'Ole, honey?' She paused to let those words make her point. 'I mean—is this Senator Banstoffsen? Oh, Senator. Please forgive me. It was a slip. I mean, the only way I can explain is to say—is—I guess that's the way I think of you all the time, I guess.' She rolled her eyes towards the ceiling in disgust and sighed silently. Her voice was all breath and lust. 'I'd sure like to see you. Yes. Yes.' She rapped impatiently with the end of a pencil on the top of the desk. 'Now. Yes. Now. Do you have a lock on that office door, lover? Yes. Ole. Yes. I'll be right there.'

Johnny Iselin was sworn in as a captain in the Signal Corps of the Army of the United States on July 20, 1942. Raymond's mother had made a powerful and interested political ally in her home state, and although he didn't know it, that was not to be the last favour he would be asked to deliver for her, and sometimes he came to be bewildered by how one simple little sprawl

on an office desk could get to be so endlessly, intricately complicated.

During the intensive training in Virginia necessary for the
absorption of vital technical and military information, Johnny
and Raymond's mother lived in a darling little cottage just
outside Wellville in Nottoway County, where she had found a
solid connection for black-market booze and petrol and a
contact for counterfeit red points to keep those old steaks coming
in. Johnny moved out of the staging area and sailed with his
outfit for Greenland in December, 1942, and Raymond's mother
went back home to handle the PR work for her man. The
recurring theme she chose for the first year of propaganda was
hammered out along the basic lines of 'Blessed is he who serves
who is not called: blessed is he who sacrifices self to bring about
the downfall of tyrants that others may prosper in Liberty.' It
was solid stuff.

She got herself a women's radio show and a women's interest
newspaper column in the *Journal*, the biggest paper in the state
and one of the best in the country. There were a lot of specialised
jobs going for the asking. Mainly she read or reprinted all of
Johnny's letters on every conceivable variety of subjects, whether
he sent her any letters or not.

The official records show that Johnny was an intelligence
officer in the Army, but his campaign literature, when Raymond's
mother ran him for governor, revealed that he had been 'a
northern Greenland combat commander.' About ten years after
the war was over, well after Johnny's second term as governor,
the *Journal* did a surprising amount of careful research on
Johnny's record, at considerable expense. They dug up docu-
ments, and men who had served with Johnny, and they virtually
reconstructed a most careful, pertinent, and accurate history of
his somewhat distorted past. A public relations officer who had
been attached to Iselin's unit, a Lieutenant Jack Ramen, now of
San Mateo, California, told the *Journal* in 1955 on a transcribed,
long-distance-telephone tape recording, which was monitored

by the *Journal*'s city editor, Fred Goldberg, and witnessed by a principal clergyman and a leading physician of the state, of the lonely incident that had lent credence to the popular belief that Johnny had seen combat while in service.

'Yeah,' Ramen said. 'I remember the day we were both at a tiny Eskimo settlement above Etah there on Smith Sound and Johnny was looking to make some kind of good trades on furs with the natives when a supply ship the name of *Midshipman Bennet Reyes* came in, covered all over with ice. They were having propeller trouble and they were due in at Etah to unload groceries and while they were standing by for repairs the skipper told them to test the guns, all the guns, everything. We find out about it when Johnny and I go aboard; we were off duty, and Johnny always operates under orders from his wife to make friends no matter where. He actually brought the skipper of that ship the stiffest piece of sealskin you ever saw and made such a big thing out of it that the guy probably even kept it. He give Johnny a half gallon of pure grain alcohol to show his appreciation, and we needed it. Man, was it cold. I can never ever explain to anybody how cold it was all the time I was in the Army and, for what reason please don't ask me, the cold absolutely does not ever seem to bother Johnny. He used to say it was because his nose was radioactive. Actually, he was always so full of anti-freeze that he couldn't feel much of anything. Anyway, Johnny hears these Navy guys cursing about having to test all the guns and he asks them if they will mind if he fires a few rounds because he has always wanted to shoot a gun of some kind, any kind. They look at each other quick, then say sure, he can fire every single gun on the ship if he likes. So he did. And he took some pretty rugged chances because if the Martians had attacked or he had slipped on the deck he could have hurt himself. Anyway, I had a job to do which was called public relations, so I wrote a little routine story about the "one-man battleship" which in a certain way was strictly true. It had a certain Army flavour, and after all they weren't paying me to do public relations for the Navy, you know what I mean? I slugged it

"From an arctic outpost of the U.S. Army," and I wrote how one lone Army officer had fired all the guns of a fighting ship on top of the world where all the forgotten battles are fought and where the Navy fighting men had been put out of action by the cruellest enemy of all, the desperate, bitter cold of the arctic night, and how when the last gun had been stilled not an enemy form or an enemy plane could be seen moving on the ancient ice cap, tomb of thousands of unknown fallen. You know. It was filler copy. Not strictly a lie, you understand. Every fact was strictly factual all by itself but—well, it was what they always said was very, very good for morale on the home front, you know what I mean? Anyway, I forgot about the whole thing until Johnny came around with a fistful of clippings and a letter from his wife which said my story was worth fifty thousand votes and he was supposed to buy me all the gin I could hold. I liked gin at the time,' Ramen concluded.

With characteristic candour, in his autobiographical sketch in the Congressional Directory of 1955, Johnny claimed 'seventeen arctic combat missions,' but when testifying in 1957 in a legal proceeding that was attempting to investigate various amounts of unusual income he had received, both as to amount and source, Johnny said (of himself): 'Iselin was on thirty-one combat missions in the arctic, plus liaison missions' and added inexplicably that the nights in the arctic region were six months long. 'Iselin saw enough battle action to keep him peaceful and quiet for the rest of his days.' Raymond's mother had taught Johnny to call himself Iselin whenever testifying or being interviewed, on the principle that it constituted a continuing plug for the name at a time when Johnny was being quoted on land, sea, and in the air, as often and as much as the New York Stock Exchange.

The question of combat would not permit any settlement. When Raymond's mother had Johnny make formal application for the Silver Star, presumably because no one else had made application for him, in a claim supported by 'certain certified copies from my personal military records,' it attracted an apoplectically outraged letter of complaint from a constituent, bitter about the violation of propriety in which Johnny had received a medal at his own request. Raymond's mother dictated, and Johnny signed, a return letter that contained this brave turn of phrase: 'I am bound by the rules which provide how such awards shall be made and as much as I felt distaste there just wasn't any other way to do it.'

However, as the years carried Big John and Raymond's mother forward through their national and international duels on behalf of a more perfect America, the most disputed part of Johnny's record continued to be the 'wound' he most blandly claimed to have suffered in military combat. Although he did not receive the Purple Heart and although the former Secretary of the Army who reviewed his personnel file disclaimed any Iselin wound in action, when Big John was asked at a veterans' rally why he wore built-up shoes (how else the big in Big John?) Governor Iselin said he was wearing the shoes because he had lost most of his heel in arctic combat. There is disagreement among those who heard him at that time as to whether he said 'lost most of my foot' or a lesser amount of tissue.

The relentless *Journal*, in the year of its gallant but futile attempt to discredit Johnny in a meaningful sense, uncovered the personal journal of an officer who had served with Johnny all during the tour, a Francis Winikus, who subsequently made a reputation as an authority on migratory elements of population in Britain and Europe. Under the date of June 22, 1944, the Winikus diary threw a white and revealing light on the circumstances leading to Johnny's wound by recording: 'Johnny Iselin has become possessed by the idea of sex. To get that interested in sex on the top of this ice cap is either suicidal or homosexual, on its surface, but Johnny isn't either. He is a persistent and determined zealot. There is a new Eskimo camp about three miles across that primordial field of ice under that gale of wind which carries those flying razor blades to cut into the face from the direction of the village. There are women there. Everybody knows that and everybody agreed it was a very good thing until we walked, secretly and one at a time, with ice grippers tied to our shoes, across that shocking three-mile course in cold worse than icy hell the old German religions called Nifelheim and came up to the igloos down wind and lost all interest in sex for the rest of the war. I was exhausted when I made the run, but I came back faster than I went over, to get away from that smell. It is the special smell of the Eskimo women and there is no smell like it because they wash their hair in stored urine, they live sewed up in those musty skins, and they eat an endless diet of putrescent food like fish heads and whale fat.

'Johnny said he was going to get around these "surface disadvantages" because he had to have a woman or the top of his head would come off. He has been practising eleven days, making that run over and back every single day. The cold and the wind simply do not seem to exist for him. All he can think of is the women. He comes back here and rests and moans and bleats with this longing, and he says proudly that *he is getting used to the stink of the women.* He says that if Eskimo men went to Chicago and smelled our women wearing those expensive French perfumes that it would sicken them, too, and that all these things are just a matter of getting used to them.

'Yesterday he decided he was ready. He crossed the ice cap again in that blackness, following a compass and watching for the lights, if any. He filled me in on the whole story this morning before they took him out in the sled to Etah, where they will hold him for pickup by relief plane to Godthaab. He was welcomed hospitably, he said, about thirty yards outside a lot of ice mounds which turned out to be igloos. Johnny doesn't speak their language and they don't speak Johnny's but he used his hands so suggestively—well, what he did with his hands when he was telling me how he showed them what he wanted makes me wonder how I will be able to get through the winter. He says they were completely sympathetic and immediately understanding and motioned him to crawl behind them into one of the blocks of ice. Before he entered, he distributed some K-ration and he told me he remembered thinking how easy this was going to be as soon as he could figure out which were the women and which were the men, because they were all wrapped in furs and their faces were as round and flat and shiny as a silver dollar. He made it into the igloo on his hands and knees, then almost fainted from the smell. He had gotten used to the smell of the women *in a high arctic wind OUTSIDE* the snow houses. The heat was tremendous for one thing: hot bricks, body heat, burning blubber, and smoking dried moss and lichens. Artfully placed around the perimeter were leather buckets of straight aged urine. Johnny said he must have stumbled into the local beauty parlour. His other quick impression was that a considerable amount of last season's fish had rotted, and, too, there was the smoky, blinding smell of long imprisoned feet. This morning as the infection turned towards fever, every now and then Johnny would say, "O my God, those feet!" There were about fourteen people in the igloo, although he feels that they could have been sitting on a few old ladies. They had slipped out of their clothing and the ripeness of all of them hit him like a stone axe and he says he keeled over although he didn't pass out. He said they immediately offered him three different people whom he decided must have been women, and some of the fellows there even seemed ready to lift him on. Although he discovered that it was impossible to get used to the congress of smells he was able to concentrate on them just being *women* and all other considerations in that tiny space actually left his mind. He said it was no question of poontang next year with a girl who smelled like flowers, it was a case of poontang now and he began to get out of his clothes. He was actually getting undressed in front of all of those people and he said he would pause every now and then to give the nearest shape that he assumed was a girl a little pinch or a tiny tickle when all of a sudden one of the Eskimos started to yell at him in *German*.

'Johnny said he doesn't speak German but he knows it when he hears it because they speak a lot of it in his home state. Then this Eskimo began to take off his furs in that way a man takes off his coat when he wants to start a fight, yelling all the time in

German and pointing at the Eskimo woman Johnny had been diddling and who was now giggling up at Johnny, when Johnny sees that this man is wearing a *German officer's uniform* under the skins. As this was the first time Johnny had ever believed that there was any enemy, he said he was absolutely flabbergasted. The Eskimos in the igloo began to yell at the German to shut up, or maybe they felt that he had impugned their hospitality by interrupting Johnny, or maybe they were sore because they liked to watch, and by now the woman had reached up and she had Johnny firmly by the privates and she wasn't letting go because for whatever crazy reason she *liked* Johnny. The noise bounced back and forth from ice wall to ice wall, dogs started barking, kids started crying, the German was yelling and weeping through what was obviously a broken heart, and Johnny said he felt very embarrassed. He realised he had been making a pass at this guy's girl right in front of the guy himself which must have hurt him terribly, and it wasn't right even if he *was* the enemy, Johnny felt. He didn't know what to do so he hit the man and as the man fell he knocked four of the small Eskimos over with him. This turned the tables. The other Eskimos now got sore at Johnny and three of them rushed him waving what Johnny calls "Stone Age power tools." He swept his arms out in front of him and sent the attackers over backward into the mob, all of this happening, he said, inside an area about as big as Orson Welles's head, with everybody howling for blood. He decided then that he wasn't going to score after all and that he'd better get the hell out of there, so he tried to dive through the tunnel which led to the full force arctic hurricane outside, forgetting entirely that the Eskimo woman had him by the family jewels and she had decided to keep those jewels for her very own. Johnny says he never felt anything quite like what he felt then and that he thought he had actually lost his reason for living. Rejecting her both physically and psychologically, he let fly with his left foot, catching her smartly in the face. She sank her over-developed teeth into his foot, then she crunched down again, then settled down to a steady munching, and he says if it hadn't been for her getting hit by someone in that yelling, milling throng behind her in the igloo she might have chewed his foot off. How he got back here in that weather with that foot I will never know. The wound had festered badly by this morning. They took him out of here for Etah about an hour ago. I guess that's the end of the war for old Johnny.'

In August, 1944, Johnny came limping home to take up his part in the red-hot campaign that 'friends' (meaning Raymond's mother and, to a conclusive extent, even though it seems absolutely impossible in retrospect, the Communist party) had been carrying forward since the day he had gone off to war. All Johnny had to do was to wear his uniform, his crutches, and his bandaged foot and shout out a few hundred topical exaggerations that Raymond's mother had written up and catalogued over the years to evade any conceivable demand. Because of the clear call from the people of his state, Johnny was permitted to resign from the armed forces on August 11, 1944.

He was elected governor of his state in the elections of 1944 and re-elected in 1948. As he entered his second term he was forty-one years old; Raymond's mother was thirty-eight. Raymond was twenty-one and was working as a district man for the *Journal*, having graduated from the state university at the head of his class.

At forty-one, Governor Iselin was a plain, aggressively humble man, five feet eight inches tall in specially shod elevator shoes. There was a fleshiness of the nose to mark him for the memory. His hair was thin and, under certain lighting, appeared to have been painted in fine, single lines across his scalp over rosettes and cabbages of two-dimensional liver spots. His clothes, from a time shortly after his marriage to Raymond's mother, were of home-spun material but they had been run up by the hands of a terribly good and quite wealthy tailor in New York. Raymond's mother had Johnny's valet shine only the lower half of his high black shoes so that it would seem, to people who thought about those things, that he managed to shine his own shoes between visits of the Strawberry Lobby and the refusal of pardons to the condemned. An abiding mark of the degree of Johnny's elemental friendliness shone from the fact that he could look no one in the eye and that when he talked he would switch syntax in seeming horror of what he had almost said to his listener. The governor never shaved from Friday night to Monday morning, no matter what function might be scheduled, as though he were a part-time Sikh. He would explain that this gave his skin a rest. Raymond's mother had invented that one, as she had invented very nearly everything else about him excepting his digestive system (and if she had invented that it would have functioned a great deal better), because not shaving 'made him like some slob, like a farm hand or some Hunky factory worker.' It is certain that over a weekend, when Big John was generating noise out of every body orifice, switching syntax, darting his eyes about, and flashing that meaty nose in his unshaven face, he was the commonest kind of common man forty ways to the ace. However, he had been custom-made by Raymond's mother. She had developed Johnny (as José Raoul Capablanca had developed his chess play; as Marie Antoine Carême had folded herbs into a sauce for Talleyrand) into the model governor, on paper that is, of all the states of the United States, and in some of those states the constituents read more about Jolly Johnny than about their own men. She had riveted into the public memory these immutable facts: John Yerkes Iselin was a formidable administrator a conserver who could dare; an honest, courageous, conscience-thrilled, God-fearing public servant; a jolly, jovial, generous, gentling, humourous, amiable, good-natured, witty big brother; a wow of a husband and a true-blue pal of a father; a fussin', fumin', fightin', soldier boy, all heart; a simple country judge with the savvy of Solomon; and an American, which was the most fortuitous circumstance of all.

Raymond's mother hardly showed one flicker of chagrin when General Eisenhower was persuaded to make the stroll for the nomination in 1952, the one unexpected accident that could have blocked her John from the White House. She broke a few little things at the Mansion when she heard the news: mirrors, lamps, vases, and other replaceable bric-à-brac. She was entitled to a flash of violence, one little demonstration that she could feel passion, and it harmed no one because Johnny was dead drunk and Raymond had marched off to the Korean War.

In the Autumn of 1952, two weeks before Raymond's return from Korea to receive the Congressional Medal of Honour, almost two months before the end of Big John's statutory final term as governor, U.S. Senator Ole Banstoffsen, the grand old man who had represented his state in Washington for six consecutive terms, succumbed to a heart attack almost immediately after a small dinner with his oldest and dearest friends, Governor and Mrs John Iselin, and died in the governor's arms in the manner of a dinner guest of the Empress Livia's some time before in ancient Rome. The exchange of last words made their bid to become part of American history, for through them Big John found his life's mission, and the words are set down herewith to complete the record.

SENATOR BANSTOFFSEN
John—Johnny, boy—are you there?
GOVERNOR ISELIN
Ole! Ole, old friend. Don't try to speak! Eleanor! *Where is that doctor!*

SENATOR BANSTOFFSEN
(his last words)
Johnny—you must—carry on. Please, please, Johnny swear to me as I lay dying that you will fight to save Our Country—from the Communist peril.

GOVERNOR ISELIN
(greatly moved)
I pledge to you, with my soul, that I will fight to keep Communists from dominating our institutions to the last breath of my life, dear friend.
(Senator Banstoffsen slumps into death, made happy.)

88

He's gone! Oh, Eleanor, he's gone. A great fighter has gone on to his rest.

The verbatim record must have been set down by Raymond's mother, as she was the only other person present at the senator's death, and she undoubtedly found time to make notes while they waited for the doctor and while the words were still so fresh in her mind, but Johnny did not use them for almost three years, during which time they had undoubtedly been carefully filed for their value as Americana and as a source of inspiration to others.

Governor Iselin appointed himself to succeed Senator Banstoffsen, to fight the good fight, and his re-election followed. He was sworn in on March 18, 1953, by Justice Krushen, after his wife had insisted that he take The Cure for two and a half months at a reliable, discreet, and medically sound ranch for alcoholics and drug addicts in sun-drenched New Mexico, following the booze-drenched Christmas holidays of 1952.

V

What is the consciousness of guilt but the arena floor rushing up to meet the falling trapeze artist? Without it, a bullet becomes a tourist flying without responsibility through the air. The consciousness of guilt gives a scent to humanity, a threat of putrefaction, the ultimate cosmetic. Without the consciousness of guilt, existence had become so bland in Paradise that Eve welcomed the pungency of Original Sin. Raymond's consciousness of guilt, that rouged lip print of original sin, had been wiped off. He had been made unique. He had been shriven into eternity, exculpated of the consciousness of guilt.

Out of his saddened childhood, Raymond had grown to the age for love. Because he was mired down within an aloof, timid, and sceptical temperament he was a man who, if he was to be permitted to love at all, was suited to find the solution of his needs only in reassuring monogamy. He had no ability to make friends. As he had grown up he was dependent upon the children of friends of the people who were his mother's garden: mostly politicians and their lackeys, and other people who could be used by politicians: newspaper types, press agents, labour types, commerce and industry edges, hustlers of veterans and hustlers of minorities, patriots and suborners, confused women and the self-seeking clergy.

By an accident, when he was just past twenty-one years old, Raymond met the daughter of a man whom his mother would not, under any condition, have entertained. Her name was Jocelyn Jordan. Her father was a United States senator and a dangerously unhealthy liberal in every sense of that word, though a member of Johnny Iselin's party. They lived in the East. They happened to be in Raymond's mother's state because it was summertime, when school teachers and senators not up for re-election are allowed time off to spend their large, accumulated salaries, and they had been invited by Jocie's room mate to use her family's summer camp while the family toured in Europe. It is certain that they had no knowledge that they would be keeping calm and cool beside the same blue lake, with its talking bass and balsam collar, as Governor Iselin and his wife or else they would have politely refused the invitation. When they did find out, they were established in the summer camp and had not been shot at so it was too late to do anything about it.

Jocie was nineteen that summer when she came around a turning of the dusty road at the moment the snake had bitten Raymond, as he lay in his wine-coloured swimming trunks where he had tripped and fallen in the road, staring from the green snake as it moved slowly through the golden dust towards the other side of the road, to the neat, new wound on his bare leg. She did not speak to him but she saw what he saw and, stopping, stared wordlessly at the two dark red spots against his healthy flesh, then moved quickly to the small plastic kit attached to the back of her bicycle seat, removed a naked razor blade and a bottle of purple fluid, and knelt beside him. She beamed expert reassurance into his eyes from the sweet brownness of her own and cut crosses with the razor blade in each dark, red spot, traversed both of them with a straight cut, then put her mouth to his leg and drew two mouthfuls of blood out of it. Each time after she spat the blood out she wiped her mouth with the back of her hand like a labourer who had just finished a hero sandwich and a bottle of beer. She poured the purple fluid on the cuts, bound Raymond's legs with two strips of a handkerchief she had ripped in half, then saturated the improvised bandage with more purple liquid, over the wounds.

'I hope I know what I'm doing,' she said in a tremulous voice. 'My father is scared tiddly about snakes in this part of the country, which is how I happen to ride around with a razor blade and potassium permanganate solution. Now don't move. It is very, very important that you don't move and start anything that might be left from that snake circulating through your system.' She walked to her bicycle as she talked. 'I'll be right back with a car. I won't be ten minutes. You just stay still, now. You hear?' She pedalled off rapidly around the same turning of the road that had magically produced her. She had vanished many seconds before he realised that he had not spoken to her and that, although he had expected to die when the snake had bitten him, he had not thought about the snake, the snake's bite, nor his impending death from the instant she had appeared. He looked bemusedly at his crudely bandaged leg below the swimming trunks. Purple ink and red blood trickled idly along his leg in parallel courses and it occurred to him that, if this had been happening to his mother's leg, she would have claimed the purple mixture as being her blood.

A car returned, it seemed to him almost at once, and Jocie had fetched her father along because it would give him such a good feeling to know that all of those warnings about the snakes in those woods had been just. A man has few enough opportunities like that when he assists in the raising of children, who must be hoisted on the pulley of one's experience every morning to the top of the pole for a view of life as extensive as that day's emotional climate would bear, then lowered again at sundown to be folded up and made to rest, and carried into their dreams with reverence.

They brought Raymond back to the summer camp, believing him to be in a state of shock because he did not speak. Raymond sat beside Jocie in the back seat with his fanged leg propped up on the back of the front seat. The senator drove and told horrendous snake stories wherein no one bitten ever recovered. The way Raymond looked at Jocie in that back seat told her well that he was in a state of shock but she was, at nineteen, sufficiently versed to be able to differentiate between the mundane and the glorious kinds of shock.

At the camp the senator made his examination of the wound and was thrown into high glee when there seemed to be no swelling on, above, or below the poisoned area. He took Raymond's temperature and found it normal. He cauterised the wounds with a carbolic acid solution while Raymond continued to stare respectfully at his daughter. When he had finished, the senator asked the only possible, sensible question.

'Are you a mute?' he said.

'No, sir.'

'Ah.'

'Thank you very much,' Raymond said, 'Miss—Miss——'

'Miss Jocelyn Jordan,' the senator said. 'And considering that you two are practically related by blood, it is probably time you met.'

'How do you do?' Raymond said.

'And now, under the quaint local custom, it is your turn to tell your name,' the senator explained gravely.

'I am Raymond Shaw, sir.'

'How do you do, Raymond?' the senator said, and shook hands with him.

'I have save your life,' Jocie said with a heavy vaudeville Hungarian accent, 'and now I may do with it what I will.'

'I would like to ask your permission to marry Jocelyn, sir.'

Raymond was deadly serious, as always. The Jordans exploded with laughter, believing Raymond was working to amuse them, but when they looked back to him to acknowledge his sally, and saw the confused and nearly hurt expression on his face, they became embarrassed. Senator Jordan coughed violently. Jocelyn murmured something about gallantry not being dead after all, that it was time she made some coffee, and went off hastily towards what must have been the kitchen. Raymond stared after her. To cover up, although for the life of him he could not have explained or understood what he was covering up, the senator sat down on a wicker chair beside Raymond. 'Is your place near here he asked.

'Yes, sir. It's that red house directly across the lake.'

'The Iselin house?' Jordan was startled. His expression became less friendly.

'My house,' Raymond said succinctly. 'It was my father's house but my father is dead and he left it to me.'

'Forgive me, I had been told that it was the summer camp of Johnny Iselin, and of all places in this world for me to spend a summer this——'

'Johnny stays there sometimes, sir, when he gets too drunk for my mother to allow him to stay around the Capitol.'

'Your mother is—uh—Mrs Iselin?'

'That's right, sir.'

'I once found it necessary to sue your mother for defamation of character and slander. My name is Thomas Jordan.'

'How do you do, sir?'

'It cost her sixty-five thousand dollars and costs. What hurt her much more than the payment of that money was that I donated all of it to the organisation called the American Civil Liberties Union.'

'Oh.' Raymond remembered the colour of his mother's words, the objects she had broken, the noises she had made, and the picture she had painted of this man.

Jordan smiled at him grimly. 'Your mother and I are, have been, and will always be divergent in our views, not to say inimical of one another's interests, and I tell you that after long study of the matter and of the uses of expediences by all of us in politics.'

Raymond smiled back at him, but not grimly, and he looked amazingly handsome and vitally attractive, Jocie thought from far across the room as she entered, carrying a tray. He had such even white teeth against such a long, tanned face, and he offered them the yellow-green eyes of a lion. 'If you weren't sure of that, sir,' Raymond said, 'you couldn't be sure of anything, because that is the absolute truth.' They both laughed, unexpectedly and heartily, and were friends of a sort. Jocie came up to them with the cups and the coffee and a bottle of rye whisky, and Raymond began to feel the beginnings of what was to be a constant, summer-long nausea as he tried to equate the daughter of Senator Jordan with the ancient, carbonised prejudice of his mother.

That summer was the only happy time, excepting one, the only fully joyous, concentrically transforming time in Raymond's life. Two pure and cooling fountains were all Raymond ever found in all that aridness of time allotted to him. Two brief episodes in his entire life in which he awoke each morning looking forward in joy to more joy and found it. Only twice was there a time when he did not maintain the full and automatic three-hundred-and-sixty-degree horizon of raw sensibilities over which swept the three searing beams of suspicion, fear, and resentment flashing from the loneliness of the tall lighthouse of his soul.

Jocie showed him how she felt. She told him how she felt. She presented him, with the pomp of new love, a thousand small and radiant gifts each day. She behaved as though she had been waiting an eternity for him to catch up with her in the time continuum, and now that he had arrived with his body to occupy a predestined place in space beside her, she knew she must wait still longer while he tried desperately to mature, all at once, out of infancy until he could understand that she only wanted to give to him, asking nothing but his awareness in return. She behaved

94

as though she loved him, a condition that could swing in suspension to fix his concentration but which, when he could understand, would need to blend with his love, matching it exactly.

He walked beside her. Once or twice he touched her, but he did not know how to touch her or where to touch her. However she saw right on the surface of him how greatly he was trying to learn, how he was struggling to lose the past so he could tell her of the glories she made him feel and of how enormously he needed her.

Every morning he waited outside her house, staring as though he could see through the walls, until she came running out to him. They spent all of every day together. They separated late, in the darkness. They did not speak much but each day she moved closer to breaking through his barriers and willed him with her love to say more each day, and she was filled with the ambition to make him safe with her love.

The summer was the second-best time in his merely twice-blest living span. The first time was not the equal of the second time because of his fear; the conviction that it would be taken from him the instant he voiced his need for it. Whatever they did together he held himself rigid, awaiting the scream of his mother's rage, and it cost him thirty pounds of his flesh because he could not keep food down as he battled to hold the thoughts of his mother and Jocie apart. His mother found out about Jocie in time, and who Jocie's father was, of course, and it was all over.

Johnny said he didn't want to be around when she told Raymond what had to be. He went back to the capital where he had a lot of work to do anyway. Raymond got home late that night. His mother was waiting for him. She was wearing a fantastically beautiful Chinese house coat. It was orange-red. It had a deep black Elizabethan collar that stood up straight behind and around her shining blonde head, in the mode of wicked witches, but it made her look very lovely and very kind and she smelled very beautiful and enlightened as Raymond dragged his dread behind him into the room, sickened to find her awake so late.

There she sits like a mail-order goddess, serene as the star on a Christmas tree, as calm as a jury, preening the teeth of her power with the floss of my joy, soiling it, shredding it, and just about ready to throw it away, and she is getting to look more and more like those two-dimensional women who pose for nail polish advertisements, and I have wanted to kill her for all of these years and now it is too late.

'What the hell do you want, Mother?'

'What the hell kind of a greeting is that at three-thirty in the morning.'

'It's a quarter to three. What do you want?'

'What's the matter with you?'

'I'm shocked to be in a room alone with you after all these years, I guess.'

'All right, Raymond. So I'm a busy woman. Do you think I work and work and ruin my health for myself? I do it for you. I'm making a place for you.'

'Please don't do it for me, Mother. Do it for Johnny. Worse I couldn't wish him.'

'What you're doing to Johnny is the worst you could wish him.'

'What is it? I'll double it.'

'I speak of that little Communist tart.'

'Shut up, Mother! Shut up with that!' His voice rose to a squeak.

'Do you know what Jordan is? Are you out to crucify Johnny?'

'I can't answer you. I don't know what you're talking about. I'm going to bed.'

'Sit down!' He stopped where he was. He was near a chair. He sat down.

'Raymond, they live in New York. How would you see her?'

'I thought of getting a job in New York.'

'You have to do your Army service.'

'Next spring.'

'Well?'

'I might be dead next spring.'

'Oh, Raymond, for Christ's *sake!*'

'No one has given me a written, printed, bonded guarantee that I will live another week. This girl is now. What the hell do I care about her father's politics any more than I care about your politics? Jocie—Jocie is *all* I care about.'

'Raymond, if we were at war now——'

'Oh, Mother, for Christ's *sake!*'

'—and you were suddenly to become infatuated with the daughter of a Russian agent—wouldn't you expect me to come to you and object, to beg you to stop the entire thing before it was too late? Well, we *are* at war. It's a cold war but it will get worse and worse until every man and woman and child in this country will have to stand up and be counted to say whether or not he or she is on the side of right and freedom, or on the side of the Thomas Jordans' of this country. I will go with you to Washington tomorrow, if you like, and I will show you documented proof that this man stands for evil and that he will do anything to win that evil——'

That was the gist of it. Raymond's mother began her filibuster at approximately three o'clock in the morning and she kept at him, walking beside him wherever he went in the house, standing next to him talking shrilly of the American Dream and its meaning in the present, pulling stops out bearing the invisible labels left over from Fourth of July speeches and old Hearst editorials such as 'The Red Menace,' 'Liberty, Freedom, and America as We know It,' 'Thought Police and The American Way,' until ten minutes to eleven o'clock the following morning, when Raymond, who had lost so much weight that summer and who had been running a sub-normal fever for three weeks, collapsed. She had talked through each weakening manifestation of defiance he had made—through his shouts and screams, through his tears and pleadings and whimperings and sobs—and the sure power of her limitless strength slowly and surely overcame his double weakness: both the physical and the psychological, until he was convinced that he would be well rid of

Jocie if he could trade her for some silence and some sleep. She made him take four sleeping pills, tucked him into his trundle bed, and he slept until the following afternoon at five forty-five, but was even then too weak to get up. His mother, having put her little boy to beddy-by, took a hot shower followed by a cold shower, ran a comforting amount of morphine into the large vein in her forearm (which was always covered with those smart, long sleeves) and sat down at the typewriter to compose a little note from Raymond to Jocie. She rewrote it three times to be sure, but when it was done it was done right, and she signed his name and sealed the envelope. She got dressed, popped into the pick-up truck, and drove directly to the Jordan camp. Jocie had gone to the post office on an errand for her father, but the senator was there. Raymond's mother said it would be necessary for them to have a talk so he invited her inside the house. The Jordans packed and left the lake by six o'clock that evening.

Jocie, who had fallen as deeply in love with Raymond as he with her, and more than that because she was healthy and normal, never really understood quite why it was all over. Her father told her that Raymond had enlisted in the Army that morning, had telephoned only to say that he could not see Jocie again and good-bye. Her father, having read the terrible letter, had shuddered with nausea and burned it. Raymond's mother had explained to him that despite their own personal differences she had come to say to him that his daughter was far too fine a girl to be hurt or twisted by her son, that Raymond was a homosexual and in other ways degenerate, and that he would be far, far better forgotten by this sweet, fine child.

VI

In February, 1953, just a little more than two months after his discharge from the Army, Raymond got a job as a researcherlegman-confidant for, and as janitor of the ivory tower of, Holborn Gaines, the distinguished international political columnist of *The Daily Press*, in New York; this on the strength of (1) a telephone call from the managing editor of the *Journal* to Joe Downey, managing editor of *The Daily Press*, (2) his relationship to Mrs John Yerkes Iselin, whom Mr Gaines admired and loathed as one of the best political minds in the country, and (3) the Medal of Honour.

Mr Gaines was a man of sixty-eight or seventy years who wore a silk handkerchief inside his shirt collar whenever he was indoors, no matter what the season of the year, and drank steady quantities of Holland beer but never seemed to grow either plump or drowsy from it, and found very nearly everything that had ever happened in politics from Caesar's ascension to Sherman Adam's downfall to be among the most amusing manifestations of his civilisation. Mr Gaines would pore over those detailed never-to-be-published-in-that-form reports from one or another of the paper's bureau chiefs around the world, which provided the intimate background data of all real or imagined political manœuvring, and sip at the lip of a beer bottle, chuckling as though the entire profile of that day's world disaster had been written by Mark Twain. He was a kind man who took the trouble to explain to Raymond on the first day of his employment that he did not much enjoy talking and fulsomely underscored how happy they would be, both of them, if they could train each other into one another's jobs so that conversation would become unnecessary. This suited Raymond so well that he could not believe his own luck, and when he had worked even faster and better than usual and needed to sit and wait until Mr Gaines would indicate, with a grunt and a push at a pile of papers, what the next job would be, he would sit turned halfway in upon himself, wishing he could turn all the way in and shut everything out and away from himself, but he was afraid Mr Gaines would decide to talk and he would have to climb and pull himself out of the pit, so he waited and watched and at last came to see that he and Mr Gaines could not have

99

been more ecstatically suited to one another had one worked days and the other worked nights.

The promotion manager of *The Daily Press* was a young man named O'Neil. He arranged that the members of the editorial staff give Raymond a testimonial dinner (from which Mr Gaines was automatically excused for, after all, he had actually met Raymond), welcoming a hero to their ranks. When O'Neil first told Raymond about the dinner plan they were standing, just the two of them, in Mr Gaines's office, one of the many glass-enclosed cubicles that lined the back wall of the city room, and Raymond hit O'Neil, knocking him across the desk and, as he lay there for an instant, spat on him. O'Neil didn't ask for an explan-ation. He got up, a tiny thread of blood hanging from the left corner of his mouth, and beat Raymond systematically and quietly. They were both of the same age and weight, but O'Neil had interest, which is the key to life, on his side. The beating was done well and quickly but it must be seen that Raymond had, if even in the most negative way, made his point. No one else ever knew what had happened and because the dinner was only a week away and O'Neil knew he would need pictures of Raymond posed beside various executives of the paper, he was careful not to hit Raymond in the face where subsequent discolourations might show. When it was over, Raymond agreed that he would not concede the dinner, at any time, to be a good idea, holding it to be 'a commonness which merchandised the flag,' but he did agree to attend. O'Neil, in his turn, inquired that if there was anything more a part of our folklore than hustling the flag for an edge, that he would appreciate it if Raymond would point it out to him, and agreed to limit the occasion to one speech which he would make himself and keep it short, and that Raymond would need only to rise in acknowledgment, bow slightly, and speak not at all.

In December, 1953, Raymond was guest of honour at a dinner given by the Overseas Press Club at which an iron-lunged general of the Armies was the principal speaker, and Raymond could not fight his way out of this invitation to attend and to speak because his boss, Mr Gaines, was chairman of the dinner committee. What Raymond did say when he spoke was 'Thank you, one and all.' The way the matter had been handled differed sharply from the O'Neil incident. Mr Gaines had come in one morning, had handed Raymond a printed invitation with his name on it, had patted him understandingly on the back, had opened a bottle of beer, sat down at his desk, and that was that.

VII

The war was over in Korea. That camera which caught every movement of everyone's life was adjusted to run backward so that they were all returned to the point from which they had started out to war. Not all. Some, like Mavole and Lembeck, remained where they had been dropped. The other members of Marco's I & R patrol whose minds believed in so many things that had never happened, although in that instance they were hardly unique, returned to their homes, left them, found jobs and left them until, at last, they achieved an understanding of their essential desperation and made peace with it, to settle down into making and acknowledging the need for the automatic motions that were called living.

Marco didn't get back to the States until the spring of 1954, on the very first day of that spring. His temporary orders placed him with the First Army on Governor's Island in the New York harbour, so he blandly took it for granted that he would be more than welcome to spend his stateside leave as Raymond's guest in Raymond's apartment. As far as Raymond was concerned, and this feeling mystified Raymond, Marco was more than welcome.

Raymond lived in a large building on Riverside Drive, facing the commercially broad Hudson at a point approximately opposite an electric spectacular on the New Jersey shore which said *SPRY* (some experiment in suggestive geriatrics, Raymond thought) to the *démodé* side of Manhattan Island.

The apartment was on the sixteenth floor. It was old-fashioned, which meant that the rooms were large and light-filled, the ceilings high enough to permit a constant circulation of air, and the walls thick enough for a man and his loving wife to have a stimulating argument at the top of their lungs without invading the nervous systems of surrounding neighbours. Raymond had rented the apartment furnished and nothing in the place beyond the books, the records, and the phonograph was his.

The bank issued rent checks for the apartment's use, as they paid all the bills for food, pressing, laundry, and liquor. These the local merchants sent directly to Raymond's very own bank officer, a Mr Jack Rothenberg, a formidably bankerish sort of a man excepting for the somewhat disturbing habit of wearing leather tassels on his shoes. Raymond believed that the exchange of money was one of the few surviving methods people had for communicating with each other, and he wanted no part of it. The act of loving, not so much of the people themselves but of the cherishment contained in the warm money passed from hand to hand was, to Raymond, intimate to the point of being obscene so that as much as possible he insisted that the bank take over that function, for which he paid them well.

Each Monday morning at fifteen minutes past ten, a bank messenger came to Raymond's office with a sealed Manila envelope containing four twenty-dollar bills, four ten-dollar bills, five five-dollar bills and thirty singles—a total of one hundred and seventy-five dollars—for which Raymond would sign. This was his walking-around money. He spent it, if he spent it, on books and off-beat restaurants for he was a gourmet—as much as a man can be who eats behind a newspaper. His salary from *The Daily Press* of one hundred and thirty-five dollars and eighty-one cents, after deductions, he mailed personally to the bank each Friday and considered himself to be both lucky and shrewd to be living in the biggest city on the Western continent for what he regarded as a net of forty dollars per week, cash.

The living expenses, rent, and such, were the bank's problem.

As much as possible, he ate every meal alone, excepting perhaps once a month when he would be forced into accepting an invitation from O'Neil, with some girls. All the men Raymond ever knew seemed to be able to summon up girls the way he might summon up a tomato juice from a waiter. Raymond was a theatrically handsome man, a well-informed man and an intelligent one. He had never had a girl inside his large, comfortable apartment. He bought the sex he needed for twenty-five dollars an hour and he had never found it necessary to exceed that time period, although he filled it amply every time. Out of distaste, because she had suggested it herself the first time he had been there, and most certainly not out of any unconscious desire to be liked, he would give the maid who ran the towels a dollar-and-a-quarter tip, because she had asked for a dollar, then would stare her down coldly when she thanked him. Raymond had found the retail outlet with efficiency. He had told the Broadway columnist on the paper that he would appreciate it greatly if one of the press agents with whom the columnist did business would secure him maximum-for-minimum accommodations atop some well-disposed, handsome professional woman. Had he known that this ritual and the attendant expense were the direct result of the release conferred on him by Yen Lo in Tunghwa, he would have resented it, because although the money meant little to him and although he enjoyed the well-disposed, handsome professional woman very much, he would just as well have preferred to have remained in the psychological position of ignoring it, because it meant getting to bed on the evenings he was with her much later than he preferred to retire and it most certainly had cut into his reading.

Marco gave him no warning. He called Raymond at the paper and told him he would be in town for a while, that he would move in with Raymond, and they met at Hungarian Charlie's fifteen minutes later, and that had been that. When Marco moved in, every one of Raymond's time-and-motion study habits

103

was tossed high in the air to land on their heads. For ten days or so everything was turned upside down.

Marco didn't believe in buying sex because he said it was so much more expensive the other way, and he was loaded with loot. Drunk or sober, Marco found matched sets of pretty girls, bright and entertaining girls, rich girls, poor girls, and even one very religious set of sisters who insisted on getting up for church in the mornings, whether it was Sunday or not, then raced back to Marco's bed again. Marco had girls stashed in most of the rooms of Raymond's apartment whenever he thought it was a good idea (day and night, night and day), severely disturbing the natural rhythm of Raymond's life. There were too many cans of beer in the icebox and too few cans of V-8. Men kept ringing the back door bell, bringing boxes or paper bags filled with liquor or heavy paper sacks of ice cubes. Everybody seemed to be an expert on cooking spaghetti and there was a film of red sauce on every white surface in the kitchen. In the foyer, in the living-room, in the dining-room (which Raymond had converted into an office), brassières were strewn, and slips, and amazingly small units of transparent panties. Marco made everyone wear shoes as a precaution against athlete's foot. He did not believe in hanging up his clothes when he was not in Army service because he said the agonising reappraisal of the piles of clothing every morning in each room made him appreciate the neatness of Army life all the more. The positive thing to be said for Marco was that although he crowded the apartment with girls and loud music and spaghetti and booze, he never invited any other guys, so what was there was fifty per cent Raymond's. The women were all sizes and colours, sharing with each other only Marco's requisite of a good disposition, and he rarely hesitated to hand out a black eye if this rule were violated.

Raymond found it enjoyable. He could not have stood it as a constant diet (and he believed that there were people who could stand it as a constant diet) and it was all extremely confusing to him at first, from his doctrinaire perspective, because the properly dressed, immaculately spoken women seemed to him to be the wantons, and the naked or near-naked babes who talked like long-shoremen seemed to be there as professional comics or entertainers on the piano or on the long-distance telephone. They were talking, talking, always talking, but never with the unpleasant garrulity of Johnny Iselin.

At first when Raymond allowed himself to get around to feeling like having a little action for himself he would grow flustered, be at a loss as to how to proceed, and he would close the door behind him in the converted dining-room he called an office and try to forget about the whole thing, but that simply was not satisfactory. He did that the very first night Marco had guests and he sat there, nearly huddled up with misery, fearing that no one would ever come in to make him come out, but finally the door was flung open and a small but strapping redheaded girl with a figure that made him moan to himself, stood in the doorway and stared at him accusingly. 'What the hell is the matter with you, honey?' she asked solicitously. 'Are you queer?'

'Queer? Me?' Strapping was definitely the word for this girl. Everything she had was big in miniature and in aching proportion.

'There are four broads out there, honey,' she said, 'and one man. Marco took me aside and told me that there was one more in here and although I ran right in here I've been worrying all the way because what the hell are you *doing* in here with very very ready broads out there?'

'Well—you see—' Raymond got up and took a slight step forward. 'I'd like to introduce myself.' The excitement was rising and he forgot to think about himself. He was aware vaguely that this was the first time he had ever been courted and if she could keep the thing within bounds everything was going to be all right. 'I'm Raymond Shaw.'

'So? I'm Winona Meighan. What has names got to do with what Marco promised I would be doing if I came here, but now I find out I may have to stand in line like at Radio City on a Sunday night?'

'I—I guess I simply didn't know what else to say. I'm just as avidly interested as you are,' Raymond said, 'but, I guess—well, I suppose you could say I am shy. Or new at all this. Shy, anyway.'

She waved her hand reassuringly. 'All the men are shy today. Everything is changing right in front of our eyes. It's become such a wonderful thing to find a man who actually is willing to go to bed with a woman that the women get all charged up and they press too much. I know it but I can't change it.' As she talked she closed the door behind her. She couldn't find any way to lock it so she pulled a heavy chair in front of it. 'So if you're shy we'll put out the lights, sweetheart. Winona understands, baby. Just get out of those bulgy pants and come over here.' She unzipped the side of her dress and began to struggle out of it impatiently. 'I have to get back downtown for an eleven o'clock show tonight, lover, so don't let's waste any more time.'

By the third night Raymond felt that he was fully adjusted to the new way of life. Winona had been extremely grateful for the extreme care he had put into his work with her and that squealing, activated gratitude, which had been coupled with an absolute insistence that he take her name and permanent address and that she write down his name and permanent address because her company was leaving in the morning for eight weeks in Las Vegas, had given him considerable confidence. After she had had to leave, both of them feeling exhausted but *triste* after the parting, he had moved quietly and weightlessly into the living room where Marco was playing at seance, explaining to the four girls that he understood, academically, exactly how a seance should operate because he had researched every necessary move and that if they would all co-operate by believing perhaps he could make something interesting happen the way things had happened in a fascinating textbook he had poured over all the way from San Francisco. It hadn't worked, but everybody enjoyed themselves and when bedtime came two of the girls joined up with Raymond as though they had all been assigned to each other by a lewd housemother and, after loads of fun, they had all dropped off to sleep and had slept like lambs.

Raymond awoke twice during the night for a few languorous moments of trying to puzzle out how come he did not feel invaded by all these bodies that were hurling themselves at him or dotting the landscape of his privacy, but he could not reach the answer before he fell asleep and, in the morning, with the girls getting ready to go off to offices or studios or dress houses or stores, no one had much more time than to wait patiently for a turn to put on lipstick hurriedly in the bathroom and rush out without any breakfast.

The extraordinary thing to Raymond was that none of them ever returned.

Marco would spend all of his day in the reading room of the Forty-second Street library, then, in the late afternoon, devote two hours to fruitful bird-dogging that was, mysteriously to Raymond, always successful, and when Raymond got back to the apartment at six twenty-two every day there would never be less than three interested and interesting girls there, making spaghetti or using the telephone.

Marco explained, on the first Saturday morning, that women were much more like men, in many almost invisible ways, than men were. Particularly in the non-involvement area in which they were many, many more times like men simply because their natural instinct to capture and hold could be suspended. Marco said that there was not a healthy woman alive who would not gladly agree to rush into bed if that action displaced only the present and did not connect with the past nor had any possibility of any shape in the future. Good health could be served in this way, he said. No fears of reputation-tarnish could threaten. It meant sex without sin, in the sense that, in the middle of the twentieth century, when sexual activity is credited to a woman by several men, creating what was termed a past could also penalise her for any sexual activity in the future. Since good health demands good sex, he assured Raymond that very nearly the entire female population of the city of New York would happily co-operate with them if approached in the proper, understanding manner.

'But how?' Raymond asked him in awe and bewilderment.

'How what?'

'How do you approach them?'

'Well, I do have the edge on others by being patently an officer and a gentleman by act of Congress, and I *am* graced with a certain courtliness of manner.'

'Yes. I agree. But so am I.'

'I approach them smiling. I tell them I am an officer passing through New York, leaving in the morning for my new station in Hawaii, and that merely by looking at them I find them enormously attractive sexually.'

'But—what do they say?'

'First, of course, they thank me. They are with it, Raymond. Believe me, they are even away ahead of me and depending on whether they need to be at home that evening to greet a loyal breadwinner, or under the clock at the Biltmore to persuade a courtier, or are committed to one or another irrevocable obligations which mar metropolitan life, they are keenly aware that one night is such a short, short burst of time in such a packed and crowded concealing city as New York.'

'But when do they say——'

'Actually,' Marco told him pedantically, 'I don't actually know until I get back here, and the door bell begins to ring, who will arrive and who won't. I always invite six. Every afternoon. So far we have not had to make do with less than three and——'

'But how do you——'

'How do I get them here?'

'Yes.'

'I explain I am using a friend's apartment. I write down the address, tear out the slip and press it into their hands, always smiling in a pleasant, lustful way, and I murmur about cold champagne and some great records. Then I pat them on the rear and walk on. I assure you, Raymond, that is all there is to it and everyone is richer all round.'

'Yes. I see. But——'

'But what?'

'Don't you ever have any *permanent* alliances?' Raymond asked earnestly.

'Of course,' Marco said stoutly. 'What do you think I am—a zombie? In London, before this last post where I met you, I was head over heels in love with my colonel's wife and she with me. And we stayed that way for almost two years.'

One night Marco took two young things by the wrists and headed off for rest. One was a Miss Ernestine Dover who worked at an exceptionally fine department store on Fifth Avenue and the other a Mrs Diamentez who was married to one of the best professional third basemen in the nation. After a while they all fell asleep.

Raymond was enjoying tremendous pleasure on a large bed in an adjoining room with a recording and variety artist, then unemployed, who was of Hawaiian, Negro, and Irish extraction and whom Marco had met that afternoon in the vestibule of a church, where he had gone to light a cigar out of the wind.

They all sat bolt upright, as one person—Raymond and June, Miss Dover and Mrs Diamentez—because Marco was yelling 'Stop him! Stop him!' in a wild, hoarse voice and trying to get out of the bed at something, his legs hopelessly entangled in the bedclothes. Mrs Diamentez recovered first—after all, she was married—and she took Marco by the shoulders and threw him over backward on the bed, pinning his torso down with her own body while Miss Dover held down his thrashing legs with hers.

'Ben Ben!' Mrs Diamentez yelled.

'It's O.K., lover, it's O.K. You ain't over there, you're over here,' Miss Dover shrilled.

Raymond and June stood naked in the doorway. 'Whassamatter?' Raymond said.

Ben was rolling and pitching, his eyes wide open, as feral as a trapped animal who is willing to leave a paw behind if it can only get away from the teeth. June swooped an old highball up from the bureau and, rushing across the room, poured it on

Marco. It brought him out. The girls climbed off him. He didn't speak to anyone but he stared at Raymond apprehensively. He shuffled dazedly out of the room and into the bathroom. He shook his head slowly from side to side as he walked, in tiny arcs, like a punch-drunk fighter, and his left cheek flinched with a tic. He closed the bathroom door behind him and they heard the lock snap and the light go on. Miss Dover went to the bathroom door and listened and suddenly the tub taps were turned on with full force. 'Are you all right, honey?' Miss Dover said, but there was no answer. After a while, although Marco wouldn't get out of the bathtub or speak, they all went back to sleep and Mrs Diamentez went in with Raymond and June.

Marco's ninth day was a Sunday. Without any warning, they were suddenly alone. All the chicks had gone to other roosts. Marco brooded over such a hangover as had not happened to him in fourteen years, since he had mixed Beaujolais wine with something called Wilkins' Family Rye Whisky. They ate steak for breakfast. Raymond opened the French windows and sat idly watching the river traffic and the multi-coloured metal band that never stopped moving along the West Side Highway. After a while, with Marco sunk into the silence of his perfect hangover, Raymond began to talk about Jocie. She had gotten married two months before. She was living in the Argentine. Her husband was an agronomist. It had run on the society page of his own newspaper and he said it as though if they had not run the item the marriage would not have been solemnised and she would be free to go to him.

Marco was ordered to Washington the following Thursday and he left without ever having seen the inside of a building at Governor's Island. He was ordered to the Pentagon, where he was assigned to active duty in Army Intelligence and promoted to major.

Of the nine men left from the patrol that had won Raymond the Medal of Honour only two had nightmares with the same awful context. They were separated by many thousands of miles and neither knew the other was suffering through the same nightmares, scene for scene, face for face, and shock for shock. The details of the nightmares and the rhythm of their recurrence were harrowing. Each man dreamed he was seated in a long line with the other men of the patrol on a stage behind Sergeant Shaw and an old Chinese, facing an audience of Soviet and Chinese officials and officers, and that they smiled and enjoyed themselves in a composed and gentling way, while Shaw strangled Ed Mavole then shot Bobby Lembeck through the head. A variation of that dream was the drill-session dream where they faced a blackboard while drillmasters took them through an imaginary battle action until they had memorised all details assigned to them. The incomprehensible part of the nightmare was that the details of the battle action they were taught exactly matched the battle action that had won Shaw the Medal of Honour. There was more.

One of these men had no course but to try to forget the nightmares as soon as they happened. The other man had no course but to try to remember the dreams while he was awake, because that was the kind of work he did, no other reason. Marco had been trained into wasteless usage of his highly developed memory. The first nightmare had come to him in bed with Miss Dover and Mrs Diamentez. It had frightened him as he had never been frightened before. He had sat in that bathtub filled with cold water until daybreak and if the humorous, noisy women had not been there he would not have been able to face Raymond that morning. The dreams started again with regularity after he got to Washington. When he dreamed the same terrifying dream every night for nine nights, and began to develop hand tremors at his work, it grew into an obsession with him which he could not share with anyone else. The Soviet uniforms haunted him. Watching his friend kill two of his men in front of all of them every night, causing himself to become part of the Technicolour print of the action, complete and edited, was like an attack upon his sanity. He could not tell anyone else about it until he felt he might understand any part of it, so that people would have some reason to listen to him. Marco began to live with the incubus, inside of it when he was awake; it appeared inside of him when he was asleep. He would fight his way out, knowing he would be returned to it later because he could not stay out of sleep; and he made detailed written records of the section of the nightmare he had just left behind, and which waited to threaten him again. He gave up women because what happened to him while he slept frightened them, and he was fearful that he would talk or shout and that the word would go out that he was slightly shock simple. He must have been getting a little strange to give up women. Women were food to Marco, and drink and exciting music. The written notes grew voluminous and after a while he transferred them all to a large loose-leaf notebook. They said things such as: Where did the interpreter, Chunjin, get a cigar? Why was he allowed to sit as an equal in a chair beside a Soviet general? Marco began to keep careful score as to how many times such things appeared in the dreams. What is that blackboard? he would note. Three different colours of chalk. Why do the Chinese know in advance and in such detail about an action which will wipe out one full Chinese infantry company? Why are the men of the patrol being worked so hard to remember so many details and different sets of details? His conflict between the love and admiration and respect for Raymond, which Yen Lo had planted in his mind, and his detailed, precise notes on exactly how Raymond had strangled Mavole and shot Lembeck had him beginning to live in dread and horror that everything which he still believed was happening in his imagination might somehow, someday, be proved to have happened in life. Marco had no thought that these things had ever happened. The notes were to keep him from unhinging, to provide the tools of his daily work to hold down his sanity. The dreams settled down to an occurrence of about three times a week in 1955, then began to step up inexorably in their appearances in 1956 until Marco was stumbling through his days on just about three hours' sleep each night. He never knew, all during that time, that he had remained sane.

*   *   *

In July, 1956, at about nine-twenty on a hot night for most New Yorkers, Raymond was reasonably cool as he sat before his opened French windows just inside the small balcony that was cleared by a strong breeze which had bowled down the Hudson River Valley. He was reading Le Compte and Sundeen's *Unified French Course*, because he had decided he would like to work directly from the notes of Brillat-Savarin and Escoffier during his recreational cooking periods, a new interest that had come to him since the many pleasant evenings when he had assisted so many expert young women in making so many different kinds of spaghetti sauce.

The telephone, on the desk beside his chair, rang. He picked it up.

'Raymond Shaw, please.' It was a pleasant male voice with an indefinite accent.

'This is he.'

'Why don't you pass the time by playing a little solitaire?'

'Yes, sir.' Raymond disconnected. He burrowed through the desk drawers until he found playing cards. He shuffled the cards carefully and began to play. The queen of diamonds did not show up until the third layout. The telephone rang again forty minutes later as Raymond was smoking and watching the queen on top of the squared deck.

'Raymond?'

'Yes, sir?'

'Can you see the red queen?'

'Yes, sir.'

'Do you carry an accident insurance policy?'

'No, sir.'

'Then tomorrow you will apply through the insurance department of your newspaper. Take all the standard benefits on a replacement income of two hundred dollars per week for total disability for as long as you have to be away from your job. Also take hospital insurance.'

'The paper carries that for me, sir.'

'Good. One week from next Saturday, on the fourteenth of

July, you will report at eleven-ten A.M. to the Timothy Swardon Sanitarium at 84 East Sixty-first Street. We want you here for a check-up. Is it clear?'

'Yes, sir.'

'Very good. Good night, Raymond.'

'Good night, sir.' The connection was discontinued. Raymond went back to Le Compte and Sundeen. He drank a bottle of Coca-Cola. He went to bed at eleven o'clock after a sensible shower, and slept dreamlessly. He breakfasted on figs and coffee, arrived at his desk at nine-forty-five, and called the personnel department immediately and made the arrangements for the insurance, naming in the life clause, his only friend, Ben Marco, as beneficiary of fifty thousand dollars if his death occurred by accident or by violence.

Senator Iselin's office forwarded a personal letter addressed to Raymond, care of the senator, to the newspaper office in New York. It was postmarked Wainwright, Alaska. Raymond opened it warily and read:

Dear Sarge:

I had to say this or write this to somebody because I think I am going nuts. I mean I have to say it or write it to somebody who knows what I'm talking about not just anybody and you was my best friend in the army so here goes. Sarge I am in trouble. I'm afraid to go to sleep because I have terrible dreams. I don't know about you but with me dreams sometimes have sounds and colours and these dreams have a way everything gets all speeded up and it can scare you. I guess you must be wondering about me going chicken like this. The dream keeps coming back to me every time I try to get to sleep. I dream about all the guys on the patrol where you won the Medal for saving us and the dream has a lot of Chinese people in it and a lot of big brass from the Russian army. Well, it is pretty rough. You have to take my word for that. There is a lot of all kind of things goes on in that dream and I need to tell about it. If you should hear from anybody else on the Patrol who writes you that they are having this kind of a dream I will appreciate if you put them in touch with me. I live in Alaska now and the address is on the envelope. I have a good plumbing business going for me here and I'll be in good shape if these dreams don't take too much of the old zing out of me. Well, sarge, I hope everything goes good with you and that if you're ever around Wainwright, Alaska, you'll give me a holler. Good luck, kid.

Your old corporal,
Alan Melvin

Raymond had himself re-read one part of the letter and he stared at that with distaste and disbelief. It offended him so that he read it and read it again: 'you was my best friend in the army.' He tore the letter across, then in quarters, then again. When he could no longer tear it smaller, he dropped the pieces into the waste-basket beside his desk.

VIII

For three years after taking the oath of office as United States Senator in March, 1953, Johnny had been moved slowly by Raymond's mother to insure acceptance within the Senate and in official Washington, to learn to know all of the press gentlemen well, to arrange the effective timing for the start of his run for re-election; in short, to master the terrain. It seems almost impossible now to credit the fact that, halfway through his first time in office, Johnny Iselin was still one of the least-known members of the Senate. It was not until April, 1956, that Raymond's mother decided to try out the first substantial issue.

On the morning of April 9, Johnny showed up at the press briefing room at the Pentagon to attend a regularly scheduled press conference of the Secretary of Defence. He walked into the conference with two friends who represented Chicago and Atlanta papers respectively. They had had coffee first. Johnny had asked them elaborately what they were up to that morning. They told him they were due at the Secretary's regular weekly press conference at eleven o'clock. Johnny said wistfully that he had never seen a really big press conference in action. He was such an obscure, diffident, pleasant, whisky-tinted little senator that one of them good-naturedly invited him to come along and thereby unwittingly won himself a $250 prize bonus, three weeks later, from his newspaper.

Johnny was so lightly regarded at that time, although extremely well known to all the regulars covering the Washington beat, that if he was noticed at all, no one seemed to think it a bit unusual that he should be there. However, immediately after the press conference writers who had not been within five hundred miles of Washington that morning claimed to have been standing beside Johnny when he made his famous accusation. Editorialists, quarterly-magazine contributors, correspondents for foreign dailies, and all other trend tenders used up a lot of time and wood pulp and, collectively, earned a lot of money writing about that extraordinary morning when a senator chose to cry out his anguish and protest at a press conference held by the Secretary of Defence.

The meeting, held in an intimate amphitheatre that had strong lights for the newsreel and television cameras, and many seats for correspondents, opened in the expected manner as the Secretary, a white-haired, florid, terrible-tempered man, strode on stage to the lectern flanked by his press secretaries and read his prepared statement concerned with that week's official view of integration of the nation's military and naval and air forces into one loyal unit. When he had finished he inquired into the microphones with sullen suspicion whether there were any questions. There were the usual number of responses from those outlets instructed to bait the Secretary, as was done in solemn rotation, to see if he could be goaded into one of his outrageous quotes that were so contemptuous of the people as to not only sell many more newspapers but give all of the arid columnists of think pieces something significant to write about. The Secretary did not rise to the bait. As the questions came in more slowly he began to shuffle his feet and shift his weight. He coughed and was making ready to escape when a loud voice, tremulous with moral indignation but brave with its recognition of duty, rang out from the centre of the briefing room.

'I have a question, Mr Secretary.'

The Secretary peered forward with some irritation at this stranger who had seen fit to take his own slow time about getting to his stupid question. 'Who are you, sir?' he said sharply, for he had been trained into politeness to the press by a patient team of wild horses and by many past dislocations, which had been extremely painful, resulting from getting his foot caught in his mouth.

'I am United States Senator John Yerkes Iselin, sir!' the voice rang out, 'and I have a question so serious that the safety of our nation may depend upon your answer.' Johnny made sure to shout very slowly so that, before he had finished, every newspaperman in the room had located him and was staring at him with that expectant lust for sensation which was their common emotion.

'Who?' the Secretary asked incredulously, his voice electronically amplified, making it sound like the mating call of a giant owl.

'No evasions, Mr Secretary,' Johnny yelled. 'No evasions, if you please.'

The Secretary owned a tyrant's temper and he had been one of the most royal of big business dynasts before he had become a statesman. 'Evasions?' he roared. 'What the hell are you talking about? What kind of foolishness is this?' That sentence alone, those few words all by themselves, served to alienate the establishment called the United States Senate from sympathy with his cause for the rest of his tenure in office for, no matter what the provocation, it is the first written law of the United States of America that one must never, never, never speak to a senator, regardless of his committee status, in such a manner before the press.

The members of the press present, who now recognised Johnny in his official status, grew light-headed over the implications of this head-on encounter of two potentially great sellers of newspapers, magazines, and radio and television time. It was one of those pulsing moments auguring an enormous upward surge in profits, when one half of the jaded-turned-thrilled stamped out their cigarettes and the other half lighted up theirs; all staring greedily.

'I said I am United States Senator John Yerkes Iselin and I hold here in my hand a list of two hundred and seven persons who are known to the Secretary of Defence as being members of the Communist party and who, nevertheless, are still working and shaping the policy of the Defence Department.'

'Whaaaaat?' The Secretary had to shout out his astonishment into the microphones to be heard over the excited keening and rumbling of the voices in the room.

'I demand an answer, Mr Secretary!' Johnny cried, waving a clutch of papers high over his head, his voice a silver trumpet of righteousness.

The Secretary had turned from beet-red to magenta. He was breathing with difficulty. He gripped the lectern before him as though he might decide to throw it at Johnny. 'If you have such a list, Senator, goddamit,' he bellowed, 'bring it up here. Give me that list!'

'There will be no covering up, Mr Secretary. You will not put your hands on this list. I regret deeply to say in front of all of these men and women that you no longer have my confidence.'

'Whaaaaat?'

'This is no longer a matter for investigation by the Department of Defence. I am afraid you have had your chance, sir. It has become the responsibility of the United States Senate.' Johnny turned and strode from the room, leaving chaos behind him.

On the following day, consistent with a booking made weeks previously and involving a token 'expenses' payment of $250, Johnny was to appear on Defenders of Our Liberty, a television programme that was a showcase for the more conservative members of the government; an interview show on which questions of a non-straightforward nature were asked before a national audience representing one of the lowest ratings of any programme in the history of the medium, the programme remaining on the air only because the sponsoring company found it generally useful and, of course, pleasant to be able to dine with the important weekly guests, following each show, when a special vice-president would make firm friends with them to continue the discussions of government problems and problems with government of a more or less specific nature over the years to come.

Johnny had been invited to appear on the show because he was one of the two senators remaining in office whom the company's special vice-president had never had to dinner, and the special vice-president was not one to underestimate.

However, on the day of his scheduled appearance, Johnny was the hottest statesman in the country as a result of thirty hours of continuous coverage and he had become an object of great importance to the television show and to its network. Wherever they could, in the extremely short time they had in which to turn around, they bought half-page advertisements in big city newspapers to herald Johnny's live appearance on the show.

Raymond's mother let everything develop in a normal manner, up to a point. Johnny was due to go on the air at seven-thirty P.M. At one P.M. she told them regretfully that he would not be available, that he was too busy preparing what would be the most important investigation the Senate had ever held. The network reeled at this news. The sponsor reeled. The press prepared to reel. After only the least perceptible stagger the special vice-president asked that a meeting between Raymond's mother and himself be quickly and quietly arranged. Raymond's mother preferred to hold this kind of a meeting in a moving car, far away from recording devices. She drove herself, and the two of them rode around the city of Washington and hammered out an agreement that guaranteed Johnny 'not less than six nor more than twelve' appearances on Defenders of Our Liberty each year for two years at the rate of $7500 worth of common stock of the sponsoring company per appearance, and for which Johnny would supply the additional consideration of 'staying in the news' in such a manner as could be reviewed after every three shows by the special vice-president and Raymond's mother jointly, to the point where the contract could be cancelled or extended, by mutual consent.

Therefore, Johnny was most certainly on hand to face the fearless panel of five newspapermen before the television cameras at seven-thirty that evening. The developments and charges of the previous day were laid on all over again, with one substantial difference concerning the actual number of Communists in the Defence Department. What follows is an excerpt from the record of the telecast:

SEN. ISELIN: Yesterday morning I—uh—discussed the—uh— Communists high up in the—uh—Defence Department. I stated that I had names of—uh—fifty-eight card-carrying members of the Communist Party. Now—uh—I say this. They must be driven out! They must be dragged out into the open from under the protection of the Defence Department!

JAMES F. RYAN (*Stamford Bee*): But you do have the names of fifty-eight actual card-carrying members—absolute Communists —who direct the policy of the Department of Defence—actual card-carrying Communists?

SEN. ISELIN: I do—uh—Jim. Yes.

JAMES F. RYAN: Well, I am just a common man who's got a family and daughters and a job. You mean to say there are fifty-eight actual card-carrying Communists in our Defence Department that direct or control our Department of Defence policy or help direct it?

SEN. ISELIN: Well—uh—Jim, I don't want to give you or—uh the rest of the American people the reassurance that there are only fifty-eight Communists high—uh—in the Defence Department. I say I have the names of only fifty-eight.

JAMES F. RYAN: It is my duty to ask this question and face the consequences of asking it later. Is the Secretary of Defence one of the names on that list?

SEN. ISELIN: I refuse to answer that question at this time—uh —Jim. And I am sure you know what I mean.

The programme was interrupted for the closing commercial right at that point, and it was an enormous success. As Raymond's mother told Johnny from the very beginning, it wasn't the issue itself so much as the way he could sell it. 'Lover, you are marvellous, that's all. Just absolutely goddam marvellous,' she told him after the television show. 'The way you punched up that stale old material, why, I swear to God, I was beginning to feel real deep indignation myself.' She did not bother him with the confusion that had immediately arisen over the differences in figures she had given him on the two days. She was more than satisfied that the ruse had had people arguing all over the country about how many Communists there were in the Defence Department rather than whether there were any there at all, and it didn't interest Johnny anyway whether the true figure was two hundred and seven or fifty-eight, until the day she handed him the speech he was to read on the floor of the Senate on April 18. In that speech Johnny said there were eighty-two employees of the Defence Department who ranged from 'persons whom I consider to be Communists' down to individuals who were 'bad risks.' On April 25, Raymond's mother reduced this figure at a press conference that had been called by the press of the nation itself, and not by Johnny's team, at which Johnny announced that he would 'stand or fall' on his ability to prove that there was not just *one* Communist in the Department of Defence but one who was 'the top espionage agent of an inimical foreign power within the borders of the United States of America.'

Johnny had taken a riding in the Senate cloakroom after he had changed the figures for the second time, in the Senate speech, and he was as sore as a pup at having been made to look silly in front of his pals. When Raymond's mother told him he was to drop the figure to one Communist, to one Communist from two hundred and seven in less than a month, he rebelled bitterly.

'What the hell do you keep changing the Communist figures for, all the time?' he asked hotly just before the press conference was to open. 'It makes me look like a goddam fool.'

'You'll be a goddam fool if you don't go in there and do as you're told. Who the hell are they writing about all over this goddam country, for crissake?' Raymond's mother asked. 'Are you going to come on like a goddam expert, all of a sudden, like you knew what the hell you were talking about, all of a sudden?'

'Now, come on, hon. I was only——'

'Shuddup! you hear? Now get the hell out there!' she snapped at him—so Senator Iselin had to face a battery of microphones, cameras, and questions, as big as ever had been assembled for any President of the United States, to say: 'I am willing to stand or fall on this one. If I am wrong on this one I think the sub-committee would be justified in not taking any other cases I ever brought up too seriously.'

If the score-card of working Communists in the Defence Department seems either tricky or confusing, it is because Raymond's mother chose to make the numbers difficult to follow from day to day, week to week, and month to month, during that launching period when his sensational allegations were winning Johnny headlines throughout the world for two reasons. First, it was consistent with one of Raymond's mother's basic verities, that thinking made Americans' heads hurt and therefore was to be avoided. Second, the figures were based upon a document that a Secretary of Defence had written some six years before to the Chairman of a House committee, pointing out that, at the end of World War II, 12,798 government employees who had worked for emergency war agencies had been temporarily transferred to the Defence Department, then that group had been reduced to 4,000 and 'a recommendation against permanent employment had been made in 286 cases. Of these, 79 had actually been removed from the service.' Raymond's mother's subtraction of 79 cases from 286 cases left 207 cases, the number with which she had had Johnny kick off. She had made one other small change. The Secretary's actual language had been 'recommendation against permanent employment,' which she had changed to read: 'members of the Communist Party,' which Johnny had adjusted to read: 'card-carrying Communists.'

Sometimes it tended to get a little too confusing until Johnny came at last to refer to it as 'the numbers game.' On one edgy day when Johnny had been drinking a little before he went on the Senate floor to speak, things got rather out of hand when he began to switch the figures around within the one speech, reported in the *Congressional Record* for April 10, in which he spoke of such varying estimates as: 'a very sizeable group of active Communists in the Defence Department,' then referred to 'vast numbers of Communists in the Defence Department.' He recalled the figure of two hundred and seven, then went on to say, almost immediately following: 'I do not believe I mentioned the figure two hundred and seven at the Secretary's press conference; I believe I announced it was over two hundred.' He thereupon hastened to claim that 'I have in my possession the names of fifty-seven Communists who are in the Defence Department at present,' then changed that count at once by saying, 'I know absolutely of one group of approximately three hundred Communists certified to the Secretary of Defence in a private communication who have since been discharged because of communism,' and then at last, sweating like a badly conditioned wrestler, he sat down, having thoroughly confused himself.

He knew he was going to catch hell when he got home that night, and he did. She turned on him so savagely that in an effort to defend himself and to keep her from striking him with a blunt object he demanded that they agree to stay with one goddam figure he could remember. Raymond's mother realised then that she had been taxing him and making his head hurt so she settled on fifty-seven, not only because Johnny would be able to remember it but because all of the jerks could remember it, too, as it could be linked so easily with the fifty-seven varieties of canned food that had been advertised so well and so steadily for so many years.

Within three months Johnny bought Raymond's mother a

case of gin for making him the 'most famous man in the United States,' and he was doing just as well all over the world. The whole thing was so successful that within five months after his first charges a Senate committee undertook a special investigation of Johnny, a public investigation that produced over three million words of testimony, of which Johnny claimed, later on, to have produced a million of those words himself.

Some important individuals refused to tolerate Johnny and said so publicly, and other bodies of elected public servants seemed to disagree with him, but when they came up to it, in the end, they equivocated because by that time Johnny had generated an extraordinary amount of fear, which he beamed directly into the eyes of all who came close to him.

IX

A short man with dark hair and skin, blue eyes, and blonde eyebrows called for Raymond at his apartment at ten-seventeen the morning of July fourteenth, 1956, the day after the investigating committee had published their report on Johnny, and a hot Saturday morning it was. The man's name was Zilkov. He was Director of the KGB, or Committee of State Security, for the region of the United States of America east of the Mississippi River. The MVD, or Ministry of Internal Affairs, is much larger. The MVD had very wide powers and functions but they hold to a jurisdiction of a somewhat more public nature *inside* the Soviet Union. The KGB, however, is the *secret* police. Its director has ministerial rank today and is a much more feared personality than Gomel, the present MVD head. Zilkov was proud of the power he represented.

Raymond opened in response to the door bell and stared coldly at the strange man. They disliked each other instantly, which was nothing against Zilkov because Raymond disliked almost everyone instantly.

'Yes?' Raymond drawled obnoxiously.

'My name is Zilkov, Mr Shaw. As you were advised by telephone this morning, I have come to drive you to the Swardon Sanitarium.'

'You are late,' Raymond told him and turned his back to walk toward his baggage, leaving the man to decide whether he would enter or wait in the corridor.

'I am exactly two minutes late,' the short man snapped.

'That *is* late, isn't it? An appointment is an oral contract. If we should happen to have any other business in the future, try to remember that.'

'Why do you have three bags? How many bags do you think you will need in the hospital?'

'Have I asked you to help me with the bags?'

'That is not the point. An accident case is not admitted to a hospital with three pieces of baggage. At the most you may bring some necessaries in an attaché case.'

'An attaché case?'

'You *do* know what that is?'

'Of course I know what that is.'

'Do you have one?'

'One? I have three!'

'Please to place your necessaries into one of your three attaché cases and we will go.'

'No.'

'No?'

'I will get there myself. I was told absolutely nothing about having to pack only the bare necessities into a leather envelope. I was told absolutely nothing about having to have to cope with a minor functionary of an obscure little hospital. That will be all. Return to your work. I will handle this myself.' Raymond began to close the door in Zilkov's face.

'Wait!'

'Wait nothing. Get your foot out of the door, you boor. Out! Out!'

'You cannot!' The short man threw his weight against the

door, but Raymond's greater weight and superior strength gradually slid the security chieftain backward. 'Stop! Stop! Zilkov cried.

'Out!' said Raymond inexorably.

'No! Please! Shaw, listen to me! Why don't you pass the time by playing a little solitaire?'

Raymond stopped pushing. Zilkov slipped into the apartment and shut the door behind him.

The Timothy Swardon Sanitarium had been a monument to personal philanthropy. Mr Swardon, dead for eleven years, had been a wealthy alcoholic whose two daughters had been caught up in the narcotics habit. He had founded the superb private hospital mostly for himself and his family, but also for the benefit of other drunks and junkies who were friends of the family, or friends of friends. Through the spontaneity of this ever widening circle, the establishment had come to the attention of Giorg Berezovo's organisation men who protected Soviet security on the eastern seaboard of the United States, and eventually two full floors of the seven-floor hospital were taken over entirely for security use; the entire establishment having been bought at a real bargain from the youngest daughter who had still not been able to kick the cocaine habit, regardless of the advantages her father had showered on her medically. Under the new management, the little haven was in its second successful year of operation as one of the few money-making operations maintained by the Soviets, thanks to the many patients still loyal to the Swardon family.

Raymond had not actually been hit by a hit-and-run driver, but the many hospital and insurance and police forms served to legitimatise his stay, or the visits of others who, from time to time, found it necessary to go to Swardon for check-ups. Raymond had taken a taxi to the hospital and had checked in as he would have into a hotel, and within a half-hour two Soviet nurses had him in bed on the sealed fifth floor. His right leg was put into a plaster cast, then in traction, and his head was bandaged. He had been put into unconsciousness by voice signal while this was being done and the memory of the morning's events was erased. The office staff at the hospital had notified the police and a squad car came by immediately to interview the cab driver who had brought Raymond in after seeing him hit by a green station wagon with Connecticut plates. Fortunately, three other witnesses corroborated the account: two women who lived in the neighbourhood and a young lawyer from Bayshore, Long Island. The personnel manager at *The Daily Press* was notified to activate both the hospital and accident policies indicated by the identification cards found in Raymond's wallet. The technicians assembled the X-rays which proved Raymond to have suffered a brain concussion and ripped calf muscles. *The Daily Press* published a short account of the accident on its back page. This was how Major Marco learned about it, and how Raymond's mother and Johnny got the news.

Raymond's boss, Holborn Gaines, dropped everything (a beer bottle and a report from the Manila office) and rushed to the hospital to see if there was anything he could do to help. The desk attendant, a Soviet Army lieutenant, upon studying his credentials and checking them against a list of Raymond's probable and therefore accredited visitors, sent him to the fifth floor just as though it were not a sealed floor. He was met at the elevator by a rugged army nurse who was wearing the traditional cap worn by graduates of the Mother Cabrini Hospital of Winsted, Connecticut, where she had never studied but which gave the establishment a certain amount of professional veri-similitude. Mr Gaines was permitted to look in on Raymond, unconscious though he was, in traction and in presumed travail, and was told the running wheeze of the profession everywhere, that Raymond was doing as well as could be expected. Gaines left a bottle of Scotch for Raymond with the pretty young nurse (five feet tall, 173 pounds, moustache, warts). He also passed the word along that Raymond was to take it easy and not to worry about anything, which the nurse was careful not to tell Raymond, in the event of possible prearranged code use. Technicians who worked directly under Yen Lo, albeit also possessing a political rating or classification, were flown in on embassy quota from the Pavlov Institute in the Ukraine. They went to work on Raymond between visiting hours, checking his conditioned apparatus from top to bottom. Five years had elapsed from the time the controls had first been installed at Tunghwa. All linkages were found perfect.

A courier took the detailed lab reports to the embassy in Washington; from there they were transmitted by diplomatic pouch to the project supervisors, who were ostensibly Gomel, Berezovo, and Yen Lo, but Berezovo had been deemed insufficiently worthy, following the disappointment that Lavrenti Beria had been to the Kremlin, and he was dead, and Yen Lo refused to look at the reports, saying with a mild smile that they could not do otherwise than certify the excellence of Raymond's conditioned reflexive mechanism, so only Gomel pored over the reports. He was mightily pleased.

Following the transmittal of the reports overseas, Raymond met his American operator who was to become his sole manager from that moment on, and whom he would never remember as having seen and whom he would never be able to recognise as his operator no matter where or when they met, because it had been designed that way. They were introduced, as it were, then the American asked to be alone in the room with Raymond. They conferred together for nearly two hours before Zilkov interrupted them. The two visitors in Raymond's room got into a heated argument, with Raymond watching them like a tennis spectator. Zilkov was a militant, bright young man. He maintained emphatically that Raymond must carry out a test assassination in order to complete the reflex check-out in a conclusive manner. The American operator opposed the suggestion violently and pointed out that it was both surprising and shocking that a security officer, with responsibility such as he held, would seek to risk a mechanism as valuable as Raymond.

Raymond listened gravely, then turned his eyes to hear Zilkov's rebuttal, which, of course, pointed out that the mechanism had been designed for assassination, that it had been five years since it had been tested, that conditions offering minimum risk for police reprisal could be designed, and that as far as he was concerned the test must be made before he would sign any certification that the mechanism was in perfect working order. The American operator said, very well, if that was how Zilkov felt about it then Raymond should be instructed to kill an employee of the hospital on one of the sealed floors. Zilkov said he would order nothing of the sort, that the table of organisation in the area was under acceptable strength as it was, as far as he was concerned, and that Raymond could damned well kill some non-productive woman or child on the outside. The American operator said there was no reason for Raymond to kill anyone unproductive—that there might as well be some feeling of gain out of this since Zilkov was insisting on the risk—and recommended that Raymond's position at the newspaper and therefore his general value to the party might be considerably strengthened if he were to kill his immediate superior, Holborn Gaines, as it was possible that, after five years as Gaines's assistant, Raymond would be given his job, which, in turn, would bring him wider influence within the inner chambers of the American government. Zilkov said he had no interest in whom Raymond assassinated so long as he worked efficiently and obediently. It was decided that Mr Gaines should die two nights hence. Subsequently, the American operator complained bitterly, through channels, that Zilkov had been reckless and foolhardy with one of the Party's most valuable pieces of apparatus in the United States, and most entirely needlessly because Raymond had been checked out by Pavlov technicians. Unfortunately the complaint was not made in time to save Mr Gaines, but within two weeks Zilkov was recalled and severely reprimanded. On his return to the United States, he could not have been more careful, both with Raymond and Raymond's operator, than if they had been his own department heads.

On the morning of the ninth day at Swardon, less than two

days before he murdered Mr Gaines, Raymond awoke as from a deep sleep, surprised to find himself in a strange bed and in traction, but even more shocked to find himself staring directly into, and on a level with, the grief-ravaged face of his mother. Raymond had never seen his mother's face as being anything but smoothly held, enforced, carefully supported, arranged, and used to help her get what she wanted as a Cadillac was used to get her where she wanted to go. The skin on his mother's face had always been flawless; the eyes were exquisitely placed and entirely clear, the whites unflecked by tiny blood vessels, merely *suggesting* malevolence and insane impatience. Her mouth had always been held well in, as the mouths of city saddle horses, and the perfect blonde hair had always framed all of this and had always softened it.

To open his eyes and find himself looking into a wracked caricature of that other vision made Raymond cry out, and made his mother aware that he was conscious. Her hair was ragged and awry. Her eyes were rabbit-red from weeping. Her cheeks shone with wet, washing away the cosmetic that always masked the wrinkles. Her mouth was twisted in ugly self-pity, while she sobbed noisily and blew her nose into too small a handkerchief. She drew back instantly at his sound and attempted to compose her face, but it could not be done convincingly on such short order, and unconsciously she wanted to gain a credit for the feat she knew would be unbelievable to him: her tears because of him.

'Raymond, oh, my Raymond.'

'Whassa matter?'

'Oh——'

'Is Johnny dead?'

'What?'

'What the hell is the matter with you?'

'I came here as soon as I could. I flew here the instant I was able to leave.'

'Where? Pardon the cliché, but where am I?'

'The Swardon Sanitarium.'

'The Swardon Sanitarium where?'

'New York. You were hit by a hit-and-run driver. Oh, I was so frightened. I came as soon as I could.'

'When? How long have I been here?'

'Eight days. Nine days. I don't know.'

'And you just got here?'

'Do you hate me, Raymond?'

'No, Mother.'

'Do you love me?'

'Yes, Mother.' He looked at her with genuine anxiety. Had she run out of arm sauce? Had she broken the arm-banging machine? Or was she just a very clever impersonator sent over to play the mother while my true mummy tries to sober up the Great Statesman?

'My little boy. My darling, little boy.' She went into a paroxysm of silent weeping, working her shoulders up and down in a horrible manner and shaking the chair she sat in. There was nothing faked about this, he knew. She must have hit some real trouble along the line. It simply could not possibly be that she was weeping over him being stretched out in a hospital. Mucus slid from the tiny handkerchief and rested on her left cheekbone. Raymond closed his eyes for a moment, but he would not tell her what had happened and felt a deep satisfaction that ultimately she would look in some mirror after she had left him and see this mess on her face.

'You are such a fraud, Mother. My God, I feel as well as I have ever felt and I know that you have been all over this with whatever doctors there are out there on the telephone days ago, and now you're at the hospital because there is probably a sale at Bloomingdale's or you're having a few radio actors black-listed and you make a production out of it like I was involved somehow in your life.' His voice was bitter. His eyes were hard and dry.

'I have to be a fraud,' she said, straightening her back and slipping several lengths of steel into her voice like whale-bone into a corset. 'And I have to be the truth, too. And a shield and the courage for all the men I have ever known, yourself included,

131

excepting my father. There is so much fraud in this world and it needs to be turned away with fraud, the way steel is turned with steel and the way a soft answer does not turneth away wrath.' She had emerged, dripping with acid, from her grief. Her face was a mass of ravaged colours and textures, her hair was like an old lamp shade fringe and that glob of mucus still rested on her left cheekbone disgustingly, but she was herself again, and Raymond felt greatly relieved.

'How's Johnny?'

'Fine. He'd be here, but that committee just finished working him over—ah, wait until that one is up for re-election.' She sniffed noisily. 'So I told him he must stay there and stare them down. You have no use for him anyway so I don't know why you bother to ask for him unless you feel guilt about something.'

'I do feel guilt about something.'

'About what?' She leaned forward slightly because information is the prime increment of power.

'About Jocie.'

'Who's Jocie?'

'Jocie Jordan. The senator's daughter.'

'Oh. Yes. Why do you feel guilt?' his mother asked.

'Why? Because she thinks I deserted her.'

'Raymond! Why do you dramatise everything so? You were babies!'

'I thought that since we're having our first meeting since I got the medal, since I got back from Korea, and I was in Korea for two years, I thought since you've been pretending to be two other people—you know, honest and maternal and wistfully remorseful about how we had let our lives go along—coldly and separately—and I thought that before we got any more honest and hated ourselves in the morning, that we might just pay Jocie the respect of asking for her—you know, mentioning her name in passing the way they do about the dead?' His voice was choked. His eyes were not dry.

As though he had reminded her of what had triggered her in the first place, she began unexpectedly to weep. The lemon sunlight was reflected from the bright white blank wall outside the window at her back and it lingered like St Elmo's fire around the ridiculously small green hat she was wearing, a suspicion of a hat that had been assembled for seventy dollars by an aesthetic leader for whom millinery signified the foundation stone of culture.

'What is the *matter* with you, Mother?'

She sobbed.

'You aren't crying about *me*?'

She sobbed and nodded.

'But, I'm all *right*. I don't have a pain or an *ache*. I am absolutely *fine*.'

'Oh, Raymond, what can I say to you? There has been so much to get done. We have so far to go. Johnny is going to lead the people of our country to the heights of their history. But I have to lead Johnny, Raymond. You know that. I know you know that. I have given my life and many, many significant things for all of this. My life. Simply that and I can see that if I were to ransack my strength—remembered strength or future strength—I could not give more to this holy crusade than I have given. Now I have come face to face with my life where it has failed to cross your own. I can't tell you how a mother feels about that, because you wouldn't understand. It made me weep for a little bit. That's all. What's that? Anybody and everybody recovers from tears, but I'm not sad and I don't have regrets because I know that what I did and what I do is for the greatest possible good for all of us.' Raymond watched her, then made the small despising gesture with his right hand, brushing her world out of his way as it came too close to him.

'I don't understand one word of what you are saying,' he told her.

'I am saying this. Some terrible, terrible changes are going to come to this country.'

He flicked at the air with his hand violently, unaware of the movement, and he closed his eyes.

'This country is going to go through a fire like it has never seen,' she said in a low and earnest voice. 'And I know what I am saying because the signs are there to read and I understand politics, which is the art of reading them. Time is going to roar and flash lightning in the streets, Raymond. Blood will gush behind the noise and stones will fall and fools and mockers will be brought down. The smugness and complacency of this country will be dragged through the blood and the noise in the streets until it becomes a country purged and purified back to original purity, which it once possessed so long ago when the founding fathers of this republic—the blessed, blessed fathers—brought it into life. And when that day comes—and we have been cleansed of the slime of oblivion and saved from the wasteful, wrong, sinful, criminal, selfish, rottenness which Johnny, and only Johnny is going to save us from, you will kneel beside me and thank me and kiss my hands and my skirt and give only me your love as will the rest of the great people of this confused and blinded land.'

He put his hand over hers on the bed, then lifted it to his lips. Suddenly, he felt himself being made soft with pity for both of them. He could not comprehend that his mother had any feelings, and it shocked him deeply.

Two days later, immediately after Raymond ate dinner in the room at Swardon with his leg still in a cast, Zilkov and the American operator came to the room with a packet of playing cards and subsequently gave him detailed instructions as to how he was to kill Holborn Gaines. The time they set was three forty-five the following morning. Gaines lived in an apartment house, alone. The house maintained a self-service elevator after one A.M. when the night man went off duty. There was no doorman. Zilkov had had a key made to fit the front door of the building and to Mr Gaines's apartment, which was one of four on the ninth floor. The security man went over the pencil-sketched, then photostatted floor plan of Gaines' small unit of three rooms and a bath, indicating where the bedroom was and suggesting that Raymond strangle him, as it was the quietest and least complicated method and, considering the close quarters in which he would have to work, the neatest. He added that Raymond must accept it as a rule, then and forever, that in the event that anyone, repeat anyone, ever discovered him on the scene of the assignment, this other person or persons must be killed. Was that clear! Zilkov may have reconsidered the risk he had decided to have Raymond run, for, to make sure this condition was understood, he asked the American operator to repeat the admonition.

As it worked out, Mr Gaines was alone but he was not asleep as he should have been to save Raymond considerable embarrassment. He was reading in bed, a four-poster feather bed, with nine soft pillows all around behind him and a shocking-pink maribou bed jacket around his shoulders; chuckling over a few pounds of confidential reports from bureau chiefs in Washington, Rome, London, Madrid, and Moscow. The windows were closed tight and, as in the office at all times, an electric heater was beaming up at him from the floor near by: in July.

As Raymond opened the door to the apartment he knocked over the tall paper screen that Mr Gaines kept in front of the opened door in the summer time. As it fell it dislodged a picture hanging on the wall; it hit the floor with a crash. There could be no doubt that someone had come to call, and Raymond cursed himself as a blunderer because he knew well that Mr Gaines would be tart about the visit, in any event.

'What the hell is that?' Mr Gaines yelled shrilly.

Raymond flushed with embarrassment. It was an entirely new feeling for him and Mr Gaines was the only living person who could have made him feel that way, because Mr Gaines made him feel helpless, gawky, and grateful all at the same time. 'It's me, Mr Gaines,' he said. 'Raymond.'

'Raymond? Raymond?' Mr Gaines was bewildered. 'My assistant? Raymond Shaw?'

Raymond appeared in the bedroom doorway at that moment. He was wearing a neat black suit, a dark grey shirt, a black tie, and black gloves. 'Yes, sir,' he said. 'I—I'm sorry to disturb you, Mr Gaines.'

Mr Gaines fingered the maribou bed jacket. 'Don't get any ideas about this silly-looking bed jacket,' he said irritably. 'It was my wife's. It's the warmest thing I have. Perfect for reading in bed at night.'

'I didn't know you were married, Mr Gaines.'

'She died nearly six years ago,' Mr Gaines said gruffly, then he remembered. 'But—but, what the hell are you doing here at—' Mr Gaines looked over at the alarm clock on the night table. 'At ten minutes to four in the morning.'

'Well—I—uh——'

'My God, Raymond, don't tell me you've come here to talk something over? I mean, surely you aren't going to pour out your heart with the details of some sordid love affair or anything like that?'

'No, sir, you see——'

'Raymond, if you feel you must resign for any reason—a circumstance which I would regret, of course—surely you could leave a little note on my desk in the morning. I hate chattering like this! I thought I had explained to you that I loathe having to talk to people, Raymond.'

'Yes, sir. I'm sorry, Mr Gaines.'

Mr Gaines suddenly seemed to remember something significant. He lifted his left hand and pointed vaguely towards the door, looking, because of the fluffy feathers all around his white hair, something like the ancient Mrs Santa R. Claus. 'How did you get in here? When I close that door, it locks.'

'They gave me a key.'

'Who did?'

'The people at the hospital.'

'What hospital? But—why? Why did they give you a key?'

Raymond had been moving slowly around the bed. At last he stood at Mr Gaines' side, looking down at him sunk into the feather bed. He felt sheepish.

'Raymond! Answer me, my boy! Why are you here?'

It was a relatively effortless job because Mr Gaines, being such an old man, did not have much strength and Raymond, because of feelings of affection and gratitude for Mr Gaines did everything he could, with his great strength, to terminate his friend's life as quickly as possible. He thought of extinguishing the bed light as he left, but turned it on again, remembering that he wouldn't be able to find his way out to the front door if he left the room in darkness.

He walked four blocks west before taking a cab north on Lexington Avenue; he left it three blocks away from Swardon. He entered the sanitarium through the basement door, off the back areaway, showing his pass to the Soviet Army corporal in overalls who had taken him under the throat with the left forearm without speaking and held until Raymond tapped his third finger twice, then showed the pass. When Raymond got to his room the American operator was waiting for him.

'Still up?' Raymond said conversationally. 'It's almost four-thirty.'

'I wanted to make sure you were all right,' the operator said. 'Good night, Raymond. I'll send the nurses in to rig you up again.'

'Do I have to have those casts put on again?'

'Those casts must stay on until you are discharged. How do you know who'll show up here as a visitor now that Mr Gaines is dead?' The operator left the room. The nurses had Raymond undressed and bandaged in no time at all.

Raymond, as it turned out, did have two more visitors before he left the hospital. Joe Downey, the managing editor of *The Daily Press*, stopped by after Mr Gaines' funeral and offered Raymond the job of writing the column, which meant a two-hundred-dollar-a-week raise in pay and a net saving of three hundred dollars a week to the paper because, naturally, they didn't figure to start Raymond at the figure Mr Gaines had finished at, and Mr Gaines had been political columnist for the paper for twenty-six years. They also offered Raymond fifty per cent of the syndication money, a net increase of one hundred per cent to the paper because under the prior arrangement Mr

Gaines had kept it all, excepting the sales and distribution and promotion percentage. To the paper's owners, Mr Downey allowed that Raymond was new and had such an unpleasant personality that it was better than five to one that no one would ever get around to telling him that he rated all the syndication money. It was fair. The reports from the bureau chiefs made up most of the columns and the paper, not Raymond, had to pay the bureau chiefs. Besides, one half of the syndication money came to five hundred and six dollars per week, which lifted Raymond's take-home pay by seven hundred and six dollars per week; Mr Downey estimated this as being a bargain because the paper would have the only Medal of Honour columnist in the business, which certainly should open the doors to information at the Pentagon, and he had that crazy stepfather who could scare people into talking to Raymond, and that mother who could get him in anywhere, even to share a double bed with the President if he felt like it, and he had had five solid years of learning his job from Holborn Gaines. Seven hundred and six dollars a week is a nice raise for a young fellow, particularly if he likes money.

Actually, the increased income took the edge off the promotion for Raymond but, the way he would handle it, he figured the money would be the bank's problem, not his.

Raymond was distraught over the murder. He had had great regard for the old man and a fondness that was unusual inasmuch as he felt fondness for only two other people in the world, Marco and Jocie, and Jocie should not be included in the category because the feeling for her was vastly different again. He just could not get it through his head that anyone would want to murder Mr Gaines. He had been a kind and gentle and helpless old man, and how could anyone do such a thing? Mr Downey expressed the police opinion that it must have been some mentally unstable political crank. 'Holly was one of the oldest friends I had left,' Mr Downey said sadly, mourning for himself.

'Is the paper going to post a reward?'

Mr Downey rubbed his chin. 'Hm. I guess we should, at that.

We certainly should. Can charge it to promotion if we ever have to pay it.'

'I want to pledge five thousand dollars of that reward,' Raymond said hotly.

'You don't need to do that, Raymond.'

'Well, I want to, goddamit.'

'Well, O.K. You pledge five and we'll pledge ten, although the board'll have to O.K. it of course, and I'll call Centre Street soon as I get back to the office so they can send out paper on it. By God, we'll pay for a general alarm, too. The dirty bastard.' Downey was doubly upset because he hated to spend the paper's money and he knew damned well that Holly Gaines, wherever he was, wouldn't approve of a goddam, boy-scout, grandstand play like that, but, what the hell, there were certain things you pretended you had to do.

Marco came in to see Raymond the same afternoon. 'Jesus, you look like hell,' Raymond said from under his head bandage and traction equipment. 'What happened?'

Marco looked worse than that. The old sayings are the best, and Marco looked like death warmed over. 'What do you mean, what happened?' he said. 'I'm not in a hospital bed, am I?'

'I just mean I never saw you look so lousy.'

'Well, thanks.'

'What happened?'

Marco ran his hand across his face. 'I can't sleep.'

'Can't you get some pills?' Raymond said tentatively—having a narcotics addict for a mother, he had developed an aversion to drugs. Also, it was difficult for him to understand any kind of a sleeping problem, since he himself could have fallen asleep hanging by one ankle in a high wind.

'It's not so much that I can't sleep. It's more that I'd rather not sleep. I'm walking around punchy because I'm scared. I keep having the same nightmare.' Raymond, lying flat on his back, made the flicking gesture with his right hand.

'Is it a nightmare about a Soviet general and a lot of Chinese and me and the guys who were on the patrol?' Marco came out of the chair like a tiger. He stood over Raymond, gripping the cloth of his pyjama jacket in both fists, staring down at him with wild eyes. 'How did you know that? How did you know that?' His voice went up and up like eccentric stairs in front of a hilltop summer beach house.

'*Take—your—hands—off—me.*' With that sentence Raymond's voice fell back into his horrid drawling manner; into his repulsive, inciting, objectionable voice that he used to keep the rest of the world on the other side of the moat surrounding the castle where he had always lain under the spell of the wicked witch. It was curdingly unfriendly, and so actively repellent that it drove Marco backward into the chair, which was a good thing because Marco had gone into a sick yellow-ivory colour, his breathing was shallow, and his eyes shone with an ever so slight sheen of insanity as he had reached out to take the shape of his oppression into the muscles of his fingers and hands and punish it for what it had been doing to his dignity, which is man's own inner image of himself.

'I'm sorry, Raymond.'

Raymond became Marco's friend again instantly, as though there had been no lapse.

'Please tell me how you knew about my nightmare, Raymond.'

'Well, you see, I didn't really. I mean, it's just that Melvin—you know: Al Melvin, the corporal on the patrol—he wrote me a long letter about a week ago. I was naturally surprised to hear from him because—well—as you know, I was never much one for fraternising, but he said in the letter that I was the only one he knew how to reach—he sent the letter to Johnny because everybody certainly knows how to reach him—because he had to tell somebody in the patrol about this nightmare or he was afraid he would lose his mind and——'

'Please tell me about the nightmare, Raymond.'

'Well, he dreams that the patrol is all sitting together. He says he dreams about a lot of Soviet officers and some Chinese brass and us being on the patrol. What is such a nightmare about that?'

'Where's the letter? Do you have the letter?'

'Well, no. I mean, I never keep letters.'

'Is that all he wrote? Is that all about the nightmare?'

'Yeah.'

'It just stops right there?'

'I guess so.'

'Man!'

'Is it like your nightmare?'

'Yeah. As a matter of fact, mine is a lot like that.'

'You guys ought to get together.'

'Right away. You don't know what this means to me. I just can't explain to you what this means to me, Raymond.'

'Well, you can't see him right away, though, Ben. He lives in Wainwright, Alaska.'

'Alaska? Alaska?'

'Yes.'

'Jesus. Wainwright, Alaska. You have to be kidding!'

'No. I wish I was, Ben. I'm not. But, so what? What's the difference?'

'What's the difference? I told you I can't sleep. You told me I look like hell. Well, I feel like hell and I'm shaking all to pieces and I think sometimes I should kill myself because I'm afraid of going insane, and then you tell me like you were talking about the weather that another man who was on the patrol is having the same delusions that I was afraid were driving me crazy, and you tell me he lives in some place called Wainwright, Alaska, where I can't sit down and talk to him and find out if he's cracking up like I am and how we can help each other, and you say what's the difference.'

Marco began to laugh hysterically, then he put his face forward into his large hands and wept into them, squeezing tightly at his cheekbones, his heavy shoulders moving grotesquely and causing the four rows of his decorations to jump up and down. He made such tearing sounds that the two Soviet Army nurses on the floor came running in. After six or seven minutes of Marco's reckless, unrelieved, and shocking sobbing, at which

141

Raymond stared helplessly, they hit him with a hypo to calm him down and get him the hell out of there.

All in all, Raymond had had a most ironic hospital stay, what with a visit from the wife of America's most gallant and noisy anti-Communist to a hospital operated by the Soviet secret police, what with a U.S. Army Intelligence officer breaking down and embarrassing the staff of the same place, what with contributing five thousand dollars to a reward for his own capture, and what with learning that two grown men were capable of behaving like children over a perfectly harmless, if repetitious, dream.

X

Johnny had become chairman of the Committee on Federal Operations and chairman of its Permanent Sub-committee on Investigations, with a budget of two hundred thousand dollars a year and an inculcating staff of investigators. He grew sly, in the way he worked that staff. He would sidle up to a fellow senator or another member of the government placed as high and mention the name and habits of some young lady for whom the senator might be paying the necessities, or perhaps an abortion here, or a folly-of-youth police record there. It worked wonders. He had only to drop this kind of talk upon five or six of them and at once they became his missionaries to intimidate others who might seek to block his ways in government.

There were a few groups and individuals who were able to find the courage to assail him. One of the most astute political analysts of the national scene wrote: 'Iselinism has developed a process for compounding a lie, then squaring it, which is a modern miracle of dishonesty far exceeding the claims of filter cigarettes. Iselin's lies seem to have atomic motors within them, tiny reactors of such power and such complexity as to confound and baffle all with direct, and even slightly honest, turns of mind.

He has bellowed out so many accusations about so many different people (and for all the public knows these names he brandishes may have been attached to people of entirely questionable existence) that no one can keep the records of these horrendous charges straight. Iselin is a man who shall forever stand guard at the door of the mind to protect the people of this great nation from facts.'

The American Association of Scientists asked that this statement be published: 'Senator Iselin puts the finishing touches on his sabotage of the morale of American scientists to the enormous net gain of those who work against the interests of the United States.'

Johnny was doing great. From a semi-hangdog country governor, Raymond's mother said, utterly unknown outside domestic politics on a state level in 1956, he had transformed himself into a global figure in 1957. He had a lot going for him beyond Raymond's mother. His very looks: that meaty nose, the nearly total absence of forehead, the perpetual unshavenness, the piggish eyes, red from being dipped in bourbon, the sickeningly monotonous voice, whining and grating,—all of it together made Johnny one of the greatest demagogues in American history, even if, as Raymond's mother often said to friends, he was essentially a light-hearted and unserious one. Nonetheless, her Johnny had become the only American in the country's history of political villains, studding folk song and story, to inspire concomitant fear and hatred in foreigners, resident in their native countries. He blew his nose in the Constitution, he thumbed his nose at the party system or any other version of governmental chain of command. He personally charted the zigs and zags of American foreign policy at a time when the American policy was a monstrously heavy weight upon world history. To the people of Iceland, Peru, France, and Pitcairn Island the label of Iselinism stood for anything and everything that was dirty, backward, ignorant, repressive, offensive, anti-progressive, or rotten, and all of those adjectives must ultimately be seen as sincere tributes to any demagogue of any country on any planet.

After Raymond's mother had written the scriptures and set the tone of the sermons Johnny was to make along the line to glory, she left him bellowing and pointing his finger while she organised, for nearly fifteen months, the cells of the Iselin national organisation she called the Loyal American Underground. This organisation enrolled, during that first period of her work, two million three-hundred thousand members, all militantly for Johnny and what he stood for, and most deeply grateful for his wanting to 'give our friends a place from which they may partake of a sense of history through adventure and real participation in the cause of fanatic good government, cleansed of the stain of communism.'

Raymond's mother and her husband held their mighty political analysis and strategy-planning sessions at their place, which was out toward Georgetown. They would talk and drink bourbon and ginger ale and Johnny would fool around with his scrapbook. He always had it in his mind that cold winter nights would be the best time to paste up the bundles of clippings about his work into individual books, with the intent of someday providing the vast resources for a John Yerkes Iselin Memorial Library. The analyses of the day's or the week's battles were always informal and usually productive of really constructive action for the immediate future.

'Hon,' Raymond's mother said, 'aren't there times when you're up there at the committee table when you have to go to the john?'

'Of course. Whatta you think I'm made of—blotting paper or something?'

'Well, what do you do about it?'

'Do? I get up and I go.'

'See? That's exactly what I mean. Now tomorrow when you have to go I want you to try it my way and see what happens. Will you?'

He grinned horribly. 'Right up there in front of all those TV cameras?'

'Never mind. Tomorrow when you have to go I want you to

throw yourself into a rage—making sure you are on camera—wait for a tight shot if you can—and bang on the desk and scream for the chairman and yell 'Point of order! Point of order!' Then stand up and say you will not put up with this farce and that you will not dignify it with your presence for one moment longer.'

'Why do I do that?'

'You have to start making the right kind of exits for yourself, Johnny, so that the American people will know that you have left so they can sit nervously and wait for you to come back.'

'Gee, hon. That's a hell of an idea. Oh, say, I like that idea!'

She threw him a kiss. 'What an innocent you are,' she said, smiling at him dotingly. 'Sometimes I don't think you give a damn what you're talking about or who you're talking about.'

'Well, why the hell should I?'

'You're right. Of course.'

'You're damn right, I'm right. What the hell, hon, this is a business with me. Suppose we were lawyers, I often say to myself. I mean actual practising lawyers. I'd be the trial lawyer working out in front, rigging the juries and feeding the stuff to the newspaper boys, and you'd be the brief man back in the law library who has the research job of writing up the case.' He finished the highball in his hand and gave the empty glass to his wife. She got up to make him another drink and said, 'Oh, I agree with that, honey, but just the same I wish you would try a little bit more to feel the sacredness of your own mission.'

'The hell with that. What's with you tonight, baby? I'm like a doctor, in a way. Am I supposed to die with every patient I lose? Life's too short.' He accepted the highball. 'Thank you, honey.'

'You're welcome, sweetheart.'

'What is this stuff? Applejack?'

'Applejack? It's twelve-year-old bourbon.'

'That's funny. It tastes like applejack.'

'Maybe it's the ginger ale.'

'The ginger ale? I always drink my bourbon with ginger ale. How could it taste like applejack because of the ginger ale. It never tasted like applejack before.'

'I can't understand it,' she said.

'Ah, what's the difference? I happen to like applejack.'

'You're so sweet it isn't even funny.'

'Not so sweet as you.'

'Johnny, have you noticed that some of the newspaper idiots are getting a little nasty with their typewriters?'

'Don't pay any attention.' He waved a careless hand. 'It's a business with them just like our business. You start getting sensitive and you just confuse everybody. The boys who are assigned to cover me may call themselves the Goon Squad but I don't notice that any of them have ever asked to be transferred. It's a game with them. They spend their time trying to catch me in lies, then printing that I said a lie. They like me. They try to knife me but they like me. I try to knife them but we drink together and we're friends. What the hell, hon. All we're all trying to do is to get a day's work done. Take it from me, never get sensitive.'

'Johnny, baby?'

'Yes, hon?'

'Do me a favour and tomorrow at the lunch break please make it a point to go into that Senate barbershop for a shave. You can stand two shaves a day. I swear to God sometimes I think you can grow a beard in twenty minutes. You look like a badger in a Disney cartoon on that TV screen.'

'Don't worry about it, hon. I have my own ways and I look my own way, but I'm very goddam American and they all know it out there.'

'Just the same, hon, will you promise to get a shave tomorrow at the lunch break?'

'Certainly. Why not? Gimme another drink. I got a big day coming up tomorrow.'

*   *   *

John Yerkes Iselin was re-elected to his second six-year term on November 4, 1958, by the biggest plurality in the history of elections in his state. Two hundred and thirty-six fist fights went unreported the following evening in the pubs, cafés, bodegas, cantinas, trattorias, and sundry brasseries of western Europe between the glum American residents and the outraged, consternated natives of the larger cities.

Early one Monday morning in his office at *The Daily Press* (for he had taken to arriving at work at seven-thirty rather than at ten o'clock now that he was the department head, just as had Mr Gaines before him) Raymond looked up and saw, with no little irritation at the interruption, the figure of Chunjin standing in the doorway. Raymond did not remember ever having seen him before. The man was slight and dark with alert, liquid eyes and a most intelligent expression; he stared with wistful hopefulness mixed with ascending regard, but these subtleties did not transport Raymond to remembering the man.

'Yes?' he drawled in his calculatedly horrid way.

'I am Chunjin, Mr Shaw, sir. I was interpreter attached to Cholly Company, Fifty-second Regiment——'

Raymond pointed his outstretched finger right at Chunjin's nose. 'You were interpreter for the patrol,' he said.

'Yes, sir, Mr Shaw.'

Other men might have allowed their camaraderie to foam over in the warming glow of the good old days, but Raymond said, 'What do you want?' Chunjin blinked.

'I mean to say, what are you doing here?' Raymond said, not backing away from his bluntness but attempting to cope with this apparent stupidity through clearer syntax.

'Your father did not say to you?'

'My *father*?'

'Senator Iselin? I write to——'

'Senator Iselin is *not* my father. Repeat. He is *not* my father. If you learn nothing else on your visit to this country memorise that fact.'

'I write to Senator Iselin. I tell him how I interpret your outfit. I tell him I want to come to America. He get me visa. Now I need job.'

'A job?'

'Yes, sir, Mr Shaw.'

'My dear fellow, we don't use interpreters here. We all speak the same language.'

'I am tailor and mender. I am cook. I am driver of car. I am cleaner and scrubber. I fix anything. I take message. I sleep at house of my cousin and not eat much food. I ask for job with you because you are great man who save my life. I need for pay only ten dollars a week.'

'Ten dollars? For all that?'

'Yes, sir, Mr Shaw.'

'Well, look here, Chunjin. I couldn't pay you only ten dollars a week.'

'Yes, sir. Only ten dollars a week.'

'I can use a valet. I would like having a cook, I think. A good cook, I mean. And I dislike washing dishes. I had been thinking about getting a car, but the parking thing sort of has me stopped. I go to Washington twice a week and there is no reason why I shouldn't have the money the airlines are getting from this newspaper for those trips and I'd rather not fly that crowded corridor anyway. I would prefer it if you didn't sleep in, as a matter of fact, but I'm sorry, ten dollars a week just isn't enough money.' Raymond said that flatly, as though it were he who had applied for the job and was turning it down for good and sufficient reasons.

'I work for fifteen, sir.'

'How can you live on fifteen dollars a week in New York?'

'I live with the cousins, sir.'

'How much do the cousins earn?'

'I do not know, sir.'

'Well, I'm sorry, Chunjin, but it is out of the question.' Raymond who had still not greeted his old wartime buddy, turned away to return to his work. From his expression he had dismissed the conversation, and he was anxious to return to the bureau reports and to some very helpful information his mother had managed to send along to him.

'Is not good for you to pay less, Mr Shaw?'

Raymond turned slowly, forcing his attention back to the Korean and realising impatiently that he had not made it clear that the meeting was over. 'Perhaps I should have clarified my position in the matter, as follows,' Raymond said frostily. 'It strikes me that there is something basically dishonest about an arrangement by which a man insists upon working for less money than he can possibly live on.'

'You think I steal, Mr Shaw?'

Raymond flushed. 'I had not considered any specific category of such theoretical dishonesty.'

'I live on two dollars a week in Mokpo. I think ten dollars many times better.'

'How long have you been here?'

Chunjin looked at his watch. 'Two hours.'

'I mean, in New York.'

'Two hours.'

'All right. I will instruct the bank to pay you a salary of twenty-five dollars a week.'

'Thank you, Mr Shaw, sir.'

'I will supply the uniforms.'

'Yes, sir.'

Raymond leaned over the desk and wrote the bank's address on a slip of paper, adding Mr Rothenberg's name. 'Go to this address. My bank. Ask for this man. I'll call him. He'll give you the key to my place and some instructions for stocking food. He'll tell you where to buy it. We don't use money. Please have dinner ready to serve at seven-fifteen next Monday. I'll be in Washington for the weekend, where I may be reached at the Willard Hotel. I am thinking in terms of roast veal—a boned rump of veal— with green beans, no potato—please, Chunjin, never serve me a potato——'

'No, sir, Mr Shaw.'

'—some canned, not fresh, spinach; pan gravy, I think some stewed fruit, and two cups of hot black coffee.'

'Yes, sir, Mr Shaw. Just like in United States Army.'

'Jesus, I hope not,' Raymond said.

XI

On April 15, 1959, the very same day on which Chunjin got his job with Raymond on transfer from the Soviet Army, another military transfer occurred. Major Marco was placed on indefinite sick leave and detached from duty.

Marco had undergone two series of psychiatric treatments at Army hospitals. As the recurring nightmare had grown more vivid, the pathological fatigue had gotten more severe. No therapy had been successful. Marco had weighed two hundred and eight pounds when he had come into New York from Korea. At the time he went on indefinite sick leave he weighed in at one hundred and sixty-three and he looked a little nuts. Every nerve-end in his body had grown a small ticklish moustache, and they sidled along under his skin like eager touts, screaming on tiptoe. He had the illusion that he could see and hear everything at once and had lost all of his ability to edit either sight or sound. Sound particularly detonated his reflexes. He tried desperately not to listen when people talked because an open *A* sound repeated several times within a sentence could make him weep uncontrollably. He didn't know why, so he concentrated on remembering the cause, when he could, so that he would not listen so attentively, but it didn't work. It was an *A* sound that must have been somewhat like a sound he had heard many, many years before, in utter peace and safety, which through its loss or through his indifference to it over the years could now cause him to weep bitterly. If he heard the sound occur once, he quickly hummed

'*La Seine*,' to push the *A* sound off to the side. His hand tremors were pronounced when his arm was extended unsupported. Sometimes his teeth would chatter as though he had entered a chill. Once in a while, after four or five unrelieved nights of nightmare, he developed a bad facial tic, and it wasn't pretty. Marco was being rubbed into sand by the grinding stones of two fealties. He was being slowly rubbed away by two faiths he lived by, far beyond his control; the first was his degree of holy reverence for the Medal of Honour, one of the most positive prejudices of his life because his life, principally, was the Army; and the second was the abnormal degree of his friendship for Raymond Shaw, which has been placed upon his mind, as coffee will leave a stain upon a fresh, snowy tablecloth, by the deepest psychological conditioning.

When Marco completed, for the want of any other word, the second course of treatment and was ordered to rest, they knew he was through and he knew they knew it. He headed for New York to talk to Raymond. He had never been able to tell the doctors the part of the dream where Raymond killed Mavole and Lembeck, on a continuous-performance basis, and he had not allowed himself to mention every phase of the four variations on the drill that had been used to win Raymond the Medal of Honour. He had written to Al Melvin and, between them, he and Melvin had spent over three hundred dollars talking to each other on the long-distance telephone, and it had brought considerable relief to each to know that the other was suffering as deeply from the same malady, but it did not stop the nightmares. Marco knew that he must talk to Raymond. He must, absolutely must. He knew that if he did not talk to Raymond about most of the details in his dreams he would die from them. Ironically, as Marco was riding one train to New York, Raymond was riding another to Washington.

Marco sat like a stone in the train chair, riding sideways in the club car. The car was about half-filled. Almost all of the seats were occupied at one end, Marco's end, by businessmen, or what seemed to be businessmen but were actually an abortionist, an

orchestra leader, a low-church clergyman, an astrologer, a Boy
Scout executive, a horticulturist, and a cinematographer, because,
no matter how much they would like the world to think so, the
planet is not populated entirely by businessmen no matter how
banal the quality of conversation everywhere has become. Some
women were present; their dresses gave the car the only embarrassing touch of colour, excepting the garish decorations on the
upper left side of Marco's blouse.

Marco had a rye old-fashioned placed on the round, metal
stand in front of him, but he hadn't tasted it. He kept wishing he
had ordered beer not to taste and he was careful not to look at
anybody, because he had stopped doing that several weeks before.
He sweated continuously. His face had very little colour. His
palms drenched his trousers at the tops of his knees. He was
battling to make a decision as to whether he wanted to smoke a
cigar or not. His eyes burned. He felt an agony of weariness. His
stomach hurt. He concentrated for an instant on not clenching his
teeth but he could not retain the thought. His jaws were tired and
some doctor had told him that he would grind the dentine off his
molars if he didn't concentrate on not clenching his jaws. He
turned his body slightly, but not his head, towards the person
sitting beside him, a woman.

'Do you mind cigar smoke,' he mumbled.

'Not at all,' she murmured. He turned away from her but
made no move to find a cigar.

'Go ahead,' she said. 'As a matter of fact, I wish you'd smoke
two cigars at the same time.'

'You must really like cigar smoke.'

'Not especially, but I think two cigars going at the same time
would *look* awfully amusing.'

He turned his body again towards the woman sitting beside
him. He lifted his eyes slowly, hesitantly, beyond the long, scarlet-
tipped fingers at repose in her lap, past a shining silver belt
buckle shaped as Quetzalcoatl, an urbane feathered serpent; past
uptilted, high-setting, pronounced breasts that stared back at him
eyelessly through dark-blue wool; past the high neckline and the

discreet seed pearls around a long throat of white Carrara marble, to a mouth whose shape he had yearned to see in living flesh since he had seen its counterpart within a photograph he had found in a German magazine twenty-three years before, rolled up in his father's effects in the trunk of a command car. In abstract, it was a sexual object. It was a witty mouth. It looked insatiable. It told him about lust which had been lost far back in mythology, lust which could endow its tasters with eternal serenity, and it was the mouth of many varieties of varying kinds of woman. He regretted having to leave off his concentration on the sight of it; with difficulty he moved his eyes upward to the questing horn of a most passionate nose; a large, formed, aquiline, and Semitic nose, the nose of a seeker and a finder of glories, and it made him remember that every Moslem who attains heaven is allotted seventy-two women who must look exactly like this between the eyes and the mouth, and he thought across the vast, vast distance of the *huanacauri* rock of Incan puberty to the words of the black, black, black song that keened: 'If she on earth no more I see, my life will quickly fade away.' Then at last his eyes came to the level of the eyes of a Tuareg woman and he rushed past a random questioning as to whether the Berlitz Schools taught Temajegh, and he thought of the god of love who was called bodiless by the Hindus because he was consumed by the fire of Siva's eyes, then he closed his own eyes and tried to help himself, to stop himself, to—SWEET GOD IN HEAVEN!—he could not. He began to weep. He stumbled to his feet. The passengers across the aisle stared at him hostilely. He knocked his drink over, and the metal stand over. He turned blindly and noisily to the left, unable to stop weeping, and made it, from behind the wet opaqueness, to the train door and the vestibule. He stood alone in the vestibule and put his head against the window and waited for time to pass, feeling confident that it would pass, when his motor would run down and this sobbing would slowly subside. Trying to analyse what had happened, as though to fill his mind, he was forced into the conclusion that the woman must have looked the way that open *A* sounded to him: an open, effortless, problemless, safe, and blessed look. What colour had her hair been? he wondered as he wept. He concentrated upon the words by which angels had been known: yaztas, fravashi, and Amesha Spentas; seraphim and cherubim; hayyot, ofanim, arelim, and Harut and Marut who had said: 'We are only a temptation. Be not then an unbeliever.' He decided that the woman could only be one of the fravashi, that army of angels that has existed in heaven before the birth of man, that protects him during his life, and is united to his soul at death. He sobbed while he conjectured about the colour of her hair. At last, he was permitted to stop weeping. He leaned against the train wall in exhaustion, riding backward. He took a handkerchief slowly from his trousers pocket and, with an effort of strength which he could not replenish with sleep, slowly dried his face, then blew his nose. He thought, only fleetingly, that he could not go back into that club car again, but that there would be plenty of other seats in the other direction, towards the rear of the train. When he got to New York, he decided, he would pull on a pair of grey slacks and a red woollen shirt and he'd sit all day on the rim of the map of the United States behind Raymond's big window, looking out at the Hudson River and that state, whatever its name was, on the other shore and think about the states beyond that state and drink beer.

When he turned to find another seat in another car, she was standing there. Her hair was the colour of birch bark, prematurely white, and he stared at her as though her thyroid were showing its excessive activity and her hypereroticism. She stood smoking a new cigarette, leaning back, riding forward, and looking out of the window.

'Maryland is a beautiful state,' she said.

'This is Delaware.'

'I know. I was one of the original Chinese workmen who laid track on this stretch, but none the less Maryland is a beautiful state. So is Ohio, for that matter.'

'I guess so. Columbus is a tremendous football town. You in the railroad business?' He felt dizzy. He wanted to keep talking.

'Not any more,' she told him. 'However, if you will permit me to point it out, when you ask someone that, you really should say: "Are you in the railroad line?" Where is your home?'

'I've been in the Army all my life,' Marco said. 'We keep moving. I was born in New Hampshire.'

'I went to a girls' camp once on Lake Francis.'

'Well. That's away north. What's your name?'

'Eugénie.'

'Pardon?'

'No kidding. I really mean it. And with that crazy French pronunciation.'

'It's pretty.'

'Thank you.'

'Your friends call you Jenny?'

'Not yet they haven't.'

'I think it's a nice name.'

'You may call me Jenny.'

'But what do your friends call you?'

'Rosie.'

'Why?'

'My full name—the first name—is Eugénie Rose. I have always favoured Rosie, of the two names, because it smells like brown soap and beer. It's the kind of a name that is always worn by the barmaid who always gets whacked across the behind by draymen. My father used to say it was a portly kind of a name, and with me being five feet nine he always figured I had a better chance of turning out portly than fragile, which is really and truly the way a girl using the name Eugénie would have to be.'

'Still, when I asked you your name, you said Eugénie.'

'It is quite possible that I was feeling more or less fragile at that instant.'

'I never could figure out what more or less meant.'

'Nobody can.'

'Are you Arabic?'

'No.'

He held out his hand to be taken in formal greeting. 'My name is Ben. It's really Bennet. I was named after Arnold Bennet.'

'The writer?'

'No. A lieutenant-colonel. He was my father's commanding officer at the time.'

'What's your last name?'

'Marco.'

'Major Marco. Are you Arabic?'

'No, but no kidding, I was sure you were Arabic. I would have placed your daddy's tents within twelve miles of the Hoggar range in the central Sahara. There's a town called Janet in there and a tiny little place with a very rude name that I couldn't possibly repeat even if you had a doctorate in geography. When the sun goes down and the rocks, which have been heated so tremendously all day, are chilled suddenly by the night, which comes across the desert like flung, cold, black stout, it makes a salvo like a hundred rifles going off in rapid fire. The wind is called the khamseen, and after a flood throws a lot of power down a mountainside the desert is reborn and millions and millions of white and yellow flowers come to bloom all across the empty desolation. The trees, when there are trees, have roots a hundred feet long. There are catfish in the waterholes. Think of that. Did you know that? Sure. Some of them run ten, twelve inches. everywhere else in the Arab world the woman is a beast of burden. Among the Tuareg, the woman is queen, and the Hoggar are the purest of the Tuareg. They had a ceremony called *ahal*, a sort of court of love where the woman reigns with her beauty, her wit, or the quality of her blood. They have enormous chivalry, the Tuareg. If a man wants to say "I love!" he will say "I am dying of love." I have dreamed many times of a woman I have never seen and will never see because she died in 1935, and to this day the Tuareg recall her in their poetry, in their *ahals*, telling of her beauty, intelligence, and her wit. Her name was Dassine oult Yemma, and her great life was deeply punctuated by widely known love affairs with the great warriors of her time. I thought you were she. For just an instant, back there in that car a little while ago, I thought you were she.'

His voice had got more and more rapid and his eyes were

feverish. She had held his hand tightly in both of hers as he had spoken, ever since he had introduced himself. They stared at each other.

'Thank you,' she said.

'You became one of my best and bravest thoughts,' he told her. 'I think you.' The taut, taut band around his head had loosened. 'Are you married?'

'No. You?'

'No. What's your last name?'

'Cheyney. I am a production assistant for a man named Justin who had two hits last season. I live on Fifty-fourth Street, a few doors from the Museum of Modern Art, of which I am a tea-privileges member, no cream. I live at Fifty-three West Fifty-fourth Street, Three B. Can you remember that?'

'Yes.'

'Eldorado nine, two six three two. Can you remember that?'

'Yes.'

'You look so tired. Apartment Three B. Are you stationed in New York? Is stationed the right word? Fifty-three West Fifty-fourth Street.'

'I'm not exactly stationed in New York. I have been stationed in Washington but I got sick and I have a long leave now and I'm going to spend it in New York.'

'Eldorado nine, two six three two.'

'I stay with a friend of mine, a newspaperman. We were in Korea together.' Marco ran a wet hand over his face and began to hum '*La Seine*.' He had found the source of the sound of the open *A*. It was far inside this girl and it was in the sound of the name Dassine oult Yemma. He couldn't get the back of his hand away from his mouth. He had had to shut his eyes. He was so tired. He was so tired. She took his hand gently away from his mouth. 'Let's sit down,' she said. 'I want you to put your head on my shoulder.' The train lurched and he almost fell, but she caught and held him, then she led the way into the other car where there were plenty of seats.

* * *

Raymond's apartment was on the extreme west coast of the island where firemen had heavy bags under their eyes from piling out four and five times a night to push sirens to brown-stone houses where nobody had any time to do anything about too many bone-weary Puerto Ricans living in one room. It was a strip of city too dishonest to admit it was a slum, or rather, in all of the vastness of the five boroughs of metropolis there was a strip of city, very tiny, which was not a slum, and this was the thin strip that was photographed and its pictures sent out across the world until all the world and the minuscule few who lived in that sliver of city thought that was New York, and neither knew or cared about the remainder of the six hundred square miles of flesh and brick. Here was the ripe slum of the West Side where the city had turned so bad that at last thirteen square blocks of it had to be torn down before the rats carried off the babies. New York, New York! it's a wonderful town! The west side of the island was rich in façades not unlike the possibilities of a fairy princess with syphilis. Central Park West was all front and faced a glorious park betrayed only now and then by bands of chattering faggots auctioning bodies and by an excessive population of emotion-caparisoned people in the somewhat temporary-looking sani-tariums on so many of its side streets. Columbus and Amsterdam Avenues were the streets of the drunks, where the murders were done in the darkest morning hours, where there were an excessive number of saloons and hardware stores. They were connected by trains of brown-stone houses whose fronts were riotously coloured morning and evening and all day on Sunday by bursts and bouquets of Puerto Ricans, and beyond Amsterdam was Broad-way, the bawling, flash street, the fleshy, pig-eyed part of the city that wore lesions of neon and incandescent scabs, pustules of lights and colour in suggestively luetic lycopods, illuminating littered streets, filth-clogged streets that could never be cleansed because when one thousand hands cleaned, one million hands threw dirt upon the streets again. Broadway was patrolled by strange-looking pedestrians, people who had grabbed the wrong face in the dark when someone had shouted 'Fire!' and were now out roaming the streets, desperate to find their own. For city block after city block on Broadway it seemed that only food was sold. Beyond that was West End Avenue, a misplaced street bitter on its own memories, lost and bewildered, seeking some Shaker Heights, desperately genteel behind an apron of shabby bricks. Here was the limbo of the lower middle-class where God the Father, in the form of sunlight, never showed His face. Raymond lived beyond that, on Riverside Drive, another front street of large, grand apartments that had become cabbage-sour furnished rooms which faced the river and an excessive amount of squalor on the Jersey shore. All together, the avenues and streets proved by their decay that the time of the city was long past, if it had ever existed, and the tall buildings, end upon end upon end, were so many extended fingers beckoning the Bomb.

Marco paid the cab off in front of Raymond's building. On an April day the city was colder than Labrador, and the wind had found teeth which tore at his face.

Marco felt like a giant. He had slept three hours on the train without dreaming and he had awakened in Rosie Cheyney's arms. He would have a very delicious therapy to tell those pate doctors about when this was all over. When it was all over but the sobbing. Big joke. All over but the sobbing, he thought, giving the driver a quarter tip. He got into the lift feeling confident that behind Raymond's mustard-coloured eyes there was an almost human understanding, not that Raymond was any monotreme but he seemed pretty much like a Martian sometimes. Fifty-three West Fifty-fourth, apartment Three B. He just wanted to hear Raymond tell how he had got the Medal of Honour. He just wanted to talk about blackboards and pointers and Chinese and that crude animated cartoon with the blue spot. Eldorado nine, two six three two. He wouldn't talk to Raymond about the murders in the nightmares. Rosie. Eugénie Rose. My Wild Arab Nose. Oh, What a Gorgeous Nose! *Cyrano:* Act I, Scene 1: Pedantic: Does not Aristophanes mention a mythologic monster called Hippocampelephantocamelos? That projection room and the American voice on the sound track and the flat, empty, half-film cans like pie plates used as ash-trays. Suddenly, he could taste the yak-dung cigarettes again and it was marvellous. If he could only remember the name of that brand, he thought, but somehow he never could. He thought about the movement of the many red dots on the screen, then of Raymond, symbolised by the blue dot, and the canned voice telling them that they were seeing the battle action in which Raymond had been willing to sacrifice his life, again and again, to save them all.

The lift operator indicated the doorway directly across the hall. Marco rang the door bell while the operator waited. Chunjin answered the door. He stood clearly under good light wearing black trousers, a white shirt, a black bow-tie, and a white jacket, looking blankly at Marco, waiting for an inquiry, not having time to recognise the major, and most certainly not expecting him. To Marco he was a *djinn* who had stepped into flesh out of that torment which was giving him lyssophobia. Not more than four-fifths of a second passed before Marco hit Chunjin high in the chest, having thrown the desperate punch for the centre of the man's face, but the Korean had stepped backward reflexively and had saved himself, partially, from the unexpectedness of Marco's assault. Because he had not thought of himself as being on duty while Raymond was out of the city, Chunjin was unarmed. However, he was a trained agent and a good one. He held the rank of lieutenant-colonel in the Soviet security forces and he had been assigned to Raymond on a crash basis. He had recognised Marco too late. He was entirely current on Marco's dossier because the major was Raymond's only friend.

The lift operator, a sturdy twenty-eight-year-old, watched the Korean carried backward and the door flung inward to bang against the pink plaster wall. He rushed in fast behind Marco and tried to pull him back. Marco held Chunjin off with his left hand and cooled the lift man with his right. Chunjin took that left arm and drew Marco into a prime judo catch and threw him high across the room so he could get at Marco's neck, coming down on it hard enough to break it in the follow-up, but Marco rolled and kept rolling when he hit the floor and slipped locks on hard when Chunjin came down, missing him.

They were both Black Belts, which is the highest judo rank there is, this side of a Dan. Marco had weight on his man, but Marco was in a run-down condition. However, he had been lifted into a murderous exhilaration and was filled to his hairline with adrenalin because he had at last been permitted to take those nightmares and one of the people in them into the fingers of his hands to beat and to torture until he found out why they had happened and where they had happened and how they could be made to stop. What worked the best was the twenty-nine extra pounds of weight and, as four neighbours watched with studious curiosity from the safer side of the door-sill, he broke Chunjin's forearm. The Korean almost took the side of his face and his neck off, not losing a beat of his rhythm during the fracture and appalling Marco that such a slight man could be so tough. Then Marco dislocated the man's hip joint as he leaped to jab his foot into Marco's larynx, and it was that second catch which brought out the great scream of agony.

He was pounding the back of Chunjin's head into the floor and asking him a series of what he thought were deliberative questions when the youngest squad-car cop came into the room first and fast, hitting him behind the head with a sap, and the entire, wonderful opportunity passed.

At St Luke's Hospital, Chunjin was adamant about two things: (1) He was emphatic in his refusal to press charges against his former commanding officer whom he had served long and intimately as orderly and interpreter, and who had most obviously mistaken him for an intruder in Mr Shaw's apartment, knowing that Mr Shaw had never employed a servant before, and (2) it would be most necessary for the hospital staff to get him out of the place not later than noon on Monday so he could shop for food, then cook the first meal on his job for Mr Shaw, because if they did not get him out he could lose his job and it was the only job he wanted in the United States of America. He could not, of course, explain that he would be shot if he lost it.

At the Twenty-fourth Precinct House at 100th Street and Central Park West, after riding the uniformed, half-conscious Marco from Raymond's apartment in the squad car, they went through his effects, found his AGO card, made his branch, and called the Military Service Bureau down town at the Police Academy, which maintained liaison between the New York police and branches of the armed forces. The bureau reached the duty officer at Army Intelligence, Washington, early in the evening. Marco was identified.. The police were told with a very special sort of a voice, effectually a pleader's voice, that Marco was one of the best men they had and that he had been having a very hard time. The voice explained, with great attention to their credulity, that Marco had picked up a sort of infection in his imagination while in the forward area in Korea, that he had run two hospital courses which had proved that he was as sane as anybody else but, well, Marco had had a hard time and anything the New York police could do that would tend to pull him together and send him on his way would be greatly appreciated by the U.S. Army.

Under proper conditions, there is no more co-operative institution than the New York Police Department, but they had had so much experience with top-blowers they insisted that Marco leave the station house in some custody which could be certified as being equable. Marco's head still wasn't very clear. He had been slugged. He had been in a rough fight and the adrenalin had turned to curds and whey in his veins. He was exhausted and he hadn't been eating very much, but he knew enough to ask them to call Eldorado nine, two six three two and ask for Miss Eugénie Rose Cheyney.

They left him in a cell while they made the call and before the cell door had closed he was asleep. Rosie got to the station house in thirty-seven minutes. Unfortunately, just as she and the two detectives came along the cell-block corridor, he had been sleeping just long enough to have reached the auditorium at Tunghwa

162

where Raymond was strangling Mavole with a silk scarf. As they stared into his cell, motionless for an instant, even the two cops were stricken with fright at the piteousness of his sounds and the imploring motions he succeeded in shaping with his hands. One detective got the door open. Eugénie Rose had gone chalk-white and was gripping her whole lower lip in her teeth to keep from yelling. She slid into the cell ahead of the second cop and got on her knees beside Marco's bunk and shook him by the shoulders, talking steadily; then, desperate to get him out of the trap he was in, she whacked him with the full strength of her splendid arm across the left cheek and he came out of it, shaking. She held him in her arms. 'It's O.K., sweetheart,' she said. 'It's Rosie. It's all right now. The dream is over. It's Jennie.' And stuff like that.

She signed out for him at the desk as though he was a ripped purse some cannon had torn off her arm. He swayed slightly as he waited for her. She shook hands like a fight manager with the desk lieutenant, the two detectives, and a patrolman who happened to be passing through, and she told them if she could ever line up any hard-to-get theatre seats for them they were to call her at Job Justin's office and she would handle it with joy. She took Marco out into the air of that freak night; a cold, cold night in mid-April that was just one of the vagaries that made New York such an interesting place to die in.

He was wearing a uniform overcoat and an overseas cap. He did not look so bad in the half-light. Everything was pressed. There was just a little blood on his right sleeve from Chunjin's face from when he had overshot with the second right-hand punch. Eugénie Rose called a taxi as if it were her own hound dog: it came to heel with a hand signal. She put Marco in first, then she got in and closed the door. 'Just drive through the park,' she said to the driver, 'and discard the conversation you've been hoarding up since the last fare.'

'I don't talk to passengers, lady,' the driver said. 'I hate people until they tip me and then it's too late.'

'I think you should eat something,' she said to Marco.

'I love food,' he answered. 'I always have but I can't swallow very well any more.'

'We'll try, anyway,' she told him and leaned forward to tell the driver to take them to the Absinthe House, a calorie and beverage bourse catering to some of the craftiest minds this side of the owl and the pussycat, on West Forty-eighth. She leaned back on the seat and looped her arm through his. She was wearing a dark-blue polo coat, some firm, dark skin, some white, white teeth, egg-sized dark eyes, and white hair.

'It was very original of you to have the Police Department call so shyly and ask for our first date,' she said softly.

'They asked me who I would—who would be willing, and I just—I——'

'Thank you. Very much.' She decided they needed more air and started to open all windows, telling the driver, 'Sorry about all this air, but it's very important. Take my word.'

'Lissen, lady, while the meter is going it's your cab arreddy. Go ahead take the doors off if its gets stuffy.' Marco's teeth began to chatter. He tried to hold them clamped shut because he wanted her to feel efficient about opening the windows, but he sounded like a stage full of castanets. She closed the windows.

'Let's pick up a can of soup and go to your place.'

'Sure.' She gave the driver the changed destination.

'You think they'll let me visit that fellow at St Luke's tonight?'

'Maybe first thing in the morning.'

'Would you come with me? It would keep me calm. I wouldn't want to hit him lying down like that.'

'Sure.'

'I have to find out where Raymond is.'

'The newspaperman you told me about? Why not call his newspaper?'

'Yeah. You're right. Well, sure. So let's go to the Absinthe House if you'd rather do that. I feel better.'

'You know what I was doing when you had the police call me?'

'I could guess, if I wasn't so tired. I give up.'

'Well, after you dropped me off and I got upstairs, and before

I took my coat off, I telephoned Lou Amjac, my fiancé"—
Marco came forward, alert and alarmed. '—and he came over as
soon as he could, which was instantly, and I told him I had just
met you and I gave him his ring back.' She held up her naked,
long fingers of the left hand, and wriggled them. 'I tried to
convey my regrets for whatever pain I might be causing him.
Then, just then, you had the police call me with the invitation to
go into the tank at the Twenty-fourth Precinct. I grabbed this
coat. I kissed Lou on the cheek for the last time in our lives that
I would ever kiss him and I ran. At the station house they told me
you had beaten up a very skinny little man but that you were a
solid type yourself, according to Washington, so I figured that if
they were willing to go to the trouble to get a comment on you
out of George Washington, you all must have had a really
successful séance while you were in the poky, and I must say it
was real sweet of General Washington with you only a major, and
I hadn't even known you two had met, but if those policemen
were the tiniest bit puzzled about you, they could have asked me
Oh, indeed yes, my darling Ben—I would have told them.'

He glared at her fiercely and possessively, clapped an arm
about her shoulders, and pulled her evocative mouth into his
while the driver, intent upon estimating within two per cent the
amount of the tip he would be paid, cleared one more stop light
just as it changed, heading east on Fifty-fourth Street.

XII

After days of wonderful, dreamless sleep upon the bed and
breast of Miss Cheyney, Marco called *The Daily Press* early
Monday morning and learned that Raymond was in Washington.
He reached Raymond at the *Press* office in Washington a few
minutes later. When he told Raymond he wanted very much to

see him, Raymond invited him to dinner in New York that evening to help him rate a new cook, then, remembering, babbled the news. 'I just remembered. Your own orderly. Yeah. Remember your orderly in Korea, the little guy who was interpreter on the patrol—Chunjin? That's my new cook! Hah? I mean, would you ever have been able to anticipate that?' Marco stated that he would not have been able to so anticipate, and inquired as to what time Raymond would arrive from Washington for the tasting.

'Estimating the travelling time from Penn Station—and I believe you'll find I won't be more than five minutes off either way—I should arrive at the apartment at—say—six twenty-two.'

'Even if you have to wait out on the corner to do it.'

'I wonder if you'd mind calling Chunjin and telling him there'll be an extra place for dinner? You're probably dying to talk to him anyway. I know you old Army guys.'

'I'll take care of everything, Raymond,' Marco said, and they both hung up.

Raymond opened the door.

'Chunjin isn't here,' he said. 'There's no dinner to offer you.'

'Or you.'

'But I did find a note. It's from him and it says you beat him up and that he's now in St Luke's Hospital.'

'One thing is for sure,' Marco said. 'There are plenty of sensational delicatessens in this neighbourhood.'

'Why, that's a marvellous idea!' Raymond said. He walked away from the door, allowing Marco to close it or not close it as he chose, and flipped open a telephone book across the square foyer. 'I never seem to be able to think of it myself. And I love it. Pastrami and those pickles and that crazy rye bread with the aphrodisiacal seeds and maybe a little marinated herring and some pot cheese with a little smoked salmon and some of that indigestible sauerkraut they make out of electric bulb filaments and some boiled beef.' He began to dial. 'On account of this I am absolutely grateful to you for getting Chunjin out of the way.'

'Ah, that's all right,' Marco said. 'Glad to do it.'

'The lift man was singing the blues so I gave him five.'

'He sure can keep a secret. He just sang a second chorus for me and I gave him five.'

'What did you hit *him* for?'

'He was determined to play peacemaker.'

'What did you whack Chunjin for?'

'That's all part of what I came to tell you about.'

'Hello—Gitlitz? This is Shaw. Right. Now hear this.' Raymond ordered food for ten, as one does when one calls a delicatessen situated anywhere on Broadway in New York between Thirty-fourth and Ninety-sixth streets, and told them where to send it.

'I've been in the hospital off and on quite a bit over the past two years.'

'Hospital? What was the matter with you?' Raymond opened a can of beer. The room was fragrant with the smell of furniture polish from Chunjin's working week-end. Marco looked very thin, but no longer drawn. The Cheyney method of soul massage had elements of greatness. He was dressed in civilian clothes, and his face had a distant, inactive look such as a man about to practice a banquet speech alone in a hotel room might have. Eugénie Rose had him coked to the gills on tranquillisers.

The authority which had come with writing a successful column on national affairs had settled Raymond considerably, Marco thought, and had made him seem taller and broader. Raymond was thirty years old. He could not have moved up the scale to a better tailor because he had always used the best. He could not have worn whiter linen. His finger-nails gleamed. His shoe-tips glowed. His colour shone. His teeth sparkled. The only fault with the lighting circuit was behind his eyes. Raymond may have believed that his eyes did light up, but unfortunately they could shine only within the extent of his art as a counterfeiter of emotions. Raymond did not feel emotion, and that could not be changed. When he was content he would try to remember how other people had looked when they had manifested happiness or pleasure or satisfaction, and he would attempt to counterfeit the appearance. It was not effective. Raymond's ability to feel anything resembling either sympathy or empathy was minimal and that was that.

As Raymond listened to Marco's story with all of his attention he could only understand that an all-out attack had been mounted against his friend and that it had almost destroyed him. He supposed he would be expected to be upset as they went on to talk about that lousy medal which had always been a lot of gas to him—tin-soldier-boy stuff: he had never asked for it, had never wanted it, and if there was some strange way that medal could keep his friend in the Army and get him his health back, then they had to make sure that he found out exactly what that was, and, if necessary to straighten this out and keep Ben safe, why, for crissake, he'd even call in Johnny Iselin. He did not say any of this to Marco. He concentrated on trying to counterfeit some of the reactions he felt Marco must expect.

'If what you've been dreaming actually happened, Ben,' he said slowly, 'then it happened to me and it happened to everyone else on the patrol.'

'Such as Chunjin,' Marco replied.

'How about an investigation?' Raymond said. 'That ought to do it.'

'Ought to do what?'

'Uncover what happened that made you dream all that.'

'What kind of an investigation?'

'Well, my mother can always get Johnny Iselin's committee in the Senate to——'

'Johnny Iselin?' Marco was utterly horrified. 'This is *Army!*'

'What has that got to do with——'

'All right, Raymond. ·I won't explain that part. But what happened is inside my head and Melvin's head and the best head doctors in this country haven't been able to shake it out and don't have even the first suspicion of what could be causing it. What could a Senate committee do? And *Iselin!* Jesus, Raymond, let's make an agreement never to mention that son-of-a-bitch ever again.'

'It was just an idea. To get started. I know Johnny is a swine better than you do.'

'Then why bring it up?'

'Because we have to dump a thing like this on the specialists. What the hell, Ben, you said so yourself—the Army can't cope with this. What there has to be, if we're going to get anywhere with it, is a big, full-scale investigation. You know—somebody has to make people talk.'

'Make who talk?'

'Well—uh—I—'

'Yeah.'

'Well, the patrol. If my Medal of Honour is a fake, and believe me I don't see how it could be anything else because it doesn't figure that I'm going to stand up in front of a lot of bullets and be a big hero for that passel of slobs, then somebody has to remember and somebody else has to make the rest of those guys remember that we've all been had. That's all. We've been had. If you can't stand the idea of Johnny Iselin, and I don't blame you, then I guess you'll just have to demand your own court martial.'

'How? What do you mean? What are you talking about?' Marco looked as though he was just beginning to understand what Raymond was talking about, almost but not quite.

'You have to charge yourself with falsifying your report that led to me getting the Medal of Honour and you'll have to demand that the Army investigate whether or not that was done in collusion with the men of the patrol. That's all there is to it.'

'They wouldn't be able to comprehend such a thing. A Medal of Honour—why, a Medal of Honour is a sacred thing to the Army, Raymond. I mean—I—Jesus, the roof would come off the Pentagon.'

'Sure! That's what I'm saying! Throw it wide open! If the Army can't understand, then, what the hell, believe me, Iselin'll understand. He'll get you off the hook.'

'No. No, never.'

'It's got to be done the sensational way just to make sure it's done and that the Army doesn't get to sit on another ridiculous

169

mistake and let you stay sick like this. What would they care? You're expendable. But they made a hero out of me so I'm not expendable. They couldn't take back a mistake as big as this one.'

'Raymond, listen. If it wasn't for those Soviet generals and those Chinese in that dream, I'd be willing to be expendable.'

'All right. That's your problem.'

'But with the chance, just the sick chance that there may be such an enormous security risk involved I have to make them dig into this thing. You're right, Raymond. I have to. I have to.'

'Why should I have got a Medal of Honour? I can't even remember being in the action. I remember the *facts* about the action, sure. But I don't remember the *action*.'

'Talk about it. Keep talking about it. Please.'

'Well, look. Let's reconstruct. We're on the patrol. You'll be at the centre of that line and I'll be off on their right flank. You know? It will be dark. I'll yell out to you, "Captain! Captain Marco! Get me some light twenty yards ahead at two o'clock!" And you'll yell back, "You got it, kid," and very soon a flare will break open and I'll pour on some enfilade fire on their column and, as everyone who reads comic books knows, I am a very good shooter. I'll start to move in on them and I'll take up one of their own heavy machine guns as I go and I'll move eight of their own grenades up ahead of me as I move along.'

'Yeah, yeah,' Marco said. 'But you don't remember *doing* all those things.'

'That's what I'm trying to tell you,' Raymond answered irritably and impatiently. 'Every time I'm directed to think about the action I always know what *will* happen exactly, but I never get to the place where it actually happens.'

'Do you remember anything about a blackboard? Chinese instructors?'

'No.'

'Memory drills? Anything about a movie projection room and animated cartoons with a sound track in English and a lot of Chinese guys standing around?'

'No.'

'You must have got a better brain-washing than I did. Or Melvin.'

'Brain-washing?' Raymond did not like that note. He could not abide the thought of anybody tampering with his person so he rejected the entire business then and there. Others, told the same set of conjectures, might have been fired into action or challenged, but not Raymond. The disgust it made Raymond feel acted like a boat-hook that pushed the solid shore away from him to allow him to drift away from it on the strong-flowing current of self. It did not mean that he had instantly closed his mind to Marco's problem. He most earnestly wanted to be able to help Ben find relief, to help to change his friend's broken mechanism, to find him sleep and rest and health, but his own participation in what he had started out to make a flaming patriotic crusade when he had first started to speak had been muted by his fastidiousness: he shrank from what he could only consider the rancid vulgarity of brain-washing.

'It has to be a brain-wash,' Marco said intensely. 'In my case it slipped. In Melvin's case it slipped. It's the only possible explanation, Raymond. The only, only explanation.'

'Why?' Raymond answered coldly. 'Why would the Communists want me to get a Medal of Honour?'

'I don't know. But we have to find out.' Marco stood up. 'Before I take this first step, before I leave here, I'd like to hear you say that you understand that I'm going to explode this whole thing with a court martial, not because—not to save myself from those dreams——'

'Ah, fuh crissake, Ben! Whose idea was it! Who gives a goddam about that?'

'Let me finish. This is an official statement because, believe me, pal, I know. Once I get that court martial started—my own court martial—it can get pretty rough on both of us.' He rolled his eyes towards the ceiling. 'My father—well, it's a good thing my father is dead—with me starting out to make a public bum out of a Medal of Honour man. Shuddup! But I have to do it. Security. What a lousy word. I look right into the horrible ace of something that might kill my country and the only word for the danger is a word that means the absolute opposite. Security. Well, as you said—with stakes like that I'm expendable. And so are you, Raymond pal. So are you.'

'Will you stop? Who thought it up? Me. Who practically made you agree to do it? Me. And you can shove that patriotic jive about saving our great country. I want to know why a bunch of filthy Soviet peasants and degraded Chinese coolies would dare to confer the Medal of Honour on me.'

'Raymond. Do me a favour? Tell me about the action again. Please.'

'What action?'

'Come on! Come on!'

'You mean go on from where I was?'

'Yeah, yeah.'

'Well—you will throw up another flare but you'll throw it about twenty yards ahead of me at maybe twelve o'clock, at maybe dead centre of the line, because you will figure I'll be moving across the terrain up that ridge so——'

'Man, oh man, this is something.'

'What?'

'Each time you talk about the action you even tell it as though it hadn't happened yet.'

'That's what I'm saying! That's the way I always think about it! I mean, when some horrible square comes out of nowhere at a banquet, the paper makes me go too, and he starts asking me about it. Come on, Ben. You made your point. Let's go meet your girl.'

Marco ran his fingers through his thick hair on both sides of his head. He put his elbows on his knees and covered his face with his hands. Raymond stared down at him, almost tenderly. 'Don't be embarrassed if you feel like you're going to cry, Ben,' Raymond said gently.

Marco shook his head. Raymond opened another can of beer.

'I swear to sweet, sweet God I think I am going to be able to sleep,' Marco said. 'I can feel it. There isn't anything about those crazy voices and those fast, blurring colours and the eyes of that terrible audience that frightens me any more.' He took his hands away from his face and reflexively reached over to take Raymond's can of beer out of his hand. Raymond reached down and opened another. Marco fell asleep, sitting up. Raymond stretched him out on the sofa, brought him a blanket, put out the lights, and went into his office to listen to the river wind and to read a slim book with the highly improbably title of *Liquor, the Servant of Man*.

Marco was still asleep when Raymond left the apartment the next morning. Eugénie Rose Cheyney called him soon after he reached his office. She asked if Marco had been sleeping quietly. Raymond said he had. She said, 'Oh, Mr Shaw, that's just wonderful!' and hung up.

XIII

Raymond's mother called him from the Idlewild Airport. She wanted him to have lunch with her. He tried to think quickly of somebody whom he could say he had to have lunch with but she said he was not to stall her, that she was well aware that he disliked people too much to be stuck for an hour or more at a luncheon table with one, so he could damn well show up wherever they let ladies eat luncheon at the Plaza Hotel at one o'clock. He said he would be there. Beyond having acknowledged that his name was Raymond when she had first spoken, it was all he said to his mother.

She was hard at work making a scene by bossing the *maître d'hôtel*, a table captain, and two waiters at a table that faced the park in the big corner room when he arrived at the Plaza at ten seconds before one o'clock. She motioned him to stand beside her chair until she finished her oration about exactly how they were to stuff the oysters into a carpet bag steak and that she would not tolerate more than eleven minutes of broiling on each side, in a pre-heated grill, at four hundred degrees. The waiters bowed and left. Raymond's mother gave the *maître d'* the full glare of her contempt for an instant, then spoke to Raymond. 'I ask you to imagine a restaurant,' she said, 'which does not list Clos de Lambrays or a Cuvée Docteur Peste!' She waved the man away, with bitterness. She permitted Raymond to kiss her on the right cheek, ever so lightly, then motioned him to his chair at the table for four, not at her right or directly across from her, but at her left, which made it impossible for either of them to look out of the window at the park.

'How have you been?' she asked.

'Fine.'

'As am I. Not that you asked.'

'When I heard you ordering a steak stuffed with oysters I had a clue.'

'The steak will be mainly for you.'

'Sure.'

'Johnny is fine.'

'You mean his physical health, I presume?'

'I do. And everything else.'

'Is he in a jam?'

'Of course not.'

'Then why are we here?'

'Why are we here?'

'Why are we having our annual meeting?'

'I am your mother, which is a sufficient reason. Why did you ask if Johnny is in a jam?'

'It occurred to me that you might have decided that you would have use for my column, which has so carefully disqualified itself from ever printing Johnny's name despite the fact that he is an assassin, pure and simple. An assassin of character and the soul. He reeks of death, you know?' Raymond exceeded his own gifts for being obnoxious and impossible when he was with his mother. His brushing gesture worked for him almost all the time, punctuating his haughtiness and scorn. His posture was as attenuated as liquid being drawn up through a drinking straw.

His mother closed her eyes tightly as she answered him. 'My dear boy, one more column of type in this weltered world spelling out Johnny's name would not be much noticed.'

'I'll remember that.'

She opened her eyes. 'What for?'

Raymond, when he was with his mother, always felt a nagging fear that he was gaping at her beauty. As they spoke, whenever they met, his eyes searched each millimeter of her skin for a flaw and weighed each of her gestures, anxious that he might discover some loss of grace, but to no avail. He was dismayed and gratified to fall back upon the mockery of her pretence at disappointment because there had been no Clos de Lambrays or Cuvée Docteur Peste, which so failed to find harmony with the fact that Johnny Iselin drank bourbon with his meals.

'Mother, in God's name, where did you ever hear of a thing like a carpetbag steak? Johnny found it, didn't he? Johnny had to find it, because in the world's literature of food there couldn't be a dish which expresses his vulgarity better than a thick, contemptuously expensive piece of meat pregnant with viscous, slippery, sensual oysters.'

'Raymond, please! Watch your language.' She leered at him.

'It's disgusting and he's disgusting.'

'The reason I asked you to lunch today, Raymond,' his mother said smoothly, 'is that I have not, actually been entirely well and my doctor has suggested a trip to Europe this summer.'

'What's the matter with you?' He stretched out the diphthongs of the drawl until its sounds reverberated nasally into his soft palate, thinking: Has there ever on God's earth been a liar like this woman? Does she at any square inch of her mountainous vanity, conceive that I can be had through the delicate health appeal? Will she produce a forged electrocardiogram? Will a malpracticing doctor with an even gaze suddenly happen to discover that we are lunching here? She would never pull anything as crude as a faint, but she could play a great scene with any given kindly old physician who had been coached in his lines.

'The doctor was a fool, of course,' his mother said. 'I went to the Leahy Clinic and to the Mayos for two separate checkups. I am as sound as a Swiss franc.'

Raymond's resentment of her made him feel as though steel burrs were forming everywhere under his skin. I am going to lose this, he thought, just as I lose them all with her. I am being blindfolded as I sit here and she will win if I cannot anticipate where she is leading me. Oh, what a woman! What a beauty she is and what a dirty fighter. She is where the world should spit when they seek to spit upon Johnny Iselin. How can I forget that? How can I look into those serenely lovely eyes, how can I be so deeply thrilled by the carriage of her exquisitely wholesome body and grow so faint at the set, the royal set of that beautiful head and not remember, not always and always and always remember that it encases a cesspool of betrayal, a poisoned well of love, and a city of deadly snakes? Why am I here? Why did I come here?

'I am glad to hear it,' he said. 'But I distinctly remember you telling me that you had not, actually, been entirely well. Just a few seconds ago. In fact, that was exactly the way you phrased it.'

She smiled at him with forbearance, showing rows of perfect white teeth. 'I said—oh, Raymond! For heaven's sake, what does it matter what I said?'

'I'd like a drink.'

'At lunch?'

'Yes.'

'You generally sulk if people drink at lunch.'

She tilted her head back and made a repulsive kissing sound with her pursed lips. A waiter sprinted towards her so rapidly that Raymond thought the man had decided to kill her, but that was not the case. He came to a point beside her and stared at her abjectly as though pleading for the knout. Raymond's mother had that effect upon many people.

'Speak up, Raymond.'

'I would like to have some beer. Served in the can.'

'Served in the can, sir?' the waiter asked softly. Raymond's mother snarled and the man shrilled 'Yes, sir!' and was off.

'And who is the more vulgar now?' she asked in a kindly tone. 'How about a can of beans, opened with a hatchet, with the can of beer?'

'Mother, for crissake, will you please tell me how come we are having lunch today?'

'Oh. Well, this fool of a doctor whom I shall expose as an alarmist, I assure you, told me that I should go to Europe for a change and whether it was from the wrong reason or not, it did plant the idea. So, since I can't go alone and since it would present too many security difficulties for Johnny to go with me, I wondered . . . and I most certainly expect you to accept for professional reasons as I will be travelling as a full, accredited representative of the Appropriations, Foreign Relations, and Finance Committees—I will be representing the Senate, you might say—and I will be there to remind the forgetful rulers of Europe and England that the United States was established not as a democracy but as a Federal Union and Republic that is controlled by the United States Senate, at this moment in our history, through a state-equality composition designed to maintain this establishment and that it exists, in the present moment of our history, to protect minorities from the precipitate and emotional tyranny of majorities. That means, of course, that I will be able to get you into places and cause you to be adjacent to people which neither your newspaper nor your column could reach in a decade of Sundays. I assure you, before you answer as to whether or not you will consent to accompany me, your own mother, on a tour of Europe at no cost whatever to you, that there is no one in the British Isles or on that entire subcontinent of Europe whom you might decide that you would like to meet— and for reasons of publication should you so choose—that I cannot deliver to you. Should you also decide that you would enjoy extending the already influential syndication of your daily writings to other languages and to foreign newspapers and opinion-moulding periodicals, I should think that could be arranged. Furthermore—' Raymond's mother was wooing him as she had wooed Johnny Iselin. Raymond's own father must have been a dreamer, indeed, to have lost her point so far back in the thickening fullness of her youth.

'I would love to go to Europe with you this summer, Mother.'

'Good. We will sail from West Forty-sixth Street on June 15, at noon, on the *United States*. My office will mail you the itinerary and hotels and indicate the shape of appointments and meetings, business and social. Would you like to see the Pope?'

'No.'

'I'll do that alone then.'

'What else?'

'Isn't this carpetbag steak absolutely delicious? Eating it is an absolute sexual experience! What a marvellous conception—steak and oysters, I mean. Johnny eats it all the time you know.'

'It figures.'

'Is there anything I can get done for you in Washington, dear heart?'

'No. Thank you. Yes. Yes, there is something. I have a friend——'

'A friend? You have a friend?' She stopped chewing for a moment and put her fork down.

'Sarcasm is the cheapest kind of a crutch to humour, Mother.'

'Please forgive me, Raymond. I was not attempting sarcasm. You must believe that. I was startled. I had never heard you mention a friend in your entire life before. I am very, very happy that you do have a friend and you may be sure, darling, that if I may help your friend I most certainly will be overjoyed to do so. Who is he?'

'He's a major in Army Intelligence in Washington.' Raymond's mother had whipped out an efficient-looking loose-leaf note-book.

'His name?'

He told her.

'Academy?' He said yes.

'Would full colonel be what you had in mind?'

'That would be fine, I guess. I hope there is some way it can be done without PI being stamped all over his personnel file.'

'What is PI?'

'Political influence.'

'Of course they'll stamp PI all over his personnel file! Are you out of your mind? What's wrong with letting the Board know that he happens to have a little muscle in the right places? Sweet Jesus, Raymond, if it weren't for PI some of the brass we call our leaders would be the oldest crop of second lieutenants in military history. I swear to God, Raymond,' his mother said in extreme exasperation, chopping savagely at a large gooseberry tart that glistened with custard filling, 'sometimes I think you are the most naïve of young men, and when I read your column, I am sure.'

'What's wrong with my column?'

She held up her hand. 'Not now. We will re-organise your column aboard ship in June. Right now let's make your friend a chicken colonel.' She looked at her notes. 'Now, is there anything —well, anything negative I should know about this one?'

'No. He's a great officer. His father and grandfather and great-grandfather were great officers.'

'You know him from Korea?'

'Yes. He—he led the patrol.' Raymond hesitated because mentioning the patrol made him think of that filthy medal again and how much his mother had made that medal mean to Johnny Iselin and what a fool she had made of herself at the White House and later what a fool Johnny had made of himself in front of the TV cameras and press cameras at that goddam, cheap, rotten, contemptuous luncheon where he had been humiliated, and all of a sudden he saw that it would be possible, too, for him to take a little bit of her skin off painfully and to kick Johnny right between the eyes with the medal nailed to the toe of his boot so that he, Raymond, would finally have a little pleasure out of that goddam medal himself, finally and at last. He was patiently quiet until she sensed the meaning of his hesitation and took it up.

'What's the matter?' she asked.

'Well, there is one thing which the Army might figure as negative. In the past. I think it's all right now.'

'He's a fairy?'

'Hah!'

'This little negative thing. You say you *think* it's all right now?'

'Yes.'

'You don't think you should tell me what it is?'

'Mother, are you going to put Johnny up for the Presidency at the convention next year?'

'Raymond, shall we make your friend a colonel or not? I don't think Johnny can make it for the Presidency. I may go after the number-two spot.'

'Will you enter him in the primaries next spring?'

'I don't think so. He has too much strength for that. I don't think I need any popularity contests for Johnny. Now—about the negative side of the major.' Raymond folded his hands neatly before him on the table. 'He's been in Army psychiatric hospitals twice in the past year.'

'Oh, that's all,' she drawled sarcastically and shrugged. 'And all the time I thought it might have been something which could present a problem. My God, Raymond! A psycho! Have you ever seen what that looks like when it's stamped across a personnel file?'

'It's not what you might think, Mother. You see, due to an experience in Korea, a very vivid experience, he has been suffering from recurring nightmares.'

'Is that right?'

'What happened to him could give anyone nightmares. In fact, it might even give you a nightmare or two after you hear it.'

'Why?'

'Because it's quite a story and I'm involved in it up to my ears.'

Her voice picked up a cutting edge. 'How are you involved?' she asked.

He told her. When he had finished explaining that Marco had decided to demand his own court martial to prove falsification and collusion in conjunction with the conferment of that Medal of Honour, savouring each word and each shocked look on his mother's face with great and deep satisfaction, she was the colour of milk and her hand trembled.

'How dare he?'

'Why, Mother, it is his duty. Surely you can see that?'

'How dare the contemptible, psychoneurotic, useless, filthy little military servant of a—?' She choked on it.

Raymond was startled at the intensity of her attack. She brought her fist down on the table top with full force from two feet above it, in full tantrum, and the glasses, plates, and silver jumped and a full water pitcher leaped into the air to crash to the floor. Everyone in the dining-room turned to stare and some stood up to look. A waiter dashed towards the table and went to his hands and knees, fussing with the sopping carpet and the fragments of heavy glass. She kicked him in the thigh as she sat, with vicious vigor. 'Get out of here, you miserable flunky,' she said. The waiter stood up slowly, staring at her, breathing shallowly. Then he left abruptly. She stood up, breathing heavily, with sweat shining on her upper lip. 'I'll help your friend, Raymond,' she said with violence in her voice. 'I'll help him to defame and destroy an American hero. I'll cheer him as he spits upon our flag.' She left him there, striding rapidly through knots of people and attendants, shouldering some. Raymond stared after her, knowing he had lost again but not knowing what he had lost. But he was not dismayed, because losing was Raymond's most constant feeling.

She went to the manager's office in the hotel. She brushed past his secretary and slammed the door behind her. She said she was the wife of Senator John Yerkes Iselin and that the two people then meeting with the manager, two barber-pinked businessmen each wearing a florid carnation, would oblige her by leaving the room. They excused themselves and left immediately, vaguely fearful of being proved Communists. She told the manager that it would be necessary to use his office and his telephone and that it would be necessary for her to have utter privacy as she would be talking about an emergency matter with the Secretary of Defence at the Pentagon, and that she would greatly appreciate it, in fact she would regard it as a patriotic service, as would indeed her husband, Senator Iselin, if he were to go to the telephone switchboard in person and direct the placement of the call to the Secretary, reversing the charges, and standing by at the operator's shoulder to make sure there was no eavesdropping on the call, a natural and human tendency under the circumstances.

Raymond paid the check and wandered about the lobby looking for his mother. He concluded that she had left so he went out of the hotel on the Fifth Avenue side, deciding to walk back to his office. When he reached the office he found a message to call Army Intelligence in New York. He called. They asked if he could help them locate Major Bennett Marco. Raymond said he believed Major Marco was presently at his apartment, as he was visiting him in New York. They asked for the telephone number. He gave it to them, explaining that they were not to give it to anyone else, then felt silly having said such a thing to professional investigators. He got busy after that on a call from the governor's press secretary and the three check-up calls that were made necessary by that call. When he called Ben at the apartment there was no answer. He forgot about it. That night, when he got home at six twenty-two, he found a note from Ben thanking him and saying that his indefinite sick leave had been cancelled and that he had been recalled to Washington. The note also urged Raymond not to question Chunjin in any way after he came out of the hospital.

In Naples, in the summer of 1958, in discussing the most powerful men in the world with Leonard Lyons, the ex-patriate Charles Luciano had said: 'A U.S. Senator can make more trouble, day in and day out, than anyone else.' The condition as stated then had not changed perceptibly a year later.

XIV

When Lieutenant General Nils Jorgenson had awakened that morning, a celebrant of his fortieth anniversary in the United States Army, he had been euphoric. When he left the office of the Secretary and the further presence of the Army's Congressional liaison officer, he was dismayed, cholerically angry, but mostly horrified. The general was a good man and a brave man. He locked the doors when he and Marco were alone in his office, then demanded that Marco confirm or deny that Marco had planned to request a court martial of himself to enforce a public investigation of circumstances involving a Medal of Honour man. Marco confirmed it. The general felt it necessary to tell Marco that he had known Marco's father and grandfather. He asked Marco what he had to say.

'Sir, there is only one person in the world with whom I have discussed this course and that was Raymond Shaw himself, at his apartment last night, and it was Shaw, sir, who urged the course and originated the conception. May I ask who has made this accusation to the Secretary, sir? I cannot understand how——'

'Senator John Yerkes Iselin made the accusation, Major. Now—I offer you this because of your record and the record of your family. I offer you the opportunity to resign from the Army.'

'I cannot resign, sir. It is my belief, sir, that the Medal of Honour is being used as an enemy weapon. I—if the general will understand—I see this as my duty, sir.'

The general walked to the window. He looked out at the river for a long time. He went to a casual chair and sat down and he leaned far, far forward, almost bent double, staring at the floor for a long time. He went to his desk and took a chewed and battered-looking pipe from its top drawer, plugged tobacco into it, lighted it, and smoked furiously, staring out of the window again. Then he went back to the desk and sat down to stare across at Marco.

'You not only will not get the court martial but I am advising you that you will have no rights of any kind.' He snorted with disgust. 'On my fortieth anniversary in the Army I find myself telling an American officer that he will have no rights of any kind.'

'Sir?'

'Senator Iselin is the kind of a man who would work day and night to block the entire defence appropriation if he were crossed on a matter as close to him as this. Senator Iselin is capable of wrecking the entire military establishment if an investigation of his stepson's glorious heroism were permitted to go through. He would undertake a war upon the United States Army which would be far more punishing and ruinous than any ever inflicted by any enemy force of arms in our history. To convey to you the enormity of the responsibility you carry, I have been ordered to tell you this, and it violates everything I stand for. Under orders, I will now threaten you.' His voice trembled. 'If you persist in urging your own court martial for the purpose of examining Raymond Shaw's right to wear the Medal of Honour, you will be placed in solitary confinement.'

Marco stared at the general.

'Have you ever had to threaten a private to force him to police a yard, Major? The Army, as we have known it, has heretofore functioned under a system utilising orders. Do you remember? I must now tell you that I have not been permitted to consider this conversation a travesty on both our lives. I have been ordered not to halt at merely threatening you. Senator Iselin has decided that I was to be ordered to bribe you. If you will agree to ignore your honour as an officer and will sign a paper which has been prepared by Senator Iselin's legal counsel which guarantees that you will not press for the investigation of this matter, I am to advise you that you will be advanced in rank to lieutenant colonel, then effective instantly, to the rank of full colonel.'

The nausea rose in Marco like the foam in a narrow beer glass. He could not speak even to acknowledge that he had heard.

The general took a paper from his blouse and placed it on the desk, on the far side of it, in front of Marco. 'So much for Iselin,' he said. 'I order you to sign it.' Marco took up the desk pen and signed the paper.

'Thank you, Major. Dismiss,' the general said. Marco left the office at four twenty-one in the afternoon. General Jorgenson shot himself to death at four fifty-five.

XV

There is an immutable phrase at large in the languages of the world that places fabulous ransom on every word in it: The love of a good woman. It means what it says and no matter what the perspective or stains of the person who speaks it, the phrase defies devaluing. The bitter and the kind can chase each other around it, this mulberry bush of truth and consequence, and the kind may convert the bitter and the bitter may emasculate the kind but neither can change its meaning because the love of a good woman does not give way to arbitrage. The phrase may be used in sarcasm or irony to underscore the ludicrous result of the lack of such love, as in the wrecks left behind by bad women or silly women, but such usage serves to mark the changeless value. The six words shine neither with sentiment nor sentimentality. They are truth; a light of its own; unchanging.

Eugenie Rose Cheyney was a good woman and she loved Marco. That fact gave Marco a large edge, tantamount to wiping out the house percentage in banker's craps. No matter what the action, that is a lot of vigourish to have going for anybody.

Eugenie Rose had had her office route all business to her home that day, because she knew Marco would call whenever he woke up at Raymond Shaw's apartment. Her boss, Justin, was overdrawn at the bank, and it irritated her that they would seek to bother him about such a thing. He was overdrawn for a tiny period every sixty days or so, at which time he always managed to make an apple-cheeked deposit that kept the bank not only honest but richer. The set construction company had called at about eleven o'clock about some bills that the general manager had questioned. She had all of his questions ready and a set of the only answers in Christendom so she was able to cut four hundred and eleven dollars and sixty-three cents from the construction of a fireplace for the main room of the castle. After that call sixteen persons of every stripe, meaning from quarter-unit investors in the next show down to press agents for health food restaurants, called to try to get house seats for specific performances, and she had to invent a new theatrical superstition to fit the problem, which was how the others had come into being, by saying that surely they knew it was bad luck to distribute seat locations for the New York run until the out-of-town notices were in. And so chaos was postponed again. When she hadn't heard from Marco by seven-ten that evening she decided that he must have tried and tried to call her while all those other calls had been coming through, so she called Raymond at home, reading Marco's handwriting as he had written the number down as though it had the relative value of the sound of his voice at her very ear. Before Raymond answered, as the instrument purred the signal, she heard the lift door open, pause, then close in the hallway just outside her door. She decided she knew it must be Marco. She slammed the phone down and rushed to the door worrying about her hair, so that she could hold it open in welcome before he could have a chance to ring the bell.

He looked terrible.

He said, 'Let's get married, Rosie.' He stepped over the threshold and grabbed her as though she were the rock of the ages. He kissed her. She kicked the door shut. She started to kiss him in return and it turned his knees to water.

'When?' she inquired.

'How long does it take in this state? That's how long.' She kissed him again and massaged his middle with her pelvis. 'I want to marry you, Ben, more than I want to go on eating Italian food, which will give you a slight idea, but we can't get married so quickly,' she breathed on him.

'Why?'

'Ben, you're thirty-nine years old. We met three days ago and that's not enough time to get a bird's-eye view or a microscopic view of anyone. When we get married, Ben, and please notice how I said when *we* get married, not when *I* get married, we have to stay married because I might turn into a drunk or a *religieuse* or a cryto-Republican if we ever failed, so let's wait a week.'

'A week.'

'Please.'

'Well, all right. There is such a thing as being over-mature about decisions like this but we won't get married for a week. But we'll get the papers and take the blood tests and post the banns and plan the children's names and buy the ring and rent the rice and call the folks——'

'Folks?'

He stared at her for a moment. 'You neither?'

'No.'

'An orphan?'

'I used to be convinced that, as a baby, I had been the only survivor of a space ship which had overshot Mars.'

'Very sexy stuff.'

'You look a different kind of awful from yesterday. Mr Shaw told me you slept all night. Quietly.'

'Ah. You talked to Raymond.'

'This morning. He is very formal about you.'

'Poor Raymond. I'm the only one he has. Not that he needs anybody. Old Raymond has only enough soul to be able to tolerate two or three people in his life. I'm one of them. There's a girl I think he weeps over after he locks the doors. There's room for just about one more and he'll be full up. I hope it's you because having Raymond on your side is not unlike being backed up by the First Army.'

'Did you have a bad time today?'

'Yeah. Well, yes and no.'

He sat down as suddenly as though his legs had broken. She descended like a great dancer to rest on the floor beside his chair. He rubbed the back of her neck with his right hand, absent-mindedly, but with sensual facility.

'You are the holiest object I have in the world,' he said slowly and with a thick voice, 'so I swear upon you that I am going to get even with Senator John Iselin for what happened today. I don't know how yet. But how I will do it will always be somewhere in my mind from today on. From today on I'll always be thinking about how I, Marco, am going to make him pay for what he did today. I probably won't kill him. I found out today that I will probably never make a murderer.'

She stared up at him. His face glistened with sweat and his eyes were sad instead of being vengeful. Her own eyes, the Tuareg eyes, were black almonds with blue centres; a changing blue, like mist over far snow. They were the eyes of a lady left over from an army of crusaders who had taken the wrong turning, moving left towards Jarabub in Africa, instead of right, towards London, after Walter the Penniless had sent them to loot the Holy Land in 1096, to settle forever in the deep Sahara, to continue the customs of the lists, knight errantry, and the wooing of ladies fair for whose warm glances the warriors sang their songs. She stared at him steadily, then rested her head on the side of his leg and sat quietly.

'Iselin is Raymond's stepfather,' Marco told her. 'He sits right there in his office on the Hill. He's the most accessible, available senator we have, you know, because most of our newspapers are published right in his office nowadays. Senator Iselin is really fond of Raymond because Johnny is a terrific salesman. Raymond has no use for him, and a lack of buyer feeling about the product has always been a tremendous challenge to a salesman. All I needed to do was to call Johnny, tell him Raymond sent me, be shown right into his office, lock the door, and shoot him through the head. Or maybe beat him to death with a steel chair.' Marco was talking quietly, through his teeth. He thought about his lost opportunity for a moment.

'Did you know Raymond was a Medal of Honour man, Rosie?' he asked almost rhetorically. She shook her grey-white head without answering. 'I wish I could explain to you what that means. But I'd have to find a way to send you back to grow up on Army posts and put you through the Academy and find you a couple of wars and a taste for Georgie Patton and Caesar's *Commentaries* and Blucher and Ney and Moltke, but thank God we can't do any of that. Just believe it because I say it, that a Medal of Honour man is the best man any soldier can think of because he has achieved the most of what every soldier was meant to do. Anyway, after Raymond got the medal, I began to have nightmares. They were pretty bad. I had come to the worst of them when I found you, thank God. The nightmares were always the same for five years and they took a lot of trouble to suggest that Raymond had not won the medal rightfully after I had sworn he had won it and the men of my patrol had sworn to it. In the end, the dreams have convinced me that we were wrong. I am sure now that the Russians wanted Raymond to have the medal so he got it. I don't know why. Maybe, if I'm lucky, I never will know why. But I'm an officer trained in intelligence work. I filled a notebook with details about furniture and clothing and complexions and speech defects and floor coverings. I talked everything over with Raymond. He got the idea that I should request my own court martial for falsifying the report and explode a public investigation so that the enemy, at the very least, would think we knew more than we knew. That idea ended this afternoon with a lieutenant general putting a bullet into his head because it was the only possible thing he could have done to make Iselin hear the Army's protest against what Iselin had done to us. I knew that general. He liked living and he had a big time at it but he saw that protest as being an important Army job and he had been trained to accept responsibility.' Marco's voice got bleak. 'So I swear on you, on my Eugénie Rose, that the day will come that I, Marco, will make Senator John Iselin pay for that, and if he has to be killed, and I can't kill him, I'll have someone kill him for me.' He closed his eyes for a few beats. 'We got any beer in the house?' he asked her.

She got some. She drank plain warm gin.

Marco drank a can of the beer before he spoke again. 'Anyway I was stopped,' he said at last. 'Before he shot himself the general ordered me to forget the court martial, so that is that. I'm frozen with my terrible dreams inside of a big cake of ice and I'll never get out.'

'You'll get out.'

'No.'

'Yes you will.'

'How?'

'Do you remember that thing I told you which no girl in her right mind would ever tell a man she had gone limp over, about how I called up the man I was engaged to and resigned from the whole idea because you happened to smell so crazy?'

'I thought you just said that to get me to kiss you.'

'His name was Lou Amjac and you happen to be right.'

'You know, you weren't attracted to me irrevocably only because I smell this way. Don't forget I cried like a little, lost tyke the instant I first looked at you. Stuff like that is a steam roller for a potential mother.'

'Have you ever done that with another woman? The smell you can't help, but I don't think I could stand sharing your snivelling with another woman.'

'Never mind. That's the kind of stuff that'll come out after we're married. What about Lou Amjac?'

'He's an FBI agent. They are good at their work. I have a whole intuitive thing about how they can help you with that notebook—The Gallant Major's Gypsy Dream Book.'

'I'm Army Intelligence, baby. We don't take our laundry to the FBI. Macy's definitely does not tell Gimbel's.'

'The way you told it to me, you *were* Army Intelligence. If the FBI can prove you have something worth going on with, then your side will take you back and you can run the whole thing down yourself.'

'Jesus.'

'Isn't it worth trying?'

'Well, yeah, but still, I don't see Lou Amjac going out of his way to help me. After all, you were his girl.'

'He might not be pleasant about it, that's true, but he's an agent of the Federal Bureau of Investigation and if you've got something in his line, you're not going to be able to shake him.'

Amjac *wasn't* entirely pleasant about Marco. In fact, he was particularly surly. Amjac was a skinny man with watery eyes and when Marco saw them for the first time he had a hot flash of jealousy go through him, feeling that maybe Eugénie Rose was nearsighted and that perhaps when she had first seen this guy she had thought he was crying. Amjac was tall. He had florid skin and sandy hair, freckles all over the backs of his hands, and looked as though he had a tendency to boils on the back of his neck. His hair was fine lanugo and he couldn't have grown a moustache if he had stayed in bed for a year. He had a jaw like a crocodile and as he sat in Rosie's small, warm, golden-draped room, which had horrible, large cabbage roses woven into the carpets and ancient northern European brewery posters on all walls, separated by mountain goat heads mounted on stained ash, he looked as though he would be happy to be invited to bite Marco's right arm off.

When he entered the apartment and had stood staring down, repelled, at Marco, Eugénie Rose had said serenely, 'This is Bonny Benny Marco, the chap I was telling you about, Lou. Benny boy, this here is a typical, old-time shamus right out of *Black Mask Magazine* name of Lou Amjac.'

'Did you bring me all the way over here in the rain just to meet this?' Amjac inquired.

'Is it raining? Yes, I did.'

'What am I supposed to do? Arrest him for impersonating an officer?'

Marco figured it would be better just to let the two old friends chat together.

'Would you like a nice plebeian rye highball, Lou?'

'Plebeian? Your friend is drinking beer right out of the can.'

'Wow, you FBI guys don't miss a trick, do you?' Eugénie Rose said. 'Do you want a rye highball or don't you?'

'Yeah.'

'Yeah, what?'

'Yeah, yeah.'

'That's better. Give me your coat. How is your elbow with the weather changing like this? Now sit down. No. Walk with me to the kitchen whilst I decant. Did your mother get back from Montreal?'

Amjac took off his coat.

'You know, I think if I was right-handed I would have had to quit the Bureau, Rose. I could hardly bend my elbow this afternoon, believe it or not. This Dr Weiler—you met Abe Weiler, the specialist, didn't you, Rose?—he may be a good man at certain things—you know what I mean—but I don't think he knows where to grope when it comes to arthritis.' He followed her into the tiny kitchen and Marco watched them go, goggle-eyed. 'My mother decided to stay over another week,' he could hear Amjac say. 'They sell very strong ale up there and since my sister's husband won't be home from the road until Monday, why not?'

'Of course, why not?' Rosie's voice said. 'Just make sure she's out before he's home, is all. He'd love to punch her right on her sweet little old-lady nose, he told me.'

'Aaaah, that's a lot of talk,' Amjac said petulantly. 'Thanks.' He accepted the stiff highball.

'Are your lads still interested in this and that about the Soviet lads? Spy stuff?'

Amjac jerked his head back towards Marco. 'Him?'

'He knows a couple,' she said. They walked back into the living room with Rosie carrying four beer cans at stomach level.

'Can he talk?' Amjac asked.

'He talks beautifully. And, oh Lou, I wish you could *smell* him!' Amjac grunted and stared hard at Marco who seemed considerably embarrassed. 'Just the same I'd like to tell you the story,' Rosie said, 'because you are gradually making Major Marco believe that after eleven years of rooming with you at the Academy he has stolen your wife, and as you know the very best in the world that just isn't the case.'

'So tell!' Amjac snarled.

She told it. From the patrol forward. She went from the Medal of Honour to the nightmares, to Melvin in Wainright, to the Army hospitals, to Chunjin and Raymond, to Raymond's mother and Senator Iselin, to Marco's court martial project and General Jorgenson's suicide. They were all quiet after she had finished. Amjac finished his highball in slow sips. Where's the notebook?' he asked harshly.

Marco spoke for the first time. 'It's with my gear. At Raymond's.'

'You think you can remember any of the faces of the men in your dreams?'

'Every man, every face. One woman.'

'And one lieutenant general?'

'With Security service markings.'

'And this Melvin dreamed the same thing?'

'He did. And that man who was sitting beside the lieutenant general is now Raymond Shaw's house man.'

Amjac stood up. He put his coat on with deliberate movement. 'I'll talk it over with the special agent in charge,' he said. 'Where can I reach you?' Marco started to answer but Eugénie Rose interrupted him. 'Right here, Louis,' she said brightly. 'Any time at all.'

'I live at Raymond Shaw's,' Marco said quickly, colouring deeply. 'Trafalgar eight, eight-eight-eight-one.'

'I cannot believe it,' Amjac said to Rosie. 'I simply cannot believe that you could ever turn out to be this kind of hard, cruel girl.' He turned to go. 'You never gave a damn about me.'

'Lou!'

He got to the door but he had to turn around. She was staring at him levelly, without much expression.

'You know I cared,' she said. 'I know that you know exactly how much I cared.'

He couldn't hold her stare. He looked away, then looked at the floor.

'With all the girls there are in the world,' she asked, 'do you think a thirty-nine-year-old bachelor who has been batting around the world most of his life wants to get married? Well, he does, Lou. And so do I. Maybe if you had been able to make up your mind between me and your elbow and your mother, you and I would have been married by now. We've been together four years, Lou. Four years. And you can say that I never cared about you and I can only answer that the cold-turkey cure is the only way for you because I have to make sure that you understand that there is only Ben; that it is as clear as daylight that Ben is the only man for me. Some day, if you keep playing the delaying game, and I guess you will, some girl may pay you out on a slow rope, then cast you adrift miles and miles away from shore and you'll know that my way—this hard, cruel way you called it—is the way that leaves the fewest scars. Now stop sulking and tell me. Are you going to help us or not?'

'I want to help him, Rosie,' Amjac said slowly, 'but somebody else has to decide that, so I'll let you know to-morrow. Good night and good luck.'

'Night, Lou. My best to your mother when she calls later.'

Amjac closed the door behind him.

'You don't just fool around, do you, Eugénie Rose?' Marco asked reverently.

*　　*　　*

Amjac was one of the four men in the large room in the New York office of the Federal Bureau of Investigation towards noon the next morning. Another man was the special agent in charge. Another man was a courier who had just come in from Washington. The fourth man was Marco.

The courier had brought one hundred and sixty-eight close-up photographs from one of the Bureau's special file. The close-ups included shots of male models, Mexican circus performers, Czech research chemists, Indiana oil men, Canadian athletes, Australian outdoor showmen, Japanese criminals, Asturian miners, French head waiters, Turkish wrestlers, pastoral psychiatrists, marine lawyers, English publishers, and various officials of the U.S.S.R., the Peoples' Republic of China, and the Soviet Army. Some shots were sharp, some were murky. Marco made Mikhail Gomel and Giorgi Berezovo the first time through. No one spoke. The second time through he made Pa Cha, the older Chinese dignitary. He pulled no stiffs, such as North Carolinian literary agents or Basque sheep brokers, because he had done so much studying so well through five years of night.

The courier and the special agent took the three photographs which Marco had chosen and left the room with them to check their classifications against information on file. Marco and Amjac were left in the room.

'You go ahead,' Marco said to Amjac. 'You must have plenty to do. I'll wait.'

'Ah, shut up,' Amjac suggested.

Marco sat down at the long polished table, unfolded *The New York Times* and was able to complete two-thirds of the crossword puzzle before the special agent and the courier returned.

'What else do you remember about these men?' the special agent asked right off, before sitting down, which caused Amjac to sit up much straighter and appear as though a dull plastic film had been peeled off his eyes. The courier slid the three photographs, face up, across the table to Marco. 'Take your time,' the special agent said.

Marco didn't need extra time. He picked up the top photo-graph, which was Gomel's. 'This one wears stainless-steel false teeth and he smells like a goat. His voice is loud and it grates. He's about five feet six, I'd figure. Heavy. He wears civilian clothes but his staff is uniformed, ranging from a full colonel to a first lieutenant. They wear political markings.' Marco picked up the shot of the Chinese civilian, Pa Cha. 'This one has a comical, high-pitched giggle and killer's eyes. He had the authority. Made no attempt to conceal his distaste and contempt for the Russians. They deferred to him.' He picked up Berezovo's picture, a shot that had been taken while the man was in silk pyjamas with a glass in his hand and a big, silly grin across his face. 'This is the lieutenant general. The staff he carried was in civilian clothes and one of the staff was a woman.' Marco grinned. 'They looked like FBI men. He speaks with a bilateral emission lisp and has a very high colour like—uh—like Mr Amjac here.'

A new man came into the room with a note for the special agent who read it and said, 'Your friend Mr Melvin has been co-operating with us in Wainwright, Alaska. He's made one of these men, Mikhail Gomel, who is a member of the Central Committee.' Marco beamed at Amjac over this development, but Amjac wouldn't look at him.

'Can you return to Washington today, Colonel? We'll have a crew of specialists waiting for you.'

'Any time you say, sir. I'm on indefinite leave. But the rank is major.'

'You have been a full colonel since sunrise this morning. They just told me on the phone from Washington.'

'No!' Marco yelled. He leaped to his feet and gripped the table and kept shouting, 'No, no, no!' He pounded and pounded on the shining table with rage and frustration. 'That filthy, filthy, filthy son-of-a-bitch. He'll pay us for this! He'll pay us some-day for this! No, no, no!'

Potentially, Marco might have been a hysteroid personality.

*　　*　　*

Colonel Marco worked with the Federal Bureau of Investigation and his own unit of Army Intelligence (into which he had been honourably and instantly reinstated upon the recommendation of the FBI's director and the Plans Board of the Central Intelligence Agency). There was no longer any question of a need for a court martial to institute a full investigation. A full unit was set up, with headquarters in New York and conference space at the Pentagon, and unaccountable funds from the White House were provided to maintain housing, laboratories, and personnel, including three psychiatrists, the country's leading Pavlovian practitioner, six espionage technicians (including three librarians), a mnemonicist, an Orientalist, and an expert on Soviet internal affairs. The rest were cops and assistant cops.

Marco was in charge. His aide, assistant, and constant companion was Louis Amjac. The other side-kick was a round type, with the nerves of a Chicago bellhop, named Jim Lehner. He was there representing the CIA. They worked out of a capacious, many chambered house in the Turtle Bay district of New York, right through the summer of 1959 but they did not get one step further than the alarming conclusions which had been reached originally by Marco. It is questionable whether any definitive conclusions beyond those reached could have been attained if Marco had been able to allow himself to tell the part of his dreams having to do with Raymond's murders, but he could see no connection, he didn't think the time had come, he couldn't keep the thought in his mind, and so on and on into many splinters of reasons why he did not divulge the information. Thousands of man-hours were put in on the project and as time went on the pressure from exalted sources grew and grew. A three-platoon system of surveillance was put around Raymond. The total cost of the project with the doctrinaire romantics in the service classified as Operation Enigma has been estimated at, or in excess of, $634,217 and some change, for travel, salaries, equipment, lease, and leasehold improvements, maintenance and miscellaneous expense—and not a quarter of it was stolen beyond a few hundred rolls of Tri-X and Hydropan film, but even accountants don't recognise such losses because all photographers everywhere are helpless about film stocks to the point where it is not even considered stealing but is called testing.

The Army flew Alan Melvin, the former corporal turned civilian plumber, from Alaska to the Walter Reed Hospital in Washington, then to the house in Turtle Bay in New York, but the interviews with him revealed no more than what had been gleaned from Marco. However, the call to Operation Enigma seemed to have come in time to have saved Melvin's sanity—even his life. The nightmares had caused a weight loss of seventy-one pounds. He weighed one hundred and three pounds when picked up at Wainwright. He could not be moved for seventeen days, while he received high-caloric feeding, but by that time he had talked to Marco. When he learned that what he had dreamed had reached such a point of credibility that it had become one more terrible anxiety for the President of the United States, it seemed as though all dread was removed instantly, enabling Melvin to sleep and eat, dissolving the concretion of his fears.

Upon his restoration to active duty Colonel Marco requested, and was granted, an informal meeting with representative officers of the Board. They explained that it would not be possible for Colonel Marco to refuse advancement to the rank he held but that it was to his great credit that he felt so strongly about the matter. They explained that such an action could disturb legislative relationships in the present climate, so extraordinary that it had to be considered the far, far better part of valor for government establishments to run with the tide. Colonel Marco asked that he be permitted to register his vociferous distaste for Senator Iselin and be allowed to demonstrate that he rejected any and all implied sponsorship of himself by such an infamous source; he wished the condition to be viewed by the Board as being and having been untenable to him as well as having been unsolicited by him and undesirable in every and any way. He added other stern officialese. He asked that he be allowed to express, in an official manner, his innermost fears that this promotion to the rank of full colonel would inconsiderately prejudice the future against his favour for an optimum Army career.

The Board explained to him, informally and in a most friendly manner, that whereas it was true that it would be necessary that his personnel file forever retain Senator Iselin's stain to explain Colonel Marco's—uh—unusual—uh—advancement, the Chairman of the Joint Chiefs, with his own hand, had appended an explanation of the attendant circumstances, absolving the colonel of any threat of shadow.

All in all, because he was human to extreme dimension, Marco secretly felt he had done pretty well out of the Iselin brush, which in no way forgave Iselin or diminished Colonel Marco's prayers for vengeance. The single negative factor connected with the mess had been the death of General Jorgenson, but that was another matter entirely and one not pertinent to his promotion. Some day, he thought fervently, he would like to see the notation made by the Chairman of the Joint Chiefs upon the personnel file of General Jorgenson before it was permitted to pass into Army history. As a soldier, Colonel Marco knew that the general's death had been a hero's death, in the sense that a Hindu priest would believe deeply in the right of a widow to burn herself upon her husband's funeral pyre, becoming a saint and joining Sati. So saved are all those who enable themselves to believe, and therefore was the military mind called a juvenile mind. It was constant; it observed a code of honour in a world where any element of devotion to a rationale summoned scorn; but the world itself knew itself was sick. -

Colonel Marco puzzled his past nightmares and decided they could make him a full general yet.

While Raymond toured Europe with his mother, Marco toured the United States with Amjac and Lehner and completed a formal canvass of the survivors of the patrol. This yielded nothing. Nightly, in the manner of a lonely drummer distracted by the boredom of the road, Marco telephoned his girl whom he had not yet had either the time or the opportunity to marry.

She comforted him. The three men moved through seven cities from La Jolla, California, to Bayshore, Long Island. Marco and Melvin had been the only two men on the patrol who had ever dreamed of it.

XVI

Mrs John Iselin's tour of Europe in the summer of 1959 with her son developed into the most shocking string of occasions, as redolent of that decade as a string of garlic pearls. Mrs Iselin achieved more for sustained anti-Americanism and drove infected wedges more deeply between America and her allies than any other action by any individual or agency, excepting her husband, of the twentieth century.

It would seem that wherever Mrs Iselin set down with her personable, strangely expressed son, she gave a different account of why she was travelling. In Paris, she was looking for inefficiency in United States Government offices overseas. In Bonn, she said she was looking for subversives in United States Government offices overseas. In Munich, she said she was looking, actually, for both, because 'any concept of efficiency in government must include complete political responsibility. If anyone should favour the Communists, then he cannot be efficient,' Mrs Iselin explained to the German (and world) press.

Mrs Iselin's only brother was, at the time of her visit to Rome in late July, the American ambassador to Italy. He extended an invitation to his sister and his nephew to stay with him and his family, which Mrs Iselin accepted via the Associated Press. 'My brother is so dear to me,' she said for publication in many languages, 'and I do so ache to see him again after a long separation, listen to his wisdom, and rejoice in his embrace. Pressure of work for our country has kept us apart too long. We are out of touch.' It was not told that what had put them in direct touch again was a specific coded order from the Secretary of State ordering his ambassador to invite his sister to be his house guest.

Mrs Iselin moved out of the ambassador's residence to the Grand Hotel on the afternoon of the second day she had been her brother's guest and immediately called a press conference to explain her action, saying, according to the transcript which was printed in full in *The New York Times* for July 29, 1959, 'In every sense of that melodramatic word I am standing before you as a torn woman. I love my brother but I must love my country more. My loyalty as a sister of a beloved brother must be moved to serve a greater loyalty to the unborn of the West. My brother's embassy is wholly directed by American Communists under direct manipulation by the Kremlin, and I pray before you today that this is a result of my brother's ineptness and ignorance and not of his villainy.'

After the press had left, Raymond languidly asked his mother what in the world had ever possessed her to do such an unbelievably malicious thing. 'Raymond, dear,' his mother said, 'in this life one can turn the other cheek in a Christian manner only so many times. A long, long time ago I told that brother of mine that I would see him nailed to the floor and today he knows that I kidded him not. I kidded him not, Raymond, dear.'

Mrs Iselin's brother resigned at once as ambassador to Italy and his resignation was at once accepted by the State Department and refused by the White House because Foster had not cleared through Jim or Jim had not cleared through Foster. For thirty-six hours thereafter the matter remained in this exquisite state of balance until, on return from the greenest kind of rolling countryside in Georgia, the President's will prevailed and the ambassadorship of Raymond's mother's brother was restored, the wisdom of the President's decision being based upon the choleric rages into which the mention of Johnny Iselin's name could throw him.

As his wife succeeded with such consistency in gaining so much space in the press of the world, Senator Iselin found it necessary to issue his own directive as to his wife's mission in Europe, from Washington. In close-up on television during his formal investigation of atheism in the Department of Agriculture he said to the millions of devoted viewers throughout the country, 'My wife, a brilliant woman, an American who has suffered deeply before this, long before this, in the name of her great and abiding patriotism, was sent abroad as unofficial emissary of the United States Senate to bring back a report on the amount of money that this Administration has spent to further the cause of communism in the Western World. It is my holy hope that this will answer the question of certain elements in this country for once and for all with regard to this matter.'

Alas, the statement did not settle the matter for once and for all, as the President insisted that his Minority Leader in the Senate make a policy answer to settle Senator Iselin's statement for once and for all. The President, being of the Executive Branch, overlooked the fact that the Minority Leader was first a member of the Senate, an establishment which has always taken a dim view of any directives from the Executive.

The Minority Leader's text was a model of political compromise. As Senate spokesman the leader denied, in a sense, that Mrs Iselin was an 'official' emissary of the United States Senate although he conceded that the Senate would indeed feel honoured to think of her as its 'unofficial' emissary at any time. 'Mrs Iselin is a beautiful and gracious lady,' this courtly gentleman said, deeply pleased that the White House was so discomfited, 'a delightful woman whose charm and grace are only exceeded by her outstanding intelligence, but I do not feel that either she or her distinguished husband would want it said that anyone not actually elected by the great people of the states of the United States to the sacred trust of the United States Senate could be said to represent that body. Say, rather, that Mrs Iselin represents America wherever she may be.' (Applause.) The gentleman received a written citation from the Daughters of the American

Struggles for Liberty for his gallantry to American woman-hood.

Citations from the presses of Europe, mainly those of a conservative stripe, took a different tack. In Stockholm, *Dagens Nyheter*, Sweden's largest and most influential daily wrote: 'What the wife of Senator John Iselin possibly might have discovered, she has already spoiled by foolishness and arrogance. She has introduced anti-American feeling far more effective than any that could possibly have been initiated by the Committee and their paid agents. The unanimous opinion of Europe is that Iselin symbolises exactly the reverse of what America stands for and what we have learned to appreciate. Iselinism is the arch-enemy of liberty and a disgrace to the name of America.'

Throughout the tour, until its closing days in England, Raymond had not so much as acknowledged the existence of his mother or his stepfather in the newspaper column that he wrote daily and transmitted by cable as he covered, with considerable cogency, a startlingly intimate view of the European political scene. *The Daily Press*, his employer in New York, was said to have had to resort to threats to force Raymond into writing and publishing a statement regarding his own position. This was the sheerest nonsense: the kind stimulated by the need of metro-politan people who feel that they simply must be seen as having inside information on everything. The fact of the matter was that Raymond's publisher, Charles O'Neil, was a more than ordinarily perceptive man. He telephoned Raymond at the Savoy Hotel in London and, after an exchange of information on the prevailing weather conditions in each country, a report of past weather phenomena, and a foretelling of what might be expected from the weather on either side of the Atlantic, O'Neil, who was paying for the call, broke in saying that he felt Raymond could have no conception of the extent of the publicity his mother's European tour had been producing all over the country, nor could he have any way of realising how closely he, Raymond Shaw, had been allied with Iselin's actions and purposes. He read from a few articles, shuddering at the cost of the telephone tolls. Raymond was aghast. He asked what O'Neil thought he should do. The publisher said he saw no reason why the cost of the entire call could not be charged to the syndicate—uh—he meant, rather, that he felt both the paper and Raymond should relent from their fixed position on the matter of Raymond's family being mentioned in his writings, and that Raymond should at once file at least one column of opinion on Iselinism and the present tour.

Raymond complied that day and the column was reprinted more than any other single piece the paper had ever caused to be syndicated and the toll charges for the call to London were absorbed by the syndicate without the slightest demurral. The column read, in part: 'I have known John Yerkes Iselin to be an assassin and a blackguard since my boyhood. He lives by attacking. He is the cowardly assassin in politics who strikes from the dark and evil alley of his opportunism. With no exceptions, the justifications for these attacks have been so flimsy as to have no standing either in courts of law or in the minds of individuals capable of differentiating repeated accusation from even a reasonable presumption of guilt. The ultimate result is a threat to national security. Iselin is laying a foundation for the agencies of American government to serve totalitarian ends rather than the Government of the United States as we have hitherto known it.'

Raymond insisted upon reading the dispatch to his mother before he sent it off. He read it in a monotone with a stony face, fearful of the response it would bring. 'Oh, for crissake, Raymond,' his mother said, 'what do you suppose I'm going to do— sue you? I know you aren't asking me, but send the silly thing. Who the hell reads beyond the headlines anyway?' She waved him away contemptuously. 'Please! Go cable your copy. I'm busy.'

Raymond was unaware of being in an anomalous position in London after his column on Johnny and his mother appeared in the States. It was reprinted in the English newspapers at once. Writing of his mother's part in what he termed their 'conspiracy of contempt for man,' Raymond had described her as 'a caricature of the valiant pioneer women of America who loaded the guns while their husbands fought off the encircling savages' in that he saw his mother and Johnny as the savages and 'if a nation's blood is its honour and its dignity before the world, then that blood covered their hands.' This appeared to be in direct opposition to basic policies of some British newspapers that had made a pretty pound indeed out of that steely treacle of Home and Mother, so that at least a portion of the press that attended Raymond's mother's farewell conference at the Savoy Hotel viewed Raymond not at all enthusiastically. Had they been able to measure how Raymond viewed them, as he viewed all the world, the shooting would have started, straight off. On the other hand, another section of the British press so detested Senator and Mrs Iselin that it quite approved of Raymond's attack upon his mother, although it would not, of course, ever permit itself to print that view.

Both sides had the opportunity to air their views, however indirectly. Before she left London Mrs Iselin told the reporters who had assembled in a large room named after a production of Richard D'Oyly Carte that she would urge her husband's Senate committee to investigate the Labour Party of Great Britain, as she had assembled documentary proof that it was a nest of Socialists and crypto-Communists and that this political party could, if returned to power, 'smash the alliance upon which the friendship of our two great nations has been based and, under the guise of honest difference of opinion, sabotage the great American purpose before the world.' It was as though the great glacier had slid down from the top of the world and enveloped the hotel. Sixty men and women stood staring at her, their chins resting comfortably on their chests, mouths wide open, eyes glazed. One gentleman of Fleet Street threw his full glass of whisky and water backward over his head in a high arc to crash in the corner of the large room rather than drink it, which is criticism indeed from a newspaperman of any country. He said, 'Madame, my name is Joseph Pole of the *Daily Advocate-Journal*. I repudiate you, your husband, and your most peculiar son.' He turned to a lady journalist on his left and took the highball from her hand. 'May I?' he asked. Then he threw the contents of the drink into Mrs Iselin's ankles.

Raymond knocked him right through the throng. At this juncture, that portion of the journalistic group which had objected to Raymond in the first place for having attacked the profitable institution of Motherhood in his column, took this chance to strike out at him, while the group which had secretly approved Raymond's utter public rejection of his mother now saw their chance to have at her themselves, and were led forward by female colleagues brandishing raised umbrellas. The result was a melée. Mrs Iselin swung chairs, water carafes, and broken whisky bottles, doing most painful damage but emerging physically unharmed. Raymond lay about him with his extraordinary strength and his natural antipathy. The news photographers present very nearly swooned with ecstasy over the turn taken, for, from every British newspaper-reader's point of view, here was Iselinism in action with British righteousness whacking it over the head.

Beginning with the very next editions the British press indulged in its own sort of good-natured London journalists' fun, which could be described by the subject of their reporting as being an experience not unlike falling nude into a morass of itching powder while two sadistic dentists drilled into one's teeth at the instant of apogee of alcoholic history's most profligate hangover. The ultimate end of all of these combative news stories was that when Mrs Iselin and her son needed to journey to Southampton to embark for home, some one hundred and fifteen London policemen, whom the world knows affectionately as 'bobbies' after their founder, Sir Robert Peel, needed to bludgeon a path through the howling mass of outraged citizenry to get them out of their hotel, following which a semi-military motor escort was formed to race them to the ship. The entire incident was a stiff test of Anglo-American relations, beyond a doubt, and somewhat scored John Iselin's own lack of popular favour in the British Isles.

While Raymond had been in Paris, in late June, a member of the French Chamber of Deputies who was co-leader of the political party having the record of greatest resistance to the government then in power, was assassinated in his *hôtel particulier* on Rue Louis David in the sixteenth *arrondissement*, baffling police and security agencies.

While Raymond was in London, on the evening before his mother's famous debate with the British press, a peer who was greatly admired for having articulated a liberal, humanistic, and forward-looking life as publisher of a chain of national newspapers and periodicals, Lord Croftnal, was murdered while he slept. There was not a clue as to the identity or motivation of his killer.

XVII

Raymond's ship docked in New York on a Wednesday in late August, 1959. He reported for work at *The Daily Press* early Thursday morning. Marco called him and made a date to meet him at four o'clock in Hungarian Charlie's, the saloon across the street from the paper, saying he would be bringing two of his side-kicks with him if Raymond wouldn't mind. Raymond didn't mind.

The four men sat at a table far in the rear of the saloon, which was a solid, practical saloon set up to sell a maximum amount of booze and, with careful attention to unsanitary seeming *décor*— a little dirt here, a little grease there—a minimum amount of food, which, after all, has a tendency to spoil after a week or so and can be a loss. The air was nearly gelid from the huge air-conditioning unit that looked big enough to chill an automobile assembly plant. A giant juke box, manufactured by The Giant Juke Box Company of Arcana, Illinois, was belting everything living right over the head with a loudly lovable old standard out of Memphis, Tennessee, in which the rhyme of the proper name Betty Lou and the plural noun *shoes* were repeated, in a Kalli-kakian couplet, over and over again. A giant juke box is constructed to make a sound like two full-sized, decibel-pregnant juke boxes going at top volume at the same time, but two separate juke boxes each playing a different tune, each in a different tempo, and, if possible, in a different language. The joint was noisy from opening to closing because Hungarian Charlie liked noise and was, in every vocal manner, very much like a giant juke box himself.

After minimum hand-shaking and ordering a highball for Amjac and Lehner and beers for Raymond and himself, Marco went right to business by asking Raymond to tell his version of the battle action, which Raymond did forthwith and in detail, utilising only the future tense in verb forms. Lehner carried the tape recorder in a shoulder sling.

'You sound as though you got those nightmares straightened out. In fact, you look it,' Raymond said warily, not sure whether it was proper to talk about such things in front of these house-detective types. Marco looked great. He had gained the weight back.

'All over.'

'Did you—was it—did that thing we were talking about help any?'

'The court martial?'

'Yeah.'

'The way it worked out, it wasn't necessary but I still have you and only you to thank for losing those nightmares. We got a different kind of an investigation started, just the way you said it had to be, and the nightmares were gone. Forever. I hope.'

'Did you investigate the medal?'

'Sure. What else?'

'Any progress?'

'Slow, but good.'

'Is it working out the way we thought?'

'Yeah. Right down the line.'

'The medal is a phony?'

'It certainly looks that way.'

'I knew it. I *knew* it.' Raymond looked from Amjac to Lehner, shaking his head in awed disbelief. 'How about that?' he asked with mystification. 'Will you tell me why a lot of Communist brass would want to steal a Medal of Honour for a complete stranger?'

Amjac didn't answer. He seemed embarrassed about something. Raymond became aware of his silence and stared at him coldly. 'It was a rhetorical question,' he said haughtily.

Amjac coughed. He said, 'It scares hell out of us, if you want the truth, Mr Shaw. We have run out of ideas and we don't know where else to look, if that gives you some idea.' Raymond swung his gaze to Lehner, who had a head like a gourd, a small moustache, and eyes like watermelon seeds, and Lehner stared him down.

'Have you talked to Al Melvin?' Raymond said. The voice of a sick child whined out of the giant juke box behind them as though trying to escape the hateful noises behind it. 'You know, Ben, Al. In Alaska.'

'Yes, sir. We have,' Amjac said grimly.

Marco said, 'Raymond, there is no known area of this case which we haven't covered in many ways. We've talked to every member of the patrol. We've travelled maybe ninety-two hundred miles around the country. We're sure Chunjin is here as an enemy agent, assigned to you as a body guard and assassin, if necessary. I have a unit in New York and Washington which does nothing but concentrate on this problem. There are seventeen of us, all told. Mr Amjac is on loan from the FBI and Mr Lehner is with us as an expert from Central Intelligence.

Working on that riddle of why the enemy should go to enormous trouble to secure the Medal of Honour for you is all I do, day and night. It's all Amjac and Lehner do. It's all the seventeen of us do, and the White House wants to know what happened in a report every week and a copy of that report goes to the Joint Chiefs. And you want to hear something off-beat, Raymond? I mean something that will throw this out of context for a moment to let you see what a unique person you have become? A copy of the report goes to the Prime Ministers of Britain and Canada and to the President of Mexico.'

'But what the hell for?' Raymond seemed outraged at this invasion, as though he were being shared by four heads of government. 'What the hell do the Mexicans and the bloody British, who tried to kill my mother, incidentally, have to do with that lousy medal?'

Lehner tapped Raymond on the forearm. Raymond looked at him, drawing his arm away. 'Why don't you listen?' Lehner said. 'If you talk you can't learn anything.'

'Don't touch me again' Raymond said. 'If you want to remain here with us, doing your clerk's tasks and waiting for your pension, do not touch me again.' He looked at Marco. 'Continue, Ben,' he said equably.

'It is our considered opinion,' Marco said, 'that we are moving into the area of action which will reveal why they wanted you to have the Medal of Honour. The patrol happened in 1951. Chunjin didn't arrive to take up his duties until '59. Eight years' lapse. Whatever is going to happen is going to happen soon. You're a marked man, Raymond. They've marked you and they guard you. We've marked you. Am I frightening you, Raymond?'

'*Me?*' Nothing frightened Raymond. A man needs to have something to lose to become frightened. Even only one thing that is his and that he values will make it possible for threat to scare a man, but Raymond had nothing.

'That's what I explained to our unit. And that's what our psychiatrists had projected on you, that attitude, that—that fearlessness, you know?—but I have to frighten you, Raymond, because we need you to think of yourself as some kind of time bomb with a fuse eight years long. You walk bare-footed on the edge of a razor. Only you will know when the change comes, when the mission is divulged, when your move is to be made, and it can only end one way. Your country, my country, this country will have to be in danger from you and you will be expected to do exactly as you have been told or will be told. They got inside your mind. They did. I swear before God.'

'Aaaah!' Raymond disliked this kind of talk. It sickened him. What kind of a world of fondlers had this become? Why did Marco have to say that those thick-necked pigs were *inside* his mind?

'I told you that we talked to every member of the patrol this summer. You know what they said about you, every one of them? That you were the greatest, warmest, most wonderful single guy they had ever met. They remembered you with love and affection, Raymond. Isn't that funny?'

'Funny? It's ludicrous.'

'How do you account for it?'

Raymond shrugged and grimaced. 'I saved their lives. I mean, they thought I had saved their lives. I suppose the poor slobs were grateful.'

'I don't think so. I've had to work all this out with our psychiatrists because I don't have a very objective view, either, but my actual memory is that there was a broad chasm between you and those men before the patrol. They didn't hate you, they seemed rather to fear your scorn, you know? You had a way of freezing their dislike and keeping them uneasy and off balance. The psychiatrists will tell you that an attitude, a group attitude as well as individual attitudes like that, can't be changed into warm and eager interest, into such admiration and deep respect merely because of gratitude. No, no, no.'

'Life isn't a popularity contest,' Raymond said. 'I didn't ask them to like me.'

'I'm going to start to prove right now that they have got

inside your mind, Raymond, because you once told me, in a joking way, that you had come out of the Army with much more of an active interest in women than when you went in—and because I have to frighten you, I will have to embarrass you, too. We checked. We are experts. Experts' experts, even. We went back over the seams of your life, looking for lint. You were twenty-two, going on twenty-three years old, when you left the Army, and you had never been laid. More than that. You had never even kissed a girl, had you, Raymond?' Marco leaned across the table, his eyes lambent with affection, and he said softly, 'You never even kissed Jocie, did you, Raymond?'

'You had men talk to Jocie? In Argentina?' Raymond wasn't outraged. Long before, he had set all his dials so that Marco could do no wrong with him, but he was extremely impressed and for the first time. He felt elated to be in connection with anyone who had looked at Jocie, had sat beside her and had spoken to her about anything at all, and to have spoken to her about him, about that wondrous summer together and about—about kissing. He felt as though his eyes had climbed into the upper space above the earth and that he could see himself as he sat in Hungarian Charlie's and at the same time watch sweet, sweet Jocie as she sat in a bower, under pink roses, knitting something soft and warm, in the Argentine.

'I had to know. And I had to make you understand that going ten thousand miles and back for the answer to one question is very little to do in the face of the pressure and the threat that is implied.'

'But, Ben—Jocie—well, after all, Jocie——'

'That's why I brought these two strangers. The only reason. Do you think I would talk about such things—things which I know are sacred to you when I also know that nothing else in this whole world is sacred to you—in front of two strangers if I wasn't desperate to get through to you?' Raymond did not answer; he was thinking about Jocie, the Jocie he had lost and would never find again.

'They are inside your mind. Deep. Now. For eight years. One

of their guys with a big sense of humour thought it would be a great gag to throw you a bone for all of the trouble they were going to put you to, and fix it up inside your head so that, all of a sudden, you'd get interested in girls, see? It meant nothing to them. It was only a gratuitous gesture, a quarter tip to the men's-room attendant, considering all the other things they were going to do inside your head and have already done from inside your head.'

'Stop it! Stop it, goddamit, Ben. I will not listen to this. You nauseate me. Stop saying that people and things and a lot of outside filth are inside my head. Just say it some other way if you have to talk to me. Just say it some other way, and what the hell are you talking about—what they have already done from inside my head?'

'Don't shout,' Lehner said. 'Take it easy.' However, he did not touch Raymond this time.

The giant juke box had found a giant guitar. It was being strummed insanely, alternating between two of the most simply constructed chords while a farmer's voice bellowed cretinous rhymes above it.

Marco stared at Raymond compassionately and held his gaze for a long moment before he said, 'You murdered Mavole and Bobby Lembeck, kid.'

'What? Whaaaat?' Raymond pushed at the table but his back was against the wall, literally as well as figuratively, so that he could not move backward to escape the words. His glaucous eyes in the long, bony face held some of the terror seen in the eyes of a horse falling on ice. He was incredulous but Marco and Amjac and Lehner knew that Marco was getting through because they knew Raymond the way a marine knows his own rifle, because they had been drilled on Raymond, his reactions and inhibitions, for hours of day and hours of night.

'You killed them. Not your fault. They just used your body the way they would use any other machine. You strangled Mavole and you shot Bobby.'

'In the dream?'

'Yes.'

Raymond was unutterably relieved. He had been greatly startled but at last things had been returned to reality. These men with Marco were captives of their belief in that unfortunate man's delusion which had almost cost him his sanity late the year before. Everything fell into place for Raymond as he understood the motivation of all of this fantasy. Ben was his friend and Raymond would not let him down. He would go right along as he was supposed to, becoming agitated now and then if necessary, because Ben looked as though he had regained his health and his ability to sleep and Raymond would have fought off an army to preserve that.

'The dream happened again and again in my sleep because it had happened so indelibly in my life. I have to frighten you, Raymond. If you can live in continuous fear perhaps we can force you to see what we aren't able to discover. Whenever it happens—this thing that has been set to happen—we have to find some way to reach you, to give you new reflexes so that you will do whatever we will tell you to do—even kill yourself if that has to be—the instant that you know what it is they have built you to do. They made you into a killer. They are inside your mind now, Raymond, and you are helpless. You are a host body and they are feeding on you, but because of the way we live we can't execute you or lock you up to stop you.'

Raymond did not need to simulate alarm. Every time Marco told him of the invasion of his person by those people it made him wince, and to think of himself as a host body on which they were feeding almost made him cry out or stand up and run out of the saloon. His voice became different. It was not the flat, undeigning drawl. It was a voice he might have borrowed from an Errol Flynn movie in which the actor faced immolation with hopeless resigned gallantry. It was a new voice for him, one he created specifically to help his friend through the maze of his fantasy, and it was most convincing. 'What do you want?' the hoarsened new voice said.

Marco's voice attacked. It moved like a starving rodent which gnaws at flaws behind the doors, mad to get through to an unknown trove of crazing scent on the other side.

'Will you submit voluntarily to a brain-washing?' that voice asked.

'Yes,' Raymond answered.

The giant juke box spat the sounds out as though trying to break the rows upon rows of shining bottles behind the bar.

Friday morning, just before noon, a psychiatric and bio-chemical task force began to work Raymond over on the fourth floor of the large house in the Turtle Bay district. The total effort exhausted and frustrated both the scientists and the policemen. The effect of the narcotics, techniques, and suggestions, which resulted in deep hypnosis for Raymond, achieved a result that approximated the impact an entire twenty-five-cent jar of F. W. Woolworth vanishing cream might have on vanishing an aircraft carrier of the *Forrestal* class when rubbed into the armour plate. They were unable to dredge up one mote of information. Under the deep hypnosis, loaded to the eyes with a cocktail of truth serums, Raymond demonstrated that he could not remember his name, his colour, his sex, his age, or his existence. Before he had been put under he had been willing to divulge anything within his power. In catalepsy, his mind seemed to have been sealed off as an atomic reactor is separated from the rest of a submarine. It all served to confirm what they already knew. Raymond had been brain-washed by a master of exalted skill. The valiant, long-cherished hope that they would be able to counterplant suggestion within Raymond's already dominated unconscious mind never had a chance of being put into work.

When it was over, the medical staff wanted to tell Raymond that the explorations had been entirely successful, on the grounds that he was able to accept suggestion with his conscious mind, but Marco overruled that. He said he would tell Raymond that he was beyond their reach, that he was going to be directed entirely by the enemy, that they could not help him but that they had to stop him and that they would stop him. Marco wanted Raymond to stay scared, as much as he disbelieved that Raymond could sustain any feeling.

After that first afternoon when Marco had poured it on him in Hungarian Charlie's, Raymond had dug in to what he was determined to maintain as a fixed position. He was a lucid man. He knew he was in excellent health, mental and physical. He knew Marco's health was a long way from what it had once been. He knew it was Marco who had been having the nightmares and breakdowns and that for unknown reasons, probably relative to the phrase 'the Army takes care of its own,' his commanders had decided to humour Marco. Well, Raymond decided, I will outhumour and outbless them. Marco is closer to me than any one or all of those uniformed clots. Raymond accordingly formed his policy. It deployed his imagination like the feelers of an insect, advancing it ahead of him wherever his mind, which moved on thousands of tiny feelers of prejudice took him in its circuitous detour that would allow him to avoid exposing himself to himself as a murderer a sexual neutral, and a man despised and scorned by his comrades. He put his back into the performance. He used all the tricks of the counterfeiter's art he could summon to project all of the surface emotions which their little playlets seemed to require of him. He bent, or seemed to bend, into their intentions to halt what he saw as a comic-book plot in which a sinister foreign power, out to destroy America, would achieve its ends by using him as an instrument. They wanted him to be scared. He would seem, when under observation, to be scared, and he worked hard for an effect of seeming as distressed and as aware as game running ahead of guns.

Fortunately, he remembered that the vegetable substitute for benzedrine, which he had taken at one time to lose weight, always gave him hand tremors, so that helped. He knew that a double dose or more of it could produce an authentic crying jag in him, with uncontrollable tears and generally distraught conduct, so that helped.

Marco's surveillance teams duly reported his purchases of this drug and the unit's psychological specialists confirmed the side-effects they would produce, so Marco was not deceived by Raymond's somewhat piteous conduct from time to time. He was very proud of Raymond, however, because he could see that Raymond was going to intolerable trouble, for Raymond, to meet Marco's urgent requirements, but the discouraging and depressing fact remained that all of them were armless in their attempt to stave off shapeless disaster.

However, there was one relentless, inexorable strength on Marco's side: in combination or singly, the Federal Bureau of Investigation, Army Intelligence, and the Central Intelligence Agency represented maximum police efficiency. Such efficiency suspends the law of averages and flattens defeat with patience.

XVIII

Eugénie Rose was in Boston with Justin's new musical show, which, secretly, had been based upon a map of the heavens issued by the National Geographic Society two years before. Marco planned to join her the next day. She and Marco talked on the telephone at odd hours. They were still dedicated to an early marriage and seemed more than ever convinced that, in a world apparently so populated, no one else existed.

It was Christmas Eve. Raymond had invited Marco for dinner, telephoning him from the office to say that he had given Chunjin the night off and that Chunjin had resisted. Marco said that was because Chunjin was undoubtedly a Buddhist and not a celebrant at Christmas. Raymond said he was sure Chunjin was not a Buddhist because he left books by Mary Baker Eddy around the pantry and kitchen and was forever smiling. Marco said he felt a sense of disappointment at that news because he had figured that if he sent Chunjin a Christmas card, Chunjin would then be obliged to send him a card on Buddha's birthday, or lose face.

Marco arrived at Raymond's apartment at seven o'clock and brought two bottles of cold champagne with him. Unfortunately for the hangovers the following day, Raymond had also put two quarts of champagne in the refrigerator. They decided they would sidle towards food a little later and settled down in Raymond's office behind the big window, and with commendable seasonal co-operation it began to snow large goose feathers, a present from the Birthday Boy himself, in lieu of peace on earth.

After two goblets of the golden bubbles, Raymond reached under his chair and, stiffly, handed Marco a large, gift-wrapped package.

'Merry Christmas,' he said. 'It has been good to know you.' Raymond, saying those words, sounded more touching than anyone else who could have said them because, while Raymond had been marooned in time and on earth and in all the pit-black darkness of interstellar space, Marco was the only other being, except Jocie, who had acknowledged he was there.

Marco ripped away the elegant gold and blue paper, revealing the three volumes of Fuller's *A Military History of the Western World* re-bound in limp morocco leather. Marco held on to the books with one hand and pounded the embarrassed, grinning Raymond with the other. Then he put the books upon the desk and reached into his pocket. 'And a merry, merry Christmas to you, too, young man,' he sang out, handing Raymond a long flat envelope. Raymond started to open the envelope, slowly and with wonderment.

'Wait, wait!' Marco said. He hurried to the record-player, shuffled through some albums, and slid out a twelve-inch record of Christmas carols. The machine conferred silvered voices upon them singing 'We Three Kings of Orient Are.'

'O.K., proceed,' Marco said.

Raymond opened the envelope and found a gift certificate in the amount of fifty dollars to be drawn on *Les Pyramides* of middle Broadway, the Gitlitz Delicatessen. The frosty carol

swelled around them as Raymond smiled his always touching
smile at the gift in his hands.

> 'We three kings of Orient are,
> Bearing gifts we traverse afar,
> Field and fountain, moor and mountain,
> Following yonder star.
> O, Star of wonder, star of night,
> Star with royal beauty bright,
> Westward leading, still proceeding,
> Guide us to the perfect light.'

Marco thought of their own three kings of Orient: Gomel,
Berezovo and that old, old Chinese who had handed Raymond
the gun to kill Bobby Lembeck. Raymond said, 'What a wonderful present. I mean, who else in the world but you could even
think of such a wonderful present? This—well—well, it's simply
great, that's what it is.' They sat down again, fulfilled by giving.
They watched the snow, listened to the *Mannergesangsverein*,
finished the first bottle of wine, and overflowed with Christmas
spirit. Raymond was opening the second bottle when he said,
steadily, 'Jocie's husband died.'

'Yeah?' Marco sat straight up. 'When?'

'Last week.'

'How'd you find out?'

'Mother told me. She had told the embassy to keep an eye on
Jocie. They told her.'

'What are you going to do?'

'I saw Senator Jordan. We're pretty good friends. At first it
was hard because Mother had told him I was a pervert and that
they would have to save Jocie from me, but, in a way, he had to
see me because he's in politics and I'm a newspaperman. After
a while, when we reached an understanding about what a
monster my mother is, we were able to get to be pretty good
friends. I asked him if I could help in any way. The paper has an
office there. He said no. He said the best thing I could do would
be to wait and give Jocie a chance to recover; then, if she doesn't

start for home in six months, say, he thinks maybe I should go down there and get her. At least go down there and ask her. You know.'

'I take it your mother isn't against Jocie any more.'

'No.'

'Some switch.'

'Try not to laugh and so will I, but that is exactly the case. Some switch. Jocie's father has become very big in his party, particularly in the Senate. Mother saw it coming before anyone else and she's done everything she can to be fast friends with him, but he isn't having any, so I guess she decided if she couldn't get him on their side positively she could cancel him out by marrying me off to his daughter, little knowing that I incite Senator Jordan against her and Johnny more than any other one agency excepting their own lovable personalities.'

'What a doll. If she were my wife, I'd probably be General-issimo Trujillo by now. At least.'

'At least.'

'So she thinks it might be a good idea for you and Jocie to get married?'

'That is the general feeling I am allowed to get.'

'How did Jocie's husband die?'

'That is a good morbid question. It just so happens he was struck down by an unknown hand in a flash riot in a town called Tucuman. He was an agronomist.'

'What has that got to do with it?'

'Well, I guess that's how he happened not to be in Buenos Aires with Jocie.'

'Have you written to her?'

Raymond looked out of the window, at the snow and the night, and shook his head.

'If you think I can, I'd like to help you with the letter.'

'You'll have to help me,' Raymond said, simply. 'I can't do it. I can't even get started. I want to write her and tell her things but I have those eight years choking me.'

'It's all a matter of tone, not so much words,' Marco explained, not having the faintest idea of what he was talking about but knowing he was light-years ahead of Raymond in knowledge of human communication. 'Sure, wait. If that feels right. But no six months. I think we should get a letter off fairly soon. You know, a letter of condolence. That would be a natural ice-breaker, then after that we'll slide into the big letter. But don't wait too long. You'll have to get it over with so you'll both know for once and for all.'

'Know what?'

'Whether—well, she should know that you want her and—you have to know whether she wants you.'

'She has to. What would I do if she didn't?'

'You've been managing to get along.'

'No. No, it won't do, Ben. That is not enough. I may not have much coming to me but I have more coming to me than I'm getting.'

'Listen, kid. If that's the way it's going to be, then that's the way. Now take it easy and, please, figure on one step at a time.'

'Sure. I'm willing.'

'You've got to give the thing time.'

'Sure. That's what Senator Jordan said.'

Major General Francis 'Fightin' Frank' Bollinger, a long-time admirer of John 'Big John' Iselin, consented, with a great deal of pleasure, to Raymond's mother's suggestion that he head a committee of patriots called Ten Million Americans Mobilising for To-morrow. This was at a small dinner, so small that it fed only Johnny, the general, and Mrs Iselin, at the Iselin residence in Washington in January, 1960. Bollinger pledged, with all of his big heart, that on the morning of the opening of his party's Presidential nominating convention, to be held at Madison Square Garden in July, he would deliver one million signatures of one million patriots petitioning that John Yerkes Iselin be named the party's candidate for the Presidency.

General Bollinger had retired from active duty to take up the helm of the largest dog-food company the world had ever known. He had often said, in one of the infrequent jokes he made (it does not matter what the other joke was), which, by reason of the favouritism he felt for it, he repeated not infrequently: 'I'd sure as hell like to see the Commies try to match Musclepal, but if they ever did try it they'd probably call it Moscowpal. Get it?' (Laughter.) He had been a patriot, himself, for many years.

Marco's unit waited out the winter and the spring without any action or any leads. In March the FBI learned that Raymond's name appeared on the final list of possible suspects in connection with the murder of the anti-Communist deputy, François Orcel, the previous June. Later that month they also learned that Raymond's name appeared on a similar listing prepared by Scotland Yard in conjunction with the murder of Lord Croftnal. The French listing included eight names of Americans or foreigners then in the United States who could be placed anywhere near the scene of the crime. The Scotland Yard list contained three such names. Both agencies asked for routine FBI check and comment. Raymond's name was the only name to appear on both listings.

In late May Senator and Mrs Iselin took a house on Long Island, anticipating the social demands of the political convention and so that, Mrs Iselin explained, she could lend a woman's touch in preparing for the imminent homecoming of Senator Jordan's widowed daughter, Jocie, she and her father being old, old friends. She confided all of this to the society editor of *The Daily Press*, after asking Raymond to ask the society editor to call her. It remained for Raymond to read the news about Jocie's homecoming as any other reader of the newspaper might and he became savage in the fury of his resentment when he reached her on the telephone. Raymonds' mother allowed him to curse and cry out at her until she was sure he had finished. He spoke for nearly four minutes without stopping, the sound of the words like a stream of bullets, his phrasing erratic and his breathing heavy. When she was sure of his pause, she invited him to a costume ball she was staging on the very day of Jocie's return from Buenos Aires. She said she was sure that he would accept because Jocie had already accepted and that it *had* been a dog's age since he and Jocie had met. She maintained her control all during Raymond's shouted obscenities and screamed vituperation; then she hung up the instrument with such vigor that she knocked it off her desk. She was drawn forward into an even blacker rage. She picked the telephone up and ripped it out of the wall and crashed it through a glass-topped table four feet away. She picked up the shattered table and flung it through the short corridor that led to the open bathroom door, disclosing warm pink tile behind the glass shower curtain. The table splintered the glass, crashed through to the tile wall, and fell noisily in the tub.

After a sleepless, tortured night, Raymond, who had decided he must get to the office at seven o'clock the following morning to do what he had to do, finally fell asleep near dawn and slept through until eleven. He nearly knocked Chunjin down, when the man said good morning, because he had not troubled to call him when he knew that Raymond never, never, never slept later than eight o'clock in the morning.

When Raymond got to the office he locked the door behind him. Utilising the nastiest voice tone in his ample store, he told the telephone switchboard that they were not to ring his telephone no matter who called.

'Including Mr Downey, sir?'

'Yes.'

'And Mr O'Neil, sir?'

'Everyone! Anyone! Can you get that through your heads?'

'Heads, sir? I have one head, sir.'

'I'm sure,' Raymond snapped. 'Then are you able to get it through your head? No calls. Do you understand?'

'Bet on it, sir. Everything. Bet your house, your clothes.'

'Bet? Oh. One moment, there. I will revise my orders. I *will* take any calls from Buenos Aires. You probably pronounce that Bewnose Airs. I will accept calls from there.'

'Which, sir?'

'Which what?'

'Which city?'

'I don't understand.'

'Buenos Aires or Bewnose Airs, sir?'

'It's the same place!'

'Very good, sir. You will accept calls from either or both. Now, would you like to revise those orders, sir?' Raymond hung up his phone as she was speaking.

'Oh boy, oh boy, oh boy,' the operator said to the girls working on either side of her. 'Am I gonna get that one someday. I wouldn't care if I was offered four times the money on some other job which had half the hours. I would never leave this here job as long as he works here. Some day, I may be a liddul old lady sittin' at this switchboard, but some day—the day will come—an' oh, boy, oh boy, oh boy!' She was grinding her teeth as she talked.

'Who? Shaw?' the girl on her left asked.

'What's the use?' the girl on her right said. 'If you get that offer for four times the money you take it. Nobody is ever gonna be able to do anything about Shaw.'

Dear Jocie,

This is a difficult letter to get written. It is nearly an impossible letter for a weak and frightened man to write, and I have surprised myself with that sentence because I have never thought that of myself and I have never said anything less than a sufficiency about myself. I will set down at the outset that I am going to open myself up to you and that it will probably be a long, long letter so that, should it hurt you to read any such things any further, you may stop now and it will all be over. To have to love you as much as I do (as I did was what I had started to write, so that I could plot its progression and its growth over the nine empty and useless years without you) and to feel my love for you grow and grow and grow and to have no place to store this enormous harvest within the emptiness, I have found that

I must carry it ahead of me wherever I go, bundled in my arms like old clothes which no one else can use and no one wants but which have warmth in them still if someone, as bleakly cold as I have been, can be found to wear them. You will return to New York next month. I have started this letter almost thirty times but I cannot postpone writing it and mailing it for another day because if I do it may not reach you. I cannot write this letter but I must write this letter because I know that I have not got the character nor the courage, the habit of hope nor the assurance that comes from having a place in a crowded world, and I could never be able to speak to you about this long pain and bitterness which——

He stopped writing. He had smudged the paper with several genuine tears.

XIX

The first break in the long, long wait through dread, even though it was a totally incomprehensible break, came in May, 1960. It happened when Marco was late for a two o'clock date with Raymond at Hungarian Charlie's booze outlet, across the street from the flash shop.

It was a fairly well-known fact to practically anyone who did not lack batteries for his hearing aid that Hungarian Charlie was one of the more stridently loquacious publicans in that not unsilent business. Only one other boniface, who operated farther north on Fifty-first Street, had a bigger mouth. Charlie talked as though Sigmund Freud himself had given permission, nay, had urged him, to tell everyone everything that came into his head, and in bad grammar, yet. Ten minutes before Marco got to the saloon, with Raymond seated at bar centre staring at a glass of beer on a slow afternoon, Charlie had pinned a bookmaker at the entrance end of the bar, a man who would much rather have talked to his new friend, a young, dumpy blonde with a face like a bat's and the thirst of a burning oil field. Charlie was telling them, loud and strong, hearty and healthy, about his wife's repulsive elder brother who lived with them and about how he had followed Charlie all over the apartment all day Sunday telling him what to do with his life, which was a new development brought on by the fact that he had just inherited twenty-three hundred dollars from a deceased friend whom he had been engaged to marry for fourteen years, which was a generous thing for her to have done when it was seen from the perspective, Charlie said, that this bum had never given the broad so much as a box of talcum powder for Christmas, it having been his policy always to pick a fight with her immediately preceding gift-exchanging occasions.

'Lissen,' Charlie yelled, 'you inherit that kinda money and you naturally feel like you know alla answers and also it puts me in a position where I can't exactly kick him inna ankle, you know what I mean? So, wit' the new pernna view, I say tuh him, very patient, "Why don't you pass the time by playing a liddul solitaire?" '

Raymond was on a bar stool twelve feet away from Charlie and had in no way been eavesdropping on the conversation, as that could have been judged suicidal. He rapped on the bar peremptorily with a half dollar. Charlie looked up, irritated. One lousy customer in the whole lousy joint and he has to be a point killer.

'What arreddy?' Charlie inquired.

'Give me a deck of cards,' Raymond said. Charlie looked at the bookmaker, then rolled his eyes heavenward. He shrugged his shoulders like the tenor in *Tosca*, opened a drawer behind him, took out a blue bicycle deck, and slid it along the polished surface to Raymond.

Raymond took the deck from its box and began to shuffle smoothly and absent-mindedly, and Charlie went back to barbering the bookmaker and the young, dumpy blonde. Raymond was laying down the second solitaire spread when

Marco came in, ten minutes later. He greeted Charlie as he passed him, ordering a beer, then stood at the bar at Raymond's elbow. 'I got held up in traffic,' he said ritualistically. 'And so forth.' Raymond didn't answer.

'Are you clear for dinner, Raymond?' Marco wasn't aware that Raymond was ignoring him. 'My girl insists that the time has come to meet you, and no matter how I try to get out of it, that's the way it's got to be. Besides, I am about to marry the little thing, ringside one hundred and thirty-nine pounds, and we would like you to be the best man.'

The queen of diamonds showed at the twenty-third card turn. Raymond scooped the cards together, ignoring Marco. Become aware of the silence, Marco was studying Raymond. Raymond squared the deck, put it face down on top of the bar, placed the queen of diamonds face up on top of the stack, and stared at it in a detached and preoccupied manner, unaware that Marco was there. Charlie put the glass of beer in front of Marco at the rate of one hundred and thirty-seven words a minute, decibel count well above the middle register, then turned, walking back to the bookmaker and the broad to punctuate his narrative by recalling the height of the repartee with his brother-in-law: 'Why don't you take a cab quick to Central Park and jump inna lake, I says,' and his voice belted it loud and strong as though a sound engineer were riding gain on it. Raymond brushed past Marco, walked rapidly past the bookmaker and the girl, and out of the saloon.

'Hey! Hey, Raymond!' Marco yelled. 'Where you going?' Raymond was gone. By the time Marco got to the street he saw Raymond slamming the door of a cab. The taxi took off fast, disappearing around the corner, going uptown.

Marco returned to the saloon. He sipped at his beer with growing anxiety. The action of the game of solitaire nagged at him until he placed it in the dreams. It was one of the factors in the dreams that he had placed no meaning upon because he had come to regard the game as aberration that had wriggled into the fantasy. He had discussed it because it had been there, but after

227

one particularly bright young doctor said that Raymond had undoubtedly been doing something with his hands which had *looked* as though he were playing solitaire, Marco had gradually allowed the presence of the game in the dream to dim and fade. He now felt the conviction that something momentous had just happened before his eyes but he did not know what it was.

'Hey, Charlie.'

Business of rolling eyes heavenward, business of slow turn, exaggerating the forbearance of an extremely patient man.

'Yeah, arreddy.'

'Does Mr Shaw play solitaire in here much?'

'Whatta you mean—much?'

'Did he ever play solitaire in here before?'

'No.'

'Give me another beer.' Marco went to the telephone booth, digging for change. He called Lou Amjac.

Amjac sounded sourer than ever. 'What the hell happened to you?'

'Come on, save time. What happened?'

'Raymond is at the Twenty-second Precinct in the middle of the park on the Eighty-sixth Street transverse.'

'What did he do? What the hell is the matter with you?'

'He rented a rowboat and he jumped in the lake.'

'If you're kidding me, Lou——'

'I'm not kidding you!'

'I'll meet you there in ten minutes.'

'Colonel Marco!'

'What?'

'Did it finally break?'

'I think so. I—yeah, I think so.'

At first, Raymond flatly denied he had done such a thing but when the shock and embarrassment had worn off and he was forced to agree that his clothes were sopping wet, he was more nearly ready to admit that something which tended towards the unusual had happened. He, Amjac, and Marco sat in a squad room, at Marco's request. When Raymond seemed to have done with spluttering and expostulating, Marco spoke to him in a low, earnest voice, like a dog trainer, in a manner too direct to be evaded.

'We've been kidding each other for a long time, Raymond, and I put up with it because I had no other choice. You didn't believe me. You decided I was sick and that you had to go along with the gag to help me. Didn't you, Raymond?' Raymond stared at his sodden shoes. 'Raymond! Am I right?'

'Yes.'

'Now hear this. You stood beside me at Hungarian Charlie's and you didn't know I was there. You played a game of solitaire. Do you remember that?'

Raymond shook his head. Marco and Amjac exchanged glances.

'You took a cab to Central Park. You rented a row-boat. You rowed to the middle of the lake, then you jumped overboard. You have always been as stubborn as a dachshund, Raymond, but we can produce maybe thirty eye-witnesses who saw you go over the side, then walk to shore, so don't tell me again that you never did such a thing—and stop kidding yourself that they are not inside your head. We can't help you if you won't help us.'

'But I don't *remember*,' Raymond said. Something had happened to permit him to feel fear. Jocie was coming home. He might have something to lose. The creeping paralysis of fright was so new to him that his joints seemed to have rusted.

The capacious house in the Turtle Bay district jumped with activity that evening and it went on all through the night. A board review agreed to accept the game of solitaire as Raymond's trigger; and once they had made the connection they were filled with admiration for the technician who had conceived of it. Three separate teams worked with Hungarian Charlie, the talker's talker, the bookmaker, and the young, dumpy blonde.

At first, the blonde refused to talk, as she had every reason to believe that she had been picked up on an utterly non-political charge. She said, 'I refuse to answer on the grounds. It might intend to incriminate.' They had to bring Marco in to bail her attitude out of that stubbon durance. She knew Marco from around Charlie's place and she liked the way he smelled so much that she was dizzy with the hope of co-operating with him. He held her hand for a short time and explained in a feeling voice that she had not been arrested and that she was co-operating mainly as a big favour to him, and who knew? the whole thing could turn out to be pretty exciting. 'I dig,' she said, and everything was straightened out although she seemed purposely to misunderstand his solicitude by trying to climb into his lap as they discussed the various areas, but everybody was too busy to notice, and he was gone about two seconds after she had said, listen, she'd love to co-operate but why did they have to co-operate in different rooms?

The bookmaker was even more wary. He was a veritable model of shiftiness, which was heightened by the fact that he was carrying over twenty-nine thousand dollars worth of action on the sixth race at Jamaica, so he couldn't possibly keep his mind on what these young men were talking to him about. They persuaded him to take a mild sedative, then a particularly sympathetic young fellow walked with him along the main corridor and, in a highly confidential manner, asked him to feel free to discuss what had him so disturbed. The bookmaker knew (1) that these were not the type police which booked gamblers, and (2) he had always responded to highly confidential, whispering treatment. He explained about his business worries, stating, for insurance, that a friend of his—not he himself—was carrying all that action. Amjac made a call and got the race result. It was Pepper Dog, Wendy's Own, and Italian Mae, in that order. Not one client had run in the money. The bookmaker was opened up like a hydrant.

Hungarian Charlie, natch, was with it from the word go.

Marco played through one hundred and twenty-five solitaire

layouts until the technicians were sure, time after time and averaging off, where Raymond had stopped his play in Hungarian Charlie's saloon. They tested number systems as possible triggers, then they settled down to a symbol system and began to work with face cards because of the colours and their identification with human beings. They threw out the male face cards, kings and knaves, based on Raymond's psychiatric pattern. They started Marco working with the four queens. He discarded the queens of spades and clubs, right off. They stacked decks with different red queens at the twenty-third position, which fell as the fifth card on the fifth stack, and Marco dealt out solitaire strips. He made it the queen of diamonds, for sure. They kept him at it, but he connected the queen of diamonds with the face-up card on the squared deck on the bar, then all at once, as it is said to happen to saints and alcoholics, a voice he had heard in nightmares perhaps seven hundred times came to him. It was Yen Lo's voice saying: 'The queen of diamonds, in so many ways reminiscent of Raymond's dearly loved and hated mother, is the second key that will clear his mechanism for any assignments.' They had it made. Marco knew they had it made. Hungarian Charlie, the bookmaker and the young, dumpy blonde filled in the background of minor confirmations.

The FBI called Cincinnati and arranged to have one dozen factory-sealed force-packs flown to New York by Army plane. The cards reached the Turtle Bay house at 9.40 A.M. A force pack is an item usually made up for magic shops and novelty stores for party types who fan out cards before their helpless quarries saying, 'Take a card, any card.' Force packs contain fifty-two copies of the same card to make it easier for the forcer to guess which card has been picked; the dozen packs from Cincinnati were made up exclusively of queens of diamonds. Marco figured the time would come to try Raymond out as player of the ancient game of solitaire that very morning, and he didn't want to have to waste any time waiting for the queen of diamonds to show up in the play.

*   *   *

An hour after Chunjin had made his report to the Soviet security drop from the red telephone booth at the Fifty-ninth Street exit from Central Park, a meeting was called between Raymond's American operator and a District of Columbia taxi driver who also served as chief of Soviet security for the region. As they drove around downtown Washington, with Raymond's operator as passenger, the conversation seemed disputatious.

Raymond's operator told the hackman emphatically that they would be foolish to panic because of what was obviously a ten thousand to one happenstance by which some idiot had unknowingly stumbled upon the right combination of words in Raymond's presence.

'If you please.'

'What?'

'This is a professional thing on which I cannot be fooled. Cannot. They have been working over him. He has broken. They have chosen this contemptuous and insulting way of telling us that he has cracked and is useless to us.'

'You people are really insecure. God knows I have always felt that the British overdo that paternal talk about this being a young country but, my God, you really *are* a young country. You just haven't been at it long enough. Please understand that if our security people knew what Raymond had been designed to do they would not let you know they knew. Once they find out what Raymond is up to, which is virtually impossible, they'll want to nail whoever is moving him. Me. Then, through me, you. Certainly you people do enough of this kind of thing in your own country, so why can't you understand it here?'

'But why should such a conservative man jump in a lake?'

'Because the phrase "go jump in the lake" is an ancient slang wheeze in this country and some boob happened on the trigger accidentally, that's how.'

'I am actually sick with anxiety.'

'So are they,' Raymond's operator said blandly, enjoying the bustle of traffic all around them and thinking what a hick town this so-called world capital was.

'But how can you be so calm?'

'I took a tranquilliser.'

'A what?'

'A pill.'

'Oh. But how can you be so sure that is what happened?'

'Because I'm smart. I'm not a stupid Russian. Because Raymond is at large. They allow him to move about. Marco is tense and frightened. Read the Korean's reports, for Christ's sake, and get hold of yourself.'

'We have so little time and this is wholly my responsibility as far as my people are concerned.'

'Heller,' Raymond's operator said, reading the name from the identification card which said that the driver's name was Frank Heller, 'suppose I prove to you that Raymond is ours, not theirs.'

'How?' The Soviet policeman had to swerve the cab to avoid a small foreign car that hurtled across from a side street at his left; he screamed out the window in richly accented, Ukrainian-kissed English. 'Why dawn't you loo quare you are gung, gew tsilly tson-of-a bitch?'

'We certainly have a severe case of nerves today, don't we?' Raymond's operator murmured.

'Never mind my nerves. To be on the right of an approaching vehicle is to have the right of way! He broke the law! How can you prove Raymond is not theirs?'

'I'll have him kill Marco.'

'Aaaaah.' It was a long, soft, satisfaction-stuffed expletive having a zibeline texture. It suggested the end of a perfect day, a cause well served, a race well run.

'Marco is in charge of this particular element of counter-espionage,' Raymond's operator said. 'Marco is Raymond's only friend. So? Proof?'

'Yes.'

'Good.'

'When?'

'Tonight, I think. Let me off here.'

233

The cab stopped at the corner of Nineteenth and Y. Raymond's operator got out and slammed the door—too quickly. It closed on flesh. The operator screamed like a lunch whistle. Zilkov stopped the cab. He leaped out, ran around behind it, and stood, wincing with sympathetic pains, while the operator held the mashed hand in the other hand and bent over double. 'It's terrible,' Zilkov said. 'Terrible. Oh, my God! Get into the cab and I'll get you to a hospital. Will you lose the nails? Oh, my God, what pain you must feel.'

XX

When Raymond returned home from the Twenty-second Precinct House, wearing damp clothes and soggy shoes, it was late afternoon. He had to order Chunjin to the kitchen because the man persisted in asking ridiculous questions. They had a brisk exchange of shouts and sulks, then Raymond showered and took a two-hour dreamless nap.

He awoke thinking about Jocie. He decided that she should be clearing customs just about then. He could not think about his letter, whether she had read it or torn it up in distaste; he could not imagine what she felt or would feel. He dressed slowly and began to pack for the weekend. He removed the gaucho costume from its cardboard box and packed it carefully. He felt a flood of panic as he folded it in. Maybe this silly monkey suit would remind Jocie of her husband. Why in the name of sweet Jesus had he ordered such a costume? It couldn't possibly resemble anything in real life, he decided. Cattle people didn't wear silk bloomers. They were for Yul Brynner or somebody who was kidding. It was probably the kind of a suit they wore to dances or fiestas a couple of times a year. Surely neither Jocie nor her husband would have attended such dances. But what the hell was he being so literal for? You didn't have to see a lot of people walking around in suits like these to know that they were symbolic of the Argentine. What would she think? Would she think he was being cruel or unkind or rude or insensitive? He fussed and pottered and grumbled to himself, conjecturing about the reactions of a woman he hadn't seen since she had been a girl, but did not give a thought to having jumped out of a rowboat into a shallow lake in broad daylight in the centre of a city because it embarrassed him to have to think of himself as having so lacked grace in front of all those strangers and those goddam policemen who had treated him as if he was Bellevue Hospital's problem and not theirs. He also would not think of it because he could not afford to get angry with Joe Downey, his boss, who could have at least had the consideration to keep the story out of all the newspapers, and if not all the newspapers, surely out of his own front page.

He snapped the suitcase shut. He carried it to the bedroom door, worrying about what the hell Jocie would think of him when she saw those idiot newspapers at the airport. He flung open the door then began a tug-of-war over the suitcase with Chunjin as he dragged both of them towards the square, tiled foyer.

'For cris*sake*, Chunjin!' It made him even angrier for having spoken to this pushy little type at all and a loud discussion started.

Chunjin did not want him to take the Long Island Railroad to his mother's house. Opposing it bitterly, he maintained that it was not sound for a rich man to wrestle with a large bag in a crowded railroad car. Raymond said he certainly was not going to put up with this kind of insubordination and if it continued for just about two more sentences Chunjin could go in and pack his own cardboard suitcase and get the hell out for good. He felt foolish as soon as he had said it because he remembered suddenly that Chunjin did not sleep in and, of course, had no suitcase on the premises.

Chunjin said loudly that he had taken the liberty of renting an automobile and the correct, dark uniform of a proper chauffeur, the jacket of which Mr Shaw could look upon as he was even now wearing it. Chunjin said he would drive Mr Shaw to his mother's house in comfort and at a level with Mr Shaw's dignity and position in the world.

To Raymond, all of this was an utterly new conception, perhaps as television would have been to the inventor of the wheel. Raymond had loved automobiles all his life, although he could not drive one, but he had never thought of renting one. He was transformed, enchanted.

'You *rented* a car?'

'Yes, sir, Mr Shaw.'

'What kind?'

'Cadillac.'

'Well! Marvellous! What colour?'

'West Point grey. French blue seats. Leather. Genuine. Rear seat radio.'

'Wonderful!'

'Tax deductible also.'

'Is that so? How?'

'You will read the booklet in the car, Mr Shaw.' Chunjin put on his dark chauffeur's cap. He took the suitcase away from Raymond without a struggle. 'We go now, Mr Shaw? Seven o'clock. Two hours to drive.'

'I don't know this house, you know. It's a rented house. I don't know about a place for you to stay.'

'My job find place. You not think. Ride and read reports from newspaper. Think about condition of world.'

Dressed as a costumer's conception of a gaucho, Raymond came down his mother's rented, winding stairs, railed in English copper, stainless steel, and lucite, and into an entrance hall that might have been hewn by a cast of Grimm Brothers' gnomes out of a marble mountain. It was studded with bronze zodiacal designs and purred with concealed neon light in an arrangement that pulled Raymond towards the great drawing room on the threshold of which Senator and Mrs Iselin were receiving their guests. The older guests who shook hands with the Iselins that night had been followers of Father Coughlin; the group just younger than them had rallied around Gerald L. K. Smith; and the rest, still younger, were fringe lice who saw Johnny's significance in a clear, white light. The clan had turned out from ten thousand yesterdays in the Middle West and neolithic Texas, and patriotism was far from being their last refuge. It was a group for anthropologists, and it seemed like very bad manners or very bad judgement on Raymond's mother's part to have invited Senator Jordan to walk among the likes of these.

Johnny and Ellie (as Raymond's mother was called by most of the guests) were costumed as honest dairy-farm folk would look if honest dairy farmers had had their work clothes built by Balenciaga. Raymond's mother had figured that the press photographs of these costumes would be viewed with great favour in the Iselin home state, where building foundations were made of butter; voters would be told that Big John never forgot where he came from. As she embraced Raymond in their mutually distasteful greeting, she whispered that Jocie's plane had run late out of San Juan but that she was now in the house next door and she had telephoned to say that she would be over no later than midnight and had asked anxiously if Raymond would be there. He felt, for an instant, that he might faint.

'Anxiously? Why anxiously? Did she sound as though she were fearful that I might be here?'

'Oh, don't be such a jerk, Raymond! If you weren't here do you think for a moment that the Jordans would come here?'

'Don't call me a jerk, Mother.'

'Go have a drink or a tranquilliser or something.' She turned to her husband. 'Raymond can certainly be a pain in the ass,' she said with asperity.

'She's kiddin' yuh,' Johnny said. 'You sure look great, kid. What are you supposed to be, one of those Dutch skaters?'

'What else?' Raymond answered. He walked through the crowds acknowledging greetings forbiddingly and feeling his heart beating as though it were trying to splinter a way out through his ribs. He walked among, but shunned contact with, the crowds on the broad lawns behind the house, all of which, excepting one section, were brilliantly illuminated with non-Communist Japanese lanterns and filled with striped tents. The dark section pulled Raymond to it. It faced the Jordan house. It was a walled-off piece of ground, as isolated as a private deck on an ocean liner. He stood there beside the wall staring across at the Jordan house without the reward of being able to observe any movement there. Frustrated, and more than usually resentful, he wandered back to the Iselin house through crowds of stout, blonde Carmens and Kansas Borgias, unhorsed Godivas, unfrocked Richelieus, and many businessmen dressed as pirates. Many of the costumes were quaint American Legion uniforms so like those of the *squadristi* of former days in Italy, encasing various sizes of fleshy prejudice which exchanged opinions they rented that week from Mr Sokolsky, Mr Lawrence, Mr Pegler, and that fascinating younger fellow who had written about men and God at Yale. The three orchestras tried to avoid playing at the same time. The Iselins had provided very nearly everything but balalaikas in the way of music. There was a 'society' orchestra, a three cha combo, and an inundation of gallant White Russian fiddlers who migrated across the grounds and in and out of the house en masse, sawing like locusts, and not only did they accept tips but they very nearly frisked the guests to get them. Raymond stopped at one of the four bars and drank a half glass of champagne. He refused offers to dance with three young women of different sizes. His mother found him later, far in a corner of the large salon, behind a pastel sofa, under two threats of Salvador Dali, a Catalan.

'My God, you look as though your head will come to a point any minute,' she told him. 'Raymond, will you *please* take a tranquilliser?'

'No.'

'Why?'

'I have a revulsion for drugs.'

'You look absolutely miserable. Never mind. A half-hour more and she'll be here. My feet hurt. Why don't we just sneak away for a few minutes until Jocie and her father arrive. We can sit in the library and sip cold wine.'

Raymond looked right at her and, for the first time in many, many years, actually smiled at her, and she thought he looked positively beautiful. Why—why he looks like Poppa! Raymond, her own Raymond, looked exactly like her darling, darling Poppa! She clutched his hand as she led him out of the salon and along the two corridors to the library, causing one woman guest to tell another woman guest that they looked as though they were rushing off to get a little of you-know-what, Mrs Iselin trailing a delicious scent of Jolie Madame because she had read that Lollobrigida wore it and she had always wished she could be short like that, and stopping only to get a bottle of wine and to tell the butler where they would be.

The library was a small, pleasant room and the books were real. The fourth wall was transparent glass and faced that walled deck of land and Jocie's house. Raymond stood rubbing his hands together, so very tall and so preposterously handsome in the short, shining boots, the ballooning trousers, and the wide expanse of white silk shirt. 'Do you *know* they got in from the airport?' he asked as he poured the lemon-yellow wine into two sherbet glasses.

'I *told* you,' his mother said. 'She telephoned me. From that house.'

'How did she sound?'

'Like a girl.'

'Thanks.'

She leaned forward tensely in the raspberry-coloured chair, splendid in pink chiffon. 'Raymond?'

'What?' He handed her one of the filled glasses. She took it with her bandaged left hand. 'What did you do to your hand?' he asked, seeing the bandage for the first time.

'I got careless in Washington this afternoon and got it caught in the door of a taxi.' He grunted involuntarily. 'Raymond,' she said, transferring the wine to her right hand and lifting it shakily. "Why don't you pass the time by playing a little solitaire?'

XXI

Marco squeezed the inside of Eugénie Rose's splended thigh, not at all sexually—well, perhaps just a little bit sexually—but mostly out of the greatest of good spirits because, after all, this time of sick fear, the work seemed to be leading to the conclusion which they had dreaded they would never be able to find.

'Hey!' Eugénie Rose said.

'What?'

'Don't stop.'

It was after midnight and it was Marco's dinner break from the unending games of solitaire, from the examinations of Hungarian Charlie, the bookmaker, and the young, dumpy blonde, from the number systems and symbol systems, and Marco knew the end was in sight.

'This time to-morrow night, oh boy! I'll have lunch with Raymond tomorrow, then a little solitaire, then a nice long chat about the good old days in Korea and a few Russian and Chinese friends of ours, then a few suggestions made to crumble up their systems and mechanisms forever—sort of removing the controls, ripping out the wiring—and, lady, it's all over. All over. All done with. Done.'

'Finished.'

'Completed.'

'Through.'

'Mission accomplished.'

'Check.'

They were in an all-night restaurant on Fifty-eighth Street, and when he wasn't clutching her hands, Rosie nibbled on cinnamon toast as daintily as a cartoon mouse. Marco was shovelling in large wedges of gooey creamed chipped beef and humming chorus after chorus of 'Here Comes the Bride.'

'That's a pretty tune you're humming. What is it?' she asked.

'Our song.'

'Oh, Benny boy. Oh, my dear colonel!'

XXII

Raymond found the cards in the desk. They were elegant rented cards that had come with the house. They had gold edges and were imprinted with the name and the grotesque crest of a hotel maintained for the expense-account set on the North Side of Chicago. He dealt out the play. The queen of diamonds did not show in the first game. As he placed the cards precisely his mother sat on the edge of her chair with her face buried in her hands. When she heard him squaring up the pack she sat up straight and her face was twisted bitterly. Raymond placed the red queen face up on top of the deck and studied it non-committally.

'Raymond, I must talk to you about a problem with Colonel Marco, and I must talk to you, as well, about many other things but there will be no time tonight. It seems that there is never time.' There was a brisk knocking at the door, which she had locked. 'Damn!' she said and walked to the door. 'Who is it?'

'It's me, hon. Johnny. Tom Jordan is here. I need you.'

'All right, lover. I'll be right out.'

'Who the hell are you in there with anyway?'

'Raymond.'

'Oh. Well, hurry it up whatever it is, hon. We have work out here.'

She walked back and stood behind Raymond with her hands on his shoulders. As he watched the red queen she repaired her face as best she could. Then she leaned over him and took the card. 'I'll take this with me, dear,' she said. 'It might bring mischief if I leave it here.'

'Yes, Mother.'

'I'll be back as soon as I can.'

'Yes, Mother.'

She left the library, locking the door behind her. As soon as she was gone something rattled at the terrace door. Raymond looked up just as the smiling, beautiful young woman closed the door behind her. She was dressed for the masquerade party, costumed as a playing card. The rich gold and scarlet cowl fell from her crown to her shoulders. Gold incrusted jewels banded the lush black and white ruff at her throat. The kaleidoscopic complex of inlays of metallic oranges, yellows, purples, scarlets, blacks, and whites fell to her bodice and below. From the top of her head, stiffly parallel to her shoulders, then falling at right angles full down the sides of her body, was a white papier-mâché board on which was printed a regal Q, a red diamond standard directly below it at the left corner, while at the right there stared a large red diamond against the shining white background. It was the queen of diamonds, his patron and his destiny. She spoke to him.

'I saw you through my window just before we left the house,' she said huskily. 'My heart almost shot out of my body. I had to see you alone. Daddy went around the front way and I slipped through that old iron door in the stone wall.'

'Jocie.' She was Jocie and she was his queen of diamonds. She was the queen of diamonds, his special lady from the stars, and she was Jocie.

'Your letter—oh, my darling.'

He moved across the room and held her by the shoulders, swaying. He looked down at her with such a force of pure love that she shivered and they were together in love forever. He kissed her. It was the first time he had ever kissed her after having possessed her completely in imaginations through nine risings of April and the deaths of eight Decembers. He pulled her down on the couch and his hands fumbled with her royal clothes and royal person while his mouth and his body sought his salvation with the only woman he would ever love, with the only woman who had ever allowed him to love her; the cardboard queen he served, and the lovely girl he had adored from the moment he had come to life beside her near a lake, near a snake, within an expanding dream.

Senator Jordan's costume was the toga and sandals of a Roman legislator, combined with a blanked expression. He stood next to Senator Iselin, equidistant from the marble walls at the centre of the foyer. The three cha combo scattered sounds over them from the bottomless fountain of its noises. When the two men spoke they spoke guardedly, like convicts in a chow line.

'I am here,' Senator Jordan said to Johnny, 'because my daughter asked me to come, saying that it was extremely important to her, that is to say, important to her happiness, that I come. There is no other reason and my presence here is not to be misunderstood nor is it to be exploited by that industry of gossip which you control. I feel loathing towards you and for what you have done to weaken our country and very nearly destroy our party. Is that clear?'

'That's all right, Tom. Glad to have you,' Johnny said. 'I was tickled when Ellie told me that we were going to be next-door neighbours.'

'And I am wearing this ridiculous costume because my daughter cabled ahead for it from Puerto Rico and because she asked me to wear it, assuring me that I would be less conspicuous at this Fascist party rally if I did.'

'It looks great on you, Tom. Great. What are you supposed to be, some kind of an athlete or something?'

'An interne. Furthermore, I hope none of this lunatic fringe

243

who are your guests tonight, and who are ringing us like hyenas to watch us chat so amiably, are getting the wrong idea about me. If they link you with me I'll take ads to repudiate you and them.'

'Don't give it a thought, Tom. If anything, old buddy, they're probably getting the wrong idea about me. They are very possessive about their politics. They're a great bunch, actually. You'd like them.'

The restless guests moved all around them. The scent of masked ambergris mixed with abstractions of carnations and musk glands, lemon rinds, and the essences of gunpowder and tobacco. Raymond's mother came like a flung harpoon through the crowds to greet her honoured guest. She shook his hand vigourously, she said again and again and again how honoured they were to have him in their house, and she forgot to ask where Jocie was. She asked Johnny to represent them among their other guests because she just had to have a good old-fashioned visit with Senator Tom. Before Johnny slunk away gratefully he mumbled amenities and moved to shake hands, which Senator Jordan had tactfully overlooked.

Raymond's mother stopped a waiter and took his tray of four filled champagne glasses. She carried it off in the opposite direction from the library, followed stiffly by the senator, to the small room which was known to the domestic staff as 'the Senator's den' because Johnny like to drink in there, unshaven.

It was a vivid room, vivid enough to make a narcoleptic sit up popeyed, with bright, white carpet, black walls, and shining brass furniture with zebrine upholstery. Raymond's mother set the tray down upon the black desk with the shining brass drawer handles, then asked her neighbour to sit down as she closed the door.

'It was good of you to come over, Tom.'

He shrugged.

'I suppose you were surprised to learn that we had taken this house.'

'Surprised and appalled.'

'You won't have to see much of us.'

'I am sure of that.'

'I would like to ask a question.'

'You may.'

'Will you carry this personal feeling you have for me and for Johnny over into other fields of practical politics?'

'What other fields?'

'Well—the convention, for example.'

His eyebrows shot up. 'In what area of the convention?'

'Would you try to block Johnny if his name is brought forward?'

'You're joking.'

'My dear Tom!'

'You are going to go after the nomination for Johnny?'

'We may be forced into that position. Your answer will help me to form the decision. A lot of Americans, you know, look upon Johnny as one of the few men willing to fight to the death for the preservation of our liberties.'

'Aaaaaah!'

'And I mean a *lot* of people. Votes. The Loyal American Underground is five million voting Americans. To say nothing of the wonderful work Frank Bollinger is doing, and with no urging from us. He says flatly that he will walk into that convention with a petition of not less than one million votes pledged for Johnny as a down payment on ten million.'

'You haven't answered me. Are you going after the nomination for Johnny?'

'No,' she answered calmly. 'We couldn't make it. But we can make the vice-presidency.'

'The vice-presidency?' Jordan was incredulous. 'Why would Johnny want the vice-presidency?'

'Why wouldn't he?'

'Because he wants power and a big stage to dance on. There's no power in the vice-presidency and the only place where there is more power than where Johnny is right now is in the White House. Why would he want the vice-presidency?'

'I answered your question, Tom, but you haven't answered mine.'

'What question?'

'Will you block us?'

'Block you? I would spend every cent I own or could borrow to block you. I have contempt for you and fear for you, but mostly I fear for this country when I think of you. Johnny is just a low clown but you are the smiler who wraps a dagger in the flag and waits for your chance, which I pray may never come. I tell you this: if at that convention one month from now you begin to deal with the delegations to cause Johnny's name to be put on that ticket, or if in my canvass of all delegations which will begin on my telephone tomorrow I learn that you are so acting, I am going to bring impeachment proceedings against your husband on the floor of the Senate and I will hit him with everything in my carefully documented book.'

Raymond's mother came out of her chair, spitting langrel.

XXIII

Jocie left a long letter for her father after she had changed and packed, before she and Raymond drove her car into New York. The letter told him that they were going to be married immediately and that they had decided to have it done quietly, even invisibly, for the entirely apparent political considerations. The letter also told him of how sublimely, utterly happy she was; it said they would return as soon as possible and beseeched her father to tell no one of the marriage because Raymond's conviction was that his mother would use it at once to political advantage, and that he felt his mother's political advantages were profitless, even detrimental, to anyone concerned.

Jocie and Raymond reached his apartment at three in the morning after driving into the city in Jocie's car. They undressed instantly and reflexively and found each other hungrily. Jocie wept and she laughed with joy and disbelief that her true life, the only life she had ever touched because it had touched her simultaneously, had been given back to her. Such an instant ago he had paddled their wide canoe across that lake of purple wine towards a pin of light high in the sky which would widen and widen and widen while she slept until it had blanched the blackness. Another day would have lighted his face as he stood there before her. She had been dreaming. She had not been waiting so long for him, she had been dreaming. She had gone to sleep beside a mountain lake and she had dreamed that he had gone away from her and that they had waited, across the world from each other, until the dream had finished. He loved her! He loved her!

Raymond mailed a concise letter to Joe Downey of *The Daily Press* concerning his first vacation in four years, explained that his column had been written ahead for five days, and announced that he would return, without saying where he was going, in time to cover the conventions.

They drove her car to Washington and parked it in the Senate garage. They took the first flight out of Washington to Miami, using the names John Starr and Marilyn Ridgeway for the manifest, then an afternoon plane from Miami to San Juan, Puerto Rico.

They were married in San Juan at 5.37 P.M., using their passports for identification in lieu of birth certificates; a condition which helped the justice to remember them two days later when the FBI office in San Juan responded to the Bureau's general alarm for Raymond. They left San Juan via PAA at 7.05 P.M. and arrived soon after in Antigua, where the presentation of one of the many mysterious cards in Raymond's wallet secured him credit and lodgings for their wedding night at the Mill Reef Club.

The following afternoon they set sail as the only passengers aboard a chartered schooner with a professionally aloof crew, on a honeymoon voyage through the islands of Guadeloupe, Dominica, Martinique, St Lucia, Barbados, Grenada, Tobago, and Trinidad.

When Raymond's mother returned to the library and found him gone, she panicked for the first time in her memory. She had to force herself to sit very, very still for nearly twenty minutes to regain control of herself. By then she needed a fix so badly that she nearly scrambled up the back stairs to get heroin and an arm banger. She changed from the costume of the dainty milkmaid, coked to the very retinas, and calmly slipped into something she could wear to the airport, thence to Washington. She leaned back and closed her eyes, her body allowing the serenity to wash over it, and she considered quite objectively what must be done to move through this catastrophe. Although she had the servants seek Raymond throughout the house and grounds and she checked his room herself, she understood best the intuition which told her that he must have fled from her, and that his mechanism had broken down. She knew as well as she could tell the time that, having been triggered by the red queen, when the red queen had been removed from his sight he would have remained in the locked room for the rest of his days in complete suspension of faculties if the mechanism had been operating as constructed. She had elaborate cause to panic.

Chunjin missed Raymond approximately two hours later than his mother did, but his alarm was relayed in the Soviet apparatus via a telephone tape recorder in Arlington, Virginia, immediately so that they knew about Raymond's disappearance before his mother could reach Washington to tell them. They had panicked, too. A general order was issued to trace the fugitive through their own organisations, but as they confined their search within the borders of the continental United States they got nowhere as the days went on and on.

The FBI resumed its interrupted surveillance of Raymond at Martinique. They were able, through some fine co-operation, to persuade two crew members to jump ship, whereupon two agents of the Bureau were signed on the schooner as working hands.

The Bureau had found Jocie's car in the Senate garage, and she and Raymond were immediately identified as connections of senators and he as the well-known newspaperman. The Bureau was about to discuss the matter with Senator Jordan when the San Juan office reported the marriage. After that the names of Mr and Mrs Raymond Shaw showed up on the PAA manifest for the skim to Antigua, then quickly after that, like gypsy finger-snapping, at the Mill Reef Club, on the right wharf, on the voyage plot filed at the company's office, then at Martinique, where the two agents boarded to protect the blissfully ignorant couple from they knew not what.

If Marco had not been the Little Gentleman about the whole thing—if he had not been so hipped on the sanctity of the honeymoon in an entirely subjective manner—he would have been one of those two agents who boarded as crew and he would have had a force deck of fifty-two queens of diamonds in his duffel, those with keen hindsight said later. However, he could see no harm coming to them while they were that far out at sea so he planned to visit Raymond at the earliest possible moment upon the honeymooners' return.

Jocie and Raymond returned to New York on Friday the evening before the Monday morning when the convention was scheduled to open at Madison Square Garden. They had been away for twenty-nine days. They moved into Raymond's apartment with golden tans and foaming joys. It took two calls to locate Jocie's father because he had closed the summer house on Long Island and had moved back to the house on Sixty-third Street. He insisted that they have a wedding celebration that evening because of the wonderful sounds and the sounds within those sounds far within his daughter's happy voice. They celebrated at an Italian restaurant on East Fifty-fifth Street. The city was rapidly tilting with the arrival of politician-statesmen and statesmen-politicians and just routine hustlers for the convention so it was no trick at all for the newspaper in opposition to *The Daily Press* to learn of the celebrating party of three, and in no time a photographer had appeared on the scene, taken a picture, and confirmed the story of the marriage. That being the case, Raymond explained earnestly to Jocie, he had no choice but to alert his own paper because it would be a bitter occasion indeed if they were beat to the street with his own picture, so a *Press* photographer and reporter were rushed to the restaurant, which heretofore had been famous only for the manufacture of the most formidable Martinis on the planet. A journalistic coincidence was duly observed in The Wayward Press department of *The New Yorker* in a subsequent examination of the national press reports published during the national political conventions. The survey noted that both newspapers reporting the Jordan-Shaw marriage at the same instant employed lead paragraphs that were almost identical. Each newspaper made a comparison with the plot of *Romeo and Juliet,* a successful play by an English writer which had been taken from the Italian of Massucio di Salerno. Both paragraphs referred to the groom as being of the House of Montague (Iselin) and to the bride as being of the House of Capulet (Jordan), then went on into divergent reviews of the murderous bitterness between the two senators, recalling Senator Iselin's startling press conference of one week previous at which he had charged Senator Jordan with high treason, brandishing papers held high as 'absolute proof' that Jordan had sold his country out to the Soviets and stating that, at the instant the Senate re-convened he would move for (1) Senator Jordan's impeachment and (2) for a civil trial at the end of which, the senator demanded passionately, the only possible verdict would be that 'this traitor to liberty and to the only perfect way of life must be hanged by the neck until dead.' Senator Jordan's only response had been made upon a single mimeographed sheet holding a single sentence. Distributed to all press agencies, it said: 'How long will you let this man use you and trick you?'

Senator Jordan did not mention the Iselin attack to the bride and groom while they were in the restaurant. He knew they would hear about it all too shortly.

Before the stories and pictures announcing Raymond's return and their wedding could appear in the morning editions, friends, agents, and sympathisers had passed the word along through channels to the Soviet security command. The command issued its wishes to Mrs Iselin, in Washington, and she reached Raymond by telephone the next morning. She chided him gently for not having told her of his great happiness and was so gently convincing in her most gentle hurt that Raymond was surprised to realise that he felt he had behaved somewhat badly towards her.

She told him that the Vice-President and the Speaker of the House were coming to the Iselin residence at three o'clock that afternoon for an unusual policy meeting relative to civil rights and that since they had decided it would be advantageous to allow the story to 'leak' to the public, she had immediately put in a bid for her syndicated son and everyone had concurred on the choice. Therefore he would need to catch a plane immediately for Washington so that they could lunch together and she could fill him in on the entire background of the meeting and the plans. Raymond readily agreed.

Jocie was a girl who had mastered every *expertise* on sleeping. He didn't waken her. He left a note explaining why he had to leave and saying he would write the piece itself in Washington that night and would be back at her doorstep before she woke up the next morning.

Raymond learned about Johnny's fantastic attack on his father-in-law from a newspaper during the flight to Washington, and he began to feel the numbness of great rage and the purest kind of joy: the substance of the attack released in him something he had always wanted to do but had always inhibited to the point where he had never recognised it before. He would go to the Iselin house and he would lock Johnny in a room and he would beat him and beat him and beat him. Another great light broke over his head. He would shave his mother bald.

Jocie learned about the attack at breakfast from the same

251

morning newspaper, in the story under the front-page, three-column picture of herself, her husband, and her father. The references to the Iselin charges were bewildering to her; she had lived so long in the Argentine that she had not developed a native callousness to any allegation made by Johnny. She dressed at once, telephoned her father, told him she would be right there, and hurried out of the house taking an overnight bag with her and leaving a note for Raymond explaining briefly and asking him to come to her father's house as soon as he could the following morning. She signed the note 'with all my love forever' and propped it up for his attention on the foyer telephone.

Colonel Marco, that constant brooder over the marriage state, deferred too long in his plan to awaken/disturb the newly-weds. When he went to Raymond's apartment with his force cards to sweep the destructions out of Raymond's mind, Raymond and Jocie had both gone. No one answered the door bell to give him information as to where they had gone. Chunjin could see the caller by opening the service door just a crack, fifteen yards along the hall to Marco's right.

Raymond's mother gave Raymond no chance to put his vengeance into effect when he reached her house in Washington. As he charged wildly into her office on the second floor—the office was decorated like the inside of a coffin—she suggested that he pass the time by playing a little solitaire, which cut him off in mid-curse. She locked the door.

The queen of diamonds showed as the fourteenth card in the first layout. Raymond listened with absorption to what his mother had to say. She questioned him and he gave her a detailed report on how and why and when he had disappeared from the house on Long Island, and she was so relieved that she laughed hysterically as he told her about Jocie's costume and his total, eternal obedience to the queen of diamonds. When she had dried the tears of nervous joy from her eyes and had fired four more short bursts of hysterical laughter she got down to business and laid out his job of work.

She had been ordered to make a full test of his reflex mechanism and, because Senator Jordan was potentially so dangerous to Johnny and her terminal plans, she had selected him for execution. She set down her orders to Raymond with clarity and economy. It was now 11.22 A.M. Raymond was to go to the Washington bureau of *The Daily Press* and talk about convention coverage problems with the bureau chief so that his presence in the city would be established. He would then have lunch at the Press Club and talk to as many acquaintances at the bar as possible. Raymond reported stolidly that he did not have acquaintances. His mother said he knew Washington newspapermen, didn't he? He said he did. She said, 'Well, you can just stand next to them and talk to them and it will be such a shock that they'll place you in Washington this weekend for many years to come.' After lunch he would appear on the Hill and find an excuse to visit with the Speaker. At five o'clock he would stop by at the press room at the White House and annoy Hagerty by pushing for a breakfast date the following morning at seven o'clock. Hagerty would not be able to accept, even if he could stand the idea of breakfasting with Raymond, because of the convention opening in New York Monday morning, but Raymond's insistence would be sure to rile Hagerty and he would remember Raymond as having been in Washington on Saturday and on Sunday. At six-fifteen he would return to the Press Club bar for forty-five minutes of startling conviviality, then he would return to the Iselin house to have dinner with friends. It would be an entirely informal dinner but with quite good people like Mr Justice Calder and the Treasury Under-secretary and that young what's-his-name criminal lawyer and his darling wife. At eleven forty-five a television repair truck would be at the back entrance to the house with his own man, Chunjin, driving. Raymond would get into the back of the panel truck, where there would be a mattress. He was to sleep all the way to New York. Did he understand that? Yes, Mother. Chunjin would give him a revolver with a silencer when they got into the city and would let him out of the truck in front of the Jordan house

253

on East Sixty-third Street at approximately 3.45 A.M. Chunjin would give him the keys to the front door and the inside door. Raymond went over a diagram of the inside of the house while his mother explained precisely how he was to find the senator's sleeping room on the second floor, after having first checked the library downstairs in the event the senator had been bothered with one of his intermittent spells of insomnia. It would all be quite as easy as the liquidation of Mr Gaines had been, but he was to take no chances and it was essential that he take every precaution against being identified, and she did not need to specify the precautions, she was sure, beyond that. After the assignment had been completed he was to return to the back of the truck and go to sleep at once. He would awaken at Chunjin's touch when they had reached the back door of this house again. He was to go to his room, undress, put on pyjamas, and immediately go to sleep until he was called and, of course, he was to remember nothing, not that he would ever be able to, in any event.

XXIV

Marco discovered that Raymond was in Washington very quickly. However, by appearing at the Press Club (where he had found himself, to his chagrin and resentment, exactly once before in the years of his political reporting) Raymond unwittingly eluded the men of Marco's unit. The unit was out in force and in desperate earnest. They knew how to unlock the mystery, that is, they held the key in their hands, but now they could not find the lock. As each day had passed since the afternoon Raymond had rented the row-boat in Central Park, and Raymond had been beyond their reach, every element of responsibility in the unit, and in the direction of the nation, had watched and waited tensely, fearing that they might have arrived at the solution too late. By going to the Hill and to the White House on a Saturday afternoon in summer, Raymond kept showing up exactly where they did not expect him to appear, so they missed him again. Fifty minutes after he had left the Washington bureau of *The Daily Press*, and after the bureau chief had taken off for the weekend in an automobile with his wife and their parrot and the information as to where and how Raymond would spend the day, two men from Marco's unit arrived to take up permanent posts waiting for Raymond to return to the office. At the White House Raymond duly registered the fact that he would be in Washington for the weekend but Hagerty said how the hell could he have time to have breakfast when there was a national convention opening Monday?

Because Raymond was known to detest his mother and stepfather under any normal circumstances and because Marco's unit calculated that he would never speak to the Iselins again after the viciousness of Johnny's smear of Raymond's father-in-law, they missed Raymond again by ignoring the Iselin house. Marco's unit ate, drank, and slept very little. They had to find Raymond so that he could play a little solitaire to pass the time and tell them what they had to know because something was about to cut the thread that held the blazing sword which was suspended directly overhead from the blazing sun.

Just before midnight, Raymond crawled into the back of the panel truck, stretched out, and went to sleep. It had started to rain. As the truck came out of the Lincoln Tunnel into New York, thunder was added and lightning flashed, but Raymond was asleep and could not heed it.

Raymond's mother had been merciful. She understood completely the operation of the Yen Lo mechanism. She knew Raymond had to do what he was told to do, that he could have no sense of right or wrong about it, nor suspect any possibility of the consciousness of guilt, but she must have sensed that he had to retain a sense of gain/loss, that he would know when the time

255

came, that by having to kill Senator Jordan he would be losing something, and that his wife, too (and so very much more dimensionally), would suffer an infinity of loss. So, out of mercy, she instructed Chunjin to let Raymond sleep until he arrived within a block of the Jordan house.

Chunjin stopped the truck on the far side of the street, opposite the house. It was raining heavily and they alone seemed to be alive in the city. Three other cars were parked in the block, an impossibly low number. Chunjin leaned over the seat and shook Raymond by the shoulder.

'Time to do the work, Mr Shaw,' he said. Raymond came awake instantly. He sat up. He clambered to sit beside Chunjin in the front seat.

Chunjin gave him the gun, to which a silencer had been affixed, making it cumbersome and very nearly impossible to pocket. 'You know this kind of gun?' he asked efficiently.

'Yes,' Raymond answered dully.

'I suggest you keep it under your coat.'

'I will,' Raymond said. 'I have never felt so sad.'

'That is proper,' Chunjin said. 'However, sir, if you do the work quickly it will be over for you, and for him, although in different ways. When the work is done you will forget.'

The rain was like movie rain. It streamed heavily against the windows and made a tympanous racket as it hit the roof of the truck. Chunjin said, 'I circle block with car, Mr Shaw. If not here when you come out you walk slowly towards next street, Third Avenue. Bring gun with you.'

Raymond opened the car door.

'Mr Shaw?'

'What?'

'Shoot through the head. After first shot, walk close, place second shot.'

'I know. She told me.' He opened the door quickly, got out quickly, and slammed it shut. He crossed the street as the panel truck pulled away, the pistol held at his waist under his light raincoat, the rain striking his face.

He felt the sadness of Lucifer. He moved in the flat, relentless rhythm of the oboe passages in 'Bald Mountain.' Colours of anguish moved behind his eyes in vangoghian swirls, having lifted edges to give an elevation to the despair. His nameless grief had handles, which he lifted, carrying himself forward towards the centre of the pain.

The doors of the house, outer and inner, opened with the master keys. There were no lights in the rooms on the main floor, only the night light over the foot of the stairs. Raymond moved towards the staircase, the pistol hanging at his side, gripped in his left hand. As his foot touched the first riser he heard a sound in the back of the house. He froze where he was until he could identify it.

Senator Jordan appeared in pyjamas, slippers, and robe. His silver hair was ruffled into a halo of duck feathers. He saw Raymond as he stood under the light leaning against the wall, but showed no surprise.

'Ah, Raymond. I didn't hear you come in. Didn't expect to see you until around breakfast time tomorrow morning. I got hungry. If I were only as hungry in a restaurant as I am after I've been asleep in a nice, warm bed for a few hours, I could be rounder and wider than the fat lady in the circus. Are you hungry, Raymond?'

'No, sir.'

'Let's go upstairs. I'll force some good whisky on you. Combat the rain. Soothe you after travelling and any number of other good reasons.' He swept past Raymond and went up the stairs ahead of him. Raymond followed, the pistol heavy in his hand.

'Jocie said you had to go down to see your mother and the Speaker.'

'Yes, sir.'

'How was the Speaker?'

'I—I didn't see him, sir.'

'I hope you didn't get yourself all upset over those charges of Iselin's.'

'Sir, when I read that story on the plane going to Washington

257

I decided what I should have decided long ago. I decided that I owed him a beating.'

'I hope you didn't——'

'No, sir.'

'Matter of fact, an attack from John Iselin can help a good deal. I'll show you some of the mail. Never got so much supporting mail in twenty-two years in the Senate.'

'I'm happy to hear it, sir.' They passed into the Senator's bedroom.

'Bottle of whisky right on top of that desk,' the Senator said as he climbed into bed and pulled up the covers. 'Help yourself. What the hell is that in your hand?'

Raymond lifted the pistol and stared at it as though he weren't sure himself. 'It's a pistol, sir.'

The Senator stared, dumbfounded, at the pistol and at Raymond. 'Is that a silencer?' he managed to say.

'Yes, sir.'

'Why are you carrying a pistol?'

Raymond seemed to try to answer, but he was unable to. He opened his mouth, closed it again. He opened it again, but he could not make himself talk. He was lifting the pistol slowly.

'Raymond! No!' the Senator shouted in a great voice. 'What are you doing?'

The door on the far side of the room burst open. Jocie came into the room saying, 'Daddy, what is it? What is it?' just as Raymond shot him. A hole appeared magically in the Senator's forehead.

'Raymond! Raymond, darling! Raymond!' Jocie cried out in full scream. He ignored her. He crossed quickly to the Senator's side and shot again, into the right ear. Jocie could not stop screaming. She came running across the room at him, her arms outstretched imploringly, her face punished with horror. He shot her without moving, from the left hand. The bullet went through her right eye at a range of seven feet. Head going backward in a punched snap, knees going forward, she fell at his feet. His second shot went directly downward, through her left eye.

He put out the bed light and fumbled his way to the stairs. He could not control his grief any longer but he could not understand why he wept. He could not see. Loss, loss, loss, loss, loss, loss, loss.

When he climbed to the mattress in the back of the panel truck the sounds he was making were so piteous that Chunjin, although expressionless, seemed to be deeply moved by them because he took the pistol from Raymond's hand and struck him on the back of the head, bringing forgetfulness to save him.

The bodies were discovered in the morning by the Jordan housekeeper, Nora Lemmon. Radio and TV news shows had the story at eleven-eighteen, having interrupted all regular programmes with the flash. In Washington, via consecutive telephone calls to the news agencies, Senator Iselin offered the explanation that the murders bore out his charges of treason against Jordan who had undoubtedly been murdered by Soviet agents to silence him forever. The Monday morning editions of all newspapers were on the streets of principal cities on Sunday afternoon, five hours before the normal bulldog edition hit the street.

Raymond's mother did not awaken him when the FBI called to ask if she could assist them in establishing her son's present whereabouts. Colonel Marco called from New York as Raymond's closest friend, saying he feared that Raymond might have harmed himself in his grief over his wife's tragic death, almost begging Mrs Iselin to tell him where her son was so that he might comfort him. Raymond's mother hit herself with a heavy fix late Sunday afternoon because she could not rid her mind of the picture of that lovely, lovely, lovely dead girl which looked out at her from every newspaper. She went into a deep sleep. Johnny called all the papers and news agencies and announced that his wife was prostrate over the loss of a dear and wonderful girl whom she had loved as a daughter. He told the papers that he would not attend the opening day of the convention 'even if it costs me the White House' because of this terrible, terrible loss and their affliction of grief. Asked where his stepson was, the

Senator replied that Raymond was 'undoubtedly in retreat, praying to God for understanding to carry on somehow.'

XXV

Sunday night Marco drank gin with his head resting across Eugénie Rose's ample lap and listened to the *Zeitgeist* of zither music until the gin had softened the rims of his memory. He looked straight up, right through the ceiling, his face an Aztec mask. Rosie had not spoken because she had too much to ask him and he did not speak for a long time because he had too much to tell her. He pulled some sheets of white paper from the breast pocket of his jacket, which had been hung across the back of the chair beside them.

'I grabbed this from the files this afternoon,' he said. 'It's a verbatim report. Fella took it down on tape in the Argentine. Read it to me, hah?'

Rosie took the paper and read aloud. 'What follows is a transcribed conversation between Mrs Seward Arnold and Agent Graham Dundee as transcribed by Carmelita Barajas and witnessed by Dolores Freg on February 16, 1959.' Rosie looked for a moment as though she would ask a question, then seemed to think better of it. She continued to read from the paper while Marco stared from her lap at far away. She read slowly and softly.

DUNDEE: Mrs Arnold, if I may say so, this is the most unusual assignment of my career. I have been awake half the night studying how I could try to explain what I have been sent here to ask you.

MRS ARNOLD: Sent by whom, Mr Dundee?

DUNDEE: I don't know. If I did know I should probably have

been instructed not to reveal that. I am a physician. A psychiatrist. I am attached to the Federal Bureau of Investigation of the Department of Justice of the government of the United States in that capacity. Here are my credentials.

MRS ARNOLD: I see. Thank you, but——

DUNDEE: I have been flown from New York for this chat with you and when we have finished I shall take the first plane back to New York. It is a terrible journey when one makes it that way. Some thirteen thousand miles of catered food and the wrong people in the seat beside one. Talkers, mostly.

MRS ARNOLD: It sounds terribly important.

DUNDEE: You may be sure of that.

MRS ARNOLD: But how can I help you? I'm not important, thank heaven. Does this involve my father?

DUNDEE: No, Mrs Arnold. It involves a man named Raymond Shaw.

(TRANSCRIBER AND WITNESS TIMED INTERVAL SILENCE OF ELEVEN SECONDS HERE.)

DUNDEE: Do you remember Raymond Shaw?

MRS ARNOLD: Yes.

DUNDEE: Will you tell me what you remember about him Mrs Arnold?

MRS ARNOLD: But—why?

DUNDEE: I don't know. There is so much we must do on faith alone. I only know that I must ask you these questions and pray that you will decide to answer. As a psychiatrist I have been assigned to work on and collect data concerning the character and personality and habits and reactions and inhibitions and repressions and idiosyncrasies and compulsions of Raymond Shaw for fourteen months, Mrs Arnold. I have not been told why. I know only that it is desperately important work.

MRS ARNOLD: It has been seven years since I have seen or spoken to Raymond Shaw, Mr—rather, Dr Dundee.

DUNDEE: Thank you.

MRS ARNOLD: I was only a girl. I mean to say I did not consciously store up information about him. I mean, to get me started perhaps you would tell me what you know about Raymond Shaw.

DUNDEE: What I know? Mrs Arnold, I know more about him than he knows about himself but I would not be permitted to tell *him*, much less you, because Raymond Shaw is classified information; his recreations and habits are top secret and his thoughts and dreams are top, *top* secret. Will you tell me about him?

MRS ARNOLD: Raymond was twenty-one or twenty-two years old when I first saw him. I thought, and I still think, he was the handsomest man I have ever seen in life, or in a photograph or in a painting. His eyes had such regret for the world. They seemed to deplore that the world had taken him upon it and had then made him invisible.

DUNDEE: Did you say invisible, Mrs Arnold?

MRS ARNOLD: That was his own description of himself, but I never knew anyone who ever saw Raymond. My own father who is a sensitive, interested man, was not able to see him. My father saw a neurotic slender giant of a child who seemed to pout and who stared rudely at every movement, the way cats do. Surely, Raymond's mother never saw him. I am not even sure that his mother ever looked at him.

DUNDEE: Still, his mother manufactured Raymond.

MRS ARNOLD: The cold, unfriendliness of him. The resentful retreater. The hurt and defiant retreater who wept stone tears behind a shield of arrogance.

DUNDEE: But he was not invisible to you.

MRS ARNOLD: No. He allowed me to see him. He was very shy. He had so much tenderness. He was nearly pathetic with his need to please, once he had been allowed to understand that it was wanted for him to be pleasing. He was so sparing with his warm thoughts, except with me. His loving and unresentful thoughts. He doled them out through that eye dropper which was his fear and shyness, then he grew until he could give spoonfuls of it until, at last, when he knew that I loved him he could have learned to give and partake of feeling and warmth and love the way the gods do.

DUNDEE: Mrs Arnold, I won't pretend to try to be casual about this. What I must ask you is tremendously important and has a direct bearing upon essential psychiatric evidence, you must be sure of that, or I would never, never, never presume to ask you such an extraordinary question, but you see we—I——

MRS ARNOLD: Did Raymond ever possess me? Did we ever sleep together? Is that the question, Doctor?

DUNDEE: Yes. Thank you. That is it, Mrs Arnold. If you please.

MRS ARNOLD: I wish he had—that we had. I wish he had and if he had I could not have told you. But he did not, so I can. Raymond never—we never—Raymond and I never so much as kissed, Dr Dundee.

Marco reached up and took the transcript gently out of Rosie's hands. He folded it and slid it back into the pocket of his jacket.

'Who was Mrs Arnold?' Rosie asked.

'That was Jocie. Raymond's girl.'

'His wife.'

'Yeah.'

He got to his feet laboriously. He could not have made it straight up into an erect position. He had to roll off her lap and the sofa to his hands and knees, then get to his feet holding on to a chair. He took the empty gin bottle to the kitchen, lurching slightly, and stored it neatly in a waste-basket. He got another bottle. On the way back to Rosie he picked up the newspaper he had brought in with him at six o'clock and which had lain, rolled up, on a table near the door. He dropped the newspaper into her lap, then sat down beside her. 'Raymond shot and killed his wife this morning,' he said.

She tried to read the paper and watch Marco at the same time. She drew astonishment from the paper and horror from the sight of Marco because he looked so ravaged. He drank a few fingers of warm gin while she read the story. When she had finished it she said, 'The paper doesn't say that Raymond killed his wife.' Marco didn't answer. He drank and thought and listened through one more side of zither music, then he fell forward on his face to the horrendous pink cabbage roses in the French blue rug. She held him and kissed him, then she dragged him by his feet into the bedroom, undressed him, and rolled him up across the bed in several stages.

XXVI

Raymond watched the queen of diamonds on top of the squared deck while his mother spoke to him.

'. . . and Chunjin will give you a two-piece Soviet Army sniper's rifle with all of its native ballistic markings. It sets nicely into a special bag which you can carry just as though it were a visiting doctor's bag. You'll take it with you to the hotel at Newark. We have come to the end of this terrible road at last, Raymond darling. After years and years and so much pain it will all be over so soon now. We have won the power, and now that they have given it to us they can just begin to fear. We may reply now, my dearest, for what they have done to you, to me, and to your lovely Jocie.'

Raymond's mother had banged a charge into her arm just before this session of briefing Raymond and it most certainly agreed with her. Her magnetic, perfectly spaced blue eyes seemed to sparkle as she talked. Her lithe, solid figure seemed even more superb because of her flawless carriage. She wore a Chinese dressing-gown of a shade so light that it complemented the contrasting colour of her eyes. Her long and extremely beautiful legs were stretched out before her on the chaise longue, and any man but her son or her husband, seeing what she had and yet knowing that this magnificent forty-nine-year-old body was only a wasted uniform covering blunted neutral energy, might have wept over such a waste. Her voice, usually that of a hard woman on the make for big stakes, had softened perceptibly as she spoke because she was pleading and her voice had new overtones of self-deception. In the years since Raymond had been returned from the Army and shock had been piled upon shock, the sanity-preserving part of her mind, which laboured to teach her how to forgive herself, and thus save herself, had been working and scheming against the day when she must explain everything to Raymond and expect to receive his forgiveness.

'I am sure you will never entirely comprehend this, darling, and I know, the way you are right now, this is like trying to have a whispered conversation with someone on a distant star, but for my own peace of mind, such as that is, it must be said. Raymond, you have to believe that I did not know that they would do what they did to you. I served them. I thought for them. I got them the greatest foothold they will ever have in this country and they paid me back by taking your soul away from you. I told them to build me an assassin. I wanted a killer who would obey orders from a stock in a world filled with killers, and they did this to you because they thought it would bind me closer to them. When I walked into that room in that Swardon Sanitarium in New York to meet this perfect assassin and I found that he was my son— my son with a changed and twisted mind and all the bridges burned behind us . . . But we have come to the end now, and it is our turn to twist tomorrow for them, because just as I am a mother before everything else I am an American second to that, and when I take power they will be pulled down and ground into dirt for what they did to you and for what they did in so contemptuously underestimating me.' She took his hand and kissed it with burning devotion, then she held his face in her hands and stared into it tenderly. 'How much you look like Poppa! You have his beautiful hands and you hold your beautiful head in that same proud, proud way. And when you smile! Smile, my darling.'

Raymond smiled, naturally and beautifully, under orders. She caught her breath in a gasp. 'When you smile, Raymond dearest, for that instant I am a little girl again and the miracle of love begins all over again. How right that seems to me. Smile for me again, sweetheart. Yes. Yes. Now kiss me. Really, really kiss me.' Her long fingers dug into his shoulders and pulled him to her on the chaise, and as her left hand opened the Chinese robe she remembered Poppa and the sound of rain high in the attic when she had been a little girl, and she found again the ecstatic peace she had lost so long, long before.

XXVII

Theodore Roosevelt said that the right of popular government is incomplete unless it includes the right of voters not merely to choose between candidates when they have been nominated, but also the right to determine who these candidates shall be.

Three major methods have been used by the parties, in American political history, to name candidates: the caucus, the convention, and the direct primary. The caucus was discarded early because it gave the legislature undue influence over the executive. The convention method for choosing Presidential candidates was first used in 1831 by the Anti-Masonic party, but the basic flaw in any convention system is the method of choice of delegates to the convention. The origin of the direct primary is somewhat obscure but it is generally considered as having been adopted by the Democratic party in Crawford County, Pennsylvania, in 1842; however, not until Robert M. La Follette became governor of Wisconsin, early in 1900, was a political leader successful in pushing through a mandatory, statewide, direct primary system.

Because no public regulation exists to control it, the national convention has developed into one of the most remarkable political institutions in the world. In no other nation on this planet is the selection of national leaders, whose influence is to be felt profoundly throughout the world, and the formulation of ostensibly serious policies placed in the hands of a convention of about three thousand howling, only cursorily consulted delegates and alternates. M. Ostrogorski, a French observer of the American political scene, wrote in 1902 of the convention system: 'You realise what a colossal travesty of popular institutions you have just been witnessing. A greedy crowd of office-holders, or of office seekers, disguised as delegates of the people on the pretence of holding the grand council of the party, indulged in, or were victims of, intrigues and manœuvres, the object of which was the chief magistracy of the greatest republic of two hemispheres—the succession to the Washingtons and the Jeffersons. Yet when you carry your thoughts back from the scene which you have just witnessed and review the line of presidents you find that if they have not all been great men—far from it—they were all honourable men; and you cannot help repeating the American saying: "God takes care of drunkards, little children, and of the United States." '

The climate of welcome in which the convention of 1960 opened was like many of those that had preceded it. Hotels were festooned with bunting. Distillers had provided all saloons with printed partisan displays, the backs of which carried the same message in the name of the other party, whose convention would follow in three weeks. The mid-town streets were choked with big-hipped broads wearing paper cowboy hats. Witty Legionnaires rode horses into hotel lobbies. Witty Legionnaires squirted friendly streams from water pistols at the more defenceless-looking passers-by. Gay delegates hung twenty-dollar call girls by their heels out of high hotel windows. Ward heelers issued statements on party unity. Elder statesmen were ignored or used depending on the need. The Pickpocket Squad worked like contestants in a newsreel husking bee. One hundred and four men's suits were misplaced by the dry-cleaning services of thirty-eight hotels. Petitions and documentations were submitted to the Resolutions Committee by farm lobbies, labour unions, women's organisations, temperance groups, veterans' blocs, anti-vivisection societies, and national manufacturers' Turnvereins. Two thousand one hundred and four hand towels over the minimal daily quota would be used, on an average, for each night the convention sat in the city. A delegate was arrested, but not prosecuted, for wrestling with a live crocodile in Duffy Square to call attention to the courage of a Florida candidate for the vice-presidency. The world's largest campaign button was worn by a bevy of lovely young 'apple farmers' from the Pacific Northwest although their candidate came from Missouri (he happened to be in the apple business). At 8 A.M., two hours before the convention opened on Monday morning, Marco conducted a drill of two hundred FBI and Army Intelligence agents and three hundred and ten plain-clothes men and women of the New York Police Department, assembled in the backstage area of the Garden where they were briefed on the over-all assignment. Marco was so frantic with worry and fear that his hand shook as he used the chalk on the large blackboard, on a high platform. After Marco's briefing, more and more detailed briefings were conducted down through the units of command to squad level, until Marco, Amjac, Lehner, and the chief inspector of the New York police were sure that each man knew what he was to do.

The twenty-seventh national convention of the party was opened by Miss Viola Narvilly of the great Indianapolis Opera Company singing the National Anthem. This one, as her manager explained, was a bitch of a song to sing, as any singer, professional or otherwise, would tell you, and, he said hotly, it like to have lifted Miss Narvilly out of her own body by her vocal cords to get up to those unnatural notes which some idiot thought he was doing great when he wrote it. Miss Narvilly's manager tried to throw a punch at the National Chairman—he had practically begged them to open the convention singing the lousy song, then not one single television shot had been taken of Miss Narvilly from beginning to end, before or after, and they had spent their own loot to come all the way in from a concert in Chicago.

After the National Chairman got some help from two sergeantsat-arms in shaking Miss Narvilly's manager loose he called the first session to order. Nearly six hundred of the three thousand delegates settled down to listen to the welcoming speech by the party's senator from New York. The Chairman made his formal address following this token welcome and the hall filled up just a little more, and the business of permanent organisation, credentials, rules and order of business, platform and resolutions got under way and filled the time nicely until the keynote speaker took over in the TV slot that had been bought on all networks for nine to nine-thirty that evening.

Although Senator Iselin and his wife did not attend the first day's session, an Iselin headquarters had been established on a full floor of the largest West Side hotel near the Garden. Also, the Loyal American Underground had established recruiting booths for Johnny in the lobbies of every 'official' convention hotel and had rented a store opposite the Eighth Avenue entrance to the Garden; the store had been an upholstery store before the convention and would be an upholstery store again. One enthusiastic newspaper reported that these recruitment booths had registered four thousand two hundred members (Mrs Iselin had thought it prudent to register the same one hundred people again and again throughout the days to insure the excitement of action at all booths), but the exact number of new recruits could not be determined accurately.

On the opening Monday, true to his word as an officer and a gentleman, General Francis 'Fightin' Frank' Bollinger headed a parade made up of state and county chairmen of Ten Million Americans Mobilising for To-morrow, down Eighth Avenue from Columbus Circle to the Garden. They were two hundred and forty-six strong from the forty-nine states, plus an irregular battalion made up of loyal wives and daughters, various uncommitted New Yorkers who enjoyed parading, and a police squad car. They marched the nine short blocks with Fightin' Frank holding in one gloved hand the front end of a continuous paper petition that stretched out behind him for eight and a half blocks and contained at least four thousand signatures, many of which had been written by the general's own family to fill out the spaces and add to the fun. Many of the newspaper reports got the figure wrong, reporting as many as 1,064,219 signatures, although at no time did any representative of any newspaper attempt to make a count. The petition urged the nomination of John Yerkes Iselin to the Presidency of the United States candidacy under the general indivisive slogan of 'The Man Who Saves America.'

Mrs Iselin arrived at Johnny's campaign headquarters at eight o'clock Monday night. For the next several hours she received the prospective candidates for the Presidency, together with their managers, in separate relays in her suite. At 1.10 A.M. she made the deal she wanted and committed Senator Iselin's entire delegate support to the candidate of her choice, accepting, on behalf of Senator Iselin, the assurance of nomination for the office of vice-presidency and losing for Fightin' Frank Bollinger the assurance of portfolio as Secretary of State.

The party's platform was presented to the convention on Tuesday morning and afternoon, together with many statesman-like speeches. Professor Hugh Bone, when writing of party platforms as delivered at conventions said: 'If the voter expects to find specific issues and clearly defined party policy in the platform he will be sorely disappointed. As a guide to the pro-gramme to be carried out by the victorious party the platform is also of little value.' The British political scholar Lord Byrce observed that the purpose of the American party platform appears to be 'neither to define nor to convince, but rather to attract and confuse.' The 1960 platform of the party committed itself as follows: for free enterprise, farm prosperity, preservation of small business, reduction in taxes, and rigid economy in government. The latter plank had been axiomatic for both major parties since 1840. Due to the insistence of Senator Iselin the platform also demanded 'the eradication of Communists and Communist thought without mercy wherever and whenever Our Flag flies.'

The roll call for the nomination got under way on Tuesday

afternoon, July 12. Alabama yielded. The nominating speech, the demonstration following that, the seconding speech, and the demonstration following that, gave the convention the first aspirant in nomination at six twenty-one. The identical ritual for the second favourite soon took up the attention of the convention to ten thirty-five. The third candidate proposed was nominated on the first ballot by unanimous vote of the convention, as had been ten candidates of the party since 1900, at twelve forty-one on July 12, 1960, when the convention was adjourned until noon the following day when it would meet to deliberate over its choice of candidate for the office of vice-president, then await the historic acceptance speeches by both leaders the following night.

XXVIII

Raymond left the hotel in Newark, where he had been told to rest, at 4 P.M. Wednesday. He carried a nondescript black satchel. He took the tubes under the river, then the subway to Times Square. For a while he wandered aimlessly along West Forty-second Street. After a while he found himself at Forty-fourth and Broadway. He went into a large drugstore. He got change for a quarter at the cigarette counter and shuffled to one of the empty telephone booths in the rear. He dialled Marco's office number. The agent on duty answered. He was alone in the large house in Turtle Bay.

'Colonel Marco, please.'

'Who is calling, please?'

'Raymond Shaw. It's a personal call.'

The agent inhaled very slowly. Then he exhaled slowly. 'Hello? Hello?' Raymond said, thinking the connection had been broken.

'Right here, Mr Shaw,' the agent said briskly. 'It looks as

though Colonel Marco has stepped away from his desk for a moment, but he'll be back practically instantly, Mr Shaw, and he left word that if you called he wanted to be sure that he could call you right back, wherever you were. If you'll give me your telephone number, Mr Shaw——'

'Well——'

'He'll be right back.'

'Maybe I'd better call him back. I'm in a drugstore here and——'

'I have my orders, Mr Shaw. If you'll give me that number, please.'

'The number in the booth here is Circle eight, nine six three seven. I'll hang around for ten minutes or so, I guess, and have a cup of coffee.' He hung up the phone and the newspaper fell from his pocket and flattened out on the floor showing the headline: MURDERS OF SENATOR AND DAUGHTER ENIGMA. Raymond picked the paper up slowly and returned it to his jacket pocket. He climbed on a stool at the soda fountain and waited for someone to come and take his order.

The agent on duty dialled a number rapidly. He got a busy signal. He waited painfully with his eyes closed, then he opened them and dialled again. He got a busy signal. He pulled his sleeve back from his wrist watch, stared at it for thirty seconds, then dialled again. The connection bubbled a through signal.

'Garden.'

'This is Turtle Bay. Get me Marco. Red signal.'

'Hold, please.'

The booming voice of the platform speaker inside the arena was cut off from every amplifier throughout the Garden. The packed hall seemed, for an instant, like a silent waxworks packed with three thousand effigies. An urgent, new voice came pounding out the horns. It contrasted so much with the ribbon of pure silence that had preceded it, after two days of amplified fustian, that every delegate felt threatened by its urgency.

'*Colonel Marco! Colonel Marco! Red Signal! Red Signal! Colonel Marco! Red Signal!*'

The voice cut itself off and another electronic flow of silence came through the system. Newspapermen immediately began to pressure the wrong officials about the significance of the interruption and the term *red signal*, and beginning with the first editions of the morning papers the term was printed again and again until it finally found itself on television variety shows as comedians' warning cries.

Marco sat backstage with an unleashed phone in his hand, within a semi-circle of agents and police. Amjac was between earphones at one telephone monitor and Lehner was at the other. The recording machines were turning. Five minutes, eight seconds, had elapsed since Raymond had made his call. Marco dialled. He was sweating peanut butter.

The telephone rang in an empty booth. It rang again. Then again. A figure slumped into the seat to answer it. It was Raymond.

'Ben?' No other opening.

'Yes, kid.'

'You read what happened?'

'Yes. I know. I know.'

'How could anyone? How could it happen? Jocie—how could anyone——'

'Where are you, Raymond?' The men ringed around Marco seemed to lean forward.

'I think maybe I'm going crazy. I have the terrible dreams like you used to have and terrible things are all twisted together. But the craziest part is how anyone—could—Ben! They killed Jocie. Somebody *killed* Jocie!' The words came out hoarsely and on a climbing scale.

'Where are you, kid? We have to talk. We can't talk on the telephone. Where are you?'

'I have to talk to you. I have to talk to you.'

'I'll meet you. Where are you?'

'I can't stay here. I have to get out. I have to get air.'

'I'll meet you at the paper.'

'No, no.'

'In the Park, then.'

'The Park?'

'The zoo, Raymond. On the porch of the cafeteria. O.K.?'

'O.K.'

'Right away.'

'They're inside my head, like you said.'

'Get a cab and get up to the Park.'

'Yes.' Raymond hung up. Marco banged the phone down and wheeled in his swivel chair. Amjac and Lehner nodded at the same time. 'The boy is in bad shape,' Lehner said.

'I'll take him now,' Marco said. 'This has to move very normally. Raymond has to be allowed to feel safe, then he has to play solitaire, so this is all mine. Give me some cards.'

Lehner took a pack of force cards out of a carton on the long work table supported by sawhorses and tossed them across the room to Marco. Lehner stuffed another pack into his pocket as a souvenir. A detail coming off duty straggled into the room. 'Whatta you know?' the first man said. 'They just handed the vice-presidency to that idiot Iselin.' Marco grunted. He turned and nearly ran towards the Forty-ninth Street exit.

Raymond was sitting in the sooty sunlight with his back to the *arriviste* skyline of Central Park South, staring at a cup of coffee. Marco felt shock like a heavy hammer as he stared at him from a few feet off. He suddenly realised he had never seen Raymond unshaven before, or wearing a dirty shirt, or wearing clothes that could have been slept in for night after night. Raymond's face seemed to be falling into itself and it presented the kind of shock a small boy's face would bring if he had had all of his teeth extracted.

Marco sat down across from Raymond at the sturdy outdoor table. There were only eight or nine people on the long, broad terrace. Marco and Raymond had a lot of room to themselves. He put his hand on top of Raymond's dirty hand with the black rimmed fingers. 'Hi, kid,' he said almost inaudibly. Raymond looked up. His eyes glistened with wet. 'I don't know what is happening to me,' he said and Marco could almost see the ripping Raymond felt. Raymond's emotion was like that of a curate with his head filled with cocaine, or perhaps like that of a man after he has had acid thrown into his eyes. The grief that shone dully out of Raymond blocked out everything else within Marco's field of vision; it was blackness which threw back no reflection.

The seals in the large pool honked and splashed. Around the seal pond grew a moving garden of zoo-blooming balloons, their roots attached to bicycles and prams and small fists. The big cats were being fed somewhere in the area behind Marco and they were noisy eaters.

'They are inside my head like you said, aren't they, Ben?'

Marco nodded.

'Can they—can they make me do anything?'

Marco nodded less perceptibly.

'I have a terrible dream—oh, my God—I have a terrible dream that my mother and I——'

Raymond's eyes were so wild that Marco could not look at him. He shut his eyes and thought of the shapes of prayers. A rubber ball came bouncing then rolling along the stone terrace. It lodged against Marco's feet. A small boy with a comical face and hair like a poodle's came running after it. He held Raymond's arm as he bent down to get his ball, then ran away from them shouting at his friends.

'Who killed Jocie, Ben?'—and Marco could not answer him. 'Ben, did I—did I kill Jocie? That could be, couldn't it? Maybe it was an accident, but they wanted me to kill Senator Jordan and—did I kill my Jocie?'

Marco could not watch this any longer. Mercifully, he said, 'How about passing the time by playing a little solitaire?' and he slid the force deck across the table. He watched Raymond relax. Raymond got the cards out of the box and began to shuffle mechanically and smoothly.

Marco had to be sure that his red queen would command the authority to supersede all others. He had never been permitted to read Yen Lo's complete instructions for the operation of a murderer. Therefore, the force deck, which had been enlisted at first as a time-saver to bring the red queen into immediate play, was now seen by Marco as his insurance policy which had to be seven ways more powerful than the single queen of diamonds that the enemy had used. Every time Raymond's play showed the red queen, which was from the first card set down, he attempted reflexively to stop the play. Marco ordered him to play on, to lay out the full, upfaced seven stacks of solitaire. At last there was arrayed a pantheon of red queens in imperious row.

Where was Jocie? Raymond asked himself, far inside himself, as he stared at the advancing sweep of costumed monarchs. The seven queens commanded silence. They began to order him, through Marco, to unlock all of the great jade doors which went back, back, back, along an austere corridor in time to the old, old man with the withered, merry smile who said his name was Yen Lo and who promised him solemnly that in other lives, through which he would journey beyond this life, he would be spared the unending agony which he had found in this life. Where was Jocie? Mr Gaines had been a good man but he had been told to make him dead. Amen. He had had to kill in Paris; he had killed in London by special appointment to the Queen of Diamonds, offices in principal cities. Amen. Where was Jocie? The tape recorder in the holster under Marco's arm revolved and listened. Raymond stared at the seven queens and talked. He told what his mother had told him. He explained that he had shot Senator Jordan and that—that he had—that after he had shot Senator Jordan he had——

Marco's voice slammed out at him, telling him he was to forget about what had happened at Senator Jordan's until he, Marco, told him to remember. He asked Raymond what he had been told to do in New York. Raymond told him.

In the end, when all Marco's questions had been answered, but not until the very end, did it become clear to Colonel Marco, what they would have to do. Marco thought of his father and his grandfather and of their Army. He considered his own life and its meaning. He decided for both of them what they would have to do.

They walked away from the terrace, past the seal pond, through the bobbing flowers in the garden of toy balloons. They walked past the bars marked YAK—POEPHAGUS GRUNNIENS—CENT. ASIA and they moved out slowly through the gantlet of resters and lovers and dreamers towards the backside of General Sherman's bronze horse.

At Sixtieth Street, on Fifth Avenue, Marco tried to anticipate the changing of a traffic light. He stepped down from the kerb two steps in front of Raymond, then turned to hurry Raymond along so that they could beat the light, when the Drive-Your-Self car, rented by Chunjin, hit him. It threw him twelve feet and he lay where he fell. A crowd began to collect itself out of motes of sunlight. A foot policeman came running from the hotel marquee at Fifty-ninth Street because a woman had screamed like a crane. Chunjin leaned over and opened the door. 'Get in, Mr Shaw. Quickly, please.' Raymond got into the car, carrying his satchel, and as the car zoomed off into the Park, he slammed the door. Chunjin left the Park at Seventy-second Street, crossed to Broadway, and started downtown. They did not speak until they reached the dingy hotel on West Forty-ninth Street when Chunjin gave him the key stamped 301, wished him good luck, shook his hand while he stared into Raymond's tragic, yellow eyes, told him to leave the car, and drove off, going west.

Raymond changed clothes in Room 301. He entered the Garden through a door marked Executive Entrance on the Forty-ninth Street side, at five forty-five, during the afternoon recess while the building held only five per cent of the activity it had seen one hour before. The candidate's acceptance speeches were scheduled to appear on all networks from ten to ten-thirty that night, and after that the campaign would start.

Raymond was dressed as he had been told to dress; as a priest, with a reversed stiff collar, black suit, a soft, black hat, and heavy black shell eyeglasses. He smoked a large black cigar from the corner of his mouth and he carried a satchel. He looked

277

over-worked, preoccupied, and sour. Everybody saw him. No one recognised him. He walked across the main lobby just inside the Eighth Avenue gates and climbed the staircase slowly like a man on a dull errand. He kept climbing. When he could go no farther, he walked along behind the top tier of the gallery seats, now empty, not bothering to look down at the littered floor of the arena, six stories below him. Carrying the satchel, he went up the iron stepladder that was bolted to the wall, climbing twenty-two feet until he reached the catwalk that ran out at right angles from the wall and led to the suspended box that was a spotlight booth, used only for theatrical spectaculars. He let himself into the booth with a key, closing and locking the door behind him. He sat down on a wooden packing case, opened the satchel, took out a gun barrel, then the stock of a sniper's rifle, and assembled the gun with expert care. When he was satisfied with its connection, he took the telescopic sight out of its chamois case and, after polishing it carefully, mounted it on the piece.

XXIX

Marco was fighting to kill time. He stalled at every possible chance as they tried to help him dress. He needed time for Raymond to find his position, for the inexorable, uncompromising television schedule to pull all of the counters into play. Marco thought about the face of John Yerkes Iselin and he made himself do everything more slowly.

His right arm was in full sling; right hand to the left shoulder. The right side of his face seemed to have come off. The skin was gone and under the snowy bandage it was as black as the far side of the moon. Four ribs had crumpled on the left side of his spine, and he was tightly taped. He was under semi-anaesthesia to keep the pain under control, and it gave him everything on the outside in parts of fantasy and parts of reality. Two men were dressing him as rapidly as he would allow them to progress, although no one there could tell that he was stalling.

Amjac and Lehner squatted on the floor around a tape play-back machine and the only sound in the room, beyond Marco's laboured breathing and his quick, deep throat-sounds of pain, was the clear, impersonal sound of Raymond's voice, backed up by children's squeals and laughter, the roar of hungry cats, the honks and splats of seals, and the gentling undersound of two hundred red, green, and yellow balloons as they cut the air at a tenth of a mile per hour. Every man in the room was staring at the machine. It was saying:

'No, I don't think the priest's outfit is supposed to have any symbolic significance. My mother doesn't think that way. Primarily, it will be good camouflage. She may have arranged to have me caught after I kill him, when, I suppose, I will be exposed as a Communist with a tailor-made record as long as a hangman's rope. Then, of course, the choice of ecclesiastical costume will keep a lot of people enraged on still a different level, if they didn't happen to plan to vote for the dead candidate. If I am caught I am to state, on the second day, after much persuasion, that I was ordered to undertake the execution by the Kremlin. Mother definitely plans to involve them, but I don't think she will purposely involve me because she was really deeply upset and affected for the first time since I have known her when she discovered that they had chosen me to be their killer. She told me that they had lost the world when they did that and that when she and Johnny got into the White House she was going to start and finish a holy war, without ten minutes' warning, that would wipe them off the face of the earth, and that then we—I do not mean this country, I mean Mother and whoever she decides to use—will run this country and we'll run the whole world. She is crazy, of course. There will be a terrible pande-monium down in that arena after they are hit, and I am sure the priest's suit will help me to get away. I am to leave at once, but the rifle stays there. It's a Soviet issue rifle.'

Marco's voice, from the tape, said, 'Did you say after *they* are hit? Did you use the word "they"?'

'Well, yes. I am ordered to shoot the nominee through the head and to shoot Johnny Iselin through the left shoulder, and when the bullet hits Johnny it will shatter a crystal compound which Mother has sewn in under the material which will make him look all soggy with blood. He won't be hurt because that whole area from his chin to his hips will be bullet-proofed. Mother said this was the part Johnny was actually born to play because he overacts so much and we can certainly use plenty of that here. The bullet's velocity will knock him down, of course, but he will get to his feet gallantly amid the chaos that will have broken out at that time, and the way she wants him to do it for the best effect for the television cameras and the still photographers is to lift the nominee's body in his arms and stand in front of the microphones like tha. because that picture will symbolise more than anything else that it is Johnny's party which the Soviets fear the most, and Johnny will offer the body of a great American on the altar of liberty, and as you know, as Mother says, there is nothing that has succeeded in the history of politics like martyrdom, for now the people must rise and strike down this Communist peril which she can prove instantly lives within and amongst us all. Johnny will point that up in his speech he will make with the candidate in his arms. It is short, but Mother says it is the most rousing speech she has ever read. They have been working on that speech, here and in Russia, on and off, for over eight years. Mother will force some of the men on that platform to take the body away from Johnny because, after all, he's not Tarzan she said, then Johnny will really hit that microphone and those cameras, blood all over him, fighting off those who try to succour him, defending America even if it means his death, and rallying a nation of television viewers into hysteria and pulling that convention along behind him to vote him into the nomination and to accept a platform which will sweep them right into the White House under powers which will make martial law seem like anarchism, Mother says.'

'When will you shoot the candidate, Raymond?' Marco's voice asked.

'Well, Mother wants him to be dead at about six minutes after he begins his acceptance speech, depending on his reading speed under pressure, but I will hit him right at the point where he finishes the phrase which reads: "nor would I ask of any fellow American in defence of his freedom that which I would not gladly give myself—my life before my liberty." '

'Where will you shoot from?'

'There is a spotlight booth that will not be in use. It's up under the roof of the Eighth Avenue side of the Garden. I haven't been in it, but Mother says I will have absolutely clear, protected shooting from it. She will seat Johnny on the platform directly behind the candidate, just a little to his left, so I'll be able to swing the sights and wing him with minimal time loss. That's about it. It's a very solid plan.'

'They all are,' Marco's voice said. 'There are going to be one or two important changes, Raymond. Forget what your mother told you. This is what you are going to do.'

There was a click. The tape in the playback machine rolled to a stop.

'What happened?' Amjac said quickly.

'The colonel stopped the machine,' Lehner said, watching Marco.

'Come on,' Marco said. 'We have seconds, not minutes. Let's go.' He started out of the room, forcing them to follow him.

'But what did you tell him, Colonel?'

'Don't worry,' Marco said, walking rapidly. 'The Army takes care of its own.'

'You mean—Raymond?'

They crowded into the elevator at the end of the hospital corridor. 'No,' Marco answered. 'I was thinking about two other things. About a General Jorgenson and the United States of America.'

XXX

A hush fell upon the delegations in the great hall as the Chairman announced that within a very few minutes their candidates would be facing the television cameras, when, for the first time together, eighty million American voters would see the next President and Vice-President of the United States standing before them. The convention thundered its approval. As they cheered the top brass of the party, made up of governors, national committeemen, fat cats, senators, and congressmen, were herded upon the platform, followed by the two nominees and their wives.

They moved with great solemnity. Senator Iselin and his wife seemed to be affected particularly. They were unsteady and extremely pale, which occasioned more than one delegate, newspaperman, committeeman, and spectator to observe that the vast dignity and the awful responsibility, truly the awesome meaning of that great office, had never failed to humble any man and that John Iselin was no exception, as he was proving up there now. When he sat down he was actually trembling and he seemed —he, of all people, whom audiences and speeches had stimulated all his life—nervous and apprehensive, even frightened. They could see his wife, a beautiful woman who was always at his side, a real campaigner and a fighter who, more than once, had looked subversion in the face and had stared it down, as she spoke to him steadily, in an undertone which was obviously too low-pitched and too personal for anyone to hear.

'Sit still, you son-of-a-bitch! He has never missed with a rifle in his life. Johnny! Damn it, Johnny, if you move you can get hurt. Give him a chance to sight you and to get used to this light. And what the hell are you sweating now for? You won't be hit until after the speech is under way. Did you take those pills? Johnny, did you? I knew it. I knew I should have stood over you and made you take those goddam pills.' She fumbled inside her handbag. She worked three pills out of a vial and placed them together on the adhesive side of a piece of Scotch tape, within the purse. Very sweetly and with the graciousness of a Schrafft's hostess she gestured unobtrusively to a young man who was at the edge of the platform for just such emergencies and asked him for a glass of water.

When the water came, just as she got it in her hand, the nominee was on the air and his acceptance speech had begun. His voice was low but clear as he began to thank the delegations for the honour they had done him.

Only the speaker's platform was lighted. Three rows in front of the speaker, as he faced the darkness of the hall, one of the men of Marco's unit was crouched in the aisle, with walkie-talkie equipment. He spoke into the mouthpiece with a low voice, giving a running account of what was happening on the platform, and if the delegates seated near him thought of him at all, they thought he was on the air, although what he was saying would have mystified any radio audience.

'She just got a glass of water from the page. She is handling it very busily. She's doing something with the rim of it. I'm not sure. Wait. I'm not sure. I'm going to take a guess that she has stuck something on the rim of the glass—I even think I can see it—and she just handed the glass to Iselin.'

On the platform, behind and to the left of the speaker, Raymond's mother said to Johnny, 'The pills are on the edge of the glass. Take them as you drink. That's good. That's fine. Now you'll be O.K. Now just sit still, sweetheart. All you'll feel will be like a very hard punch on the shoulder. Just one punch and it's all over. Then you get up and do your stuff and we're home free, honey. We're in like Flynn, honey. Just take it easy. Take it easy, sweetheart.'

Marco, Amjac, and Lehner climbed the stairs. Lehner was carrying a walkie-talkie and mumbling into it. The nominee's speech was booming out of the speakers and Amjac was saying, as though in a bright conversation with nobody, O Jesus God, they were too late, they were too late. Marco moved clumsily under his bandages but he held the lead going up the stairs.

As they got to the top level they were scrambling and they started to run along behind the gallery seats towards the iron ladder as the nominee's voice reverberated all around them, saying: '. . . that which I would gladly give myself—my life before my liberty,' and Amjac was screaming, 'Oh, my good God, no! No!' when they heard the first rifle shot crack out and echo. 'No! No!' Amjac screamed, and the sounds were ripped out of his chest as though they were being sent on to overtake the bullet and deflect its course when the second shot ripped its sound through the air, then everything was drowned out by a great, enormous roar of shock and fear as comprehension of the meaning of the first shot reached the floor of the arena. The noise from the Garden floor was horrendous. Lehner stopped to crouch against the building wall, pressing the earphones to his ears, trying to hear the message from the man in front of the platform on the arena floor. 'What? What? Louder. Aaaaaaah!' It was a wailed sigh. He dragged the earphones off his head, staring numbly at Amjac. 'He shot Iselin, then he shot his mother. Dead. Not the nominee. Johnny and his wife are stone cold dead.'

Amjac wheeled. 'Colonel!' he shouted. 'Where's the colonel?' He looked up and saw Marco moving painfully across the narrow catwalk towards the locked black box that was the spotlight booth. 'Colonel Marco!' Amjac yelled. Marco turned slightly as he walked, and waved his left hand. It held a deck of playing cards. They watched him come to the door of the booth and kick at it gently.

When they reached the catwalk, Marco had disappeared into the booth. The door had closed again. Amjac started across the catwalk with Lehner behind him. They stopped short as the door opened and Marco came out. He couldn't close the door behind him because of the sling, but they could not see through the darkness inside. They backed up on the catwalk as he came towards them, and then they heard the third shot sound inside the booth—short, sharp, and clean.

'No electric chair for a Medal of Honour man,' Marco said, and he began to pick his way painfully down the iron ladder listening intently for a memory of Raymond, for the faintest rustle of his ever having lived, but there was none.

MONTE CARLO

Stephen Sheppard

It is May 1940 when Harry Pilikian, a young American, drives his Rolls Royce through the French night. By the time he reaches the principality of Monaco, the Germans have invaded France — and the war begins in earnest.

In neutral Monte Carlo, for the next two years, an uncertain peace prevails. The Italian army pays a token visit, Gestapo men move about in plain clothes, and refugees from all parts of the world — the rich, beautiful and bizarre — gather to sit out the war in safety and comfort.

But amidst the glitter and elegance of this famous resort, the menace of engulfing war is never far away. And those who fled to Monte Carlo for sanctuary are inescapably drawn into the anguish and horror of the conflict . . .

BESTSELLING FICTION FROM ARROW

All these books are available from your bookshop or news-
agent or you can order them direct. Just tick the titles you
want and complete the form below.

☐	THE COMPANY OF SAINTS	Evelyn Anthony	£1.95
☐	HESTER DARK	Emma Blair	£1.95
☐	1985	Anthony Burgess	£1.75
☐	2001: A SPACE ODYSSEY	Arthur C. Clarke	£1.75
☐	NILE	Laurie Devine	£2.75
☐	THE BILLION DOLLAR KILLING	Paul Erdman	£1.75
☐	THE YEAR OF THE FRENCH	Thomas Flanagan	£2.50
☐	LISA LOGAN	Marie Joseph	£1.95
☐	SCORPION	Andrew Kaplan	£2.50
☐	SUCCESS TO THE BRAVE	Alexander Kent	£1.95
☐	STRUMPET CITY	James Plunkett	£2.95
	FAMILY CHORUS	Claire Rayner	£2.50
	BADGE OF GLORY	Douglas Reeman	£1.95
	THE KILLING DOLL	Ruth Rendell	£1.95
	CENT OF FEAR	Margaret Yorke	£1.75

Postage ———

Total ———

BOOKS, BOOKSERVICE BY POST, PO BOX 29,
AS, ISLE OF MAN, BRITISH ISLES

Please enclose a cheque or postal order made out to Arrow Books
Limited for the amount due including 15p per book for postage and
packing both for orders within the UK and for overseas orders.

Please print clearly

NAME...

ADDRESS...

....

Whilst every effort is made to keep prices down and to keep popular
books in print, Arrow Books cannot guarantee that prices will be the
same as those advertised here or that the books will be available.